THE WICKER WITCH

CHERYL LOW

Crystal Lake Entertainment
www.CrystalLakePub.com

"*The Wicker Witch* will keep you enthralled, twisted, turned and smitten until the very last. Set in a town where the impossible becomes possible, the story plays out with ever-increasing tension, rising to a devastating climax that will play with your mind and stay with you long after you finish the final page."

— Catherine Cavendish, author of
Those Who Dwell in Mordenhyrst Hall

"*The Wicker Witch* is an intricate story about generations of tragedies and dark secrets. It has the harrowing atmosphere of Stephen King's *Storm of the Century* while completely being a Cheryl Low original. You should pick this up immediately."

— Mercedes M. Yardley,
multiple Bram Stoker Award winner

"*The Wicker Witch* is a stunning feat of storytelling. Low masterfully crafted an immersive, moody tale that left me feeling every bit as trapped on that mountain as the characters!"

— Somer Canon, author of
You're Mine and *Picking You Out of My Teeth*

Torrid Waters is the pulp and extreme horror imprint of Crystal Lake Entertainment. For this book, the author has supplied the following trigger warnings: violence, blood, gore, reference to past suicides, monster, grief, assault, attempted sexual assault, teen death, children in danger, bodily trauma, spiders.

CHAPTER ONE

Wicker was a town carved into the side of an angry mountain. The settling of it had been a war against trees, storms, and wolves, but nothing could stop people from climbing its sides and fighting for their place on Mount Grayson. Whether it had been the seams of gold inside the mountain, or the trees felled and hauled down to the sawmill near its base, there was money to be made. And something in the challenge, in the way nature itself offered ripe bounty but bucked against the people that came reaching for it, only spurred them to want it more.

Charlotte Crowe had left once, in rebellion to all those ancestors that stayed before her. She had driven away with no goal but to have the mountain behind her.

But the mountain was gravity, and eventually everyone came back.

The windows of the little cabin rattled in their frames while heavy rain battered the roof. She should have gone to the family house and weathered out the storm there, behind sturdier walls and in the company of people who loved her. But she rarely went into that house anymore and sometimes the comfort of being loved was worse than even a bone deep chill. Sometimes it made her skin raw and her chest tight. Sometimes, she needed to be alone, because the truth was, she was never really alone. No one could be alone with that many secrets.

The wind whistled down the pipe of the wood stove. The flames hissed, struggling to keep their feast burning.

Charlotte remained stretched out on the narrow bed, boots and jacket on just like her daddy taught her. No one wanted to get caught in their pajamas in a storm, and no Crowe ever got caught, period. She curled her arms up behind her head, scanning the small space of the cabin in the orange glow of the stove.

It seemed as though she could hear the whole mountain tonight. She imagined the wind that battered her shack rolling over the treetops, trying to bend them to the ground from the twin peaks down to the river at the bottom.

It never sat right with her, to call the peaks of their mountain *twins*. If they were twins, then one was a growth hanging onto the other. Grayson was the mountain, vast and covered in an ocean of green so deep and dark that whole cities could be lost there. Its peak rose beyond the forest, into a cap of ice often cloaked in clouds. She had been up a few times but found that stretch of the mountain to be foreign and unsettling.

Somehow, it bore no relation to the world she'd grown up in. The mountain beyond their lesser peak was a crown to impress those below, but it meant little to the people of Wicker. Few of their residents ever bothered hiking that high.

Mount Bell was the lesser mountain, the benign tumor on the neck of Mount Grayson, jutting up from the woods with stone and dirt to loom over the town of Wicker. Bell was the peak they knew, the peak they climbed, and the one they looked to when they cast their gazes high. Everything beyond Bell was beyond Wicker and of no consequence to the people who lived there.

That was how it was living in Wicker, there was nothing beyond the mountain.

Even when she ran away from it, the rest of the world had felt like pretend. The way a place is different on vacation than when you live there. Charlotte could never really live anywhere but Wicker. She could only be a tourist in the rest of the world. And when she came home after four years roaming North America, it was a relief to be once again wrapped in her secrets, surrounded by people that reminded her of lies and loss, because that was home.

She had once overheard her momma and some of the other ladies in the quilting circle complaining about how the people of Cyprus, the city at the base of the mountain, had started coming up to Wicker for day trips to take in the nature. The people of Cyprus used to keep their distance back when the two settlements were new. The pastors of Cyprus used to warn their flocks not to go past the river. They told them God had not made it up that mountain, and the people of Wicker had preferred it that way.

The words had stuck in Charlotte's head because they were true. God had not made it up to Wicker. There had never been a church, and few residents had ever bothered going down to Cyprus to convene with religion in the pews.

A particularly strong wind shook the shack and for a second, Charlotte thought it might actually blow down. Her thoughts jumped to that story about little pigs and a wolf. She supposed this cabin would be the equivalent of the straw hut the first pig built. It was more than a hundred years old, and no one would call it a cabin anymore. It was a shack. The Crowes had retired it half a century ago. It was used by children pretending to camp far from home, teens looking for a sense of privacy, and husbands banished from their beds. On the northmost edge of their property, far from the other houses, it offered the illusion of isolation. No one lived there permanently. She'd had to clean out a bunch of junk and make some repairs when she started crashing there after she moved back to the mountain.

Her phone lit up, the screen casting blue light across one side of the room. Charlotte reached for it automatically, fumbling it off the bedside table and holding it up over her face.

Greenleigh: Still alive?

With a smile, she tapped out a reply to her best friend.

Charlotte: No.

Greenleigh: Want me to come get you?

Charlotte snorted. Rebecca had already invited her down from her shack to weather the storm at the Greenleigh house.

They'd been best friends since they were kids, and Rebecca had always been the responsible counterpart to Charlotte's *jump-first* mentality. After a few decades together, Charlotte really should have learned to just listen to her.

Charlotte: No, mom. I'm good.

As if to disagree, the cabin creaked. It was loud enough that she looked away from her phone to the ceiling. It sounded how she imagined a boat at sea would, straining against a force pressing from all sides. She even thought she heard the waves sloshing against the walls. When it didn't stop, she sat up and turned, boots to the floor.

The walls *groaned.*

Charlotte squeezed her phone and rose to her feet.

The fire hissed and dimmed, the shadows of the room growing deep. She walked softly across the floor, suddenly afraid of the world hearing her. Something dragged across the outside of the wall, smooth and endless like the body of a world-eating snake. She reached out and pressed her palm to the old wood. Nerves clawed up her back, painful and making her head twitch when they reached her neck. The wall shuddered under her hand and began to bend inward, like a living beast pressing into her touch.

Her pulse rammed against her throat. Her mind reached for explanations but nothing good came forward. The best possibility was that she was losing her mind because the alternative would mean…

The fire went out and the room went black.

Everything got louder in the dark.

The floorboards creaked like they were coming apart, twisting and snapping. The windows popped in the frames, shattering and bursting inward on the wind that rushed past. Her hands shot up in the dark, the roar of the storm deafened by the rending of the cabin around her.

Charlotte screamed when the ground literally moved under her feet. Rain hit her face before her brain could fully accept that the roof was gone. Her shack had broken apart. She scrambled back, arms flailing in the night for something, *anything*, to grab hold of. The storm was suddenly all around her—no more flimsy walls to separate her from it. She fell to her knees and the world continued to spin. Her hands and knees pressed through cold mud to find the floorboards beneath, rain beating down on her and the full cry of the storm pounding against her eardrums.

The spinning stopped almost as quickly as it began, her heart beating so hard in her chest that she felt sick. She gasped for air and coughed up rain. Her fingers flexed against the wood under the mud, trying to convince herself it was there. The cabin wasn't whole. It wasn't even the entire base. A wall and a corner had been left behind. Maybe most of the roof too? Her hands moved across the floor at her knees, sliding through loose mud. The tall trees swung overhead, back and forth with the wind like it was just a dance for them—just another night on the mountain.

Charlotte lifted her phone, trying to rub the mud off it and onto her jacket. The rain had already soaked through her hair, running down her face and off her lips and chin. She shook, but it wasn't the cold; not yet. Her shivers were one-hundred percent adrenaline. Her cabin had come apart. A mudslide? She hit the flashlight button and light burst from her phone, washing over what remained of the floor. She stood wobbly, expecting the structure to teeter, but it sat firm even if it was at a slope. She walked down it, squinting through the rain to see where she'd ended up. It couldn't be far from where she'd started. It had only been a few seconds of sliding.

The light bounced off metal to the left and she stared hard until finally realizing it was her truck rolled and half-buried in mud, the tailgate and back wheels sticking out almost vertically.

Her first thought was to the loss of it and the expense of having to get another one, which almost immediately dragged a panicked laugh up from her chest. She could have easily been rolled and buried in mud herself. In fact, this was a fucking miracle.

She was still standing. Nothing broken.

She smiled slowly, the cold finally digging into her bones to make her shake. This was insane. This would be a wild story to tell once she figured out how to get to a road.

Something moved behind her truck—a shadow darting from it to the trees.

Charlotte jerked her phone light after it but only illuminated the trees and rain pelting soupy mud.

Her light dimmed. She flicked her gaze to the screen. It was wet and streaked in mud. Was the battery low or was it rebelling against all this abuse? The phone turned off completely.

The trees creaked all around her and the wind screamed. She couldn't see anything in the dark, under the clouds.

The floorboards behind her groaned.

The nerves along the back of her neck remained painfully tight. She'd mistaken it for adrenaline and cold but realized suddenly that it was fear. It cut right to her gut, and she almost dropped her phone when she swung around to stare at the night. It was too dark to see. Anything could be in front of her, and she wouldn't know it. Unless she reached out with her hands.

Her thumb pressed hard into the power button along the side of her phone, willing it to come back to life—silently begging it not to abandon her in the dark all alone.

Only she wasn't alone.

Charlotte Crowe was never alone.

Something scraped across the floorboard right in front of her, taking a step closer. The sound was so solid, like a stone in Charlotte's throat, choking her. Another, unhurried, drag and step. She imagined a stag, lost and disoriented in the storm, only it was too loud…too heavy. Her eyes strained against the dark, looking higher and higher as she searched desperately for the outline of antlers.

The wind never relented but now she could hear a low humming on it.

It was almost a voice.

The steps stopped, close enough that if she reached out, she really would touch whatever was standing on the broken floor of her shack with her.

Charlotte thought of that story her momma used to tell again. *God never made it up the mountain.* But the people of Wicker had. And in their oldest stories, there had already been something on the mountain, long before they arrived. Something old and terrible.

She lifted her hand slowly, up her body, until she clamped her palm over her mouth to smother a scream gathering in her lungs. Why was she thinking of monster stories now? It could be anything. It could be *nothing* but her mind playing tricks in the dark.

The humming grew louder…or maybe closer? It wasn't quite a voice, and it wasn't quite a song. The wrongness of it brought tears to her eyes and made her legs shake, threatening to give out on her.

The thick clouds overhead shifted, and the moon slowly peeked through, fingers of white light reaching out into the night.

Charlotte's heart ratcheted so hard and fast that for one horrible second, she thought she might faint. She wanted to scream and beg the moon to look away. She didn't want to see whatever stood in front of her and, more than that, she did not want it to see her.

But the moon looked where the moon wanted, and no one could stop it.

The trees lit up, black and tall. They whipped side to side overhead, and the wind screamed again rather than humming. Light spilled across the muddy floorboards and the half wall. It filled the space around her, and Charlotte stared, tears rolling off her lashes, at nothing.

Nothing.

She stood there for a few more seconds, waiting for the creature she sensed so keenly to appear, but it didn't. She'd allowed her mind to play tricks on her. Maybe the breaking of the cabin had broken something in her? She unclamped her hand from her face and turned, using the moonlight to find her bearings. If she couldn't figure out which way she was pointed, she would have to sit there until sunup. The idea of being there in the dark any longer made her want to run foolishly in any direction just to escape.

It didn't take Charlotte long to find her way south. South would take her down to her family's property. She would either hit a road or one of their houses if she kept true.

Now she just had to pick her way across the mud. She scraped her boot along the edge of the floor, where the planks had broken off, but froze when she saw the tracks in the mud.

She crouched to squint at them, fingertips tracing the shapes but not touching. A cloven hoof inside a human footprint, the two turned in opposite directions. As soon as she saw it, the clouds moved again. The moon looked away, throwing her back into darkness.

Charlotte gritted her teeth and gingerly stepped off the floorboards. She only sank up to mid-calf and told herself to be grateful for it, because no matter how deep it was, she couldn't have convinced herself to stay put on that platform and wait. The walk was long and hard. She stumbled several times but kept going, refusing to admit even to herself that she was running away from something. She wasn't *running*, after all. She couldn't have run in that mud even if she wanted to. But knowing that only made the ball of fear in her gut bigger.

Eventually, the cold and the exhaustion hit her. Then came the strain in her thighs every time she pulled a foot up from the mud. And the only fear in her was that of getting lost in the storm.

Whatever had happened at the cabin—whatever had seen her in the night—had looked away. The weight of it was gone and, in its absence, the ideas of sanity pressed in like a steady stream to fill all the spaces that would become madness if left to be believed.

She had been through something frightening and life-threatening. She had imagined the sounds, the feelings, and even the sight of those tracks in the mud. The mind could do crazy things.

But deep down, Charlotte Crowe knew there was no place for sanity in Wicker.

CHAPTER TWO

They had forgotten her.
They had forgotten the rules.
They had forgotten her hunger.
The witch would remind them all.

CHAPTER THREE

The sun was barely up and Rebecca Greenleigh was already driving her truck around the eastern side of the mountain. She'd received several calls during the night about mudslides. Actually, she'd been grateful when their phones lost service almost an hour ago. It gave her time to take stock of the mess in peace and decide what to do about it before talking to anyone else.

At least the rain had let up. Rebecca couldn't imagine the clouds had much left in them after the onslaught that came in the night. Before she'd lost contact, she heard the river had flooded and damaged the bridge down to Cyprus.

Hannah, her wife, had nearly lost her mind over the news. She wasn't from the mountain, so the idea of being trapped there frightened her. Rebecca, on the other hand, was relieved to have the bridge closed for a while. It would end the conversations about evacuation from her better half.

Greenleighs did not abandon the mountain. They did not evacuate or hide. They didn't even move away. Some Greenleighs left, went to college, and then came back to where they belonged. Hannah didn't understand, and that was okay, because Rebecca did, and so would their son.

Rebecca's ancestors had been among the proud, last few standing of the original settlers. They had cleared away the trees to build the town of Wicker, and her grandfather had shot the last wolf on the mountain fifty years ago. Her whole life, she had been told the forest was her domain, the mountain her throne, and the little town her responsibility. The family house, once a log cabin, had been rebuilt over the generations into a modern residence with sliding glass doors and a high sprawling deck, but it did not look out over the side of the mountain like most.

The Greenleighs had not turned their windows toward the slope, to look down at the world beneath, but into the thick woods at their backs. Her grandfather had told her never to forget that the woods were wild, that not so long-ago wolves had made easy meals of grown men. That at least once a decade, a bear wandered close to town, or a stag struck by a car kicked the passengers to death.

"We live on the mountain," he'd said. *"We killed the wolves, but the woods are always wild, no matter what we take from them. There is a wild that cannot be killed. A wild that does not age or grow weak. It is always there, always looking back at us."*

He had stood on the deck some nights and watched the trees at the edge of the yard, staring into them, and Rebecca had wondered, with more curiosity than fear, if he saw the wild staring back.

He died before she could find the words to ask, and her father had never looked at the woods the way his had.

Sometimes she stood on her deck—the same deck and in the same spot as her grandfather, and she stared into the trees. Whatever was there that held his gaze, she had yet to find. She loved her mountain, but she saw no wonder in it.

Flashing blue lights danced in her windshield and she slowed her truck into a crawl through the mud.

The sheriff's car was parked in the mouth of the little road leading to the tourist cabins.

Rebecca stopped and put the truck into park, leaving the engine on and the heater running when she jumped out.

Only a few steps and she realized the doctor's car and another truck were parked just ahead of the sheriff's, two of the men talking at the edge of the thick mudslide and pointing at the mess. One of the cabin walls was flat on the ground and half-buried.

Billy Benson leaned against his truck at the end of the gathering, his arms crossed over his thick chest and his chin tucked low. He grunted a greeting, and Rebecca came closer. Benson owned the cabins and rented them out to tourists, but this wasn't the season for guests. Despite that, Rebecca had no doubt there had been someone staying up there. It was in the flush of color on Benson's cheeks, peeking out from the edges of his thick beard. Why else would the sheriff and the doctor be there?

"Did you lose all four cabins?" she asked, hands in her pockets.

"Yep."

"How many guests?"

Billy Benson dragged a breath and managed to look even more tense. "Five, staying in two cabins. Warned 'em 'bout the storm. Didn't think—"

"You had no way of knowing," Rebecca agreed. She might have patted his shoulder if there had been any moment in all her life that she'd seen anyone touch Benson outside of a fight. She'd never even seen his *wife* lay a hand on him.

Sheriff Summerfield joined them, the doctor on his heels. Rebecca immediately missed the old sheriff, the one who had been wearing that hat and badge since she was a kid until just a few years ago. He had had a warmth about him and a certainty that put everyone at ease. Bryan Summerfield had an anxious neediness that set her on edge. He tipped his hat like he was in a damn western.

"*Greenleigh*," he said. "I tried to call the mayor about getting some people up here to help look for the lost tourists, but I'm not getting through."

She resisted the impulse to roll her eyes when he called Jane *the mayor*. Yes, she was the mayor of Wicker. Rebecca had even voted for her. But that didn't mean anyone called her by title instead of by name. Wicker was home to only a few hundred people, and they all knew each other well enough not to bother with formalities. Summerfield himself had been born on the mountain, his ancestors among the townsfolk for four generations.

"It's good you came. We can use the help," he went on, pink-cheeked and almost excited to have such an important, if not grim, task at hand.

Rebecca took a step back. "Had no idea about the tourists. I was just heading over to the old sanitorium to check on the damage and the stocks."

Summerfield looked immediately put out, but the doctor nodded quickly. Doctor Paulson had attended the births of more than half the township. He knew each and every one of them and never forgot a name. He also never panicked or overreacted, and today he was the perfect balance to Summerfield's eagerness.

"With the bridge to Cyprus out, a good stock of food could be handy," he chimed.

Summerfield frowned, thumb hooking into that thick belt of his. "I think looking for survivors is more important…" he mumbled, not quite saying it loud enough to make a point of it.

Doctor Paulson huffed, his breath forming thin whisps in the morning air. "No reason to keep her from her business. Cabins have been wrecked and we've already spotted a couple bodies in the mud, Bryan. The deputies are headed up with the gear, and we'll do fine searching on our own." He put his hand on Summerfield's shoulder, leaning close and adding in a softer voice. "Not likely to be any survivors after last night from this mess, especially out-of-towners."

If the missing had been Wicker born, the doctor might have had more faith in them hanging on through the night, even in a mudslide. If they'd been Wicker born, Rebecca would have dropped everything to wade out into the mud in her boots and jeans to start looking. She tried not to pick that fact apart and reveal anything to her psyche about herself she'd rather not deal with. She had shit to do, and it didn't include looking for tourists. In fact, with the phones out and these mudslides, she should get a group going property to property just to make sure no other houses had been swept away or buried in mud.

She took another step back. "I'll check in when I'm done."

Benson grunted a *goodbye* that sounded a lot like his *hello*.

The doctor smiled and waved her off. "Let us know if we need to start rationing our food!" he half-joked.

It wouldn't be the first time they'd been trapped on the mountain after a storm, stretching their food stocks to make it last until the road off the mountain could be plowed. But it was usually on account of snow, not mud. The last mudslide had been in 1947, but that one had come from even higher up the mountain and not quite reached any of the Wicker properties.

Rebecca got back into her truck and continued down the road that curved along the side of the mountain. After seeing the cabins in ruins, she expected to find the old sanitorium buried or ripped apart. Her family had turned the facility into emergency storage for the town after closing it down decades ago. They rotated the contents out regularly to keep them from going bad, either using them at the Wicker town hall meetings, festivals, and school potlucks, or donating the canned goods to organizations in Cyprus.

She rounded the last bend and pulled up onto the small gravel parking lot in front of the brick structure. She turned off the engine and for a second just sat there, staring at the building. It looked fine. She had been so sure it would be damaged, but it wasn't. At this rate, she could start the chore of checking on all her neighbors. She just had to drive past the turn off and the sheriff without getting recruited to search for strangers.

Never one to half-ass anything, Rebecca got out of her truck and went up to the front door, flicking the keys on her ring until she came to the right one. Inside, she turned on the lights, but nothing happened. *Fair enough*, she thought. Half of Wicker had lost power last night. Of course, most homes had their own generators too. She grabbed one of the flashlights Hannah had hung on the wall near the door for just such an occasion. She flicked it on and took a look up and down the empty halls.

Her steps echoed when she made her way toward the old patient rooms where they'd locked up the supplies—mostly canned goods and toiletries. She checked the first room and then the second. Everything in place. But she paused, still leaned into the second room, when she noticed the absolute darkness but for her flashlight beam. She aimed it toward the windows, barred on both sides but otherwise unobstructed. And yet, no light shone through.

She closed the door and marched down the long hall to the back of the building. She tried to open the door, but it wouldn't budge.

Flashlight swinging at her side, Rebecca jogged around to the front door again. The wind was picking up, shaking water loose from the branches above. She ran around the side of the building and jerked to a stop at the back, where there should have been an abandoned garden with stone benches and the old graveyard tucked back into the trees. Mud heaved up and over the grounds, reshaping it and stripping away all colors but for shades of brown. It had hit the back of the building and piled up almost to the roof, completely burying the back wall.

She would have cared about the mess if she weren't also looking at the sharp angles of coffins sticking out of the ground.

Rebecca ran her gaze over them, despite the voice in her head screaming to look away. She was going to see something she couldn't unsee. Several of the old coffins were broken open. But she couldn't look away. She told herself it was because it was her responsibility to handle any situation on Greenleigh land, but she'd be lying if she didn't admit to a little morbid curiosity. How old were the bodies in the Green Tree Sanitorium graveyard? It had been opened in 1866, and she had noticed as a kid that there was at least one grave for every year it had been open—ninety-two graves in total.

She stared at the open coffin nearest to her, slammed up against another that was still nailed shut as far as she could tell. She expected to see a gruesome body inside, decayed and leathery, or maybe even just bones and hair, but there was nothing but more mud.

She walked out into the yard, the mud squelching under her boots and soon up to her ankles. She grabbed the lid of another narrow coffin, already broken and barely hanging on. Giving it a hard jerk, she peeled it back from the box.

Rebecca stared down at the contents. She knelt and reached in, moving the rocks around and picking up a few of the trinkets—an old, battered pocket-watch, a silver wedding band, and a belt buckle coated in char. She thumbed it in her gloved palm. It didn't make sense.

She stood upright, dropping the contents back into the coffin and looking around the yard. Coffins everywhere but no bones in sight—no remains. Maybe they had been swept away? But what about the one that had been closed? She had opened it herself. A fluke, maybe?

Rebecca scrutinized the rest in sight. A few were shut more firmly than the one she had opened. There was no chance the storm had emptied their contents and reburied them in the face of the mountain. She clenched her teeth and turned back, marching out of the mud.

She had a crowbar in the back of her truck. She just needed to see one to put her mind at ease. One body in a coffin to know that the others had been washed away. She'd pay some of the loggers to help her dig the old coffins from the mud after the storm had passed and put the grounds to rights before winter.

But first, she needed to crack open one of those pine tombs and see. She wouldn't let herself think about what she was looking for or what alternative there could be other than the mudslide ravaging the old coffins. She busied her thoughts with the seemingly endless list of things she needed to check on, repair, and handle—this ruined graveyard not the least of them.

Climbing through the mud to get to the nearest whole coffin wasn't an easy task. She wasn't a large woman by any standards. The mud was almost up to her knees and every step dragged her deeper. But Rebecca Greenleigh would not be dragged anywhere by anything. She pushed forward until she reached the coffin, tapping the crowbar against the lid and catching her breath.

Large, black birds cawed in the trees, clinging to branches that swayed in the wind.

Repositioning the crowbar in her hands, she wedged the curved end into the seam between the lid and the box. It took her whole weight to strain the old nails until they wrenched up from wet wood with a groan. She repeated the movement until one full side of the lid had given way. It hadn't been loose. Unless there was a hole on the other side, there was no way the storm could have emptied this one. She didn't even bother to brace herself against the sight or stench of rotting contents. At this point, it would be a relief. A quiet, horrible relief that she would never share with anyone.

She pulled the lid, splintering the wood and lifting it like a bad tooth that just wouldn't completely let go. She had to hold it open to look inside.

Her breaths were deep and her gaze sharp.

The coffin was empty.

CHAPTER FOUR

Just as old as the legends of settlers on the mountain, was the story of the Wicker Witch.

Every year a handful of ghost hunters and paranormal investigators came traipsing up the mountain to visit the little footbridge north of the town, where half a dozen trails led hikers into the wilderness toward Mount Bell. Anyone who grew up in Wicker knew the spot well. Every kid played on that bridge, squealing with the thrills of fright.

They say, if you stand on the bridge in the narrow clearing and look up into the woods near the jagged peak of Mount Bell, you might spot the curls of smoke from the witch's hut. Most of the old stories, passed down from one child to the next, one generation after another, recommend crossing the bridge backward with your hand over your eyes. No peeking, because if you happen to spot the witch's house, she might look down and see you in return. Good kids never peeked when a witch was involved…but most kids weren't good, not really. Most kids stared up into the woods, squinting and searching the treetops. They swore they saw the hut and then spent the better part of a day running around the forest with their friends trying to find it.

But no one ever found the house of the Wicker Witch, of course, because it wasn't there.

Charlotte Crowe had searched when she was a kid. She had walked and biked all the trails and gone off into the woods looking for the Wicker Witch until she turned fifteen and decided that boys were more interesting than witches. At least they were in abundance, and the ones hiding were not the ones she wanted to find, anyway.

Coming down the north side of the Crowe property, she couldn't keep her thoughts from straying back to those old fairy tales. The ground was soggy but most of the mud was in her boots and on her clothes now. She'd walked past the mudslide and then kept going until the dark grew lighter with the coming dawn, until she recognized trees and boulders and finally the backside of that little house where her aunt lived. It was a short walk from the main house, but the main house was too crowded, and she was too wet and tired to deal with that many questions.

She came around the side of the building, distantly surprised by the quiet. The dog should have announced her arrival. She knocked hard and then stepped back. As eager as she was to be inside, only a fool would try to barge into Henrietta Crowe's home.

The little house had been on the Crowe property for more than sixty years. Charlotte's grandad had built it when her grandma told him she couldn't stand living under the same roof as him anymore, threatening to finally divorce him and move away. Her grandad had built the little house behind the big house and lived there for as long as Charlotte had known him. Her grandparents had stayed married. In fact, they'd been a rather happy couple. Grandad took all his meals at the big house and sometimes even stayed the night. But after her grandma passed, he'd stayed in the little house, following her to the grave within a year.

It was only empty for a few months before Charlotte's aunt, Henrietta, moved in.

"It's me, Aunt Henri," Charlotte called. She was definitely being too loud that early in the morning, but if she didn't want to run the risk of being shot, it was best to be clear. Crowes had always possessed a *shoot first* mentality and the dangers of that did not exclude their own kin.

A succession of locks rolled back on the door before it inched open. "Lotte?" a gravelly voice called through the opening.

"Last I checked." Charlotte kicked branches off the covered deck. It was still raining but the wind had let up.

The porch light came on, as bright as a lighthouse shining in her face.

The door creaked open fully and a little woman pushed her way out. Her coat was too big for her, the sleeves rolled to her wrists and the hem nearly reaching her knees. Charlotte couldn't help but notice they were wearing the same kind of boots and wondered if she would *be* Aunt Henri someday. She could see herself living out her final decades in the little house, probably with the same shotgun. Which of her nieces and nephews would bring her food and check on her to make sure she wasn't dead yet? She would bet on Miles, but time could change a lot of things. She was pretty sure Aunt Henri wouldn't have bet on her when she and her siblings were still small.

She probably expected it to be Edgar.

A lot of people had expected things of Edgar that never happened.

"Look at you!" Aunt Henri rasped, still standing in the doorway and not yet inviting her in. "What happened?"

"Landslide," Charlotte answered. Or was it a mudslide? It was a lot of mud… "Shack's in pieces and my truck rolled. Had to walk down."

"Jesus…" Henri still hadn't budged and then seemed to realize all at once that Charlotte wanted to come in. Her eyes widened and her crooked fingers squeezed the door harder, like Charlotte might try to push her way in. She *wouldn't*…but if she'd wanted to, that arthritic grip on the door wouldn't stop her. "You're not coming in here like that! You're covered in mud, girl!"

She couldn't exactly argue with that. Instead, she looked down at herself and weighed her options. She could walk into the big house, track mud wherever the hell she wanted and probably make it to the shower. But no one ever went into the big house and came back out without anyone noticing. Her younger brother, Victor, his wife, and their four kids had moved in with her dad there a few years back.

"What if I take everything off? Will you let me in to shower?"

Aunt Henri curled her lip like she might say *no* anyway but finally waved a stalling hand. "I'll grab towels!" She left the door open and shuffled away into the cabin.

Charlotte peeled off her jacket and then her boots. The laces squelched. Her jeans were almost impossible to get off, but she managed it. Most of the mud had gone with the clothing by the time Aunt Henri came back, cold finally digging down into her bones and making her shake from head to toe. The woman nodded and shoved a towel into Charlotte's arms, signaling her in.

The little house was a one room cabin with a full kitchen and bathroom. It was a palace compared to the one Charlotte had been sleeping in. But when she closed the door, the windows rattled against the wind and she couldn't help but think of the little pig in that story, running for the second house that still wouldn't be enough to stop the wolf.

She went straight for the bathroom and got into the shower. The water burned even before it got hot, her skin aching with cold. She washed up quickly but then lingered to warm up. She still couldn't believe she'd survived her shack sliding off its foundation like that. She should probably be dead right now.

By the time she got out of the shower, she could hear coffee percolating through the thin door.

She rubbed her dark hair so it wouldn't drip and then wrapped the towel around herself.

The main room smelled like coffee when she opened the door and a small pile of clean clothes had been put on the nearest chair for her. She pulled them on, not the least bit surprised to find that they were her own clothes. She had a habit of leaving laundry at different houses, which was suddenly great as she wasn't likely to find the bag of sweaters and jeans she'd had stowed away in the shack up the hill.

"Mind if I throw my wet clothes in the wash?" Charlotte asked, zipping up her jeans before pulling on a shirt.

Aunt Henri pulled two mugs out and put them on the counter beside the coffee machine. "If you hose the mud off them first…"

Charlotte yanked a sweater on over her head. "Deal."

The TV was on but the sound muted. There was a blanket on the recliner while the bed in the far corner was still made. Aunt Henri had fallen asleep in front of the TV again. Charlotte crossed the room and stepped out onto the porch, crouching long enough to fish her phone from the pocket of her muddy pants before heading back inside. She used the damp towel from her shower to rub it clean. It still wouldn't turn on. It was a miracle she'd left her laptop at Harvey's, or it too would have been buried in the side of the mountain like her truck and her shack.

Aunt Henri poured her coffee while Charlotte checked to see if one of the chargers crowding the extension cord would fit hers. Three different charges and none of them worked.

"Have you seen Bill?" Aunt Henri asked. It came out with a snap, almost like an accusation, but Charlotte knew better than to take offense.

Giving up on her phone, she shoved it into her pocket and headed to the kitchen. "Which Bill? Billy Benson? Bill Latham? Bill Brandon?" Charlotte teased.

Aunt Henri glared. It was a good glare too. She had dark, pitless eyes and wrinkles inside her wrinkles. Her gray hair was braided into one thick plait and hung over her shoulder. "I don't give no shits about those Bills, and you know it." She harrumphed and picked up her coffee cup.

Charlotte knew her aunt wanted to retreat back to her recliner in the living room. She wasn't in the mood for company. Aunt Henri rarely was.

Charlotte poured her own coffee, only filling half the cup before opening the refrigerator and taking out the milk.

"You're wasting milk and wasting good coffee," Aunt Henri berated, nose wrinkled even more than usual. She turned and started the slow march to her chair.

Charlotte put the milk away after adding it to her mug. The house seemed so quiet. Where *was* Bill? She glanced around the cabin like the Pitbull-mix might be curled into a corner. He wasn't. "You lost your dog?"

"Fuck you," Aunt Henri groused, setting down her mug before sinking into her seat. "I didn't lose him. He ran off."

Charlotte shrugged and took her usual spot on the couch. "Result is the same. Did he run off before the storm?"

"During. He needed to go out, so I let him, but he didn't come back." She frowned hard and shook her head. "Ain't like him."

Charlotte took a long drink of her coffee. She probably should have gotten a glass of water after that hike down through the woods, but hot caffeine always won out. "Maybe he got lost in the storm? I'll call around and see if anyone has him." Bill was eighty pounds with a head like a brick. Wherever he was, he was fine, but Aunt Henri was right; it wasn't like him to go running off. He'd never been interested in chasing animals in the woods. Bill liked his soft bed and abundant snacks.

Aunt Henri put her mug down on the side table, hands shaking, and set about the slow task of extracting a pack of cigarettes from the breast pocket of her jacket. It was one of Edgar's old jackets—red and black wool. Every year Charlotte hoped it would wear out and her aunt would get a new one, but she knew that wasn't likely. The jacket held up, and even if it did have the decency to wear, Aunt Henri would never toss it. Edgar had been her favorite.

She finally got a cigarette out of the pack, put it between her lips, and then held the pack out to the side in silent offer. Charlotte took it and deftly tugged one from the crumpled plastic before tucking the pack back into her aunt's pocket, never quite touching the jacket. Aunt Henri handed her a lighter from the side table. There were always a few floating around the tables and at least one next to the cut glass ashtray. Charlotte lit them both up before handing it back.

Aunt Henri had left the mountain once too. She never said much about those years though. Even after Charlotte returned, something that should have given them common ground to speak on, it hadn't. Wherever Henrietta Crowe had gone and whatever she had done in the world outside Wicker, she kept it to herself. In return, she never asked Charlotte about her own adventure. Not where she'd gone, or, more importantly, why. Everyone else asked, but never Aunt Henri. Charlotte suspected the old woman *thought* she knew—probably thought it was for whatever reason she had gone. Wanderlust? A need to escape? A desire to explore? Whatever it was, it was wrong.

Charlotte took a lungful of nicotine and tar, watching her aunt frown at the TV as she smoked beside her. "I'll walk over to Alice's place and see if they've seen Bill. If he wandered over there, you know Miles would have brought him inside for the night."

Aunt Henri nodded. "That boy's always trying to steal my dog…"

"Kids like dogs."

"Then his momma should get him his own. If Edgar were here, he'd get the boy a dog and sure as shit wouldn't be stealing mine."

Charlotte exhaled smoke and tried to ignore the ache in her gut at the mention of what Edgar would do. Her older brother was gone. He'd been gone for eight years and unlike either of them, he wasn't coming back.

"You get a job yet?" Aunt Henri asked.

Charlotte smiled around her cigarette. For once her aunt's brutal conversational style worked in her favor—getting her away from thoughts of Edgar. "I have a job, Aunt Henri." Neither her dad nor her aunt understood how she made money online doing formatting and cover designs. She had shown them her webpage a hundred times and tried to explain it, but they either honestly couldn't grasp the idea or they just refused to. She suspected it was the latter and until she started working at the gas station again, they would pretend she was jobless.

Living on the mountain had a lot of benefits, but it also meant everyone in her town knew her—or thought they did. At the very least, her neighbors all knew too much about her. She was the sixteenth generation of Crowe on the mountain. Daughter of Gerard and Carol Crowe. Middle child with two brothers, Edgar and Victor. The townsfolk had called her the *trouble kid* of the three, but, in hindsight, she hadn't done anything worse than her brothers. Gender had been what tipped the scale of her crimes. Of course, she hadn't realized that until her mid-twenties. As a teen, she thought of herself as a storm, because that's how Wicker treated her. *Close your shutters, lock your doors, put away your breakables—Charlotte's here.*

She had enjoyed being a storm. It lowered a lot of expectations. Her momma had been delighted when she brought home good grades, sure Charlotte would flunk out of school because of that bad attention span of hers. And her dad had been proud of her for the very little achievement of not getting pregnant—which backfired terribly for him when she continued not to get pregnant, or married, through her twenties and into her thirties.

Her momma had passed eight years back, but her dad was still ensconced in the big house. He slept in her momma's sewing room at the back of the house, unable to go into their bedroom. No one went in there, not even after Vic and his family had moved in. He couldn't convince the old man to turn the room into something useful and he wasn't willing to do it himself.

Gerard Crowe was the epitome of stubborn and the perfect patriarch to a family *known* for being stubborn since they stepped foot on the mountain. Some families had survived by cunning and practicality, by planning ahead and working together, but the Crowes had survived by being unmovable— as though it was a refusal to die that bought them their place in Wicker. Charlotte had always hated the way her father and uncles talked about it like being pigheaded was a skill. But time had taught her that she was no better. Charlotte was a Crowe through and through.

The family motto, muttered and shouted by Crowes for two-hundred years, was, *Crowes don't make deals with devils.* Charlotte considered it a testament to her lineage of stubborn people. When they couldn't win an argument or explain why they wouldn't do something someone else was telling them was best, they simply snapped those words off and walked away. She had heard her father, her aunt, her momma, and her brothers end arguments on those words her whole life. Charlotte had bitten them back on a dozen occasions, refusing to say them herself.

"Don't fall asleep on my couch 'til you find Bill," Aunt Henri said and only then did Charlotte realize she'd closed her eyes.

She mumbled a swear and rolled to her feet, tapping ash off her cigarette and onto the tray. "Yep. On it." She put the cigarette between her lips and went to find socks and dry shoes.

CHAPTER FIVE

In 1762, a witch fled up the mountain from a settlement that would one day be called Cyprus.

She wasn't really a witch, of course, but her community had cried the word, and the word had stained their tongues and blackened their hearts.

She fled in the night, shoeless and beaten, and sure to swing for nothing but the accusations of her neighbors—wild, senseless, claims that her mere presence had killed a cow, soured milk, and caused two households to fall ill.

When she reached Wicker, she begged for mercy in the face of certain ruin. There was no reason to hope that these people would help her. If the families she had known all her life could condemn her, then why would strangers be any different?

But these strangers were more than different; they were the settlers of Wicker.

There was no God in Wicker, and the people there grew kinder for his absence.

They did not call her a witch.

They knew a witch was a far cry from a living person. They knew that no man could root her out and not even God could end her life.

CHAPTER SIX

Alice hadn't been able to sleep.

She hated the mountain when the weather turned bad. Sometimes she hated the mountain even when the weather was perfect. Around three in the morning, she abandoned all hope of sleep and padded out to the living room. Edgar had picked the couch. She hadn't liked it before, but she couldn't imagine getting rid of it now. She sat in the same spot she always did, nearest the door. Tucking her legs up under her, she scrolled through social media apps for what felt like minutes but actually amounted to hours.

She scrolled until her feed wouldn't refresh. Nothing changed, no matter how hard she flicked the screen. The little network icon on her phone had gone dark. Alice put it down before she could throw it and wake Miles.

She restarted the router and waited.

The house was too quiet under the battering of the storm outside. It was like all the silence had been herded and pushed into her home, locked in by the winds outside and building pressure in her skull.

Alice squeezed her eyes shut.

The wind battered the house and howled between the trees. It sounded like wolves far away in the woods. A branch cracked and she sucked back a breath, bracing as though it might hit her roof and come crashing through that delicate bubble of safety. A part of her wished it would, that it would rip her home in half and crush her. Even if it didn't end her, the ruined house would be a good excuse to move in with her mom in Cyprus. It might be the only way she could ever leave. Would the sounds of the city be different than those of the woods? Would the quiet inside her be less deafening?

Edgar wouldn't like it if he came back and found that she'd abandoned the mountain and his family... But he wasn't coming back. Everyone said he would someday. They said that sometimes people from Wicker just left for a while, but that they always returned. His dad and his brother liked to talk about him coming back like it was a given, like he was just out there sowing oats. But Alice knew in her gut that they were wrong.

Edgar was dead.

Nothing but death would have kept him from Wicker. She had known from the start that she'd never be able to talk him into living in Cyprus, let alone going someplace farther away. If she wanted to be with Edgar Crowe, she would have to live on his family land—on his mountain. She hadn't minded when he was there with her. But without him… Without him, she was suffocating in all that fresh mountain air. Eight years had passed since he disappeared, each one stretching longer than the last.

She went over that morning in her head again. She'd made a habit of it, afraid that time would change it in her mind or make her memories blurry. He had gotten up early to go hunting, and she'd filled a thermos with coffee. It had been a last-minute decision to take Miles with him. She hadn't wanted her little boy to go. He was so small and only five years old. That had to be too young for hunting. He couldn't hold a rifle and he might not be able to stay quiet. He might upset Edgar.

Alice hated when she thought that. Edgar didn't have a temper. He was one of the calmest people she'd ever met. He was level and steady and she had loved that about him. But it was still the thought that leaped across her mind. Miles would yammer or cry and Edgar would be angry that he had to give up and come home early.

But she hadn't been able to talk him out of taking Miles with him.

Alice stood on the front step that morning, mist clinging to the ground between trees, and watched her husband and son load up into his truck. Edgar had flashed her a smile and a wink and pulled away. She had smiled back despite that lump that grew in her chest and the tears rising behind her eyes.

Had part of her known something bad would happen?

Hours later, Rebecca Greenleigh brought Alice's son home to her. She said he'd been alone, sitting on a bench in town. She said she'd taken him with her to the diner to warm up and wait for his dad to come back. But Edgar hadn't come back.

Rebecca Greenleigh was a liar.

Alice had confronted her many times over the years, trying to get the truth from her, but she wouldn't bend. Alice had tried pleading and begging for the truth. She'd offered absolution if Rebecca had been sleeping with Edgar. She offered to keep it a secret too, if only she would tell her the truth about what happened to him.

But Rebecca never changed her story, and everyone believed her.

They all believed Edgar was still alive. *Everyone*, Alice supposed, but herself and whoever had killed him.

She didn't notice the creaking sound until it broke through her thoughts, so loud that for an instant she imagined her entire house straining under the grip of one giant hand. Her lids burst open, the sound still ringing in her ears with a low hiss like a beast trying to laugh. Daylight clawed at her vision, making her reel back in her corner of the couch. Her hand flew to her face, covering her eyes as she blinked to clear her vision.

The front door opened, letting in a gust of wind before slamming shut. She turned her head toward it, scowling at the woman that walked in.

"Sorry. Were you sleeping?" Charlotte asked but didn't stop or offer to leave. She walked right into the kitchen, disappearing behind the wall that separated it from the living room.

"No," Alice answered but realized it might be a lie. She had obviously fallen asleep. "What time is it?" She rubbed her face and blinked at the windows. Gray light pierced the swaying treetops outside.

Charlotte fiddled with something in the kitchen, water from the sink and something in the cupboard. "Almost six."

Alice rolled her eyes. Six was practically noon for Charlotte. Did she ever sleep?

The coffee machine crackled in the kitchen.

"I'm gonna borrow Dad's truck and take a look at the damage in town. Do you want me to pick anything up for you?"

Alice hated how helpful Charlotte was sometimes. She showed up like she was welcome, like they were really family. But where was she when Alice's whole life came crumbling down? She'd been gone, running from the mountain to see the world below. She hadn't come back just because Edgar was gone—hadn't come back until a couple of years later and then she'd never asked about him, never talked about him, never even patted Alice's shoulder and told her he'd be back like the rest of the family had done. Charlotte had just gone about life like it had always been this way. She came over and fixed things. She drove Miles places. She offered to help.

But if she was really going to help, she'd offer to find Edgar, wouldn't she?

Alice pushed herself to her feet and stretched, trying to leave her dark mood where she'd sat—like it was something she could just step out of. That seemed fair since she knew it would still be there waiting to wrap around her as soon as she sat down again.

"Why do you have to borrow your dad's truck?" Alice asked rather than answering her question. It was a small defiance, but it made her feel a lot better.

When she came around the corner into the kitchen, Charlotte was leaning against the counter, waiting for the coffee. "Mine got rolled in the storm. Shack came apart too."

Alice stared, trying to imagine that. She had to be joking. Charlotte was weird. She could definitely be joking. Alice was not going to bite if that was the case.

The Crowe dragged her gaze over Alice and then glanced away discreetly.

Alice resisted the urge to claw her long hair into some sort of order. *Fuck, Charlotte.* If she was going to barge in on her, then she couldn't very well expect her to be dressed and ready for company. And who was Charlotte to judge? She always looked like she'd just woken up from a nap—her clothes wrinkled and hair messily pulled up. At least when they'd been in high school Charlotte had worn makeup and colored her hair. Ever since she came back to the mountain, she hadn't even tried. Charlotte was nothing special, and Alice hated how comfortable she was with it.

More than that, *more than anything*, Alice had hated how much Edgar had liked his little sister. No one else had ever made Edgar laugh the way Charlotte could, and he'd talked about her all the time. At first, when Charlotte came home, Alice had been worried she would grieve Edgar and that it would be larger and louder than her own grief. But then she hadn't grieved at all, and that was worse.

Alice took a coffee cup from the sink and rinsed it out, using her fingers to clean yesterday's stains away. "Any damage done to the big house?"

"Not that I noticed. Just a lot of downed branches. I saw one on your roof. It doesn't look too big. I'll get it down when the weather clears up."

Alice nodded, still trying to shake the funk that clung to her like mud. It made her skin cold. She didn't always mind having Charlotte over. If nothing else, she broke up the torturous quiet inside the house. But this morning she was grating her nerves just by being there.

The coffee machine hissed, announcing a brewed pot of caffeine.

Alice winced, remembering that hissing laugh at the end of her waking dream.

Charlotte poured. "You feeling okay?" She held out the pot and waited.

Alice extended her mug and watched the dark liquid slosh in. "Headache," she lied.

Charlotte nodded and put the coffee pot back before opening the refrigerator. She kept a jug of vanilla creamer at Alice's house. She couldn't leave it at her own house anymore because Vic would drink it all, despite insisting he hadn't touched it. He'd swear up and down that he never drank creamer and it would ignite another screaming match between the siblings Edgar had always known how to make them stop, but it seemed like no one else did.

Alice knew Vic was lying about the creamer because he used to come by her place a lot to help out around the house after

Edgar disappeared. He had a sweet tooth and he'd dip into her creamer if he didn't think anyone would find out. He looked nothing like Edgar, too wide and too soft in the face even with the beard he grew to hide those boyish cheeks. Still, she liked to think he had a thing for her.

For a year or two, he'd been spending more time at her place than up at the big house, until his wife got jealous and probably forbade him from coming over on his own. Alice had spread rumors that Vic was in love with her a few years back but denied being the source with a level of fury that stopped anyone from suspecting her. She wasn't sure why she'd done it. Sometimes she believed he really had been obsessed with her, and sometimes she knew she just wanted people to think about her.

A door creaked inside the house, followed by another opening and closing. Miles was up. Alice only ever woke him if he had school, but he still never slept in for long. She liked when he was asleep. She could imagine he was still small, and maybe if he was still small then that morning where her life fell apart might not have happened yet. Edgar might still be there, quietly reading on the porch.

She sipped her coffee. It was bitter and disgusting but she made herself swallow it down. It was normalcy. Offensive and staining her tongue.

Alice missed the storm.

CHAPTER SEVEN

Charlotte lingered at Alice's house a while longer, until she was pretty sure her dad would be on the porch having his morning cigarette. Momma had banned smoking in the house long before any of the kids were born. She hadn't made a lot of hard rules, but that one had stuck even after her death. When Charlotte was still a kid, her dad had foolishly run through the house with a lit cigarette once to answer the phone. Her momma hadn't baked for two months after that.

Charlotte walked from Alice's house across the front of the property and back up to the big house situated at the end of the dirt road. Halfway there, she realized she'd forgotten her coffee at Alice's and seriously considered going back for it. The only thing that stopped her was knowing that if she went back now, she would stay and hide from the rest of her family. If

Alice wasn't in a particularly bad mood today, Charlotte would probably have done just that.

Alice's moods were important to keep track of. Sometimes they got along great, and Charlotte could spend all day hanging out with her. Other days, like today, it felt like Alice hated her.

At least the storm had cleared some of the old toys and tacky decorations from Alice's overgrown front yard. If Charlotte found them on the roofs, she'd toss them out before her sister-in-law could reclaim them.

Alice had bouts of wanting to fix up the property. She liked to start projects. A few years back, she bought all those ugly fairy statues for the yard, hellbent on hand-painting each one. Most were unpainted, broken, and lost in the weeds now. Two springs ago, Alice brought home sacks of soil, dozens of little plants, and deep pots that were *still* cluttered along the side of the house. Then there was the time she took the knobs off all the cabinets to repaint them. They were ideas that got far enough to leave a mark but never completed. The cabinets in the kitchen still didn't have knobs, and after two years, everyone had gotten used to pulling them open from their edges.

Charlotte tried to help—tried to finish a project or just put it back the way it was when Alice gave up. Her meddling had gone unnoticed, until Charlotte had put Miles's new bike together after it sat in pieces for three months in the living room after his birthday. She and Alice had had a screaming match right in the yard, between hideous fairy statues and blooming weeds.

They hadn't spoken for almost half a year after that. Oh, they had seen one another almost daily, Charlotte often picking up and dropping off Miles or sitting across from them both at family dinners with her old man at the big house. It turned out, one of the few things she and Alice had in common was the ability to hold on to grudges.

There hadn't been some heartwarming conversation to end the silent feud either. One day, when Charlotte said, "Good morning," as always, Alice finally said, "Good morning" back, and that was the end of the fight.

Charlotte didn't try to finish any of Alice's projects anymore—unless they were for Miles. She would take on Alice's anger for Miles any day.

So, she wouldn't go back for her mug today. She'd wait and maybe go over and see how she was doing tomorrow.

Gerard Crowe was on his porch, lighting a cigarette, when she reached the big house. Her dad raised one curious, bushy, brow at the sight of her. "On a walk, girl?" he called, but didn't get up. Getting up was harder for him now.

"Truck got totaled in the storm. Mudslide, I think."

He frowned hard, and she could already see him thinking about getting up to the truck and fixing it.

Charlotte laughed at the idea and stopped just below the first step of the porch. The big house was three stories and in there, somewhere, was her bedroom. The same room she'd had since she was a kid. Her dad reminded her often that it was there, waiting for her to come home, and she nodded and pretended she had come home—that she lived there, but she hadn't slept in her own bed once since coming home six years ago. She'd slept on the porch a hundred times, slumped in the same chair her dad sat in now, but not inside the house. There were ghosts in there. Her momma's, her brother's, and her own.

"It's wrecked," she repeated. "Can I borrow your truck?"

He had stopped driving earlier that year, not that any of them had talked about it directly. Just when she was sure she'd have to bring it up, for his own good and the well-being of others, he had started telling her when he needed to be someplace. Charlotte had taken to driving him, either in his truck or hers.

He nodded, brow creased and probably still thinking about her truck. "Key's in the visor. It's all yours, girl."

Sounds rustled in the house, a kid shouting for a parent with the distinct cry of unfairness afoot.

Charlotte stood her ground. Her younger brother had made a solid effort to fill the big house in the absence of his siblings. He and his wife had four kids, all under ten years old.

But, despite the rising ruckus inside, something was missing.

"Where are the dogs?" she asked.

Her dad rolled his eyes and took a drag off his cigarette. "The bastards all ran off in the storm. They'll find their way back."

Maybe Bill had run off with the other dogs? It was strange, but she convinced herself they'd be back in time for feeding.

"Cereal!" a shrill voice howled inside. It was a demand, not a request.

Charlotte laughed before she could stop herself and took a couple steps back. "You need anything from town?"

He waved an empty pack at her. It was the same brand her aunt smoked—not that they would ever share.

She nodded and turned for the truck. It was never locked, and the keys were always right where he said they would be—tucked into the driver's side visor. By the time she was pulling away from the house and crawling down the dirt road toward the paved street, Miles had emerged from Alice's house. The teen pushed his bike through the mud and weeds across his yard.

He lifted his head to throw a smile at the approaching truck. He looked so much like his father that it cut at her heart every time. The boy had the same sharp features and black curly hair. The same dark eyes, but with so much more light inside them. His hat pushed his curls down and pinned them close to his face, his cheeks already pink from the cold wind. He shoved his bike toward the beaten road.

Charlotte reached across and popped the door open in invitation. The fourteen year old was quick to hoist his bike up into the back of the truck. Just a year ago, he couldn't have done it on his own.

He hopped into the front seat with a big smile and buckled up without being asked. "Good morning!"

"Morning. Where are you going in this weather?"

Miles shrugged. "Momma said I could ride on the trails with Karl."

Charlotte nodded and started driving again. By *Karl*, Miles usually meant their whole miniature gang of friends. Even when Karl couldn't make it, Miles still called it *hanging out with Karl.* Charlotte wasn't sure if Alice knew that or not, but she didn't think it mattered either. "The trails are probably a mess."

Miles nodded but didn't look at all dissuaded from his plans. "I'm meeting them in town near the bus stop."

He wouldn't outright ask her to drive him there. He would just ride with her until she stopped, wherever that might be, and then get out and take his bike the rest of the way.

"I think I can get you there," she said, pretending to be unsure. The bus stop he was talking about was on Green Street, the same street that ran through the heart of Wicker. The post office, the grocery store, the diner, the bar, and the sheriff's office all lined up in brick buildings on Green Street.

Miles laughed and dug around in his pocket, pulling out a granola bar with the nutritional content of a donut.

Charlotte spotted the smudge on his jaw just before she turned onto the paved street past their mailbox. She took one hand off the wheel to grab his face, thumbing it once. He whined and batted her away. "You fall on your face?" she asked.

Miles laughed again and bit the granola bar in half, cramming it into his cheek as he chewed. "More like my face fell on this jerk's fist…"

Charlotte tried not to smile. Miles had always had a way with words. Well, not *always*. There were a few years there when he just made sounds and blew bubbles. But once he got talking, things had gotten interesting. "Which jerk?" One of the perks of a small town like Wicker was knowing every jerk, their parents, *and* their grandparents.

In Wicker, families took care of feuds like cherished pets. The Lathams and Asbies hadn't spoken in nearly a century over a land dispute. The Ludds had nearly driven all the Douglases off the mountain over a messy divorce that happened in the 1940s. And the Philipses and Crowes had a habit of shooting each other. So far, no one had died, but one of Charlotte's great uncles had lost a finger and, according to legend, Griffith Philips lost an ear in 1872. The fights were always over petty offenses and considered one-off incidents rather than a real feud, but Charlotte was convinced both sides were ready to draw on the other *because* of the long-standing habit.

No better than her ancestors, Charlotte was more than willing to make a whole family their enemies over kids fighting if one of those kids was Miles. It wasn't really okay to admit to having a favorite nephew or niece, but Miles was obviously hers.

The kid shook his head, chewing. "You wouldn't know him."

She almost argued, thinking this was some childhood naivety on his part before realizing *the jerk* wasn't from town. Wicker had its own elementary and middle school, squished into one in the little neighborhood behind the Green Street buildings. It was the same school where Charlotte had gone and where Charlotte's parents had gone before her. But Wicker sent its youth down the mountain to the high school in Cyprus after eighth grade. They took a bus, leaving at 5:30 on the dot every morning and arriving at 7:16 on a good day. A dozen times a year, the kids from Wicker were late to school because of the bus and bad weather slowing it down.

The one thing Wicker teens were never late for was that bus—though plenty of them managed to miss the bus home in hopes of sleeping over at a friend's house in the city.

But not Miles. He never missed the bus home because, even if he had friends in Cyprus, missing the bus would mean staying the night at his maternal grandmother's.

"Are you being bullied?" Charlotte asked.

Miles finished his granola bar and shoved the wrapper back into his pocket. "Huh? Oh. Not really. Karl got into a fight with one of the city kids and I tried to break it up." He laughed a little and pointed at the bruise on his jaw. "Got this for trying."

"And how did that go?"

Miles shrugged. "Momma was mad. She says if I stick my nose into other people's business it's going to get hit."

Charlotte bit back a mean smile, fingers tightening on the steering wheel. "Yeah, well, you couldn't just stand there, could you?" Of course, he *could* have, but that wasn't who Miles was. "Better to get hit doing the right thing than walk away feeling like an asshole."

Miles giggled, the way he always did when she swore. Soon he wouldn't. But right now, he was fourteen and still found it funny. Greenleigh, Hannah, and Lila were all good at using pretend swears around the kids—lots of *"poop"* and *"meanie"* and *"darn."* Charlotte was of the opinion that some people weren't *"meanies"*—they were *"assholes."* And some situations called for a solid *"damn it"* and no amount of *"darn"* would ever do. But, obliging the mothers in her life, she didn't let the kids swear just because she did. Charlotte did all sorts of things her nieces and nephews weren't allowed to do— eating cookies for dinner and swearing like her Aunt Henri only being the tip of the iceberg.

But Alice was not a *pretend swearword mom.* In fact, she swore more than Charlotte. But Miles had somehow gleaned the situation of cuss words and childhood from the other kids in the family. Charlotte had never heard him drop even a *"shit"* around her. Which was a relief, because she had no idea if she was supposed to care if he did. Would Alice care?

They turned onto the highway that ran up the mountain from Cyprus, going right past Wicker before curving to the east. The road tucked around the first peak, Mount Bell, with its last turn off for mountain trails before wrapping around the mountain and descending the north side in a straight shot to nowhere but long stretches of farmland. But on the south side of the mountain—their side—the highway skirted drop-offs with magnificent views of treetops streaming away in an endless sea of green. On dark nights, Cyprus could be seen twinkling in the wilderness at the bottom of the mountain, just on the other side of the Aurora River.

It had been Charlotte's experience that unless she wanted to leave town, there were not a lot of roads to drive. A handful of residential streets looped around the town center, and a dozen dirt roads split from the highway onto private properties and trails on both sides of Wicker.

She turned onto Green Street and slowed the truck to a crawl, almost stopping when she caught sight of Mount Bell looming over the town. Half the peak was gone, still a jagged rock formation sticking out of the side of Mount Grayson but different than before, sharper. She had known the shape of the mountain her whole life but today it had changed, a chunk of it broken off and swept down through the woods in the storm.

"If it starts raining again, come back to town and I'll come get you," Charlotte said, remembering that their phone connections were lost. "You can wait at the diner."

Miles nodded, sitting up taller to look for his friends. "I see them!"

She parked along the street at the first spot she found. It looked like everyone was gathering, either to buy supplies or share news. A large metal post bearing the power line had tipped over and now rested against the brick post office with a precarious wobble every time the wind brushed past. "Be careful," she reminded, getting out and helping her nephew pull his bike from the truck. She got a muddy tire track on her jeans.

"Bye! Thanks!" Miles shouted, already on his bike and pedaling away.

His friends called to him when they saw him. Karl waited but the Philips girls got on their bikes and started pedaling up the road. She thought that might be strategy though, since one of them was barely off her training wheels and would quickly be passed by the others.

The group headed north, toward the hiking trails the kids of Wicker had been playing on for five generations now. Charlotte had no way of knowing then, that not every kid would make it home that night. If she had even the slightest idea, she would have grabbed them all up and dragged them home. If she could even begin to guess at the darkness on their mountain, she would have made a run for Cyprus with her whole family.

But, like everyone else in Wicker, Charlotte did not know what lived on their mountain with them—what had been there all along, waiting to bring ruin and death.

She stuffed her hands into her pockets and walked up the sidewalk, smiling wide when she saw a familiar truck.

"Greenleigh!" Charlotte called, louder than necessary, when she saw her friend heaving a box into the back.

Rebecca Greenleigh didn't jump. She hadn't jumped no matter how many times Charlotte tried to scare her over the last thirty years. Instead, she turned and ran her gaze over Charlotte, her smile tucked carefully in the side of her mouth. "Oh good, you survived," she said with a tone that suggested disappointment.

Charlotte shrugged. "Takes more than weather to kill Crowes." She'd heard several relatives say those exact words before. The pride of Crowes was second only to their stubbornness. "Although it did manage to kill my truck, my shack, and my phone."

Greenleigh's eyebrows went up and the hint of a smile vanished. "Your shack blew down?" She had hated the shack and even gone so far as to offer to help her build something better. A thought crossed her features, darkening her expression. "Mudslide?"

Charlotte nodded, leaning against the side of her friend's truck. She told the story in detail, trying it out and finding it was quite the absurd tale—even without the part where she spooked herself into thinking that there was something with her in the dark.

Greenleigh looked shocked but she didn't call her a liar. She knew better. Crowes never told lies they could be caught in, one of their many characteristics and one that Rebecca Greenleigh would know well.

Both the Greenleighs and Crowes had been among the founders of Wicker, pressed up against one another on the mountain for nearly twenty generations.

In all that time, Charlotte and Rebecca were the first of their lines to form a friendship.

Crowes and Greenleighs did not get along. It wasn't a rule so much as a fact. They never fought, not really, but there was a grudge between them as old as the town itself—so old and unspoken that the facts of it had been long lost. As girls they had both asked their respective grandparents about the offense and, while both grandparents were set on not wanting the kids to hang out, neither could remember why.

In all those generations, there had been no marriage between the two families or even between their cousins under different surnames. They were possibly the only families in Wicker with no tie to one another but the mountain itself.

It had been a town-wide scandal when Charlotte Crowe and Rebecca Greenleigh, only eight years old at the time, became best friends. Charlotte still remembered how it started, when Frank Wilde pushed her down in the third grade and ripped up her drawing. No one in the world could remember why he did it, but Greenleigh had walked up to him and dumped a jar of blue paint on his head. The two girls had been inseparable ever since. They had ridden busses together, driven their first cars together, tasted their first wine coolers together, and weathered the loss of parents together. Nothing could break their friendship. Charlotte knew it for a fact because she had tested it plenty.

The town had even given up being bothered by them. It probably helped when Rebecca brought home a girlfriend before heading off to college. That had been a much larger scandal than Crowes and Greenleighs. The town was even *more* shocked when she returned to Wicker, married to Hannah, and took over the family business. The Greenleighs owned most of the mountain between the river and Wicker, and a little more than half the sawmill. There had been a moment when the other original families of Wicker thought Rebecca would be the end of the long line of Greenleighs, the last of her blood on the mountain—until she announced she was pregnant.

Their little town had a lot of questions—none of which would Greenleigh or Hannah answer. Of course, *Charlotte* knew they'd picked out a sperm donor from a clinic in Cyprus. But it was the principal of the matter, and if Greenleigh and Hannah didn't want to explain, they wouldn't, and neither would she. It had been six years since they had William, but every so often someone tried to wheedle the details out of them.

"The bridge is down," Greenleigh said, looking around at the busy street rather than right at Charlotte. She was acting strange. Was she worried about the bridge?

"Is Hannah freaking out?"

Greenleigh shrugged. "I haven't seen her all morning. But she'll be at the emergency alderman meeting."

Charlotte nodded, watching her carefully. Her thoughts were obviously elsewhere. It wasn't like Greenleigh to worry about the bridge. Wicker got cut off from Cyprus sometimes. Even if people were saying that the bridge was out, it was probably an exaggeration. It was more likely blocked, or the river had risen above it.

Charlotte finally turned her head to get a look at what her friend had been loading into the bed of her truck. She expected food stock but instead found an axe, shovels, chains, tarps, and cans of kerosine. *A lot* of kerosine. She didn't even try to school her reaction, eyebrows lifting high and eyes turning on Greenleigh. "You need help with something?"

To Charlotte's surprise, her friend considered the offer.

"Maybe," she said and then, "Yes."

Charlotte straightened. Greenleigh looked almost nervous. "Is everything okay with Hannah and Will?"

"Yeah. They're fine. Can you meet me back here in an hour?"

Charlotte nodded. It wasn't often Greenleigh needed anything from anyone. "Absolutely."

Greenleigh closed the back of the truck and started walking in the direction of the school. She was so preoccupied with her own thoughts she hadn't even said goodbye. It was strange. Worry clawed at the back of Charlotte's thoughts—but if Greenleigh was still going to an alderman meeting, it couldn't be anything too bad.

Charlotte walked down the street, peeking in through the big windows of the grocery store. The aisles were uncharacteristically packed and the shelves half-emptied. Metal carts brimmed with food and toilet paper, creating a snaking line that vanished into the depths of the store. She considered going in and elbowing her way to a stockpile of canned soup and pasta but kept walking. They had plenty of reserves at the big house and if that really ran out, she could just go over to the Greenleigh house.

The Greenleighs had a stockpile worthy of an apocalypse, and that wasn't even taking into account the storage of supplies at the old sanitorium. They were determined to be capable of helping the town in any emergency. Charlotte had gaped at the garage of food and supplies the first time she saw it as a kid, and then she and Greenleigh had eaten so many boxes of vanilla wafer cookies that they puked in the backyard.

Sheriff Summerfield stood in the doorway of the bar across the street, holding it open and talking to someone inside. Was the bar open early?

The sheriff threw his voice low when he spoke, trying to command authority. Not an easy task since anyone her age and over had known him as a kid. It was hard to listen to a man who was once, very clearly in memory, a boy who ate gum he pulled up from under tables and benches.

Charlotte ducked into the corner shop at one end of Green Street. It had no sign, but through the dirty window any passersby could make out the shelves of books. A narrow, wood door led into a musty room with very little free space.

Two well-worn plush chairs were wedged under the window, with boxes of books piled around them. Almost all the books packed into the little shop were used, some printed in the last few years while others were decades old. There was no particular order to how they had been crammed into the ceiling high shelves—or, none she had deciphered, anyway.

Harvey Darling sat behind a high, solid oak counter in one corner with his legs crossed at the knee. He held a book up—something beaten by time, the pages a sallow yellow and the cover frayed into soft fluff at the edges. Charlotte tipped her head to the side to make out a spaceship and a dragon on the cover. He smiled, still reading, his wide mouth bright red with lipstick. Harvey pointed at a plate beside the vintage cash register, not looking away from his page. "Brownie?"

"Oh, you always did know how to flirt with me." She shrugged off her jacket and flung it over one of the old chairs.

His smile grew, gaze flicking up from the pages to her. His pupils were blown wide, melting into his already dark irises.

Harvey Darling, known in Wicker simply as, *Darling*, had been the little boy who came home every day with a new bruise, broken glasses, or drenched in soda. This town would have broken him, quite literally, if it had ever been possible to break a Darling. Harvey was the perfect mix of fun and insane as a kid, always keeping the other boys on their toes.

He had been a beautiful child who grew into a pretty teen. That girlish face coupled with his utterly shameless habit of doing and saying exactly what he wanted got him into a lot of trouble. When they were twelve, the other boys took their rage out on his long hair. They cornered him in the bathroom and cut it off with safety scissors stolen from the classroom art supplies. Harvey hadn't shed a tear or complained; he just left it choppy until it grew back. Since then, when his hair grew long and he was looking for a change, he hacked it up just like those boys had decades before. The culprits of the first crime, grown men now, steered clear of Darling when he did, averting their eyes from the reminder that he still hadn't forgotten.

He wore eyeliner in high school and got his lip pierced at fourteen, sticking out in Wicker as well as Cyprus. He'd been in fights at school almost weekly but walked away from them with a bloody smile, like it was all in good fun—a price gladly paid to be exactly who he was. It unnerved the other boys.

Charlotte hadn't given him much thought, being a year behind him in school, until the Halloween festival when she was fifteen. He showed up in platform heels, black tights, a corset, and vampire fangs. Her crush was instantaneous—and when she saw her chance, she dragged a chair over to him, climbed up, and dipped him in her arms. It hadn't been her first kiss, but it was the first one seared into her mind like a streak of lightning across skin. She suspected he'd gone along with it for the show they were giving and for the effort she'd made in coming at him with a prop.

In Charlotte's life, Darling had been her one-man sexual revolution. She could do anything, and he was always game. He would never judge, never be cruel, and never leave her hanging. She pretended they were just friends killing time together, but they both knew she intended to kill all her time with him, right down to the last second.

She picked up one of the brownies from the plate. "Heard the bridge is down."

He nodded, black hair in wild waves around his face, falling out of the tie at the back of his head. "I went and looked at it. The river is flooded. But the water tower is fine and most of Wicker has power now," he reported casually, not particularly worried—though, in his current high, it was unlikely he would be worried about a meteor falling on them. "Everyone has a generator anyway," he added with a shrug.

Charlotte smiled and took a bite of gooey chocolate. Darling liked to bake, and he was good at it. He could have worked at the bakery if his name had been different. No one was going to hire a Darling in Wicker, not even their own Darling.

"A couple tourists died in a mudslide up past the sanitorium," he reported.

Charlotte blinked. "Really?" Why hadn't Rebecca mentioned that?

He nodded. "They brought what they could find of them down to the morgue a little while ago."

Charlotte winced and couldn't help but think about her own run-in with the storm. If she'd been buried in that mud, would anyone have realized she was missing yet? With everything going on, maybe it would have taken a couple days before anyone even thought to go looking for her.

"You okay, Lotte?" Harvey asked, voice edged in concern and eyes narrowed on her.

She met his gaze. Her fears were wrong. It would not have taken Harvey long to realize she wasn't answering texts or rolling into his shop for sweets. "Can I crash at your place tonight?"

"Of course." He looked surprised, and she knew it wasn't because she wanted to stay with him; it was because she'd asked. She had most of her stuff at his trailer. Greenleigh liked to make jabs about how Charlotte had moved in, but the only one who wouldn't admit it was Charlotte herself.

The copper bell over the door chimed and Roger Gary walked in. He tossed each of them a nod before disappearing down one of the narrow aisles of books. Charlotte leaned against the edge of the counter, nibbling brownie, until he came back with a paperback in hand. He put it on the counter with two twenty-dollar bills sticking out of the pages.

Darling swept up the book, and the money vanished. He snatched something from under his counter and a small plastic bag—slipping both the book and the extra something into it before passing it to Roger. "Have a nice day."

Roger pushed away from the counter before hesitating, eyes darting to the plate of brownies.

Darling grinned and fanned his hand toward the treats in offering.

Roger's smile pressed his round cheeks high. He took a brownie before nodding to both of them again and leaving.

Darling's bookstore was popular, despite being located in a tiny town where very few people cared to read books—let alone books about space cowboys and dragon oaths.

"How's your cousin's farm?" Charlotte asked before taking the last bite of her brownie.

Darling groaned and slid off his stool. "Everything they had indoors is fine, but it sounds like the valley took a beating." He shrugged in that casual 'it's not really my problem' way. He just sold the product. It was their job to grow it and bring it down the mountain to him and other distributors.

Before the bookstore started selling books and weed, it had been a storage facility for the grocery store next door. Supposedly, the Garys, who owned the grocery store, had stocked moonshine made by the Darlings during prohibition and sold the jars to the locals of Wicker as well as those from Cyprus willing to drive up for a drink. Of course, none of the Garys would admit to any past connection—nor to the bootlegging—but Darling swore to it. He'd even shown her the tunnel under the floorboards of his bookshop, where the moonshine deliveries had been dragged in.

Darling's cousins, like his mother, lived outside of Wicker— outside of any town at all. They liked to think of themselves as wild. And, having seen them a few times, Charlotte would not disagree. She had seen bears and deer, and the Darlings of the gray mountain were just as wild, if not a bit wicked to boot.

Harvey's mother had given him to his father, a Wicker resident, when he was four, making him the only town Darling. The rest only came through when making deliveries to the bookstore or heading down to Cyprus, and they never stopped in at the bar or diner. Everything north of the Wicker town borders, just past Mount Bell, belonged to the Darlings. Not legally, but all the same. According to the stories, the Darlings had been living on the mountain long before the first settling families arrived—before the town itself.

Back in 1902, when a brutal snowstorm buried the town, almost a quarter of the Wicker residents had died. Those that were too sick or too frail to tend their fires were found frozen after the storm. More than one house had burned in that frigid winter, leaving no survivors and the dark rumors that the families had set their own homes on fire just for some warmth after their wood stocks ran out. But the worst stories had come from the families who lost only one member. In the archives, those dead were all listed as having frozen—in homes where everyone else had stayed warm. The bodies were not autopsied before being taken down the mountain and cremated.

Everyone who grew up in the town since noticed the brittle silence surrounding that storm. Where usually their parents and grandparents loved to tell the tales of their survival on the mountain, that particular winter remained vague and rarely mentioned. They had survived—that was all, and nothing else would ever be said about it. Except that, despite the cruelty of that winter, it was rumored that not a single Darling up the mountain had died. They had food and warmth and, from their vantage, had watched the smokestacks go out in the town—watched as the folks of Wicker froze and perished, with no mercy in their hearts for them.

The Darlings had been on the mountain first—and they meant to be there last.

Harvey Darling, on the other hand, was a lighthearted man who declined even to go hunting when invited by his friends. He preferred to bake, smoke, and read rather than play the old family game of *last one standing on the mountain*. And yet the town never forgot the blood in his veins. Most everyone had seen his smile at one point or another, sometimes after a fight, with blood on his teeth. He smiled like the fight had been friendly and he was glad for it.

He smiled like nothing hurt him and all attempts brought him amusement.

He smiled like a wolf—*like a Darling*.

Harvey came around the counter to her, hooking an arm across her back and leading her toward the plush chairs. "So, are you going to tell me why you're driving your dad's truck today?" he asked, deep voice in her ear just before he fell into one of the chairs and pulled her into his lap.

From that spot, Charlotte could see out the clean top corner of the dirty window, clouds still gathering in the sky—lighter than yesterday with only tendrils of dark gray swirling like the memory of a storm. She relaxed the way she only ever could with him.

"I've got an hour to kill," she conceded vaguely, never one to offer too much of herself. "So, I was sleeping in the shack last night…"

CHAPTER EIGHT

When Mr. Harrison Wicker forged a path up and over Mount Grayson in 1694, adding it to his notes on the land, he did not know the witch was already there. He thought he was the first. More than twenty-thousand years since the first humans roamed the land, more than a hundred years since the first invaders arrived on the continent, and yet Mr. Harrison Wicker fancied himself the first just about everywhere he ever went.

When a settlement donned his name eight years later, he decided to return. He proclaimed the Gray Mountain to be the prettiest place he'd ever discovered. Discovered. Like it had been unseen before he arrived. Like it had not been a part of the landscape of the world for nearly a thousand human generations before he marched across it.

The witch did not know he was offensive when she ate him. He was just another rabbit in the woods. The witch's woods, because Mr. Harrison Wicker may have thought he discovered the mountain, but the witch had built it.

CHAPTER NINE

Miles met up with his friends in town and together they took their bikes up Green Street, almost to the top where it spit onto the highway heading north out of town. A dirt parking lot with big wooden signs indicating the hiking trails and history of Mount Bell invited them into the woods. He and his friends never actually made it up to the smaller peak at the top of the winding trails, but they had gone all the way over to the viewpoint a few times and thrown rocks down to the Aurora River far below.

They all knew their parents didn't want them going there.

Well, Josie and Sage's dad had said they weren't allowed to go over to the cliff without him. And Jon's parents had told him the same thing, but Karl thought Jon was lying and just too scared to go. Karl's dad never said anything about where he should go, as long as he came back before dark, and Miles had told his momma once about going to the viewpoint, but she hadn't said anything about it. He wasn't sure she'd actually been listening.

They had to push their bikes across the muddy path from the parking lot through the trees, up to the old witch bridge.

All the trails split off after the bridge, snaking between boulders and trees. The bridge itself was just six feet of old planks set across a ditch that sometimes filled with water but today was swollen with muck.

The sun winked in his eyes before disappearing between the clouds again, gathering over the first summit and completely hiding the top of Mount Grayson.

His mom had been in a bad mood that morning and had just shrugged when he asked if he could go ride bikes with his friends. The streets were muddy, and the trails would probably be worse, but that had never stopped them before.

Karl and Jon waited on the other side of the bridge. Jon was worried about the mud ruining his shoes and Karl was pretending not to hear him. Josie and Sage rushed past Miles, crossing the bridge. Each of the Philips girls held one hand over her eyes and used the other to steer her bike. They only managed not to bump into one another because they had done this exact blind-rush across the bridge a hundred times. Sage was three years younger than them, but Josie wouldn't leave her behind no matter how the boys whined about waiting for her.

"Come on!" Karl called, grinding out the words with impatience.

Miles closed his eyes and started walking across. His aunt and uncle said he was supposed to cross the bridge backward—that was how they'd done it when they were kids—but all his friends just covered their eyes.

The trick was not to peek. If you opened your eyes and saw the witch's house, she might see you too. He had *never* peeked. He told his friends he did, but he hadn't really. Josie had looked once, hands on her hips and nose wrinkled when she squinted up the mountain at Mount Bell where the witch's house was supposed to be. Karl had asked if she saw it. He was a fan of peeking too. But unlike Karl who always claimed to see the smoke from the witch's chimney, Josie had seen nothing and been disappointed. Still, she covered her eyes every time since.

The wet planks creaked in high tones underfoot. Karl's voice grew farther away. He was probably rushing off to the trails to see how they looked for riding. And then the other voices started stretching away from Miles too. His heart beat faster. Were they leaving him behind? He told himself it was okay. It didn't matter. He would catch up in a minute.

But he was still walking, the boards still creaking.

It never took this long to cross the little bridge.

The wind moved hard against his side, making him wobble and stop. With his eyes closed, he was unbalanced. His face started to sweat under his palm. For a horrible second, he was sure he would fall off the bridge and into the gooey, gross mud that had gathered in the ditch. What if his bike fell on top of him? What if it pushed him down and drowned him in the dirty water? He could almost taste it, that earthy grit against his teeth.

"Karl?" he called, and his voice echoed back on him, making him jump.

His breath came in faster and that too echoed, bouncing off walls he knew weren't there.

Open your eyes, a patient voice suggested.

He twisted right and then left.

Another gust of wind and he dropped his hand from his face to hold onto his bike with both. Daylight made his eyelids orange and the sway of trees cast shadows back and forth across them. "Josie?" he called for his most responsible friend, his voice embarrassingly thin now.

The bridge creaked again, but he hadn't moved. Someone else walked closer, their steps hard and heavy like large stones thudding down on the planks. A thick shadow loomed over him, pressing back the orange daylight. The wind continued to roll back and forth, but the shadow didn't sway.

Open your eyes, the voice whispered again—not a real voice but something in his head. His mind was playing tricks on him. He was scaring himself. That was what Aunt Lotte would say, wasn't it? Like when he tried to convince himself there were no monsters in the dark only to stare hard and outline the shapes of them with his imagination, creating something from nothing.

Miles cringed, holding so tightly to the handlebars of his bike that his hands ached. He clenched his teeth and forced down a deep breath. There was nothing there. There couldn't be. And he was probably only steps from the other side.

Miles started forward, toward the shadow. It was only in his head. He would just walk forward until he reached the end of—

His bike stopped. Someone had grabbed hold of it. His breath hitched, heaving from his lungs in tight gasps. He tried to shake the handlebars, but the bike wouldn't budge. His fingers uncurled slowly from the rubber grips, long enough to let it stand all by itself, and then he clung to them again to keep *himself* upright.

Tears gathered against his closed lids. "Karl?" he shouted. "Josie?" He didn't care how his voice pitched and cracked.

The names rolled back at him, but this time it wasn't an echo; it was someone else's voice, ragged as though strangled and laughing at the same time. *"Karl? Josie?"*

His eyelids flung open, daylight searing his pupils and tears spilling over his lashes.

There was no one on the bridge in front of him. He was exactly in the middle, the distance just as short as ever, and he could see his friends up ahead at the crossroad of trails, arguing over their options. They hadn't heard him calling. They hadn't seen anything. It had all just been in his head.

Miles took a step and just then a heavy hand came down against his back. He screamed, too much fear already gathered against the back of his throat to hold it in now.

Laughter rose behind him. The hand closed into a fist on his hoodie, dragging him up onto his toes. Sam Caller wrenched Miles's bike from his grip and shoved it off the bridge and into the ditch. The sixteen-year-old was already as tall as most dads, easily dwarfing Miles.

"You fuckin' pussy!" Sam howled. His three friends crossed the bridge, two carrying backpacks and one with a six-pack of beer. All three were grinning and one of the boys even stopped to spit over the edge on Miles's already sinking bike, air bubbling up from the thick mud.

Karl, Josie, Sage, and Jon doubled back, their faces twisted in a collection of anger and fear.

"Hey!" Josie was first to shout, pushing through the older teens to the bridge while her little sister stayed back with the bikes. "Get away from him!"

Miles struggled, trying to smack away the hand on the back of his hoodie. Sam jerked harder, ripping seams and dragging Miles to the side of the bridge. He was going the direction of his bike. His breath lodged hard against the back of his throat. His sneakers squeaked against the edge of the planks, trying to stay on while Sam leaned him over the thick mud.

"You want me to let you go?" Sam said.

Miles twisted toward him rather than away, clutching at the arm he had been batting moments before.

Sam's face was pink with excitement, making his freckles pop out and his zits blend in. His head was shaved, peach fuzz coating the dome, and his blue eyes glittered with mischief. He gave Miles a ruthless shake and licked his chapped lips. He was going to drop him. Miles knew it and his heart cringed behind his ribs.

Miles's gaze slipped over Sam's shoulder and up the mountain, caught by a curl of smoke, light gray and twirling from the treetops. Following it down, he could see the little shape of a dark house just at the base of Mount Bell's peak where the rocks jutted free of the woods.

He *knew* it was the witch's house without question because he knew she was looking back at him. He *felt* her smile, rolling through the woods, shivering in the air, the ground, and the trees. It pushed tears from his eyes in a new wave of horror because her attention felt slick and poisonous. His head filled with a hissing, writhing cry, the pounding of hooves, and the gut deep howl of a wolf.

Miles landed in the mud feetfirst and sank to his waist. He might have fallen to the side and gone under if he weren't already tangled with his bike, the metal bruising into his hip and knee at awkward angles.

Josie yelled, "Asshole!"

Karl ran onto the bridge and shoved Sam, despite the older teen being twice his size.

Sam laughed and grabbed Karl by the arm, but Karl swung his other fist and punched Sam in the crotch. They had seen it in Karl's dad's collection of Bruce Lee movies. Karl laughed hysterically at every dick-punch and had decided it was what evil people deserved.

Sam let out a high-pitched wheeze of surprise, his knees pinching together, and Karl burst into glorious laughter. Sam still managed to twist the arm he had captured and tossed Karl off the other side of the bridge. The boy went in and disappeared beneath a wetter patch than where Miles had landed, mucky water flinging into the air. When Karl popped up, drenched in mud, he was still laughing.

Sam hobbled off the bridge, swearing, and Jon ducked to the side, holding tight to his bike and looking like he might piss himself. The teen disappeared into the woods, on the heels of his friends, and Miles was pretty sure Jon didn't dare breathe until Sam was out of sight.

Karl scrubbed a dirty hand over his face, scraping off enough mud to open his eyes. He smiled under the bridge at Miles. "Did you see that?" he roared, grinning from one big ear to the other.

Miles smiled back, forgetting the odd vision from the bridge—the Wicker Witch replaced with the moment his best friend revenge-punched Sam Caller in the dick.

Sage walked both her and her sister's bikes over and let out a disappointed sigh. "Does this mean we're going home?"

Josie ignored her and squatted on the bridge, looking down at Miles. "Pass up the bike first," she said, arms out.

It took both Josie and Jon to pull his bike up and dump it on solid ground.

Karl convinced Jon to give him a hand out of the mud. Jon, always the easiest one to dupe, took Karl's hand and was immediately hauled in.

Josie stood on the bridge, eyeing the mess of them, and all three boys feared she would leave them there, stuck like flies on paper. Ultimately, she helped Miles out first, and then Jon, and then together they all pulled Karl out without getting tossed in themselves. By the time the five of them were pushing their bikes back to town, no one would be able to guess which, if any, of them had not gone into the mud.

CHAPTER TEN

The group found one of the picnic tables and sat on it.

Last summer, Sam and his friends had dragged all the picnic tables to one spot and stacked them up. After that, Mayor Philips and her aldermen had the picnic tables chained to trees so they couldn't be stolen or moved. She was a bitch, but today it had kept the tables from being swept away in the storm.

Blades of grass stuck up from the layer of mud covering the ground and Sam tried to stamp them back down. He sipped warm beer and pretended to like it. Honestly, he didn't know why anyone drank beer. It tasted nasty. But he would never admit that. Just last month, when Harry cringed at his first sip, they had all made fun of him.

Ashley dug a plastic baggy out of her backpack, fingering a dry joint to set between her blue-painted lips. Danny pulled a lighter from his jacket and offered her a flame. They had been dating for a month and this was how they always lit up.

Sam rolled his eyes, pretty sure that they'd practiced so it would look natural. He thought it looked stupid.

"Gotta piss," Sam said, jumping up from the table and trudging off into the trees.

He hoped the roads *never* got cleared because if the buses couldn't get up and down the mountain, then they didn't have to go to school. His aunt had a bunch of small kids in her house to take care of—her own and the ones she babysat for her friends—so she never cared where he went as long as he came back by eight.

Sam kicked a rock, picked a tree, and unzipped. He chanced another glance back, making sure no one had followed him to try to play a prank on him. Sam had claimed the role of group trickster, and it left him paranoid that they would do to him what he would most certainly do to them.

The trees creaked when the wind pushed through the woods. He had to shift sideways to make sure his stream didn't come back on him and wet his sneakers. Mud was one thing; piss was another.

He whistled at the close call, giving himself a little jump and shake before zipping up and starting back toward his friends. The ground sank a little with each soggy step. He stopped when he spotted tracks in the mud. He bent over and blinked, but there was no mistaking the human footprints. Had someone been running around barefoot out there? The only other people they'd seen had been those shits on the bridge.

Sam squinted, brow pinching when he noticed that inside each footprint was a pointy cloven hoofprint going the other direction.

"Hey, guys! Come see this!" he called.

Had a deer been following in someone's tracks? What were the chances of that happening on accident?

The trees creaked but his friends didn't answer.

Sam groaned and stood upright again. He left the tracks and marched back to the table chained to the big tree. He stopped in front of it. They were gone.

The trees swayed in the breeze, more wet leaves spinning to the ground.

He turned a full circle, but they really were gone. He didn't even spot the flash of a bright rain jacket ducking behind a tree. He held his breath, straining to hear but not getting even a mischievous giggle.

"Funny! Come out!" he said.

Sam waited. There was no answering laughter or whispers. In fact, the forest had gone quiet. There were no birds or squirrels. There was only the creaking of branches in the wind and the endless dripping of water off leaves and pine needles onto wet ground.

"Fine. Screw you guys, I'm going home," he said with a big groan, so they'd know he was unimpressed. He stomped away for four minutes before realizing the trail had vanished underfoot and he was just walking through the woods.

Stopping, he flashed his gaze around the forest floor. All the trails were gone. All the boulders coated in generations of graffiti were suddenly nowhere to be seen, along with the big landmark trees that just about everyone in Wicker had carved their initials into.

Sam spun around in a full circle twice, feeling the first sickening waves of panic slosh in his stomach. He had been out there almost every day of his life. He knew the area. And yet, he had no idea where he was. For the first time in his life, Sam Caller was lost.

"Ashley? Harry?" he called, voice cracking. He coughed to clear it.

The trees creaked, far away and getting closer, making the hairs on the back of his neck stand on end and his skin wash cold.

Something was coming.

"Dad!" he called, choking on the word when it escaped him, forgetting for an instant that the man had moved down the mountain years ago and never come back. Tears stung his eyes and he scrubbed at them before they could fall.

"Someone!" he called, forgetting all his anger. "Anyone, please!" he shouted and then sucked a breath as though he could take back the words, draw back in the sounds he had made and time itself—because he *felt* the moment something heard him.

He stood frozen, cold right down to his bones with terror. *Something* had heard him all right. It reminded him of the time he and Danny had seen a grizzly and the big old bear sat right up and looked at them.

He staggered through the trees, head whipping from side to side. He could sense something watching him, but he couldn't spot it.

He tripped over a thick, upgrown root and pushed his hands at the ground to right himself. That was when he spotted the strange tracks again, the hoofprints inside footprints. He stared at them for too long, trying to make sense of them before deciding to go in the opposite direction of the human prints.

Sam scrubbed at his eyes with the sleeves of his jacket, trying not to cry. He wanted to get back to a trail, *any trail*. He walked faster and faster until he started running. The muscles in his thighs burned and his breaths came harsh and wheezing. The creaking of the trees all around grew louder, closer, but there was no wind.

Then the whole forest darkened as though one giant hand had reached up to block the bright cloudy sky. He staggered to a stop in a thicket of overgrown, tangled trees. He had never seen that place before, or anything remotely like it. The trees grew into and out of one another. They were crooked, their thick trunks wrapping around each other and branches curling down as though reaching for the shadows near the ground rather than the light up above.

Looking through them, Sam could see a clearing at the other end washed in daylight. A rock wall, maybe part of Mount Bell's peak, gleamed brightly with an open cavern and a chimney stack.

His tears ran freely down his cheeks. He wanted to look away from the opening, but he couldn't. The smoke curling from the chimney ruined any hope he had of it being a trick of the eye or a natural formation. Smoke rose in pale twists, and the mad thought that this was where clouds came from—from *this* chimney—struck him. And depending on what burned, the clouds would come out white and fluffy or black and heavy with rain.

Sam swallowed hard, realizing only then that he was making a thin, keening sound in the back of his throat. He backpedaled away from the old, tangled trees and the strange little house.

He wasn't supposed to be there.

No one was supposed to be there.

A wind shoved up against his back, stopping his retreat and trying to drive him forward. Sam cried out, almost screaming. He shook his head hard.

He noticed then the tracks on the patch of mud between the twisted trees. The strange hoofprints inside footprints were everywhere, walking back and forth until every inch of the ground had been covered in them.

Sam took deep, gulping breaths until he was sure he would choke on air.

The eerie silence broke and sound returned to him all at once—not just his own little whimpers and cries, or the ever-nearing creaking of trees, but a clattering of wind chimes. They burst across his eardrums and his head whipped up. Chimes dangled from the bent trees, glinting white and red and brown, hanging from knots of string and swaying violently in the wind.

He shook his head, that senseless song of chimes speaking to him, asking something horrible.

Sam spun around, turning his back on that dark, twisted place, and ran.

He ran harder and faster than ever before, trying to keep his direction downhill at every incline. Eventually he would hit a trail or a road. Eventually he would see something he recognized.

He ran until his throat burned, lungs aching, and he tasted iron on the back of his tongue.

The woods grew dark again.

He stopped when he stared through his tears into that knotted gathering of trees, the dark cottage on the other side waiting for him.

His hand flew to his mouth to smother the scream bubbling up in his chest.

It wasn't possible.

He had run away from it, in the opposite direction and downhill. But somehow, he was facing uphill again, and the wind chimes called from overhead, deafening—*screaming*. He heard voices in their clatter, crying down at him in a furious song of death.

His hands cupped his ears, pushing his palms flat and trying to focus on his own pulse, but he couldn't quiet the chimes. They became a thousand voices, all yelling in his head at the same time. He couldn't make out their words, some angry and some frightened, all of them flooding his mind.

And then the shadows on the ground ahead moved and the chimes went silent. The wind continued to blow, and the chimes still swayed and crashed together, but the sound had been turned off again.

The shadows on the ground writhed until shoulders arched up from the mud like a giant mountain lion stretching beneath.

An arm snapped up from out of the darkness and grabbed at the earth. A second followed, and together they hoisted a body up. Long arms and narrow torso stretched, sharp hips pushing to one side as it tested strong legs. The shadows clung to the monster's head in waves of hair, mud glistening wet on the almost-human body. Eyelids opened and Sam's breath caught in his throat. She stared right at him.

Tears burned down his cheeks.

Her head tipped from one side to the other, like a bird considering him. Then those mud-slick lips pulled into a grin, so unbearably human but for the gleam of teeth—too long and too many with points.

Hunger rippled in the air around her like wings unfurling. It was overwhelming. All he wanted to do was run, scream, and beg. But Sam could barely breathe, body shaking in tight convulsions where he stood.

She moved toward him in little steps that somehow jumped distances, closer and closer and then right in front of him.

The monster was so tall that it had to lean down to look him in the eye, and when she did, he *heard* her. She sounded like wind and waves and the grinding of stones. She sounded like the beginning and the end. And just when he was certain he could take no more, his thoughts went silent but for one blaring scream of pain.

Sam looked down between them at the creature's mud-coated hand sliding into him, tearing open jacket and shirt like they were nothing but cobwebs. Blood gushed down his front, and all the warmth he had ever known slipped from him.

He grabbed at her shoulders, his fingers tangling in hair but his palms finding skin and bone. She felt fragile but when he pushed, she didn't move. Something in her hair crawled over the backs of his hands and he screamed again, her hand driving deeper into his soft stomach.

When he tried again to push away, she pressed in closer, like he had drawn her to him. His heart hammered with so much fear that it made his stomach roll, his vision blurring at the edges, but he couldn't look away when she curled her arm inside of him.

He could only feel the wound, the pain and wrongness setting off fireworks in his spine, but he imagined her snaking her hand and wrist between his organs, squirming higher and higher in his chest until he was gasping in time with his frantic heartbeat.

His ribs strained when she forced her hand into the space behind them, wrapping long fingers around his heart. His lungs straining against her arm, not enough space left inside to expand. In a final effort to plea for his life, Sam Caller lifted his head and looked the Wicker Witch in the eye. Her lips parted and her teeth were the last thing he ever saw, mouth opening wide and coming for his face.

CHAPTER ELEVEN

In 1961, Nathaniel Greenleigh shot the last wolf on the Gray Mountain.

The wolf did not know his name, but the wolf had known it was the last. The humans had grown in numbers since the witch was lost. The balance of the mountain was no longer in the favor of wolves. The humans took the food to fill their sheds in stores for winter. They prowled aimlessly and ceaselessly. The witch had also been ceaseless, but never aimless.

The wolf was the last creature on the mountain that remembered the witch. It died with the only memory of what had built the mountain, what owned the mountain, and what still slept inside the mountain.

CHAPTER TWELVE

The Wicker Board of Aldermen included Kenny Feldman, Deborah Rogers, Parker Whitley, Gary Freeman, Hannah Greenleigh, Rebecca Greenleigh, and the mayor, Jane Philips. Jane's husband, Wyatt Jr., attended as well, though he wasn't officially a member. He was more a silent partner, brooding in the corner while the rest of them discussed the state of the town after the storm.

There had been mudslides and minor damage, Benson's cabins and the trailer park the worst of it, and a few out-of-towners the only casualties. The most pressing issue was the bridge to the south and finding out if the service roads and foot bridges to Cyprus were washed out as well. Luckily, no houses had taken more than a casual beating—though Deborah Rogers's eldest son had a tree crush his shed.

Rebecca heard it all but struggled to focus. If the phones had been working, she would have texted to tell her wife she couldn't make it to the meeting. She had things to take care of out at the sanitorium. But not showing up at all would only worry Hannah and bring her running out to find her. Rebecca didn't want that. She wasn't even sure how to explain, but she knew she didn't want Hannah to see the upturned graveyard of empty coffins.

Empty.

Rebecca had pulled the lids off as many as she could and found not a single bone. Just little sacks of belongings and mud.

Her knee bounced under the table while her fingers remained tightly knitted together on the surface.

The meeting was taking forever.

Jane was talking about splitting up and going door to door to check in on the residents. Most would find it intrusive, maybe even suggestive that they couldn't look after themselves, but it still wasn't a bad idea. Many of the residents were spread out and isolated on their own lots of land set back into the woods. It was better to check on them now than to realize in a week that they'd been washed away in the storm.

A warm hand slid over Rebecca's thigh under the table, squeezing gently.

She stopped bouncing the leg and glanced to the side at her wife.

Hannah had that worried crease in her brow and Rebecca wondered if she'd missed something—something worse than the disaster at the tourist cabins, which had been the first topic of discussion at the table. Dead tourists were tragic, but Wicker was far from some *Jaws* town with an economy hinging on *summer dollars.* Tourists were a byproduct of staking claim to a beautiful spot in the world. Fortunately, their spot was so unhospitable and isolating at times, that out-of-towners rarely decided to stay for long. The residents of Wicker had a hard enough time convincing their significant others from Cyprus to move up.

"Are you okay?" Hannah mouthed.

Rebecca blinked. She loved her wife for always being able to read her, but as much as she wanted to unload all her thoughts and worries, she certainly wouldn't do it with an audience. She nodded and hated the feel of the lie. She didn't lie to Hannah. She didn't lie to much of anyone. Her grandmother used to say the truth was all she needed. If she'd done wrong, there was no point in hiding it. If the truth hurt, it was still better than happiness made of lies.

But that grandmother hadn't been a Greenleigh by birth, and Rebecca was starting to suspect honesty wasn't necessarily a Greenleigh trait.

Why are the coffins empty?

She would tell Hannah about the sanitorium tonight, after she'd cleaned it up.

Was cleaning it up a lie?

Maybe.

But it was still her land and her mess. Had she inherited a lie just like she'd inherited the land and the responsibility?

Rebecca decided, for now, that it didn't matter. She would clean up the mess. There were no bodies, after all, so the coffins were just wood stuck in the mud outside the old building. There was nothing sacred about them and no need to rebury them.

She unlaced her fingers, leaning back in her seat and placing one hand over Hannah's on her leg. The worried crease in the other woman's brow did not fade but she returned her attention to Jane and the other aldermen. They discussed having a town meeting soon but put off the decision about timing until tomorrow.

Hannah wrote down notes with her free hand, nodding and talking about opening up one of the classrooms for the kids to play in while the adults met to discuss the downed bridge and the tragedy at the cabins—if and when they had a town meeting.

Under other circumstances, Rebecca would have enjoyed how her wife was beginning to fit into the Wicker community. It had taken some convincing to get Hannah to move to Wicker after college. Hannah had tried to negotiate for a home in Cyprus, near her own family and the church. They'd met under that roof, in stained glass light. Rebecca's family had come down for service every Sunday, weather permitting, just as she, Hannah, and their son did now. But Rebecca was not going to set up her home anywhere but on the mountain proper—right where a Greenleigh had been since Wicker was first settled. The house had been rebuilt a few times, but it was the same spot. She would not be the one that abandoned the post.

Sometimes she worried that was why Hannah had finally agreed to move. She had realized that as much as they talked about it, there was never really any negotiation. There were only two outcomes. Either Hannah moved to Wicker with Rebecca, or she did not, and Rebecca would go home without her.

Rebecca hoped never to make her wife regret the choice to follow her.

Hannah had flourished on the mountain. She said she was happy, at least. But how could Rebecca not worry from time to time? How could anyone who truly loved someone not worry that their smile was thinner than they realized?

She squeezed her wife's hand absently, fighting the impulse to reach out and tuck the strand of blonde hair that escaped her braid behind her ear. They were opposites in so many ways—but not in any way that mattered. Hannah's eyes were deep brown and Rebecca's pale green. Hannah favored light colors and soft styles while Rebecca had always liked dark shades and functional clothing. Despite that, Hannah wore one of Rebecca's knit sweaters today. It was a looser fit than her own. She wasn't ready for anyone to ask about the weight she'd put on. Even though she was coming up on the three-month mark, it was hardly time to announce a baby to their friends. Maybe in a week or two after the mess of the storm had blown over.

They'd gone through IVF this time, using Rebecca's egg and another donor. They'd talked a lot about having a second and maybe even a third kid someday, but Rebecca had been surprised when Hannah wanted to carry this one. With William, Hannah had been happy not to do the actual birthing part. She'd handled just about everything else, and Rebecca had assumed that was how they'd be bringing all their kids into the world.

Hannah had researched IVF and presented Rebecca with the idea last year. She hadn't even suggested they skip IVF and just use a donor and her own eggs like Rebecca had done with William. Hannah must have known that Rebecca wanted to put more Greenleighs on the mountain and worse, Hannah had known that the name alone wasn't enough. Her wife knew her too well, and sometimes Rebecca worried it would break the other woman's heart.

Was the truth that hurt really better than the soft cradle of lies? Rebecca had lived by the belief that it was until she fell in love. Nothing made her want to lie more than the idea of hurting Hannah.

Hannah brought up evacuating to the group, suggesting they have a strategy ready in case it was necessary. The rest of the board paused long enough to look at the non-Wicker born member with a mix of pity and amusement—though they were smart enough not to comment.

Jane patted Hannah's hand, the two having been fast friends since Hannah first moved to the mountain. Jane herself had moved up only a couple years earlier. "If it comes to it, I'm sure we could get you down to Cyprus or go north to Graveston," Jane said.

"I only mean…" Hannah started, a little flustered by their looks. "What if there was a medical emergency?"

Kenny Feldman shrugged inside his thick sweater, one of the many knitted for him by his wife with intricate designs but terrible colors. "We have a doctor."

Hannah pressed her lips.

After a pause, they returned to listing candidates for checking the paths down and the lesser bridges.

"My boys can take Waverly path on four-wheelers and check the bridge there," Deborah decided.

Hannah's frown smoothed out, gone as quickly as it had formed, and she wrote it down, nodding.

When the official meeting concluded and the discussions bled into gossip, Rebecca leaned over to Hannah. "I have to go take care of things at the sanitorium. I might be late getting back to the house tonight, so don't worry."

The crease in her forehead returned. "You were there all morning. Is it that bad?"

"I'll get it taken care of today so people can get to the supplies if they're needed. I'll take a look at our yard tomorrow."

"Our yard is fine, Becca. It's just a few branches."

Hannah was the only person who had ever called Rebecca Greenleigh, *Becca.* Her parents, just like the congregation in Cyprus, had called her Rebecca while just about everyone in Wicker had taken to calling her Greenleigh. Lotte had started that when they were teens and it spread, probably because she was nearly the last Greenleigh at that time—only herself and her dad left.

She liked how the town thought of her as *the* Greenleigh now. She loved the name, but she also loved the way her wife said *Becca.* "Still. Leave it and I'll handle it tomorrow." She touched Hannah's cheek. "Get home before dark if you can.

It's probably going to start raining again, and I don't want you and Will stuck in the mud without reception."

Hannah smiled. It was full of love and trust. Rebecca would tell her everything about the sanitorium tonight. She kissed Hannah's forehead quickly as she stood, heading for the door without excusing herself from the group.

She checked her watch when she stepped onto the sidewalk, a cold wind barreling past. It was almost noon. She needed to get moving if they were going to get everything done at the sanitorium—and she desperately needed it to be done tonight. She didn't want to wake up tomorrow and still have it on her plate. She wanted to drop off the keys for the building with Jane and tell her to have at the stockpile if needed.

Rebecca crossed the street, walking toward her truck but eyeing the corner bookshop at the far end of the buildings. As if sensing her, the door swung open, and Charlotte appeared. She flashed Rebecca a grin, and Rebecca wondered how long her friend would be grinning when she realized what she'd signed herself up for.

CHAPTER THIRTEEN

Charlotte expected them to drive to the Greenleigh house. She'd had plenty of time to think about what they were doing and come to the conclusion that it had to be some sort of clean-up. Maybe a tree had fallen? While Crowes were fine with leaving a mess to clean up on another day—Greenleighs were not. They actually believed they were responsible for the mountain and took pride in the care of their property. Anything less would be a blight on the family name.

But they were not heading to the Greenleigh house. They were soon on a backroad toward the cabins. Her thoughts jumped to the tourists. Harvey had filled her in on that particularly dark bit of news while they watched the clouds outside his shop window.

"Jesus, are we digging them out of the mud?" The words flew out of Charlotte's mouth.

"What?" Greenleigh gripped the steering wheel tighter, gaze slicing toward Charlotte and then back to the road.

"Harvey said the deputies found one of the tourist's bodies this morning, but the rest were still missing..." Did she really have to explain? What else could Greenleigh think she was talking about?

The other woman actually relaxed a fraction. "Oh. No. I mean, yeah, they found part of one of them but that's not what we're working on."

Charlotte twisted sideways in her seat to stare at her. "*Part of?*"

Greenleigh had to slow the truck to a crawl through the mud, the road almost impossible to see. But there were tire tracks—probably made by the same truck earlier that day—and she followed those past the turn off for the cabins. Several trees were down, some almost completely buried under the slide of mud and rocks.

"Holy shit..." Charlotte exhaled, leaning forward against the dash to see one wall of a cabin leaning against two trees up ahead.

It was only then she noticed the mud speckled with debris, jagged planks torn from the structures, pipes, bricks, and the bright blue glow of a rain jacket only half-buried. She couldn't help but think of the little shack she'd been in the night before and how it had broken apart in the storm. She could have ended up just like the out-of-towners, buried and lost in the mountain—trapped there forever. The idea made her suddenly queasy and itching to run.

They drove past it and Charlotte was grateful she hadn't unwittingly volunteered for clean-up. The last thing she wanted was to find someone's body. *Part of?* The unanswered question rattled in her head, but she kept it to herself this time because if she voiced it again, there was a good chance Greenleigh would answer. Nothing had ever made Rebecca Greenleigh queasy.

The road cleared when they took another turn, winding down toward the old sanitorium tucked out of sight and mind. Charlotte leaned back in her seat and exhaled relief. Okay, so she probably needed help clearing debris from the entrance to the building or…

They pulled up in front of the stone structure. There was no mud or debris, nothing more than orange leaves and pine needles piled into wet clumps against the walls. Instead of parking in front of the entrance doors, Greenleigh drove along the side and backed up near the far end.

Dred pooled in Charlotte's stomach. Her friend had barely spoken to her since she got in the truck and wouldn't explain what they were doing until they got there. If she had been anyone else, Charlotte might be worried for her personal safety at this point. But this was Greenleigh—*her Greenleigh*—and she would follow her anywhere. Especially if she needed help.

They got out. The wind still pushed through the trees, knocking a seemingly endless quantity of water from branches and leaves to pelt the ground. Greenleigh opened the back of the truck and started pulling on work gloves, but Charlotte walked toward the back of the building. She couldn't just stand there in the quiet and wait patiently to be told what was going on.

A mudslide had rolled over the back of the property, churning up the ground and the trees, heaving headstones from the sanitorium graveyard and…

Her breath caught in her throat, becoming a physical lump that ached under her skin.

The old coffins stuck up like yellow teeth from the rotting maw of the mountain.

Part of her mind screamed to look away before she really did see a dead body, but the rest of her thoughts knew it was too late. She was looking. There was no turning away from it now. But the horror she braced for never hit. There were no bodies that she could see. Almost all the lids had been pulled off, some by the storm and some pried open, but there were no corpses. Not even bones.

Greenleigh came up beside her, surveyed the yard. "There are extra gloves in the truck. We're pulling the wood debris out and piling it in the parking lot."

Charlotte gaped at her friend. "The wood debris?" she repeated. "Greenleigh… Those are coffins." As if she had somehow missed it.

Greenleigh's jaw flexed and only then did Charlotte realize she was carrying a shovel. She trudged out into the mud. Charlotte could see the tracks from where someone—*Greenleigh*—had been out there earlier. The mud seemed firmer now, not sinking quite as deep as those first lines of travel.

Charlotte watched her make her way to one—not the closest nor the farthest—and start pulling at the flimsy planks. She lifted the lid and tossed it in Charlotte's direction before grabbing hold of the almost vertical coffin with both hands. She wiggled it side to side and the old wood creaked and squelched in the mud. When it wouldn't come free, like a stubborn tooth, she picked up her shovel and started digging it out.

It never even occurred to Charlotte to walk away. She could have. She'd walked every inch of Wicker and could sure as shit walk herself home from there. If it had been just about anyone else, she would have. Instead, she went to the truck and took off her sweater.

She noticed the smudge of mud on her jeans again, the one left by Miles's bike tire. She would have snorted a laugh at how stupid that was now, if she weren't about to climb into an upturned graveyard. She pulled on a pair of heavy work gloves, grateful she'd worn rainboots.

Charlotte Crowe picked up an ax and followed her friend out into the mud. She chose a coffin—*debris*—and started hacking until the pieces were small enough to pull free and toss toward the truck.

They worked without talking for hours. Greenleigh had brought a bucket out and set it somewhere between them. They tossed everything that wasn't wood into the bucket— nails that had come loose, the little bags of trinkets, and stray items like flasks, lighters, cigarette cases, and glasses. When Charlotte found an old shoe, she hesitated, and then finally tossed it into the pile with the wood. There was no point in asking. She understood what they were doing. The shoe was burnable.

She held her tongue and worked, questions piling up inside her head. Her arms were sore and her legs cold, but she kept working. These coffins had belonged to the patients of the Greenleigh Sanitorium, not Wicker residents. Her first desperate explanation had been that the families of the dead had simply wanted to bury them close to their own homes. But everyone knew the patients had been unfortunates without any family that cared for them in life. It wasn't likely any would bother tending to them in death. And even if they had, why would the Greenleighs bury empty coffins?

They got farther and farther from the truck, hurling planks in the right direction until the last coffin was pulled. On their way back to the truck, they picked up the last of the debris. They were losing daylight by the time they moved all the wood pieces into one pile near the middle of the parking lot. The final stack was higher than they were tall, and Charlotte avoided looking too long at the shoes tossed in between planks. She leaned against the side of the truck, exhausted, her breath forming in the air.

Greenleigh sprayed a full bottle of kerosine onto the wet mess. Charlotte hadn't been convinced it would burn until she remembered the six bottles of kerosine in the back of the truck and realized Greenleigh would make sure that shit burned.

"Am I allowed to ask the obvious question yet?" Charlotte finally spoke and her voice sounded ungodly loud in the quiet that had grown between them.

Greenleigh lit a match and flicked it into the pile. The fluid went up in a blaze, black smoke rolling off the pile. "I don't know why they're empty." She backed up to the truck when the fire took, eating away at those thin boards with loud pops. Flames stretched and hissed against the wind.

Charlotte pulled off her muddy shirt and flung it onto the fire. The cold air bit at her bare, sweat-damp skin before she pulled her sweater back on.

"We can't put the headstones back," Charlotte said, just in case Greenleigh had some delusion of getting everything *just right.*

"I'll have it taken care of later. The mudslide moved the headstones."

Charlotte didn't like the hollow ring in the other woman's voice. She came up beside her and nudged her shoulder. "It's done. If you don't know, then we'll probably never know, right?"

Greenleigh stared at the fire.

Charlotte knew they'd be standing there until everything had burned down to ash. "Do you want me to theorize about—"

"No, please," she said, exhaling hard, like the exhaustion of the day had only just now hit her.

Charlotte nodded. "Okay." If she didn't want to talk about it, they wouldn't. If she wanted to pretend the coffins had never turned up—hadn't been mysteriously empty—then Charlotte would never bring them up again, but they were going to be standing there for a while watching the fire. She thumped the bucket of junk with the toe of her muddy boot. "What about this shit?"

Greenleigh finally looked at her, frowning disapprovingly.

If Greenleigh was willing to acknowledge that they'd just dug up and destroyed a bunch of coffins, she would probably tell her not to call the last belongings of these people *shit.* But since she *wasn't* acknowledging any of that, she just pressed her lips and said it with her eyes.

Charlotte pretended not to hear the unspoken beratement. She crouched and dug around in the bucket, picking up one of the flasks she'd tossed in earlier. The silver had tarnished into dark reddish-brown.

She shook the flask, but nothing sloshed inside. "Who keeps an empty flask? Isn't that bad luck or—" The lid popped off and a roll of paper almost fell out. Charlotte caught it in her free hand before it could land in a puddle on the parking lot ground.

Greenleigh stared but didn't try to take it from her or tell her to put it back.

Charlotte dropped the flask back into the bucket and unrolled the paper. It was thin and torn on one side where it had been ripped from a book. The ink was faded, and the tight cursive hard to read. Her breath came faster when she finally made out the words.

> *They will kill me.*
> *They killed the man I roomed with. They took him out into the woods at night and she came for him. We heard him screaming.*
> *It wasn't the wind. It was him.*

They fed him to the Wicker Witch.

Every couple of months they put another one out, another one that doesn't come back, another one they say died of illness none of us have.

Please, God, save me.

Please, God, stop them.

It was signed but she couldn't even begin to guess at the name, the signature too looping for her eye. She let the paper roll up on itself again, if only to stop herself from reading it over and over. She was tempted to put it in the fire, but it had very likely been a person's last written words. Greenleigh held out her hand and Charlotte passed her the note—far from the notes they had passed in classes and on busses as kids.

Greenleigh read it and her face screwed up in what looked like anger, but Charlotte knew it was confusion. "It doesn't make sense."

"Well, it *was* a sanitorium..." Charlotte tried to lift the weight of those ominous words. There was no witch. But had the Greenleighs been killing people off for some other reason? "Maybe he was just crazy."

The easy statement might have been enough to brush off the letter if they weren't standing in front of a bonfire built out of empty coffins.

CHAPTER FOURTEEN

Rebecca sat in the Greenleigh study at the big desk her great-great-grandfather had carved.

They kept meticulous notes of every business the family had been involved in going back to the seventeen-hundreds when three Greenleigh brothers arrived on the mountain with a group of friends and set about building Wicker. The room housed documents historians would drool to get their hands on—documents Rebecca fanned across the surface of the table.

The newspaper article about Jessup Crip laid on top, yellowed with age. He had been a patient at the sanitorium in 1947. He had escaped and walked down the mountain during a storm. Cyprus had run an article about the insane patient roaming the streets of their town when the Wicker Greenleighs failed to keep him contained. It was the only incident of its kind but almost immediately after, the Greenleighs announced the sanitorium would be closing its doors. The remaining patients were relocated to other facilities at the expense of the Greenleigh family.

Rebecca had assumed it was because of the embarrassment the article had caused, but now she wondered if her ancestors hadn't been afraid of too much attention coming up the mountain. What had they been doing with those people? Why fake their graves?

She groaned and closed her eyes. One hand cradled her forehead, her thumb pressing hard against her temple.

Where were the bodies?

The sanitorium had been run by members of the Greenleigh family, with no other staff. There had been no physician or psychiatrist involved. They hadn't even hired outside the family for cleaning and care. In earlier articles about the facility, when it was new, the Greenleighs had called it an *'opportunity to do volunteer work close to home.'* And until that morning, Rebecca had never thought twice about it. Now, she couldn't help but dwell—wondering what they were hiding. They had a dark legacy of hanging themselves, though it wasn't known outside the family. As far as she knew, not even the Wicker townsfolk had realized it. But it was all there in their private records. Four Greenleigh men, in four different generations, had used the same tree on their property to end their lives. They left no notes and there was nothing written down about why they had done it. Their siblings or children simply cut them down, made up a story about falling off a roof or out of a tree, and took them down to Cyprus for burial.

No one in Wicker was ever buried on the mountain. The only graveyard had belonged to the sanitorium, to strangers, and it had been full of empty coffins.

Rebecca started putting the papers away. They had no answers for her. But now she wondered if the men that had hung themselves in her family had known something about it—something they couldn't live with.

Her great grandfather had cut the hanging tree down. It was a stump she played around as a child. Her father had always told her to come away from it, but she only realized why when she inherited the house and the Greenleigh study. It was a trove of answers, but it was far from enough.

The wind battered the windows and she stopped mid-motion, folders in hands. Rebecca thought she heard a howl. She was wrong, of course, because there had not been wolves on the mountain during her lifetime. She had never heard them before.

It was the wind. Even when she heard another howl, she told herself it was the wind.

CHAPTER FIFTEEN

The residents of Wicker went to sleep that night believing the worst of the storm had passed and that tomorrow would be an easier day.

They were wrong.

CHAPTER SIXTEEN

Harvey Darling drove home to the trailer park. Most of the residents had abandoned it either before or after the storm.

The lot was a large circle of packed dirt surrounded by woods. Only a dozen trailers were still parked there, moonlight pooling on the stretches of bare ground and bouncing off metal shells and tinted windows. A quarter of the clearing had been swept by the edge of one of last night's mudslides, trailers rolled onto their sides and slammed into one another. Fortunately, they were already empty.

Most of the trailers had been brought up and parked in the lot decades back for loggers from Cyprus to use. Over the years since, a handful of those trailers were bought by locals looking to get a little distance from their generational homes higher up the mountain, but it never seemed to be far enough. The mountain was big, but it wasn't *that* big.

Harvey knew his own Wicker relatives had wanted him to leave and, if he was being honest, he'd only stayed in the beginning to spite them. It wasn't that he was angry, exactly, he just didn't want to go, and he wouldn't go just because they wanted it. So he was there, waiting for a reason to want to leave.

That reason almost came eight years ago when Lotte left town after her momma passed away. If she'd asked, he would have gone with her. If she'd asked, he might have realized then what he knew now—that he'd go anywhere with her.

But she hadn't asked, and he hadn't pressed because she had looked so lost. If she wanted to go alone, to find herself or just run, he wouldn't stop her or insist on going with. Yet, that resolve had worn thin in the two years she was absent from the mountain.

He'd thought they were just really good friends before she left. The sort of friends who shared secrets and beds. But when she was gone, he realized they'd been more than friends and Wicker was a hollow place for him without her. The only reason he hadn't left in those two years was because he didn't know where she was; he wouldn't have had a shot in hell of bumping into her again in his life if he didn't stay right where he was.

He wasn't sure if it was a curse or a habit, but the Wicker born always came home eventually. Harvey wondered sometimes if that tether would noose him too. Was he Wicker enough to be bound to the mountain? Did Darlings have the same tie?

He knew less about the Darlings than he did about the people of Wicker. As much as the townsfolk saw him as a Darling, the Darlings saw him as something else, something in-between that could never be fully trusted. They checked in from time to time and brought him plenty of pot to sell, but he'd only been up to the Darling property a few times and they'd watched him like a hawk. They could never be sure about his loyalty and that was fair because Harvey was not loyal to them. Not to them, and not to Wicker.

Really, he'd only ever been loyal to himself…himself, and one other person.

He turned the key, killing the engine and plunging himself into the darkness of the mountain.

His truck door groaned open. It felt like peeling himself out of a rusted toy car every time and he loved it. The heels of his boots squished down in the mud on the way to his trailer door. He unlocked it. Not a lot of people in Wicker would bother to lock up their homes, but Harvey did. It wasn't that he had anything there worth taking; he had just dealt with these people long enough to know that leaving his door open would be considered an invitation for vandalism.

The metal hull was spray-painted in slurs and *DARLING* a dozen times over. In the summer, he and Lotte did their own tags over the rest, adding nonsense quotes and poems to the mess.

He stood in his doorway and unzipped his boots, thumping them against the outer wall to knock some of the mud off before putting them down inside.

The night was eerily quiet.

It wasn't just the lack of other residents in the park tonight, it was the lack of their dogs. The only thing moving was the wind, knocking trees back and forth and whistling threats after last night's chaos. He stood in his doorway another moment, leaned out and listened to the tail end of the storm still holding on to the mountain.

You had your fun, he thought. *Go.*

But it felt like it was waiting. Like it was smiling.

The wind picked up and something in the deep shadows moved, darting from one tree to another at the edge of the clearing. Or at least, he thought it had.

His hand moved up the wall inside the trailer, palm on the light switch but not pressing. If he turned on the lights in the trailer, it would push back the darkness around him, but he wouldn't be able to make out any differences in those shadows at the edge of the park.

Another moved—too low to be a person.

There was a shot gun in the corner by the door, shells already racked, but he didn't reach for it. There was something out there, but it wasn't close.

The rumble of an engine turning onto the narrow dirt road to the park caught his ear, but he didn't turn to look in its direction, still squinting at shadows. Then the car lights washed over the park and a dozen sets of eyes in the trees glimmered white, caught for an instant, before darting away into the woods.

The missing dogs, maybe? But why be so sly? Why not go home to their beds and their food bowls?

The truck bounced on the rough ground and pulled up beside his.

Harvey flicked on his trailer lights and leaned against the doorframe. He wasn't surprised to see Lotte climb out of her daddy's truck, but he was surprised to see her flecked in mud like she'd been out playing in it. She looked tired and cold, that question always there in her eyes when she came to his place—like she was worried she might be intruding. Like the place wasn't half full with her clothes. Like her computer and favorite mug weren't permanently stationed at the little table in his trailer.

He held one arm out to her, and she took it, letting him hoist her up into the trailer. She was cold like a corpse. He didn't like it, quick to push her toward the shower and more than happy to join her when she suggested it.

CHAPTER SEVENTEEN

Once again, Alice Crowe could not sleep. She lay awake in bed, staring at the ceiling and trying hard not to look at the empty spot beside her.

After all those years, she still stayed on her side of the mattress, Edgar's side left bare and cold. Even his bedside table had gone untouched, preserved just as he'd left it. His vintage alarm clock had stopped ticking five years ago. His book— some macabre tome about the end of the world, nukes, and a war between good and evil—lay half-off the edge with the faded receipt wedged between the pages where he had left off reading, so close to the end that it was a tragedy in and of itself. Alice had forgotten what it was called, unwilling to pick it up and look at the front or even get close enough to lean over and see the thick spine. Even Edgar's charger was still plugged into the wall, though his phone had never been found.

She got up when she couldn't take it anymore. It wasn't even two and already she'd given up on sleep.

Miles had been covered from head to toe in dried mud when he came home today. His clothes were still out on the front step in a pile where she'd made him strip down before coming in. She thought about bringing them inside but only made it as far as her spot on the couch.

The walls creaked and she looked around with the first shudders of unease.

Hadn't the storm passed?

Alice rose from her seat, but this time took her glower with her. She went to the window and pushed back the curtain. It had stopped raining and the bright moon cast long shadows from the branches to the ground.

Her fingertips touched the window, cold seeping into her digits and circles of condensation gathering around them on the glass.

Something crawled along the mud-slick road right at the end of her yard. Alice leaned closer to the window, breath fogging it until she had to swipe it clean with her sleeve. A dog, maybe? Hadn't Miles said something about all the dogs having gone missing? The creature dragged itself forward, thin and gangly. Muddy limbs stuck up into the air, and Alice jumped where she stood.

It was not a dog.

The limbs stretched skyward and then bent down like the legs of a giant, sleek spider, digging into the filth at its sides for leverage.

Her breath caught in her throat, her hand pressing so hard to the glass that her knuckles ached. The shape slowly rose, higher and higher, until it stood on two legs. Sharp shoulders pressed back in a jerking motion not unlike a bird shaking out its wings, only it had no wings. It tipped its head up, a mop of sopping hair whipping in the wind.

It was a woman, outside in the middle of the night.

Alice's hand fell away from the window, about to turn toward the front door and rush out to yell at the idiot. Maybe Alice would even drag her inside. Already her mind raced down a list of names of women in Wicker who it could be, not that she could imagine any reason on earth why they would be playing in a storm instead of home with their families, fast asleep.

But before Alice could move, the figure turned toward her.

For a long stretch of seconds, she couldn't breathe. At once, and without reason, she understood that it was not a woman at all. It stared at her through the dark and the storm, eyes glinting green like a cat's reflected in the night. It looked right into Alice and saw everything.

Cold washed over her, holding her where she stood. She felt the rain pattering down her skin and the wind lashing like tongues of ice across her cheeks and neck even though she was safely inside. A whisper curled in her ear, not quite a voice, but a howl echoing off stone walls until it choked on mud.

Alice wanted to look away but couldn't. She wouldn't dare. Fear burrowed deep in her chest like a desperate, thin animal searching for food. She sobbed, tears streaming down her cheeks, certain she could provide a meal.

CHAPTER EIGHTEEN

The sun was up, somewhere behind the trees and the clouds, and so was Rebecca Greenleigh.

She had already been on the roof and pushed the larger branches off. No damage done. Back on the ground, she dragged the downed limbs to a pile on the front yard, away from the long gravel driveway. She tried hard not to think about carrying shards of coffins into a similar pile last night.

It felt good to do yardwork, reaffirming reality and her place in the world. It also helped put distance between herself and the question of what her ancestors had been doing with the sanitorium. Rebecca had buried the bucket of trinkets, the note inside the flask included, in the woods on her own property before finishing the drive up to the house the night before.

She had told Hannah everything except *that*—told her about finding the coffins and not knowing why they were empty, and that Charlotte had helped her clean up the mess. Hannah had not asked if it was a secret because she knew asking would make it one and Rebecca didn't want it to taste that foul. She just wanted to put it away.

"I've got coffee in the thermoses," Hannah announced, the heavy front door swinging shut behind her.

Walking to the car, she had a matching thermos in each hand. She put one on the roof while she unlocked and opened the front door. Jane Philips had dropped by just before six in the morning to tell them about a missing teen. Sam Caller had gone into the woods last night with his friends and never come home. What with all the mud and the dead tourists, his aunt was having a fit and sending family and friends door to door across the mountain. His uncle was already in the woods looking for him. If they were lucky, he'd be found before they could organize a search party.

"I know the diner is going to be open and giving out coffee to anyone searching but… Well…" She lifted and dropped an eyebrow, putting the thermoses into the cupholders.

Rebecca smiled. She did know. Her wife was very particular about her coffee. In fact, Rebecca had never known anyone to drink more of it than Hannah. She started with a cup, first thing in the morning, and usually finished her evenings with an espresso shot before bed. She even bought coffee-flavored ice cream and her favorite dessert was tiramisu. But there was no coffee in her thermos today. Hannah had stopped drinking coffee cold-turkey as soon as she decided to get pregnant. The thermos was camouflage so no one would notice and guess that she was pregnant before they were ready to break the news.

Hannah had dressed in what she considered *"woodsy sensible"* wear. Kneehigh navy rainboots, jeans, and a white down vest over a long-sleeve shirt. Rebecca had never considered anything white sensible, but she also knew better than to argue about clothing choices. Especially since Hannah would be manning the snacks and childcare portion of the search and not actually slogging through the woods herself.

"Where's William?" Hannah asked, coming to stand beside her in the yard and following her gaze up to scowl at a branch half-broken and hanging down the side of the ponderosa nearest the house. It was just high enough to be out of reach.

"Backyard. He went to check out the wreckage for me." She smiled as she said it. Their son was always eager to help. She hoped the trait stuck and wasn't just a part of being six for him.

"Anything else broken?" Hannah asked, arm curling around Rebecca's waist and their hips bumping together.

"No. We got lucky the mudslide didn't hit any houses," she said and then wished she hadn't, remembering how it had swept those cabins down like a tidal wave. There shouldn't have been any tourists there this time of year. It should have been a shame rather than a tragedy.

Hannah nodded, understanding the unspoken shift and giving Rebecca another squeeze before starting toward the side of the house. Somewhere under the mud and twigs was a stone path that led around to the back.

Rebecca was two steps to the car when Hannah stopped walking, gaze turned down as though inspecting her own boots. "Becca?"

The note of worry in her wife's voice brought Rebecca across the yard to her without question.

"Is that from a dog?" she asked, pointing at the ground.

There had been a lot of reports of missing dogs the day before; it wouldn't be surprising to discover one or two wandering around.

Rebecca came up beside her and looked. Her heart lurched up into her throat when she blinked at the mud, trying to change what she saw, trying not to hear the echoes of howling still trapped in her skull from the night before.

The prints were definitely made by a large canine paw, but unlike dogs, they had left a single-track—the back paws almost stepping over the marks left by the front. And once she saw the first, she noticed more and more in the mud, circling the side of the house.

Rebecca followed them, almost running toward the backyard.

"William!" Hannah called, their son's name breaking from her chest like the starting shot in a race, sending shivers across Rebecca's skin.

Hannah veered off from her side when they came around to the backyard, darting up the stairs of the deck to the sliding back door of the house while Rebecca continued down the slope to the yard, following the tracks until they disappeared into the grass.

"Will!" Hannah's voice carried from inside.

"What?"

Rebecca stopped and stared at her son. The little boy stood in the backyard with the stubby end of a broken branch in both of his gloved hands. His small body was still half-leaned in the effort to drag it away from his toys.

William had been named after Rebecca's brother, who had been older than her by birth but since he died young, she out-aged him with time—leaving him forever the baby. Her parents had never fully recovered from his death and Rebecca had struggled with that when she was younger, before she had a child of her own and could imagine that gaping, bleeding hole the loss of him would leave in her.

Her mother had taken to drinking, quietly—like even her self-destruction and misery had to be done thoughtfully. And when she crashed her car on the long road up from Cyprus, no one had even whispered about drunk driving. She had been a Greenleigh, a good woman, and a heartbroken mother. Plus, Rebecca's father would have scorned anyone who said anything else, and Matthew Greenleigh had not been the sort of man anyone in Wicker would dare to cross. He had been considered fair, but his judgement final.

During her whole upbringing there had never been any discussion about Rebecca's future, about returning to Wicker after college to take over the family businesses, oversee their interests in the sawmill and keep guard over their mountain. It had only ever come into question when she brought Hannah home the summer after high school. Matthew Greenleigh had looked at his daughter differently that day, a question in his eyes, trying to decide if she was still the same girl he'd known all her life.

"Nothing changes," she'd told him, answering before he could ask.

Whatever worry had been there dissipated with a nod and a thin smile. *"I guess you'll be the last of us then?"*

She had never been sure if she really heard that note of amusement when he asked about their family line, but at the time she had laughed and told him she'd find a way. Afterall, what would the mountain be without a Greenleigh on it? Rebecca's father had lived long enough to see his grandson, to hold him and smile with tears in his eyes when she told him the name they had given him. A brain aneurysm had taken Matthew Greenleigh later that year, swiftly and without warning.

Rebecca's William didn't look much like her brother, any more than any Greenleigh might resemble another. Brown hair, brown eyes, and thick lashes—still, he reminded her of the other boy's memory sometimes and it made her eager for him to grow a little bigger and pass up the ghost of his namesake.

Rebecca flashed her confused son a smile but called back to Hannah, "He's over here. He's fine."

William blinked at her with his big, doe eyes and let go of the branch. "I was helping," he explained, almost defensive.

She nodded, about to tell him what a great job he was doing when she felt it, even before she heard it. She *felt* the growling, setting fire to the nerves up her back like lightning crawling over her skin. William's eyes grew even wider, sliding past her and into the trees just as Rebecca twisted around to follow the sound.

The dark of the woods stared back at her, the canopy so thick that even in the morning light she could barely see anything. And then she made out the white glint of teeth in the shadows. They were finger-long and pointed, fitting perfectly together and gleaming brighter and brighter the longer she stared. Black fur blended perfectly into the shadows between the trees, the beast's body crouched low to the ground and rising slowly as it leaned forward. A black lip quivered against the growling that rolled up and past. It took a step closer, out of the woods, and those yellow eyes flared.

William pressed his whole body against the back of her right leg, his hands groping at her waist, her jacket, and her arm as though he would climb up her.

Rebecca couldn't look away from those yellow eyes, but she grabbed the back of her son's jacket and slowly hauled him up her side until he clung to her shoulders. His little rainboot dug into her hip and his fingernails bit into her neck but she didn't wince or rearrange him. She pivoted slowly to keep her body between him and the wolf, taking a step back, and then another, working her way toward the stairs of the deck.

The growl grew louder and a long, pink tongue snaked out between teeth to flick at the air, smacking its own muzzle.

Rebecca heard Hannah's boots on the deck overlooking the yard behind her. "Han," she barely got the word out, her throat painfully dry, but she wouldn't cough to clear it. "Get the rifle…"

Impossible! her mind screamed, even as she stared at the animal. It took one step for every two she backed away, losing no distance at all. William cried into her shoulder, his body so tightly wrapped around hers that she was sure she could let go and he wouldn't fall.

There were no wolves on Mount Grayson. There hadn't been since the 1960s. She had spent her whole life hiking and hunting in the forest and never seen one—never seen even a single track.

But there it was. *Looking* at her. *Growling* at her. And she didn't have to touch it to believe it. She felt it in her bones, that gut-twisting horror of having something predatory stare back at her. Her skin was on fire, her eyes watered, and her stomach knotted.

The heel of her boot hit the first step of the wood staircase along the side of the deck, stopping her steady backward stride. Her breath hitched in her throat, and the wolf snapped into motion—lunging forward. Two bounding strides and it was in the air, jumping for her.

The gunshot clapped across the yard and the wolf fell hard to the side, sliding in the mud with blood bursting across wet fur.

William screamed and Rebecca turned, taking the steps two at a time until she was halfway up to the deck. She put the boy on his feet and shoved him upward until he was running on his own, up to the top and straight through the open slider doors into the house.

Hannah was at the corner of the wood railing nearest her, Rebecca's rifle still aimed. She took another shot, body jerking with the recoil and breath puffing in the cold air.

Rebecca stared down just as the wolf was knocked to the ground again, lips still curled back and teeth gnashing angrily. It kicked against mud and grass. More blood spilled on the ground, dripping in thick streams from the beast.

"Han," Rebecca demanded, and her wife handed over the weapon, taking backward steps to block the sliding door into their home with her body. One hand groped at her throat, fingers finding the gold chain there and grabbing hold of the little cross.

Rebecca checked that the rifle was loaded and walked down to the middle of the stairs, where they came to a platform before turning down into the yard. The wolf reached the first step. Blood dripped off its teeth when it snarled up at her. It was at least three and a half feet high, ears pressed back flat. She could easily imagine it tackling her to the ground—ripping her jacket and stripping flesh from bone. It growled and the ferocity of that sound rippled the air between them, shuddering through her own chest.

"Becca..." Hannah breathed her name somewhere out of sight, probably still holding the line at the door of their home with their son tucked inside.

Where did it come from?

She took aim and its snarl grew as though it knew her heart—as though it saw her will and hated her all the more for it.

The shot rang out, echoing off trees and disappearing into the wind.

The bullet blew straight down through the wolf's skull and the beast landed hard on its chest, legs sprawled and jaw clapping shut against the ground.

She waited.

For what? It's dead.

But still she waited, half-expecting it to growl even now. It didn't. Blood oozed from its head and maw, puddling on the ground.

In the quiet that followed, she recognized the sounds of William crying inside and Hannah's hushed voice promising their son that everything was okay.

Rebecca stood there for a long time, just staring at the wolf. It was so big. How could it have grown so large in her woods without anyone seeing it? Without even a whisper of tracks being spotted on the trails? Without a single hunter noticing the beast prowling the trees? Was it really alone? Were wolves *ever* alone?

"Rebecca?" Hannah asked.

She looked up at her wife standing at the top of the stairs, William in her arms and wrapped around her. "Are there more?" she whispered, like maybe the wolves were listening.

Maybe they were.

"I don't know."

"You said there weren't any—"

"There weren't." Rebecca was sure of that. She had known it as a fact. But proof that they had been wrong was bleeding out in her yard, threatening the foundation of her reality and of the safety she had known on her mountain.

"Maybe we should go down to my parents," Hannah said softly, even though they both knew the bridge to Cyprus wasn't an option. She would have to drive two hours north and then another six around the mountain to get to Cyprus.

Her wife's go-to response of escape was a splash of cold water, waking Rebecca from her own fright. "Because of a dog?"

"That is not *a dog*," Hannah snapped, steel in her voice again.

Rebecca loved that steel. She had known Hannah was made for the mountain, for the Greenleigh name, because of that steel. "We're meeting with the rest of the board this morning before the search party, right? I'll let them know and they can decide what to do about it."

She wanted to sound steady and maybe even casual about it—as though her own certainty would brush away any of her wife's worries—but Rebecca was still winded, blood pounding in her ears from the adrenaline of just how close she had been to something horrible. If she had been a few minutes later, would the wolf have taken William? Even the touch of that thought was too horrifying to linger on, her mind reeling back from it and focusing anywhere else.

"What do you mean?" Hannah said.

"We'll have to figure out if it's a wolf or not, and if we need to be worried. No one has seen them in more than fifty years. It could just be a rogue that came over the mountain." It was a flimsy theory, but it felt easy to swallow and even Hannah relaxed a little for hearing it. "Put Will in the car and then help me drag it to the garage?"

Hannah chewed her lower lip, looking for a moment like she might argue before nodding and stomping through the house with William still in her arms.

Rebecca kept her rifle in hand and stepped around the dead wolf. Her pulse jumped but she wouldn't let herself run. She headed to the garage on the other side of the house, gaze skimming the tree line on her way. For the first time in her life, she wondered why no one had ever put up a fence—some big wood construction to keep nature from walking right up to their home. The thought was fleeting and stupid, feeling very much like the thought of someone else—someone who wasn't a Greenleigh. They didn't need fences. They were not hiding from the mountain because they were at home on it.

Going in the back door of the garage, she pulled out a plastic tarp. They would roll the dead animal up and drag it inside. Jane Philips would probably send her husband, Wyatt, to take a look at it after the meeting. She imagined a few others would be curious enough to come see, and hopefully they would insist it was a dog and not a wolf. Then she too could pretend it was someone's overgrown monster of a pet. Maybe one of those wolfdogs—an offense to both species and a symbol of mankind's need to feel special. Like dogs weren't good enough already? Did people really need the fantasy of a wolf obeying them? Ignoring that the very thing they envied in wolves was the thing they had to breed out of them if they had any hope of possessing one.

A breeze pressed past her when she left the garage. The trees shuddered and, in the rustle of leaves, Rebecca heard someone humming. The back door to the garage thumped against the wall. She had left it open so they could drag the animal inside with less fuss. Rebecca ignored the sensation of someone watching her. She pushed it back with all the other nerves and tipped her chin high. With her rifle cradled in one arm and a plastic tarp gripped in the other hand, she marched across her yard.

The humming rolled on the wind, slithering through the trees and raising goosebumps on her arms. It wasn't Hannah's voice. It wasn't a voice at all but a tangle of sounds imitating melody—like a perfect mistake.

She rounded the deck and came to a stop, staring at the patch of flattened grass and mud at the base of the steps.

Rebecca dropped the plastic.

The puddle of blood was still there, slowly sinking into the ground.

"Where is it?" Hannah asked, having returned to the top of the deck. She gaped down at the empty spot.

A breath shuddered past Rebecca's lips, her gaze following the drag marks all the way to the trees.

"*Becca?*" Hannah shouted but didn't budge from the deck.

Rebecca stared into the woods, but for the first time in her life she didn't dare step into them—certain that something waited just inside.

"Get in the car," Rebecca said.

"Where did it go?"

"Something dragged it away." Something big.

"*Something?*" Hannah's voice cracked a little and Rebecca didn't need to turn and look to know those beautiful eyes would be bugging out of her wife's head right now.

"Maybe a bear." Yes. That was possible. Bears were known to stray into Wicker land. It was rare, but it happened. Maybe the storm had flushed the wildlife from the other side of the mountain over?

She backed away from the woods, gaze skimming the shadows for movement. Her breath caught in her throat and she almost stumbled. There, between the trees and the bushes stood a silhouette. It was nothing but darkness, so completely still that it couldn't possibly be a person, and yet she felt it staring back at her. Her pulse thudded inside her skull and her joints locked for a string of agonizing seconds. She couldn't will herself to move. Her heart beat so fast it made her nauseous.

Then the wind stole through the forest, shifting the branches overhead and showing the shape to be nothing more than a crooked sapling.

Whatever had come for the wolf, had gone. No one would believe it had been a wolf without proof. She had barely believed it when she stared right at it. Still, she would have to tell the Board of Aldermen. What if there were more?

Rebecca's whole body hurt when she turned her back on the woods and walked around her house, ignoring the pins-and-needles sensation of danger right behind her every step of the way. She closed the garage, packed her rifle into the trunk of the car, and then finally settled into the front seat. Thankfully, Hannah would not bring up bears or wolves with William in earshot, which afforded Rebecca a little more time to come to terms with the idea that everything she had believed about her woods was wrong.

CHAPTER NINETEEN

Charlotte went inside the big house long enough to start the coffee machine and hear her dad rustling around in the back of the house. She'd gotten some sleep at Harvey's trailer but had woken up early, thinking she heard the missing dogs running around outside. The dogs weren't there. Maybe she'd heard them in a dream? Since she was already up, she went home to check on her family.

She didn't mean to hold her breath in long stretches between tight little gasps in the house. She didn't mean to keep her eyes down and her steps quick either. And she tried hard not to think about why—why seeing the place where she'd grown up made her stomach twist. Why laying eyes on her momma's belongings or their family portraits all over the walls choked her with grief and shame.

She stepped out onto the porch and closed the door behind her, dragging a deep breath of cold morning air. She shook out her hands and shoulders, and then sat down on one of the deck chairs. The sun was coming up, daylight glinting through the trees. Fog clung low to the ground, leaving a chilly dew over every tree, blade of grass, fallen leaf, and plank of wood. It all glittered in those first rays of morning, delicate and only seconds away from evaporating.

Branches rustled in the wind, dropping leaves and rainwater. Something clanked together, creating a thin sporadic melody that clawed at Charlotte's nerves. Her gaze flashed between the trees. There was no one out there. Unless they were hiding?

The sound fluttered through the woods again. It was high in the branches.

Charlotte rose slowly from her seat. Since when were there sounds out there that she didn't know? She touched the railing along the deck and leaned out, staring at the white objects dangling in clusters from the lower branches of the trees. They were too high to get to without a ladder, but she was certain they had not been there when she came in twenty minutes ago. It had been just as windy then, but she had heard no chimes. And that was exactly what they were, wind chimes. More than a dozen of them littered the branches that she could see, singing to the breeze that passed through them. They weren't metal, but they didn't sound like wood either.

She squinted hard but couldn't make them out clearly. They were too high up to be something the kids had done. Had her brother and some of his idiot friends put them up? And if so, why? How had she not noticed them before?

The door opened and Charlotte whirled around, startled.

Her dad stepped out onto the porch with two mugs of coffee gripped in one large hand. "What's got you jumping?"

She took one of the coffee cups from him while he closed the front door and then traded it for the one five shades lighter. Before she could explain, he glared at the trees and walked to the front of the deck. "What the hell are those?"

Charlotte took a mouthful of coffee, the warmth sliding down her esophagus like a spill down the front of her shirt. The heat of the mug reminded her fingers how cold they were, spreading an ache through her palms. "No idea. Vic and his friends must have done it."

He grumbled something under his breath, frowning at the trees like they might give up the truth of it. "I'll get the ladder."

"Drink your coffee," she suggested. "Vic put them up so he can get them down."

He hummed, unconvinced.

"You know…Jane will want to hold a town meeting soon. Do you want to go?" Charlotte asked, sitting back down on one of deck chairs.

Her dad followed, sitting next to her. "No. Waste of time. Bunch of kids pissing themselves because they can't drive down to Cyprus." He snorted, drank his coffee, and slumped back into his chair. He sank into his jacket.

The jacket used to fit him well, but he'd shrunk over the last five years. When she wasn't looking at him, Gerard Crowe was still a big man who could fall out of the tree with a laugh, steer his truck with his knees, and scare off any monster fool enough to hide in his kids' rooms. He would always be in his forties in her head, and sometimes it was hard to see the changes even when she looked straight at him.

"We got plenty of food stored up and, if needs be, your brother can take the long road north," he went on, nodding to himself.

Charlotte sipped her coffee to keep from arguing. Vic would only take the long drive for supplies if Wicker ran out of cigarettes or energy drinks. Until then, Charlotte or Lila would be the ones taking the two-hour drive north to the grocery store in Graveston. But her dad was right, it wasn't likely they would need to go anytime soon.

"You hear about the dogs?" her dad asked against the lip of his mug.

"What about them?"

"Vic and the boys went down to take a look at the bridge last night. It's flooded over."

"I heard about that. What about the dogs?"

"Well, they got service on their phones when they were down at the river. Made some calls into Cyprus while they were there, and it turns out all the dogs are over on that side."

Charlotte stared at her dad, smile quirking one side of her mouth. "What?" It sounded like a joke she didn't understand. They'd had plenty of storms in Wicker, but their pets had never turned traitor and run for the city.

Gerard nodded like he heard her thoughts. "Was in the news on that side, I guess. The dogs were at the shelter, but local friends and family have been picking them up to keep until we can get across to fetch them back."

Charlotte shouldn't have been as surprised by that as she was. It was easy to forget that Wicker had any connections beyond the mountain itself, but they all had friends and relatives by marriage in Cyprus, and a good chunk of the city worked for the Wicker sawmill at the base.

"Anyone told Aunt Henri yet?" Charlotte asked, still gunning for a way to distract her dad from the wind chimes.

Gerard's eyebrows rose. Like her own brother, her father often forgot his sister existed when she wasn't in the room.

"I'll let her know," he decided, and Charlotte hid her smirk. She'd grab the ladder and get the chimes down as soon as he was up the hill.

Quiet stretched between them until she broke it on impulse. "Hey, Dad, do you remember when I was a kid and I asked you why the Greenleighs went to church and none of us did?" The words were out of Charlotte's mouth before she could catch them. She hadn't even thought about them before they escaped.

Gerard grunted something close to a laugh. "Because they're guilty. No one else needs to crawl down the mountain and ask for mercy."

Charlotte looked at her father, closer than she had in years. He spat the words with such certainty and venom that there could be no doubt he meant them. "But what are they guilty of?"

He noticed her watching him then and a frown creased his face. "It's just old stories."

Her heart pounded faster. Since when were there stories in Wicker they didn't tell?

He waved her off and she knew he'd end it there if she let him. She almost wanted to. Instead, she asked, "Does it have something to do with the sanitorium?"

He jolted, like a little shock had come up from the ground and gone right through him. His face smoothed and drained of anger. "Why?"

It was like hitting a wall, that question. How could she explain? She couldn't. If she told him any version of what she had seen and done last night, he would tell everyone he knew—which was everyone in Wicker. She looked away first, gaze flicking between the trees gently sloping toward the front of the property and Alice's house near the street.

Gerard Crowe grumbled, "That Greenleigh is going to be the death of you."

It was something her momma used to say, sometimes laughing and sometimes with a serious note that startled Charlotte.

They heard the car before they saw it turning up their long drive. Gerard worked himself out of his chair, managing it just before the vehicle came to a stop in front of the house behind Vic's truck. They didn't get surprise visitors often, and definitely not before seven in the morning.

Marie Latham hopped out of her car but left it running and the door open. Her breath formed in the air like she'd been running rather than driving. "Hey, Gerard," she called, hurrying toward the deck but not climbing the steps. She nodded to Charlotte when she spotted her. "Any chance you've seen the Caller boy out here?"

Marie's usually curled hair was limp and falling around her face. Charlotte got up from her seat when she noticed the woman wasn't wearing a lick of makeup. Charlotte had seen the woman, now in her early sixties, at the sewing circle her momma used to go to just about every other week since she was a kid. She had *never* seen her without makeup before. Marie Latham had bags under her eyes and no eyebrows. She wore pajama pants and a down jacket that had to be either her husband's or her son's by the size of it.

"Sam?" Charlotte asked, just to be sure who they were talking about. There were plenty of Callers, but they were mostly girls. Still, Sam seemed too big and too mean to call a *boy*.

Marie nodded, something hopeful and desperate in her eyes.

"No," Charlotte answered.

Marie exhaled hard, deflating right before their eyes. "He was up at the trails with some other kids yesterday, but they said he took off on them. He never came home last night. His aunt is worried he got lost, and his uncle and a few others are out looking. Jane's got some of us going house to house, but we're going to meet in town and form a search party if no one finds him by eight."

Gerard nodded gravely. "I'll get Vic up and we'll head into town," he said, turning around and hurrying inside before Charlotte could even react. Her dad was definitely not up to searching the woods for a lost boy after a storm. She wasn't even sure he was up to the colossal challenge of waking Vic.

Marie offered a brittle smile, apology in her eyes, but she was already taking steps back toward her car.

"I'll see you in town. Hope you find him before that though," Charlotte said, and she meant it. She sure as shit didn't want to spend her day looking for his dumb ass. The *boy* was a bully.

"Can you let Alice know for me? Eight o'clock!" She was in her car, the door closed, before Charlotte could even nod.

Charlotte drained her coffee and put the mug on the deck railing.

The chimes laughed overhead. Charlotte shot them a glare, wondering if she had time to get them down before heading out.

CHAPTER TWENTY

A little past seven, Rebecca and Hannah were in the school auditorium with the other aldermen. There had been no sign of Sam Caller. He might really be missing. Rebecca knew she couldn't have been the only one expecting him to be found sleeping at a friend's and hiding from his aunt and uncle.

Now that they were seriously talking about forming a proper search party, she couldn't stop thinking about the wolf in her yard.

The more minutes passed, the more certain she was it couldn't have happened. It couldn't have been a wolf, and it couldn't have taken that many bullets and gotten up like it had. And then something else had dragged it away. It was insane and she didn't know how to begin to explain it to the others.

Hannah kept glancing at her with the question in her eyes.

Rebecca held her thermos in both hands and stopped listening. She could still hear the wolf growling, like a sound that never quite faded—always there in her ear. Like the beast was right behind her.

She had to keep herself from glancing back over her shoulder when her skin prickled down her spine. It wasn't there. But it was so hard not to look.

What sort of animal could have dragged that wolf off her yard that quickly? She hoped it was a bear—better that than more wolves.

Jane, Hannah, and a few others were planning to set themselves up in one of the classrooms to watch the kids of anyone joining the search party. The diner had offered to let them use their space for a base of operations since it was right on Green Street.

Jane worked up a list of residents she expected to come help in the search. They decided everyone would go in pairs and carry a whistle or airhorn in case they found anything.

Rebecca imagined all of them scattered in the woods, hooting out the boy's name and, for the first time, she wondered if a wolf had eaten him. The thought was so jarring that she actually jerked a step back. "We should take rifles," Rebecca blurted out.

Kenny was in the process of taking a sip of his coffee and spilled it down his front, swearing under his breath and looking around for something to dab the mess up with.

"Why?" Deborah asked.

All eyes were on Rebecca, waiting.

"The storm might have pushed some of the animals from the northern side of the mountain," Rebecca explained as stiffly as she could, still thinking about the way that wolf had risen back onto its legs with two bullets already in it. "We had a wolf on our property this morning." She almost cringed when she said it. It sounded stupid even to her. She didn't have to look to see all their faces pulling with smiles—all but Hannah who had seen it, and Wyatt who acted like smiles were a level of intimacy reserved for his wife.

"Very funny," Mr. Freeman said with a rough voice that suggested it was *not* funny, but he was willing to smile along if it got them back to business.

"It's not a joke," Rebecca said calmly. "We both saw it."

"But we shot it," Hannah added quickly, as though it could be forgotten now. Was that why Hannah hadn't wanted to talk about it in the hall before the meeting? Had she decided to forget it? Considering how the memory stuck in Rebecca's brain, repeating and growing with every minute that ticked by, she could see why someone would put it away. She wanted desperately to forget it and pretend it hadn't happened.

"It was probably a dog," Deborah decided with a stern nod. "A lot of dogs went missing before the storm. My boys were able to make some calls when they went down to the river yesterday. The Cyprus Police Department said nearly a dozen dogs had shown up during the storm but maybe a few are still up here in the woods? They could be lost."

"It was not a dog." She knew what she saw. It was not a dog.

"You killed it?" Mr. Freeman asked.

Rebecca hesitated. They *had* killed it, hadn't they? She kept thinking about the first two times it was shot and rose back up.

"Yes," Hannah answered for her. "But—"

"Wyatt, could you go with them to take a look at it?" Jane asked, turning toward her husband. "If we really do have a wolf, we should let people know—"

"Nonsense!" Mr. Freeman burst. "There are no wolves on the mountain. You're just going to scare everyone."

Rebecca sipped her coffee to keep from saying that they *should* be scared.

"If it was a wolf, it might have been the last," Jane suggested, optimistic as always. "But it's best to check."

"It's gone," Rebecca said. "After we killed it, before we could drag it to the garage, something took it."

Another horrible silence descended on the group.

"Took it?" Deborah repeated slowly, not looking the least bit convinced.

Rebecca met the older woman's gaze. "Took it. Dragged it off into the woods. It might have been a bear—"

"Oh, so now we have a bear too?" Deborah snapped and then sneered. "The storm has gone to your head."

"Have you ever known me to spin a story?" Rebecca replied, voice rising only the smallest bit, but it was enough to alarm Deborah Rogers. Rebecca rarely lost her temper—rarely argued at all. She said what she had to say and, more often than not, left it at that. But this wasn't up for debate. She knew what she had seen—no matter how much she didn't want to believe it. "I saw a wolf. It was as close to me as you are now, and I shot it in the head. It was at least two-hundred pounds and *something else* in the woods dragged it off in a matter of minutes without much of a sound. Do you have any suggestions what might have done that, if not a bear?"

The group went quiet again.

"We could form a hunting party," Jane suggested. "We'll put out the word of a bear sighting."

"I didn't see a bear," Rebecca reminded, staring at the other woman.

Jane didn't shy away from that stare—she never had. "We won't say who saw anything, but it will be easier to believe than a wolf."

Rebecca looked away before she wrinkled her nose. She didn't like it, but she understood. No one in Wicker would believe she had seen a wolf. In a few years, Hannah probably wouldn't either and she had been there; she had seen it.

Mr. Freeman started, voice high with irritation, "We're supposed to be forming a search party for Sam Caller, not a hunting party for a—"

"Jesus Christ! You don't think the Caller boy got eaten, do you?" Parker Whitley spoke for the first time since the 'good mornings' portion of the gathering.

Jane inhaled sharply and Deborah glowered.

Parker pressed his mouth shut but his eyes were still big, likely imagining the horror in the woods.

Rebecca took another sip of her coffee and then stood up. Hannah looked at her, all her own anger and frustration cleared from her features and replaced with only love and worry. She touched Rebecca's wrist the way she did when she wanted to ask if she was okay but hesitated to draw too much attention. Rebecca nodded once and waggled her thermos, now mostly empty. "I'm going across the street to get more coffee from the diner." It was a thin excuse presented to the aldermen.

No one argued or pointed to the pot of coffee on the side table.

She left the meeting room and padded past the offices to the front door. She didn't exhale until she was outside, washed in autumn gray light and the brisk breath of a wind.

Green Street was more lively than usual, cars parked haphazardly in front of the grocery store down the street. Two blocked in her own vehicle. Sheriff Summerfield stood between another two trucks, shoulders pressed back and chest out, ordering people to park farther down the road. Richard Silver waved him off with a laugh, leaving his truck right where it was, almost in the middle of the street.

"Did you find any tracks?" a voice came from her left.

Rebecca swung around to stare up at Wyatt Caro Philips Jr. They had been more-or-less forced into a friendship ever since Rebecca moved back to the mountain. Their wives were kindred-spirits of sorts, likely to be friends until they died. Rebecca and Wyatt had been dragged to family barbeques, holidays parties, kids' birthdays, and game nights. Now she and Wyatt went hunting together on their own every year and the two families shared a cabin farther down the mountain, midway to the sawmill.

"What?" Rebecca asked when she realized he had said something—either that or she had something on her face because he was staring.

He frowned tightly, a slight gesture beneath his dark beard. "The bear. Did you find tracks?"

"I didn't see a bear," she said, sounding more defensive than she meant to. She had known no one would believe her. It shouldn't have stung as much as it did.

"You didn't check?" He sounded honestly surprised.

That surprise was flattering. She should have checked to see what had taken the wolf, but she hadn't wanted to go anywhere near the trees then. She hadn't even let herself think about doing it. She had just put the plastic tarp away, locked up the garage, and left.

"What color was the wolf?"

"Why?"

He stared at her, eyes pale blue and lashes thick and long, contrary to the otherwise gruff exterior he had sculpted.

"Black. With yellow eyes." She would never stop seeing it in her mind. She would never stop hearing it. She understood now why wolves had become legends. Why it had been the great monster of the forest in all their stories, even more frightening than the bears or mountain lions. "The wolf left tracks circling the house and, when we were in the backyard, it came out of the woods."

He nodded twice, the way he did when he made a decision, and Rebecca realized that he actually believed her. He wasn't poking fun or trying to make her see that it was just a dog. "Let's go then," he said, voice low in a near mumble. If you didn't listen to Wyatt, you didn't hear him.

He walked past her, toward his truck parked at the edge of Green Street, on the north side of the traffic jam poor Sheriff

Summerfield was failing to disperse. Rebecca followed him, empty thermos still in hand. "Where?"

"We're going to tell Richard Silver and the rest of those assholes over there to bring their hunting rifles on the search just in case any wildlife is around. Won't need to ask 'em to tell everyone else. It'll get around."

"They won't believe I saw a wolf." It wasn't anything personal. They wouldn't have believed *anyone* about a wolf on Wicker.

"Won't have to. They like carrying their guns and they'll fill in the blanks how they please." He fished his keys from his pocket, flicking them around his fingers. "And then we're going back to your place. I want a look at the tracks before it rains again."

CHAPTER TWENTY-ONE

Charlotte trudged through the woods in her rubber boots. They carried flashlights and water bottles in their backpacks just in case the search went on into the night. Everyone started on the footpaths just above Wicker and branched off from there in pairs. Greenleigh had been Charlotte's designated buddy since kindergarten, so naturally they walked together. She wanted to remark on the nostalgia of it, but there was a chance of someone overhearing and Greenleigh scolding her for inappropriate timing.

Greenleigh had insisted on carrying her hunting rifle and urged a number of others to do the same as they split up to comb the woods. Jane reminded everyone of the bear sighting a couple years ago, but no one took it seriously. Sure, bears were seen in the woods around Wicker once a decade, but there hadn't been any actual attacks.

"You really think that's necessary?" she finally asked. Greenleigh had never been worried about bears before, not even after that time she'd had to shoot one near town.

"Sam!" Greenleigh called the boy's name out into the woods, echoed distantly by others doing the same. For a long while, she didn't answer, leaving the question hanging between them and uncharacteristically avoiding eye contact. "Last night, I thought I heard howling," Greenleigh said, keeping their even pace and scanning the ground to the right while Charlotte looked over the left.

"The wind?" Charlotte asked. It wasn't like Greenleigh to jump to conclusions, and they both knew there were no wolves on the mountain anymore. Greenleigh should know best since her family boasted having killed the last of them in the name of protecting Wicker. "Wolf ghosts, maybe?" Charlotte snickered before another cursory call, "Sam!"

The echo of the search party calling his name moved slowly up the mountain while another group moved down. Charlotte had wanted to be one of the downward moving groups, but Greenleigh volunteered them for hiking up instead. The Greenleigh family had managed to pass down that noble sense of responsibility for Wicker to Rebecca. Charlotte sympathized—her parents had passed down a talent for sarcasm and chain-smoking. Though Charlotte had managed to bring her smoking down to the casual "secret" cigarette, she feared that she would never shake that bone-deep legacy of sarcasm.

"If I tell you something, you can't tell anyone…" Greenleigh whispered.

Charlotte swiveled toward her, surprised by that tone. She sounded unsure. Greenleigh hadn't sounded unsure of anything since they were twelve and Charlotte talked her into skipping school. "Yeah. Is this about yesterday?"

Greenleigh's brow pinched. "What? Oh. No." She called out, "Sam!"

Charlotte's mind raced. Greenleigh sounded like the whole *'burning empty coffins'* of yesterday had been nothing. What the hell was this about if *not* that?

"I saw a wolf," Greenleigh said.

Charlotte had to strain to hear her. Greenleigh scanned the trees around them, maintaining that steady, slow stride up the slope. "What are you talking about?"

"I saw one. Hannah saw it too. It was in our yard."

"Holy shit," Charlotte huffed, shoving her hands into the pockets of her jacket and looking around the forest—not just searching for a boy but for a fairytale monster. "Was it big?"

"It was huge. It came right up to the deck and we shot it."

Charlotte nodded even though what she really wanted to do was shake her head and walk away. "Why haven't you told anyone?" What if Sam Caller was taken by wolves?

"I did. I told Jane and the board." Greenleigh hesitated, her mouth tight in a stubborn frown. "I shot it in the head. It was dead."

"Okay…"

"And then it disappeared."

Charlotte grabbed the sleeve of her friend's jacket, jerking her to a stop and pulling until she looked at her. If it had been anyone else, Charlotte would think she was playing a joke on her—but Rebecca Greenleigh didn't joke like that. "So…you saw a wolf. You shot it. It got up and went back into the woods? Maybe you missed?"

"No."

Charlotte forced a laugh. "Maybe you shot it, but it didn't take. I saw a documentary about a crocodile that got shot in the head and lived. The bullet messed with its brain and made it all sweet."

She tipped her head to the side and glared at Charlotte. "Crocodiles are never *sweet,* and this thing was dead. I shot it *dead* and then when I came back it was gone. Something dragged it away."

Charlotte stared at her. Greenleigh had never claimed to see anything she hadn't—not even when they were kids. She had stood on the witch's bridge and stared into the woods like the rest of them but never once said she saw even a hint of a house or a wisp of smoke. "Okay… But isn't that even more reason to warn people?"

"I told the aldermen," she reminded. "Why do you think they're toting guns out here on the search for Sam?"

Charlotte suppressed a shudder, realizing they really were looking for remains and not a living boy. Either the town officials didn't believe Greenleigh had seen a wolf or they didn't want to tell the rest of Wicker. Suddenly, she was even more grateful she had partnered up with her best friend. They started walking again, quiet except for when they shouted out the missing kid's name, feeling less and less like it would help. If he had been eaten by a wolf or a bear, he wasn't likely to call back.

"Wait." Greenleigh's voice went low, head turning to the right.

Charlotte froze, listening. They could hear the other groups, calling out for Sam and stomping their way through the wet woods. And just when Charlotte was about to ask Greenleigh what she thought she had heard, it came again, a small *thwack, thud, whistle.*

The wind playing tricks?

The sound was familiar.

They inched along toward it, stopping on a patch of muddy ground where the sound sang loudest. Hollow wood whistled in the breeze, twisting and clanking together. They looked up at the ugly chime hanging from a branch.

"Shit," Charlotte whispered, remembering the smaller chimes in the trees that morning. She had forgotten about them once the search for the missing boy started. She had taken them down before heading into town, afraid that if she left her dad alone he'd try to do it while they were all away from the house. The chimes in her trees had been grotesque little things, made out of small bones, smooth stones, and dry wood laced together with mud-crusted strings. She'd put all of them in a bag and tossed them into the back of the truck to worry about later.

Later had come too soon.

The wind chime above them was much bigger than the ones Charlotte had taken down. The thick, red string twirled around the branch half a dozen times before being knotted. Charlotte reached up, trying to grab the longest of the flutes to tug the whole awful thing down. She needed that sound to stop.

"What are you doing?"

"I don't know. It could be evidence?" Charlotte suggested, stretching onto her toes, almost popping her shoulder but only flicking it with her fingertip.

It dripped on her. She came back down to her heels and stared at the glob in her palm. It wasn't the brown mud she had expected. It was dark red, smearing brightly against her skin. She rubbed the lump of gore with her thumb. Her breath quickened and goosebumps rose along her arms. She rubbed the film of slimy red off the hard piece.

It's just a rock. Or a large splinter. Or…

"It's a tooth," she whispered.

"Holy fuck," Greenleigh burst, startling Charlotte. She had stopped saying the *f-word* all together when William was born. It was all *"fudge"* and *"frick"* now. Even when she sent a text it had stars instead of letters. She turned, expecting Rebecca to be beside her, looking at the tooth, but she had backed up, head tipped skyward to stare at the chime in the tree.

Charlotte wrapped her fingers around the tooth and hurried to her side. Part of her mind screamed not to look, but she couldn't stop herself. She twisted around, standing shoulder to shoulder with the other woman, and stared at the chime. It twirled in the air with long pieces she had mistaken for wood. But there was no mistaking the curve of a jaw or the shape of teeth still nestled in place among patches of dark meat. The wind pushed by and the jawbone twirled, *thwacking* against the other pieces.

They both jumped when an airhorn sounded off not far from their right. Each pair had been given the handheld emergency airhorns when they went out to search. It was supposed to mean someone had found something—ideally, Sam Caller.

Greenleigh grabbed her hand and pulled her toward the sound, away from the gore. But Charlotte still had a tooth pressed into her other palm, bringing that horrible thing with her no matter how far they went.

"Maybe they found Sam," Greenleigh panted out the words, half-strangled in her throat.

Charlotte stared back over her shoulder at the nightmarish wind chime, sick with the certainty that *they* had found Sam— that she had his tooth in her hand.

She let Greenleigh pull her away from the sight. They would report it. Someone else would cut it down.

Other hikers rushed toward the call of the horn too, knees lifting high to run on the wet ground. They converged in a clearing and Charlotte's stomach rose high in her chest, her heart pounding and skin washing cold. This clearing had been beautiful once, with tall grass and a sea of wildflowers in the summer. It was too far from any of the streams and benches for the teens to hang out in, but hikers liked to snap pictures there.

The storm had reduced it to a thick layer of mud, the grass gone and the muck leaving swirls where it had settled. It would harden here and eventually all those wildflowers would come back. But today, atop the muck and debris, lay a body.

Greenleigh squeezed Charlotte's hand, dragging her forward. Charlotte didn't want to get closer. She didn't want to see it, but Greenleigh did.

The voices of the hikers rose into screams and shouts, echoing out confusion.

Everyone's sounds warped and sloshed against Charlotte's ears.

The withered body looked like something from a mummy movie. Skin clung to the bones like jerky, and someone poured out their water bottle to wash the mud away from the eyeless face. Charlotte's breaths dragged in and out of her lungs, ragged and losing rhythm. She stared at it. At the way the arms were curled forever against its chest, the long legs bent, almost tucking knees to neck.

Her vision blurred.

The voices of Sheriff Summerfield and Doctor Paulson pushed against her eardrums, vibrating into her skull.

"Too big."

"Can't be Sam."

"Been dead long."

"Who is it?"

"Who is it?"

"Who is it?"

Her vision homed in on the jacket dressing the corpse, heavy wool with a checkered pattern, the reds washed out into pinkish brown. For a long second all she could see was that pattern and then she doubled over, her hands pressed into her knees when she puked into the mud—her coffee-vomit nearly disappearing into the wet ground. Disappearing, but not gone. Nothing was ever really gone.

CHAPTER TWENTY-TWO

Charlotte sat on the edge of the couch, resisting the strong impulse to run away.

Everyone in the big house gathered around the dining room, some spilling out into the living room. She was at the edge of it, just outside the group, listening and feeling sick long after she had puked up everything.

Her dad shook his head again and again, sitting at the kitchen table with tears in his red-rimmed eyes. Vic paced in and out of the kitchen. He was just as teary as their dad but pressing his feelings into a tight mold of anger rather than the soft accommodating shape of heartbreak.

Sheriff Summerfield stood facing her dad, his back to her. The jacket from the body they found that morning was in a plastic evidence bag on the kitchen table—the table where they ate. Charlotte wasn't sure she would ever eat there again.

Alice pawed at the jacket through the plastic. "The color…"

"It's been weathered," Summerfield explained gently.

"It's his," Vic ground out, nodding his head madly. "It's Edgar's jacket."

There were other plastic evidence bags and Summerfield took a few out of the box to show them. A hunting knife. Boots. Jeans. His shirt, barely more than a whisp of rag. And his wristwatch, the one gifted to him by their father when he turned sixteen.

But no wallet or keys.

"He was murdered," Alice whispered.

Summerfield turned his hat in his hand but nodded slowly. "It looks that way, ma'am. The body is at the morgue with the doc, but it looked like there were bullet holes."

All of Vic's blistering anger broke with a cry and Lila was there to comfort him, her husband having to bend down into her embrace.

Alice continued to stare at the jacket through the plastic under her hand. Her eyes shimmered, but she hadn't cried. "I want to see him."

"I don't think that's a good idea…" Summerfield said quietly, hesitating over something this dark. Wicker had had its share of dead bodies, but they had always been fresh— sometimes pulled from car wrecks or the very rare hunting accident, but mostly just people getting old and passing away. Eventually, time just runs out.

Charlotte felt sick again.

"I'll go with her," her dad said.

She shook her head but didn't say anything—couldn't.

Alice stood up and started carefully putting the evidence bags into the box, as though she was packing a suitcase. "No, Gerard, I'll go. I need to go alone."

Sheriff Summerfield jumped to help, picking up the box. "If you're sure. I can drive you."

"No, Charlotte will drive."

Charlotte's head shot up. "What?"

No one answered her. Summerfield headed out with his box of evidence and the door stood open in his wake.

Her dad started talking about funeral arrangements. The body would need to be sent down to Cyprus for cremation.

Vic still had tears on his face when he pointed out that the body was evidence. They'd have to do an autopsy. He had been murdered.

Charlotte tried not to flinch at the word and the thrill of outrage in her brother's voice. He grasped at it like a lifeline, better than the pain cracking his heart, she supposed.

Alice pulled her coat on, each movement unhurried and full of decision. Charlotte didn't like any of it and tried to disappear into the couch.

"Let's go," the other woman said, walking toward the front door.

Lila, Vic, and her old man were digging into a conversation about suspects and timelines, voices fast and wild. They didn't seem to notice her and Alice anymore.

Charlotte shook her head. She couldn't do this. She couldn't go to the morgue. Alice should have taken a ride with

Summerfield when she had the chance—but Charlotte choked on those words when she met her gaze.

Alice stared back at her, waiting. Those hateful eyes struck her like an open palm. *"This is your fault,"* they said. *"You found a corpse instead of a man."*

Charlotte pulled herself up from the couch. She got a jacket from the downstairs closet because she knew that if she went up to her room, she'd hide like a child.

Together, they shuffled out of the house like ghosts, barely even aware of each other when they were sitting side by side in the cab of the truck. The drive to the little medical office was quiet, not even the radio on. It was dark out. No one had found Sam Caller. They had cut down the gruesome wind chime and brought it back to town along with the body. Some of the townsfolk were still out searching. The rest suspected they had found him in those pieces in the tree, or maybe they had just had enough of dead bodies for one day.

Charlotte had had enough of them, that was for sure. But there she was, parking in the lot behind the doctor's office next to the sheriff's truck.

"You have to come in with me," Alice said.

Charlotte shook her head, tears starting to come up again. There was a lump in her throat, growing until she was sure it would choke her to death. "I can't. Please. I already saw it."

"I can't go alone," Alice snapped angrily.

Charlotte wanted to lash out. It had been Alice's idea to go alone! She had turned down the others. She had dragged Charlotte with her. And now here she was, looking across the threshold, and she didn't want to do it?

"You owe me this," Alice hissed.

Charlotte's head whipped to the side. What did she mean by that? Charlotte was too afraid to ask. She turned off the engine and got out of the truck.

As soon as they opened the door to the doctor's office, they heard voices from somewhere inside. The waiting room and reception were dark, the only light leading them down the side hall toward the morgue at the back.

"I'll have to send samples to the lab to see if the pieces belong to the Caller boy, but with the bridge down someone will have to take them the long way around," Doctor Paulson's voice echoed. They were talking about the bone wind chime. People had gathered to gawk at it when the deputies cut it down, pointing out a broken jaw and ribs and two femurs. They were human bones and fresh blood.

"Do what you have to do. We need to know. Andrew is still out there looking for his nephew, but now he and his friends are armed and looking for an enemy," the sheriff replied. "The whole town is talking about bears and wolves and dead bodies."

"No animal did this, Bryan," Doctor Paulson whispered. "I've never seen anything like this."

Sheriff Summerfield groaned, the sound bouncing off the clean tile walls down the hallway. "Do you think it could have been the Darlings?"

"That is a terrible idea to throw out there, boy. I've never seen them hurt anyone that didn't go up to their territory, and even then, they never did anything like this."

The sheriff hummed with uncertainty and Charlotte could practically feel him grabbing for an explanation. "I'm having all the little wind chimes around town collected. They'll be on your desk by dawn, and you can take a look and see if any of them are—"

"Human?" the doctor finished when the sheriff seemed to stumble for the word.

So, the Crowes hadn't been the only family to discover chimes in their trees. Charlotte came around the corner and into the doorway in time to see Bryan's head bobbing in a nod.

Alice wedged past her, having no interest in the mysterious and gruesome wind chimes. Her face was stiff, her eyes glassy, and her hands clenched tightly together and pushed in against her stomach.

Both men straightened at the sight of her, eyes filling with sympathy.

"Mrs. Crowe." Sheriff Summerfield welcomed her into the room. He had called her *Alice* for years but not today. Today she was *Mrs. Crowe* because her husband was on a slab.

Charlotte stopped exactly one step into the room, because so far that was all Alice had demanded of her.

Doctor Paulson warned Alice that the body had decayed. He must have died at least five years ago.

"Eight," Alice corrected hollowly.

The doctor nodded sadly but asked her again if she was sure about seeing the body.

She was.

He pulled one of those meat-locker handles and opened a square metal door. The slab rolled out, little wheels whizzing and the white plastic bag jiggling.

Charlotte couldn't look away, no matter how much she didn't want to see her brother's corpse again. But there was something wrong with it this time. She could tell even with the body still inside the bag.

She took a step closer. Closer to Alice's back. Closer to the slab.

Doctor Paulson pulled the heavy zipper of the thick plastic as delicately as he could. He peeled back the layer but, before he could lay it down smoothly, his hand jerked away. He jumped as though the body had snapped at him.

They all gaped.

The withered corpse had been curled when they found it in the mud. She remembered the way they had gently moved it into the first plastic bag out in the field, struggling to make the odd angles fit. And the clothing in the evidence bags had all been cut away later. She had assumed the body was still curled, but now he was stretched out, skin no longer leather clinging to bone but a sickly gray rubber. The corpse was gaunt but not the mummy she had seen before. Even the eye sockets, previously sunken holes, were now gently closed lids.

It was definitely Edgar. He had a short crop of hair, dark and wavy, and thick lashes. And his lips, though gray, were the same shape as ever—crooked into an almost smile. In his forehead was the dark hole a bullet had made, its twin in his chest somewhere below his heart.

Alice let out a sob and reached for the body.

Charlotte latched onto her arm, suddenly desperate to hold her back, terrified the corpse would jump to life if she got too close. But she couldn't hold Alice back, and even when she flung herself onto his bare chest, he didn't come to life. No matter how much Alice might have wanted him to, he didn't wake.

Edgar was still dead.

The doctor and sheriff exchanged looks, but neither dared to say anything while Alice sobbed over the body.

Edgar was still dead, Charlotte reminded herself. But what the hell was going on?

After nearly thirty-minutes of crying, petting, hugging, and kissing, Alice finally let go of the corpse. She hadn't noticed any of their surprise at the state of him and it seemed none of them, Charlotte included, would say anything about it. Alice told the doctor she would be back tomorrow. The doctor told her that wasn't necessary, but she wouldn't hear it. Alice would be back, and Charlotte could only hope she wouldn't have to come with her. She couldn't bear it. She couldn't look at his body again.

On the short ride home, along the dark mountain roads, they didn't say a single word to one another.

Charlotte stopped in front of Alice's house and waited, making no move to turn off the engine or offer to come inside with her. Alice got out of the truck, making a string of sounds that imitated words, and Charlotte was just grateful she hadn't wanted to talk about it.

Do corpses change like that? No. Definitely not. Maybe she'd lost her mind and imagined it being skeletal in the field?

Or imagined it looking like him in the morgue? No. The doctor had been just as shocked. She could ask him about it tomorrow, but that would mean going back to the doctor's office—the same building as the morgue. She wasn't sure she could stand to be that close to Edgar's body again.

The front door opened before Alice reached it, Miles rushing out to her. His eyes were tear swollen and, through the window, Charlotte watched his mouth move with a flood of words. Alice just slipped past her son and into the house, leaving the boy standing there, alone and confused.

Charlotte got out of the truck but left the engine running. She didn't even close her door, just took a few steps toward the house to meet her nephew on the stone path. He ran the short distance and slammed into her, his head hitting her sternum. She hugged him tightly and let him cry for a long while before telling him to stay the night at the big house. His mom needed time. It was a bullshit explanation for something so much more complicated, but honestly it was all she could give him—all she could understand herself. She had no idea what Alice was feeling or what was going through her head.

She told Miles he could have her room at the house so he wouldn't have to bunk with any of his cousins.

"What about you?"

"I'm not going in yet." She couldn't go in. There were so many people in the big house. Too many that would be grieving. She wasn't ready to hear Vic demand justice for their brother. She didn't want to see the heartbreak etched into their dad's face.

She waited until Miles got his things and then drove him up to the other house. The door was open, the living room lights still on. She waited in the truck while he went in, not turning around in the driveway until the door closed securely behind the boy.

The problem with Wicker had always been the smallness of the town. There was nowhere to go—nowhere to drive off to. It was ten o'clock and nothing was open tonight, not even the bar.. She drove small lazy circles through the town before finally coming to the half-deserted trailer park.

Charlotte squeezed the steering wheel. What was her plan?

She didn't want to wake up Harvey to get into his trailer. It was too late to go to Greenleigh's. Hannah would give her a pass after finding her own brother's body today, but she still didn't want to wake them up. She could sleep in the truck.

Turning off the engine, she swore under her breath. She just needed a minute to put her thoughts together—or maybe to bury them again. The truck door opened with a pop, and she swung herself out, staggering away from the vehicle and gasping down air like she'd been drowning. She just needed to catch her breath and clear her head. She just needed to breathe.

Charlotte pressed her hands into her sides and squeezed her eyes shut.

She let out a gush of air from her lungs as though trying to empty herself. *Empty* would be nice. *Empty* would be welcome. But in the darkness behind her lids, she saw Edgar.

Not the corpse from the woods or even the man laid out on the metal table in the morgue. She saw her brother, warm and alive and smiling at her. At first it was his usual smile, the easy one that he only ever had for her and Victor. And then, in a faraway memory, she heard a gunshot. She stood between the trees in mid-morning, the air cold in her lungs, and watched her brother. They had gone out hunting together a hundred times, but this was the last time. Edgar was fourteen but carried himself with all the authority and certainty of a sixty-year-old. Momma liked to say her Edgar had been an old man from birth.

The gunshot rang in her memory again. The same one, *again* and *again*.

They had been hunting up past the northern trails. He had taken aim, but she couldn't see the buck anywhere. Just a doe and her fawn.

The gunshot cracked between her ears, making her heart gallop in her chest now just like it had when she was eleven.

The doe ran off and Edgar hurried across the distance. Charlotte ran after him. She stopped short, so shocked she couldn't even cry.

Edgar's chest rose and fell. His breath came deeper—heavier, like he had run a mile. His knuckles turned white, squeezing the rifle to his chest. He moved closer, standing over the dying fawn and staring down at it. His eyes darkened when the creature kicked and bleated, struggling against death—too new to life to be anywhere near ready. Edgar stood there for what felt like forever, watching it suffer. Watching it fight the inevitable. His cheeks turned pink, and his mouth opened a little. Charlotte couldn't take her eyes off him, mesmerized and horrified at the same time.

It died. And when it did, Edgar's mouth twitched with the strangest smile. He looked back at her, and she knew he had shown her something about himself that no one else had seen—a secret. Edgar's secret.

"Lotte?"

Charlotte jumped, jarred from her memory. Her eyes flung open and the dark was thicker than she expected, her memories so ruthlessly bright.

The glow from one of the still-standing trailers came into focus, a door open and a familiar body leaning out. "Lotte?" Harvey Darling said again, an edge of worry in his voice now.

She drew in a breath and found a thin smile. "Yeah. I was just…" She realized he might not have heard about the body. He hadn't been out looking for Sam Caller. No one would have thought to ask the town Darling for help. He was like a wolf the people had raised. They enjoyed him enough but never expected him to do more than take care of himself.

She thought about the sheriff whispering in the morgue about the mountain Darlings possibly being behind the missing boy and the bone chimes. Maybe it was deeper than not thinking to ask Harvey for help? Maybe some of these people were afraid to ask—afraid he had other allegiances?

He leaned half out the door in nothing but a pair of sweatpants. His hair was a mess of black waves sloppily pulled back and his mouth seemed to glow red against the night. Tattoos ran up his right side, following the shapes of ribs with quotes from fictional characters and dead philosophers.

"They found Edgar," she said, standing in the lights of his trailer. "He's dead."

Darling's expression fell but he didn't look entirely surprised either. He reached out with one long arm, palm up, and waited just like he always did. She exhaled relief and took those last steps to him. He pulled her up into the warmth and the comfort of someplace else—someplace none of her problems had ever been.

CHAPTER TWENTY-THREE

Rebecca heard the wolves again.

They howled, making their existence known as though the trees had missed them. They howled and then stopped, leaving a vacuum of still night. She imagined them listening, waiting for the flutter of panic in the hearts of their prey and the rustle of bodies fleeing from their terrible hunger. And then they howled again, just to hear the echo of themselves. The whole town must have heard them tonight. No one would doubt the wolves were back on the mountain anymore.

She stood in the dark family room, staring out the big sliding doors onto the deck that overlooked the yard. A slope of grass edged in their own gardens, chicken coup painted bright white, and lush dark forest at the end. Rebecca had never seen anything sinister about her mountain or those trees before the wolf had emerged from the storm. Now they had a missing boy, a dead body, and those awful chimes.

She had pulled all the wind chimes from her trees when they got back from the search—bird skulls and tiny bones on string. She buried them at the edge of the garden.

The whole town buzzed about murders by sunset. The body of Edgar Crowe had been found with a bullet hole in his head. And then there had been that horrific bone chime in the trees. It had to be Sam Caller, didn't it? It was fresh. But there were also some of the tourists still missing, assumed to be buried in the mudslide.

Hannah wanted to go to her parent's home in Cyprus. If the bridge weren't out, she would probably have taken William down the mountain last night. Quietly, to herself only, Rebecca was glad the bridge was unpassable. She loved Hannah, but she didn't understand what it meant to live in a place like Wicker. Just because they had the means to run away when times were hard, didn't mean they had the right to. In Wicker, they would suffer together and survive together, or they would all die alone. That was what her grandparents had said. And what her parents had said. That was the code of honor passed down through generations of Greenleighs.

At least, that was what she had thought. But those empty coffins still clawed at the back of her mind. What had they done with the bodies? Why pretend to bury them?

A shimmer of light in the otherwise smooth, dark, tree line at the edge of her yard caught Rebecca's gaze. She leaned closer to the glass. Eyes, bright green, glinted back at her from down there in the forest. It could be anything. A deer, most likely.

She flicked the latch on the door and slid it back, stepping barefoot onto the cold, wet wood of her deck. Her mother had overseen the landscaping of the yard and rebuilt the deck when Rebecca was eight. Before that, the woods had pressed right up against the house.

Standing at the railing, she stared down her yard and into the trees, not unlike a queen surveying her land. The wind stopped and for a moment it wasn't raining—not even misting. There came no creaking of trees or screeching of owls. No hum of life at all. Nothing.

Rebecca could not remember *ever* standing outside and hearing nothing.

She had never been afraid of her forest, not even when she was little. Rebecca was the girl that went trudging out into the woods, leading the search for the mythical cottage of the witch. She and Charlotte had spent years looking, before growing bored with the fairytale and moving on to other adventures.

Those green eyes were in the darkness again, staring up at her, and suddenly the silence broke for a soft, distant humming. It wasn't a tune she recognized. She clutched at the railing, leaning out until the edge bruised her ribs. "Hello?" she called down.

"Hello?" a voice called back from the trees, wispy and ragged like a wind. But just as soon as she heard it, she doubted it. It wasn't quite solid, and the trees groaned as though to remind her what real sounds were, but the humming was still there beneath, pressing at her ears like words she could almost make out.

Her breath caught in her throat as she made out the silhouette of a person at the edge of the forest. *Her forest.*

"Hello?" Rebecca called again, the word rough in her throat.

A wind rustled the woods back into life and this time no strange echo found its way up to her. The green eyes vanished, but she was still seeing the shape in the shadows—afraid to glance away and lose it—waiting for it to move and prove itself there.

"Becca?" Hannah's tired voice made her jump and spin around. She stood in the doorway wrapped in a light robe, hugging herself with one arm and holding onto the sliding door with the other. Her blonde hair was in a high, loose knot on top of her head and her face was still glossy from her night cream. "What are you doing?"

Rebecca turned back toward the yard and the woods, panic rising in one tight ball in her chest when she was suddenly sure she would see whatever had been in the woods right in front of her now.

It wasn't, of course. There was no shape in the shadows, or glowing eyes, or mystery sounds. Just the same sounds she had heard all her life—the trees and the things that lived in them. "Nothing."

"Babe, come back to bed," Hannah said, voice soft from sleep.

Rebecca nodded absently and backed away from the railing and the woods. Hannah hooked an arm around her waist, tugging her inside and closing the door. She latched it and started to pull the curtain. Rebecca caught her wrist and shook her head. "Leave it."

Hannah blinked back at her, really waking now. Her arm squeezed Rebecca, hugging her to her side. "Okay." She touched her cheek, fingers warm against the cold that had soaked into Rebecca's skin. Hannah made a small, cooing sound of worry and kissed the other cheek. "Maybe they'll find that boy tomorrow," she said, trying for optimism.

Her wife had guessed at what was keeping Rebecca awake and, for once, gotten it wrong. But Rebecca didn't argue. Sam Caller was dead. She knew it and half the town had accepted it, but the optimists would hold on until proof came.

Hannah kissed the corner of her mouth, the way she did whenever she worried about her.

Rebecca smiled at the familiar gesture. She held Hannah's face in her hands and kissed her. It was okay if Hannah was optimistic and frightened because Rebecca would be practical and fearless.

When the kiss broke, Hannah tried to tug her down the hallway toward their room. "You can still get a couple hours of sleep."

Rebecca stopped at the edge of the family room, looking back at the wall of big windows and the wild outside. It still felt like it was staring back at her. "I don't think I can sleep," she confessed. "I'm just going to sit out here."

Hannah didn't let go of her, hesitating until Rebecca was sure her wife would argue.

But she didn't. Hannah grabbed a blanket from the back of a chair and pulled her along to the couch. They snuggled up and soon Hannah was asleep in Rebecca's lap, the house falling quiet and still once more.

Rebecca stared out the windows, at the dark shapes of trees.

And even when she did fall asleep, she could still hear the humming.

CHAPTER TWENTY-FOUR

Charlotte woke up on a stiff mattress with one flat pillow and too many quilts. Even before all the events of the night came back to her, she realized she was at Harvey's. Rolling onto her back, she inhaled a lungful of coffee and cake smells

She shifted onto her side, blinking against the morning glow. When she opened her eyes, she could see straight across the tin-can trailer. The bed was tucked into one end, the kitchenette and dining table for two taking up the middle, and two doors on the far side led to a storage room and a bathroom. Harvey's lean body occupied the space directly ahead, naked but for a pair of floral print oven mitts. He pulled a tray of cake from the oven, the warm scent of cinnamon and brown sugar filling the trailer. The pan clanked down on the stove. His hair was flat on the side he had slept on and tangled on the other, hairspray holding it all in place when he bent to snap the oven shut. Shaking off one mitt, he plucked up a cigarette from the pink, ceramic ashtray on the counter and delivered it to his lips.

Harvey sometimes made her think of what people would be like if they had each been left to their own—to grow exactly how they wanted.

He had been raised in Wicker by the vaguest of technicalities.

Despite being left with his father's family as a kid, the Travers had never given him their name. Whether it was done in fear of offending the Darlings or because they didn't want to share it with him, no one but the Travers could say. The only real rules put on Harvey had been that he go to school. The Travers had done their best to keep him from influencing the other kids in their family, making it clear he wasn't their sibling or cousin. He was something else. They fed him and sheltered him and clothed him, but they hadn't cared what he did with himself or who he became. When he graduated from high school, they gave him five-hundred dollars cash and wished him luck in life—a polite way of telling him to leave.

As far as Charlotte knew, Darling had no more interaction with the Travers in town than he did with strangers. He didn't even seem upset with them.

She wondered sometimes if the Darlings really were something different than the rest of them—something closer to wild.

He smiled around the cigarette hanging on his lip. "You're being a creep."

Charlotte grinned, cheek still to the pillow and body curled under a pile of covers. He refilled his coffee.

Leather jackets hung from the walls of the trailer and stacks of jeans were piled in one corner, with boots and heels littering the floor. If anyone who didn't know him came looking, they might imagine a parade of lovers having gone through, but she knew the heels were his. He wore them into town at least once a week. Most everyone in Wicker was used to it, though a few still spit and cursed under their breaths. But no one threw punches at Darling anymore, not since high school down in Cyprus. Wicker had a natural born fear of Harvey, though he had done nothing to earn it. He was different, sure, but more importantly, he was a Darling. Kids had been cruel, but once they all grew up, they started treating him like the adults did—with unease. No one knew why the Darlings had left him in Wicker and no one could tell if the town had done right by him or not. So, either they made friends with him, or they looked the other way.

Charlotte hadn't been able to take her eyes off him since that high school Halloween festival.

He left his cigarette in the ashtray on the stove and came over, coffee in hand. She lifted the covers so he could crawl back into bed. He rested his back against the wall, and she settled against his chest, listening through his skin to the first sips of his coffee. With his free hand, he combed fingers through her hair, dragging the brown strands back from her temple. He thumbed the scar there. He always did.

"It's a shame we never made it to prom," Harvey thought aloud about a night that seemed forever ago.

Charlotte closed her eyes. "They wouldn't have let us in anyway."

"You don't know that. I looked amazing in that dress."

"You did." She smiled against his skin.

Her momma had hated that she was going with Harvey Darling but hated it even more when he showed up at the house wearing a dress to match Charlotte's. She'd never seen so much tulle in her life. Hers had been an offensive yellow and his had been the sweetest pink. She'd done his eyeliner, and he'd curled her hair. Charlotte's dad had tried to console her momma with the prevailing town theory that Harvey was gay and thus no danger to their daughter. Charlotte wasn't sure what world her parents had grown up in, because hers had never been that black and white.

"But you did look great with blood on your face," Harvey added.

"That's a weird thing to say." She stole the coffee cup from him and sat up.

They had been in the parking lot of the hotel hosting their school's prom, just getting out of the truck, when someone threw a rock and nailed her right in the head. A string of minutes had vanished from her memory while she sat there, on the pavement, holding her head. Harvey told the story like it was a good time, but she had never seen him so pissed. He had pushed her hand to her head and told her to keep it there, and then he picked her up and put her back into the truck.

"Best prom ever," he said now, more than a decade later. "Hospital visit, stitches, bloodstains, and pancakes at Denny's."

"And the part where I threw up the pancakes at Denny's and we went back to the hospital because you thought I had a concussion…"

He laughed. "And the part where I brought you home and your brother thought I'd hit you."

She started to laugh but the sound thinned when she remembered the serious look on Edgar's face when she came home with a black eye, a bandage stuck to her head, and blood down the side of her dress. She still had their dresses in her closet in the big house. She'd had to let hers out, but they wore them to the annual Greenleigh Halloween party sometimes and called it Zombie Prom.

"Lotte…" he started, concern in his voice.

"Do you want to run away with me?" she whispered before she could stop herself, looking up at him. She hated the mountain and sometimes, just to herself, she hated everyone that loved it. There was something wrong with it, not just with her own family and her, but with the dirt and the trees.

Harvey's smile fell away, his eyes on her. "You're going to take me with you this time?"

She expected resentment or accusation in his voice or in his expression but found nothing but the patient affection that had always been there. "When the bridge is fixed, we should go to the beach. Any beach. Just go."

He nodded, smile slowly returning. "Never been before," he admitted.

"Me neither."

He raised an eyebrow. "Not even on your great escape? Two years off the mountain and you never made it to a coastline?"

Charlotte shook her head. "Wasn't sightseeing." She lifted the mug she'd stolen from him to her lips and took a sip. She almost spit it out, body convulsing in disgust. "What the fuck is in this?"

He grinned. "Peppermint and rum. I'm experimenting."

"No," she straddled him and stretched to the side, putting the cup on the counter and pushing it as far away as she could.

He caught her hips before she could fall back onto her side again. His thumb stroked under the hem of her shirt, against her skin, flicking at the thin elastic band of her underwear. He bit his lip with his right incisor. She'd always thought his teeth were longer than average, a part of that Darling image, maybe? Did they all have long incisors? Most had that plush mouth, capable of pulling into wide, daunting smiles.

His hips rolled under hers and her mind went blissfully hazy.

"Stay?" he asked.

She never knew if he meant a minute, a day, or a lifetime when he asked that.

It didn't matter.

She dropped her head down and kissed him.

CHAPTER TWENTY-FIVE

Bryan Summerfield was a good man. He *knew* it because his momma had always called him her *good boy*. Even his dad had said it a couple times. And everyone knew that good boys grew up into good men. There was no other way they could turn out. It was natural, like a tree growing toward the sky.

As if that weren't enough, Bryan knew he was good because throughout his life he'd had friends that weren't so good. They had stolen candy from the plastic bins at the grocery store, but never Bryan. They had picked on some of the younger kids when they got to the top of elementary school and again at the top of middle school, but not Bryan. Bryan always looked away. Almost always, anyway.

His hand flexed at his side. Open and closed. Open and closed. He remembered the feel of that stone against his palm, the sharp edge pressing into skin that used to be softer—before his fingers had callouses. Why was that moment always the one that came back to him? It wasn't the worst slip he'd ever made—was far from the worst thing he'd ever seen.

Bryan soothed the rise of guilt with memories of worse deeds by other boys. Tom Claymoth, one of the kids he'd befriended in high school in Cyprus, had cornered a freshman in the locker room their senior year. Bryan and a couple others had stood around, sentinels pretending they weren't a part of it even when their bodies made up the walls of a cage locking the smaller boy in. Tom had spent months terrorizing that kid. Bryan hadn't understood why, but he hadn't wondered either. Good boys didn't understand shit like that, so he didn't try. He just stood there and looked away when the kid started crying. Tom hadn't even touched him, but it was already enough to make him choke on sobs, to scream at them to leave him alone. *Them*, like Bryan had something to do with it.

Tom hit the kid when his voice rose too high, when the echo pitched against the ceiling and rang off metal lockers. The thudding sound of skin against skin was better, softer, easier to stomach than the crack of that boy's voice. But Tom had gone too far that day. He had an endless well of rage inside that had to be let out sometimes, had to go somewhere. Bryan didn't care because it was never directed at him. But that time, he had broken the kid's nose and the kid had gone crying to the teacher after they left. Tom, Bryan, and their two other friends had all been called into the principal's office the next day. Their parents were called and words like *suspension* and *zero tolerance* were bandied about.

Bryan's parents had to take the day off from their jobs and drive down from Wicker. They were steamed-up by the time they got there, his dad all quiet fury while his momma refused to sit, glaring at any adult who thought they could speak ill of her son. Bryan was a good boy, after all. And even when the kid with his broken nose had been asked repeatedly, there had never been any version of events where Bryan had actually *done* anything.

So, Tom had been suspended for a week and Bryan's parents had suggested he not spend so much time with the Cyprus boy; they didn't want Tom rubbing off on him. Bryan had nodded, but he hadn't been worried about that. Seeing how bad Tom could be made him feel better, assuring him of his own place in the world. Tom was too angry. Tom was maybe even bad. But Bryan wasn't like him.

He wasn't a kid anymore, either. He had moved back onto the family property after his dad passed away four years ago. Everyone said how good he was to come home and look after his momma, as though his house behind Green Street had been far away. The Summerfields weren't among the first families to settle Wicker, but they had been there nearly as long. And now he was the sheriff of Wicker. He had the hat and the badge and the car with the decals. He was a good man. A man other men should look up to.

But did they?

He stood in the dark kitchen, staring down at the sink. It was clogged and the murky water swirled with mud, blood, and chunks of gore. Wind rolled in from the open back door.

Had he left it open all night? No. He had been out there, in the woods.

It was cold inside. The fire had gone out and the night had crept in. Why wasn't his momma complaining? She was always quick to complain.

His hand flexed at his side. Open and closed. Open and closed. Trying to convince himself the stone wasn't there anymore.

That stone haunted him—a ghost of a bad deed that suggested maybe he wasn't as good as he believed. Why had he thrown it that night? And why had it been so satisfying to cut her laughter short and see her body crumple to the ground in the parking lot? She'd been limp when Darling put her back in his truck and drove off. They never made it to prom and he wondered all weekend if she was dead—and more importantly, if anyone had seen him do it.

He heard hooves clicking across the floor of his kitchen, bringing him back to the here and now. Something was coming in from the open door and pausing at his back. There was a cracking, creaking sound behind him, prickling the skin up his neck and into his hair. It didn't speak this time, but he knew what it wanted.

He lifted his hand and looked down at it, palm up. More than a decade later and he could swear he still felt the weight of that stone, but all he saw was the thin scar the edge had made when he squeezed it too tightly before throwing it.

"I want off the mountain," he said, voice breaking like that boy in the locker room under Tom's fists.

The Wicker Witch hummed and he knew the price. He knew it because he had seen it in his dreams—images of horror dancing in front of his mind's eye while he sleepwalked to her lullaby.

Why him? Why did she sing to him? Maybe he was special. Not everyone would get the chance to walk off this mountain. Not everyone would get a deal.

And maybe it was more than that. More than just a chance to save himself—it was a chance to show mercy.

Yes.

Good men showed mercy.

He turned without looking at the witch in his kitchen because he knew he would go mad if he did. He walked out the front door without his jacket or his phone. He cut across the soggy yard to his squad car, knees shaking at first but growing steadier with every step taken. He mopped a hand over his sweaty face when he sat in the front seat, and then he started the engine. He'd forgotten his hat, he realized, but didn't go back in for it. If he went back in now, he'd never be able to do what needed to be done; he'd never get off the mountain.

The sun still hadn't come up. He'd be the first one to the office. He'd unlock the door, turn on the lights, and start the coffee machine just like always.

Just like always.

He pulled away from his house. He would come get his momma when everything was done and by nightfall they'd be in Cyprus. She wouldn't want to leave Wicker, but he would carry her if he had to. And he wouldn't stop in Cyprus, either. He'd keep driving. He'd drive until they hit a coastline and then maybe…maybe when he could stand ankle deep in waves, looking out at the edge of the world, he would be able to breathe.

CHAPTER TWENTY-SIX

Summerfield wasn't the only one to make a deal in the night.

The witch whispered because she had waited too long, and she was sick of their game. She wanted out of the deal she had struck long ago, and the only way out was to get rid of the players.

She had agreed not to lay talon or tooth on the original families of Wicker, and in return the rabbit had promised to stock her woods with more to hunt. The rabbit had kept its word and the bargain had dragged on. Now, the original blood was still living among her trees, but she had no more patience for rabbits she could not touch.

She could not hurt the original blood, but she could whisper.

Let the rabbits eat the rabbits and when they were done, the wolf would have its fill.

CHAPTER TWENTY-SEVEN

Alice sat up, wincing at the ache in her spine. She was on the floor in her bedroom, in a pile of Edgar's old shirts. Her head throbbed and she pressed her fist against her skull as though she could push back that ache with brute force. It didn't work.

She stood, still wearing yesterday's clothes. Her closet was open. Had she pulled everything out and onto the floor? Yes. She remembered that. Her husband had been dead all these years and she shouldn't be keeping his things anymore. No reason to wait for him to return. He wasn't coming home.

The tears started again, a lump in her throat so real that she struggled to breathe around it.

Edgar was never coming home.

She staggered out of her bedroom and froze in the hall, the eerie melody of lazy chimes inside her house.

She inched down the hallway, daylight seeping in through the curtains in the front room, stretching long shadows toward her. Her breath quickened.

Little bone chimes hung from her ceiling, dangled off picture frames, lay strewn across the floor, and were piled on the dining table.

"What the hell?" she wheezed out with no one to answer.

She reached up to pull one of the chimes down and winced back, pain shooting through her hand. Sticky, red scabs tipped her fingers, oozing blood from the sides. Had she bitten them in her sleep? Not just chewed her nails down but gnawed at her fingertips? She couldn't remember doing it. Couldn't remember much other than despair and the exhaustion of her own misery.

A firm knock on the door made her jump. She swiveled toward it, clutching her hand to her chest and staring at the solid wood barrier like she had never seen it before.

"Alice, I know you're home," Lila called through the door. Was it already past ten or did she make exceptions to her personal schedule for family deaths?

Lila knocked again, firmer this time. When Alice made no move to answer, Lila tried to open the door.

Alice stiffened. How was she supposed to explain this? Her house was full of creepy little wind chimes like the ones pulled from the trees yesterday.

The door rattled in the frame, locked.

Alice narrowed her eyes at the bolt. She never locked it— couldn't remember even a single time she had since moving in.

Lila groaned in irritation on the other side. "Alice!" she called, trying vaguely to imitate an understanding tone while beating the door with her fist.

Alice inched to the barrier, sparing another uneasy glance for the mess in her house before unbolting the door and opening it just a little, only enough to stick her head out.

Lila took a step back, surprise creasing her face before she put on a smile. It was an awkward sort of smile, like an alien imitating human gestures. "I came to check on you," she said.

Alice swallowed back a frown. "I was sleeping." Her voice was hoarse, and she coughed to clear it.

"It's almost nine and Miles has been over at our place," Lila said, her voice multiplying inside Alice's skull until she winced.

Alice suddenly knew Lila had been unable to sleep last night. She had tried, curling up in bed beside her snoring husband and shutting her eyes to the world—but she couldn't block out the rattle of the window in the frame, battered by the wind, or the voice inside that rattle that whispered in her ear. The witch was singing a siren song to the town. Alice didn't know how she could know that—but she did.

Just like she knew Lila had not been able to understand the call. She had heard it and it had kept her awake, stirring that nervous energy deep inside her. Lila had tried to soothe herself with social media only to be reminded that there was no connection. She was alone and unable to hide from that gnawing sense of unease. So, she spent the morning renewing all the wiccan traditions and beliefs she had forsaken after high school. And after she was done lighting her candles, touching her stones, and donning her charms, Lila had silently declared herself and her home safe from all evils.

But she hadn't *felt* safe, not really. That nagging instinct was still there, like a warning bell she couldn't stop from ringing. So, she had decided the problem was Miles—or rather, *Alice* for not looking after her own son.

"My husband is dead," Alice reminded. How could she know all those things? Maybe she was just guessing?

"Well, he's been gone for a long time…" Lila said, as though offering some bit of wisdom Alice might have missed that would snap her right out of her crushing depression. "And Miles is still over at our house."

Alice blinked at the woman, imagining what it would be like to slap her. The crisp sound of her palm striking Lila's cheek and the look of shock on her stupid face would almost be worth the lifetime of drama.

"He's with his aunt and his grandfather," Alice said, voice becoming sterile even to her own ears.

"Do you want me to send him back over?" Lila asked, trying to peek around her and into the house. There was no chance of that, Alice had wedged herself between the door and the frame.

"No," Alice said flatly, aware that on any other day of her life she would have bent to the pressures of this woman. She would have been furious inside but smiled apologetically and hurried to retrieve her son. They were family and that meant Alice had to play nice with them if she didn't want to end up cast out and alone in this stupid town. A part of her knew that wasn't possible, not with Charlotte and Gerard in the mix. But the fear was still real and would usually have driven her to action—but not today.

"Well, you can't just stay here and wallow," Lila tried again.

Alice wanted to groan. She wanted to roll her eyes and scream. Most of all, she *really* wanted to lash out at her—so eager to judge another mother and pretend she herself wasn't a sinking ship in the Bermuda Triangle of bad parents.

"My husband is dead," Alice heard herself say again, tired now.

Lila's thin lips pulled into a line, but before she said whatever shit was in her head, she spotted Alice's hand on the door. "Jesus, what happened to your fingers?"

Alice didn't look at them, still staring at the ridiculous woman. She had seen her at every holiday dinner and every family gathering. She had babysat her kids and suffered through pretending at a friendship that never went beyond her compliance with Lila's delusions. If Victor had died, Alice would have had to hear about it every day for the rest of her life, but she knew Lila wouldn't feel an ounce of the heartache she did. She would remarry in a heartbeat, fall in love all over again, and then bring up her dead husband when she needed to win an argument or gain attention. She would keep going, because Lila was strong the way only people who never loved anyone or anything more than themselves could be. It was almost as enviable as it was hateable.

"My husband died," Alice said for the third time, and then closed the door in her face.

This time, she made sure to lock it, and the solidness of the bolt sliding into place felt good.

CHAPTER TWENTY-EIGHT

Miles sat on the stairs, watching the goings-on of the first floor. His cousins had woken up early, first the little girls, Summer and Winnie, and then eventually Jeremy and Greg. The girls had lost control of the TV to the boys almost immediately, a small fight turning into high screeching voices that brought Uncle Victor down from his room to break them up. He told the girls to play with their tablets instead and let the boys play video games on the TV. Summer sulked and, for a few seconds, Miles was afraid she would cry. But Winnie stomped over to the bucket of toys in the corner and pulled the whole thing onto its side, spilling bright plastic guts everywhere.

The duo settled into their own world of whispers and giggles.

When Lila came downstairs, Miles tried to be invisible. She had been up early, and he had heard her moving around the house, whispering to herself, and then he'd heard the humming that wasn't her at all. It was the witch. He knew it but didn't think anyone would believe him.

After Lila left to check on his momma, Miles could still hear the humming. It was in the kitchen now, with Uncle Victor.

Victor started the coffee machine. "Miles, you want cereal or waffles this morning?" his uncle called. He had been smiling all morning, but it was thin and nowhere near his eyes—like when Miles's momma smiled.

Miles couldn't see into the kitchen from the stairs, but the lights flicked on and cast the man's big shadow.

"Not hungry," he answered, holding his phone in both hands but the screen had gone dark. The internet wasn't working so there wasn't really much to do with it. Still, he kept turning it on and checking.

"Waffles!" Jeremy shouted from the living room and Greg echoed him.

"I don't want waffles," Summer sniffled, suddenly on the verge of crying again. It wasn't unusual for Summer to cry a lot. Once her feelings were hurt, they stayed tender all day.

Miles watched his uncle's shadow slide across the empty dining room, folding over the table and chairs. And then a second shadow moved too—tall and slender—following him in the kitchen. No one else seemed to notice it. No one else heard the humming either.

Miles held his breath, fingers pressing into the glass of his screen. It came to life, but he didn't look away from the shadow.

He crept down the stairs on bare feet, shoulder to the wall when he moved around it, and peeked into the kitchen.

Uncle Victor had the refrigerator door open, pulling out milk and eggs. There was no one else with him. Miles exhaled relief and shoved his phone into the pocket of his hoodie.

The big man turned toward the counter, kicking the refrigerator door shut.

And there stood the shadow figure.

The air rippled in dark folds around it, like it was a living smudge on the world. It was definitely a person-shape, with long arms and legs. It stood upright as though it had been crouching behind the door, stretching up and up until its head almost brushed the ceiling. It turned toward Uncle Victor, looking over his shoulder to watch him cook. It was still hunched, too tall for the house.

The humming grew louder now that Miles had his eyes locked on the source. The song was a tangled melody that he could neither follow nor forget.

Uncle Victor turned toward the creature, but he didn't see it. He walked closer, crossing the kitchen for the pantry. The shadow slid back to allow the man to pass, watching him, leaning over and whispering something even as the humming continued.

Miles took a step back and then another. Why couldn't Uncle Victor see it? Why couldn't anyone else hear it?

The shadow turned suddenly, head snapping toward Miles. He froze, feeling the weight of that gaze bearing down on him.

One shadowy arm lifted in a gesture so familiar that he understood even if there was no finger to hold in front of a mouth. And then the darkness in that face split into a toothy grin. He sucked a breath and stumbled back. Uncle Victor turned to look at him in surprise but before he could say anything, the front door swung open and Aunt Lila stormed back in.

Miles looked at her and then back to the kitchen, but the shadow behind Uncle Victor was gone.

He swallowed hard and sank back into the house, toward the stairs. "I-I'm going back up…" he muttered.

Aunt Lila stalked toward the kitchen. The sounds of simulated gunfire filled the living room and Greg groaned as he lost the game they'd started up. Still, standing on the staircase, Miles could hear the grownups in the kitchen.

Aunt Lila's voice was low and biting. "She won't come get him."

"Who?" Uncle Victor didn't whisper, oblivious.

Aunt Lila huffed. "Alice!"

Miles held his breath at his momma's name.

"She just lost her husband," Uncle Victor did whisper this time.

"That doesn't mean she can leave her kid over here for us to look after," she said quickly, and heat rushed to Miles's face.

"Of course, it does," Uncle Victor argued. "And it's not like Miles is any trouble."

"It's not right," she pressed. "She's being selfish."

"Oh, it's okay," he tried to soothe her, a smile in his voice, but Aunt Lila was having none of it.

"She's giving me a headache. I'm going upstairs…"

Miles backed up the steps.

"You sure? I'm making breakfast," Uncle Victor said.

Miles turned and finished climbing to the second floor, slinking back into Aunt Lotte's room and closing the door like a barricade against the whole house.

He held his breath when he heard Aunt Lila walking down the hall. She was whispering again, muttering under her breath. He waited, wondering if the humming would follow her. He watched her shadow move under the door, terrified that he might see a second trailing her. But he didn't. Whatever the smudge was, it had gone. It had been there in the morning, watching them and whispering, and it had left.

But the witch had seen them.

He pulled his phone out of his pocket. Still no connection. Sitting down on the floor, he leaned his back to the foot of the bed and tried to lose himself in one of the bright, repetitive games on his phone. Eventually, his grandpa would get up or until Aunt Lotte would come home. Miles would stay right there and wait until then, and everything would be okay.

CHAPTER TWENTY-NINE

The moment Charlotte stepped into the house, a wave of grief crashed over her. Not her own grief but the living ocean of it gathering between the walls. The kids moved through it with vague confusion, aware something had changed but unable to really grasp it. They were sluggish, eyes glazed, but moving in their usual patterns around the living room. The girls played with their toys and the boys stared, slack-jawed at the television, controllers in their hands.

Charlotte's dad was in the garage, and she wondered if the drowning presence of sadness and death had driven him out or if he had gone to spread the miasma. The whole house reminded her of when her momma passed away eight years ago.

Vic and one of his friends were at the kitchen table, whispering about big concepts like revenge and justice. Edgar had been murdered and that Sam kid had gone missing. Someone was terrorizing the town with grisly chimes. They seemed to like the word *terrorize*, because once one said it, they tried to fit it into every sentence.

Charlotte slipped by, hoping to go unnoticed. She went upstairs. It was the first time she'd been that deep into the house in weeks, maybe even months. She knocked on her own bedroom door before opening it.

Miles sat on the floor, legs crossed and mouth pressed into a tight crease that could become a frown at the slightest turn. He had his hat on, even indoors. "Aunt Lila wants me to go home."

She leaned against the wall. "You are home," Charlotte said.

He looked up, eyes red from crying. "Is my momma okay?"

She nodded, deciding *"okay"* was a vague enough word for it not to be a lie. Alice wasn't dead, after all. That put her in the realm of *"okay," she guessed.* "She's sad," she said. "She needs some time."

He looked back down at his phone in his hands. "Uncle Vic says we can't go outside and ride bikes."

"Want to have Karl over?"

"Can't. His dad won't let him go anywhere."

She chewed her lip and considered his dismal situation. She didn't want to be in this house, so why would he? "Wanna go see if there's any ice cream left at the diner?"

He brightened. "Really?"

She nodded but pressed a finger to her lips. These were treasonous words considering she had other nieces and nephews under the same roof. Favoritism was a dangerous game. Miles smiled, and it was worth it. "Go down and grab your coat. I'll meet you on the porch. *Don't blab.*"

He nodded hurriedly and ran past her, out of the room and down the hall.

She closed her door and stood in the hall, waiting until he was down the stairs to turn deeper into the house. She walked the short distance to the room across from hers—Vic's bedroom. She didn't knock, pushing the door into an open swing that had it thudding against the wall.

Lila was on the bed, one arm slung over her eyes. "I have a headache," she complained without even peeking to see who stood there watching her. Charlotte stalked into the room and her sister-in-law finally looked up at her, surprise flitting across her features. It settled quickly and pressed into contempt. "You finally came home. You know your dad's real broken up about Edgar, not to mention the rest of us—"

"Lila," Charlotte interrupted, voice just loud enough to actually shut her up. "You don't ever send Miles home."

Lila sat up, forgetting her headache. "His mother—"

"*You don't ever send Miles home,*" Charlotte repeated. "This is the family house. You get to stay here because *you* are family, and Miles gets to stay here because *he* is family. And if there is ever any question about it—if ever you don't understand—*he's a kid.* He stays as long as he wants to stay, and you don't say shit to him unless it's something nice. You hear me?"

"You're making a big deal out of nothing."

"You're still not listening."

"If you want to take care of Miles, then you should be here to do it, not just leave him for me to feed and look after," Lila said sharply. "I already have four kids."

Charlotte tried really hard not to roll her eyes. She wasn't sure if she managed it or if she just pressed the impulse into an eye twitch. "Don't fuck with me, Lila. Treat the kid right or just look the other way."

Lila balled her small fists, gathering a possible tirade, but ultimately choked it back. They didn't usually talk and definitely never like this.

After another moment, Charlotte left. She was down the stairs in a flash.

"You're taking Miles?" Vic called from the kitchen, half in the refrigerator.

"Yeah. But he'll probably be staying over here for a while. He'll be in my room."

Vic grunted something like a *"yep."* He wouldn't have been involved in trying to kick the kid out. Her brother was a lot of things, but cold-hearted wasn't one of them.

Charlotte left the house, and it felt a lot like escaping. It always did.

Miles shot to his feet from where he had been sitting on the porch and followed her down the path to the truck.

She almost asked if he wanted to take his bike, in case he saw some of his friends in town but decided against it. One kid was missing, most likely dead, and the whole town was riled-up about Edgar's murder. They had killers on the loose, not to mention possible wolves. Probably not the time for riding bikes.

Was it inappropriate to take Miles out for ice cream when everything was so messed up? Maybe, but what else could they do?

"Someone killed my dad?" Miles asked.

She started the truck and waited for him to buckle up, not answering. She drove down the property, his head swiveling to the side to stare at his own house as they passed it. The blinds were drawn, his momma inside with her own grief.

He exhaled when they were past it, turning onto the paved road. For a while, they sat in silence, and she hoped that meant he'd dropped the subject.

"I heard Uncle Vic and Lila talking last night," he said, clearly not giving up.

Charlotte exhaled slowly, white knuckling the steering wheel. "Yeah. Do you remember anything about the day he left?" she asked, not sure she wanted to know. Everyone had already asked him, she was sure of that, but she never had. They had never talked about that day. She and Miles rarely ever even talked about his dad.

The kid shrugged. He had only been five years old at the time. "We were going to go hunting. I'd never been. The gunshots were really loud. I had to cover my ears."

She stared ahead, turning off the old highway and onto Green Street, slowing down as they neared the center of Wicker.

"And then I remember Mrs. Greenleigh taking me to the diner. We had breakfast. She let me order whatever I wanted.

And then she took me home," Miles said, sounding curious. "Did he really leave me in town?" He glanced toward the bench where Rebecca had found him sitting all alone that morning, years ago. "Or was he already dead?"

Charlotte drug in a breath and held it tight, remembering her brother's withered body in the mud. "I don't know what to tell you, kid. He died, but you're okay." She tried and failed to find the right words—to offer him some sort of closure. She'd had almost a decade to come up with something to say and yet there she was, at a loss.

He stared out the window but stopped asking her about his dad.

She parked along the street, a few windows down from the Evergreen Diner. On the sidewalk, she dropped her hand onto Miles's head and wiggled his hat over his curls. The kid smiled and bumped into her before she nudged him toward the glass door. The cowbell hanging on the inside handle clanged loudly, announcing their entrance.

"Do you think they have donuts?" he asked, already stretching his neck to try to get a look between the people sitting at the counter.

Charlotte clapped a hand to her chest. "This is why you're my favorite. You know my heart!"

With a laugh, Miles led the way in.

"Good morning!" Amanda, the diner's manager, and only fulltime waitress, called when she caught sight of Charlotte and Miles. "Sit anywhere you like, sweethearts. I'll find you."

A group of kids were laughing in one of the booths and Charlotte felt Miles's attention turning their way even before she looked. The Philips girls, Josie and Sage, sat across from William Greenleigh. They had a boardgame set up on the table between them with cards in plastic sleeves, tiny tokens, and figurines. Josie crowed and Sage slouched into a pout. Jane Philips straightened in a nearby booth with members of the board of aldermen, Greenleigh and Hannah among them. Jane shushed her daughter in the other booth, reminding her that they were in public and Amanda had been nice enough to let them set up their game.

For a second, the kids hadn't noticed Miles, and he was caught between them and his aunt. It was a tether being pulled, dragging him in both directions and setting his child heart into a conflict of allegiances that would last only a split-second.

"Go on. I'll send over donuts if they have any," Charlotte said.

He heaved out a breath with a big smile and ran over to the table.

They cried out his name in delight and the girls were promptly shushed again.

Charlotte sat at the counter, next to Jordan Sutton. They were neighbors—the comfortable kind who waved but almost never talked. He was working his way through a breakfast plate with two sunny-side-up eggs, two links of sausage, two pieces of crispy bacon, and a biscuit drowning in gravy. He took a drink of his coffee. "Morning," he said.

"Morning."

"Heard about Edgar," he said, voice rough like the rest of him.

Charlotte glanced at him. This went beyond their usual exchange of one-word greetings, and she did not like it. He was ruining a good thing.

"Sorry," he huffed out and then stabbed one of the eggs on his plate, the yolk gushing out to mix with the pale gravy.

"Thanks," she said awkwardly. Was this going to happen now? Would everyone have to say it?

Amanda came over to stand on the other side of the counter. "I heard about your brother, sweetheart. I'm so sorry. How's your daddy doin'?"

Of course, they would all have to say it. It would be weird if they didn't, right? "He's okay. Thanks."

Amanda hummed like she doubted it but moved on. "What can I get you?"

"Coffee with cream and sugar. Plate of bacon and whatever donuts you have to the kids' table," she thumbed over her shoulder, toward the little gang.

Amanda grinned. "Donuts and bacon, Lotte?"

"The bacon's for protein."

Amanda nodded slowly, mouth pinching to press back a smile. "Got it. On it. Should I bring him a glass of milk too?"

Charlotte lit up. "Oh, yes! Good thinking."

"And what about you? Breakfast?" She put a mug on the counter and half-filled it with coffee before sliding the cream and sugar in front of her.

"Got any cake?" Charlotte *sensed* Jordan Sutton judging her from behind his forkful of gravy and biscuit.

"I've got some peach pie from last night left," Amanda said.

Charlotte wrinkled her nose. She didn't like pie. "French toast?"

Amanda smiled, winked, and jotted the order down before plating up a few donuts for the kids.

Charlotte poured cream into her coffee, the white swirling down into the dark liquid until it all evened out.

"I saw it last night, standing outside my window," a man at the table to her left whispered, the distress in his voice making it hard not to hear. She recognized him but couldn't remember his name. He lived on the mountain but was a couple of decades ahead of her. One of the Brandons, maybe?

"Shut up," Thomas Wilshire snapped at him over his coffee. "You were drunk."

"But it was there, like the one we saw in the woods," he pressed, voice cracking like he might cry.

Thomas leaned across the table and Charlotte only barely heard the words he ground out, "Don't spread that shit around. We didn't see anything."

Charlotte jumped when a hand touched her arm.

Greenleigh's eyes went big with her own surprise, retracting her touch.

"Sorry," Charlotte said, trying to offer a laugh but it came out thin.

Greenleigh frowned, sitting on the stool to her right. "Are you okay?"

"Yeah. Just thought I'd get the kid out of the house," she explained absently, nudging her head in Miles's direction.

Greenleigh's gaze followed the plate Amanda delivered to the kids' table. "Donuts?"

"And milk," Charlotte defended. "What are you doing here? Run out of food already?"

She smirked just a little bit. "Not yet. We're attending this *not-so-secret* board meeting." They both glanced toward the corner booth. Hannah shot them a glare, pitching an eyebrow at her wife in a silent reminder that she was supposed to be sitting at the meeting, not hanging out with her friend at the counter. Greenleigh nodded once but didn't move. "How's your family doing?" she asked instead.

Charlotte groaned in answer.

"How's Alice?" Greenleigh changed her question only slightly.

Charlotte stared at her friend. Greenleigh almost never asked about Alice. They didn't exactly get along. They'd never had a fight or anything, but they didn't mesh well—especially not after the day Edgar vanished and Greenleigh brought Miles home. "Pretty sure she's a mess."

Greenleigh nodded grimly. She couldn't have expected any better. "Did you hear about Andrew Caller?" she asked.

"The missing kid's uncle? No." They were still calling him *"missing"* even though Charlotte was pretty sure she had held his blood-slick tooth yesterday. She could still feel the shape of it against her palm. Her fingers curled, stroking skin and reassuring herself it wasn't there anymore.

"He didn't come back last night," Greenleigh said quietly, even though most of the people there would have heard about it already. They didn't just go to the diner for a good meal; they went for the latest gossip.

Charlotte blinked at her friend. Andrew Caller, like most of the people born and raised in Wicker, knew the woods well. Only children and out-of-towners got lost.

"He was out with the search party after dark but never came back to the meet up point. Some think maybe he fell and got hurt or went beyond the search zone into Darling territory…" Her voice dipped at that.

No one hunted on Darling territory. No one even hiked it. The kids who went running the trails looking for witches and monsters wouldn't even go that far north. Everyone knew not to go past Mount Bell. They had cut no trails beyond it and made it clear to visitors renting cabins that it was off limits. They usually lied and said it was private property or a national park reserve—anything that might keep people from straying onto Darling land.

"Jane wants the sheriff to go up and talk to the Darlings, find out if they've seen Sam or Andrew," Greenleigh said the boy's name with a sort of sick contempt, because she too knew he was dead. Like all Greenleighs before her, she had very little patience for time-wasting—and looking for a dead boy was definitely a waste of time now that Andrew Caller had vanished too. "But no one's been able to get ahold of the sheriff this morning. He's probably hiding under his desk from this mess."

Something *thwacked* against one of the big front windows, making all the occupants of the diner jump. Everyone exchanged glances, searching for the offending party among the guests in the booths. Most eyes swept over the table of kids, expecting to find a guilty face among them.

Thwack!

This time they all saw the bird fly right into the glass, hitting hard enough to shudder the pane.

The youngest Philips girl at the kids' table started crying and her mother hurried over to join the booth, arms enfolding both of her daughters and words pouring out in a soothing melody.

"Momma," Will called, standing up on the booth and pressing his small hands against the glass. Greenleigh was across to him in a flash, grabbing the back of his jacket, but she froze when she followed his gaze out the window.

She wasn't the only one. Everyone in the booths were staring out and up.

Charlotte inched closer. A dark swam bobbed high in the air above the street, undulating almost rhythmically.

No, not a swarm. A flock. The birds twisted in the air, rising and falling in a frantic rush. Some of the birds seemed to be chasing the others but it was too fast to make out clearly. And then the cloud of birds dipped and dove toward the window.

Thwack. Thwack. Thwack.

Miles jumped up from the booth and backpedaled.

The birds continued to strike the windows, blocking the daylight out one by one to bring sudden night onto the diner. Voices rose in screams and shouts that struggled to compete with the battering of small bodies against glass.

Charlotte had her hands on Miles. She turned him from the bizarre sight and hugged him to her chest.

The windows shattered one after another and the birds poured in.

Charlotte pulled Miles to the floor, covering his head and pushing them both in under one of the booths.

Plates and mugs fell off tables, breaking on the floor. Waffles and scrambled eggs bounced on the flopping bodies of birds. The coffeepot hit the floor near her boot. The glass broke and the orange plastic handle twirled in a puddle of decaf and glass.

Miles clung to her, burying his face in her neck like he had since he was little. She curled her arms over their heads, her back pressed into the pole of the table so hard that her spine ached in protest.

The birds continued to pour in, smashing into everything and anything before falling to the floor, piling on top of one another until her boots were buried under black wings.

Crows.

Dots of brown, blue, and red littered the floor as sparrows, woodpeckers, and owls joined the ruin, but their numbers were dwarfed by all those large black birds. Some were still flopping, wings beating in a struggle to rise again.

Just as suddenly as it had happened, it stopped. The overhead lamps swung back and forth. The screaming sobs of the smaller children pierced the diner in the wake of all that flapping and crashing, finally rising above the sloppy thump and beat of the birds not quite dead on the heaps.

Charlotte watched a thrush atop the pile, its neck clearly snapped and little body gone limp. It kicked and twitched. She watched its neck crack back into place and in another second it was on its feet again, clicking its beak a few times before flying away. She crawled out from under the table, Miles still wrapped around her. The mess of dead birds stirred all around them. A big brown owl crawled out from under the pile, hissed, and flew away. Sparrows, woodpeckers, thrushes, and finches joined the retreat.

The people who had been sitting nearest the door rushed out, shouting and screaming, but the rest of them simply rose and looked on in confused horror as the birds collected themselves and left.

All the birds, it seemed, except for the crows.

She stared at the half dozen on top of the table, sleek black feathers shimmering in the daylight from the broken windows. And then she noticed the spiders, just as black and smooth, crawling over their bodies. Hundreds of them.

"Fuck," the word jumped from Charlotte and not even the moms in the room shot her looks for it. She grabbed Miles and made a hasty retreat, using her boots to shuffle hollow-boned carcasses out of the way to the front door.

As soon as she was on the sidewalk, she shuddered and pulled Miles in front of her. She used her bare hands to sweep over his whole body from his hat to his shoes, making sure there wasn't so much as a feather sticking to him.

"Wh-What happened?" he asked, voice rattling in his little chest.

She shook her head. She didn't know. But he expected her to know. He stared like he *needed* her to know. "They might have been sick. Could have been a parasite or something. Or maybe they just got confused and didn't see the windows." It was weak and she knew it, but it was all she had.

He nodded like he could make that work, and she put his hat back on him after shaking it out.

Everyone else had streamed out of the diner behind them and gathered on the street.

Charlotte cast her gaze through the broken windows, at the dark piles of birds inside, and then up at the sky.

It was clear. Not a bird in sight.

CHAPTER THIRTY

Charlotte, Jane, and Hannah walked the kids down the street to the doctor's office.

Jane took over as soon as they walked in. She herded the kids from the waiting room into exam room two and then set the nurse to work while she went to get paper cups of orange juice from the kitchenette and grab the doctor. Hannah was already talking about blood tests and infectious diseases. In the company of the two most motherly mothers she knew, Charlotte had taken to nodding and hoping neither noticed they'd accidentally dragged *her* along.

Charlotte kept out of the way while Doctor Paulson asked each one of the kids a series of questions, making them track a pen light with their eyes, and list out numbers and their parents' names. He had them wiggle their limbs and their fingers and toes to see if anything hurt. All together they had a couple of scratches and bruises, but nothing broken. No significant injury in the mix.

They were all set to leave, mostly calmed down from the shock of the scene by the routine of their checkups, when the doctor caught Charlotte's gaze. "I'm sorry, Miss Crowe, but could you stay a bit?"

Jane continued her duties by directing the kids into the waiting room for stickers at the receptionist's desk, but Hannah lingered in the doorway.

"There's something in the morgue I'd like to discuss," he said when the kids were out of the room, his voice hushed just in case they were still listening.

Charlotte's stomach dropped. No. She couldn't deal with Edgar's body—especially not with Miles there. He couldn't see that. She didn't even want him to realize the body was in the same building as him.

Hannah coughed, clearly uncomfortable for having eavesdropped. "I can take Miles to the house with us to play games. I'm watching the rest of the kids today..." She made the offer sound natural—like she and Charlotte had an understanding of some kind. The only understanding they'd ever had was that they both loved Greenleigh. Was this act of kindness somehow under the umbrella of that love?

"Would you mind?" Charlotte tested, unsure. "Miles is staying at our place for a while. Alice isn't feeling great, you know..."

Hannah nodded hurriedly, not needing the details. "Sage and Josie are staying the night anyway. Miles is welcome to sleep over too. They can have a slumber party."

As far as she knew, Miles and his friends didn't usually hang out with William Greenleigh. There were too many years between them. But considering everything going on, exceptions were bound to be made. "That would be great. I'll let Alice know. If anything changes, just give us a call and we'll come get him."

Hannah's brow pinched. "The phones aren't working."

"What? Oh, shit. Right."

"If he wants to come home early, we'll bring him back to your house."

Charlotte nodded slowly, accepting the plan. "Okay. Yeah. Thank you."

Hannah smiled, polite as ever, and then turned out of the office. She took a few steps into the waiting room and announced the sleepover. She was almost as good at directing people as Jane.

Miles looked back to catch Charlotte's eye, uncertain again just like he had been in the diner before joining his friends. A dozen questions filled those brown eyes, begging her to understand. She flashed him a smile and a wave. "Have fun!"

He grinned back.

"This way, Miss Crowe," Doctor Paulson said, already down that long hallway running to the back of the building.

She glanced one last time toward the exit, counting the steps it would take her to escape, before following him.

"I'm so glad you're here. The sheriff was supposed to be over this morning, but I haven't seen him." He disappeared through a swinging door.

Charlotte frowned. Why would she be a good replacement for the sheriff in *any* situation? "Yeah, he seems to be off the grid today." She stopped just inside the morgue, breath catching in her throat.

A crisp white sheet draped over a body on a metal table near the center of the room. She could see the shape of a large man through the fabric. Was that Andrew Caller? Had they found him?

"Did you figure out what happened to Edgar? Why his body…changed?" she said, grinding out the words, feeling sick and unable to look away from the dead man in the room.

The doctor shook his head, pacing. He had looked edgy when he came to see the kids, but she had chalked it up to a bad night and no sleep. Now he oozed anxious energy, unbound by whatever thin restraint he'd been using before. She noticed the sweat sticking his shirt to his back and the dew on his brow all the way up his scalp to the receding line of his gray hair.

"Last night I sent a few of Deborah Rogers's sons with my samples north, to take the long way over the mountain and around to Cyprus but they came back." His voice dropped low, almost trembling. "The road was blocked on the north side of the mountain, just as it starts the descent. They said it was blocked with downed trees and abandoned trucks. The trees were cut…" He wheezed out the words in a whisper, like someone might be listening. Charlotte wished she *wasn't* listening.

"Why are you telling me?" she demanded, suddenly angry. Shouldn't he have kept Jane if he wanted to talk about Wicker business? If Deborah Rogers knew, then so did the town council.

He blinked at her dumbly, caught by surprise, and then he used his sleeve to mop the sweat from his forehead. He took two steps to the body on the table and pulled back the sheet before she could ask him not to.

She held her breath for so long that her lungs burned. Her eyes watered when she finally let that exhale out. The dead man wasn't Andrew Caller, but she recognized him. Edgar looked even better than he had last night, his face a smooth oval and his cheeks and eyes no longer sunken. He had a gray pallor but was otherwise perfect—just as he had looked the last time she saw him.

She took a step closer, terror twisting in her gut. Her hand twitched at her side, resisting the impulse to reach out to him. Tears blurred her vision and her breath came in shallow sucks. The hole in his head was gone. *Gone.* Healed over. Not even a scab left behind.

"That's not possible."

The doctor let out a gust of air tangled up with a whimper and a laugh. Tears glistened in his eyes. "Oh, thank God you see it too. I thought I was losing my damned mind! I would think it was a prank, you know, someone swapping out the bodies at night, if it weren't always Edgar."

She winced at her brother's name, still staring at him, terrified he might sit up any second now. She stared hard at his naked chest, willing it not to move—to stay breathless.

"It's just not possible and I haven't been able to tell anyone. With the phones down, I can't even call the sheriff and the office is still locked up—"

Charlotte stopped listening. Not taking her eyes off of Edgar, she inched closer. She couldn't help but think of that morning eight years ago when she woke to a muffled, gagging sound downstairs. On her feet before she could think, she'd raced blindly toward it. Her vision cleared just when she lurched into the doorway of her momma's room, pushing it open wide. But Momma wasn't making any sounds. None at all. She was gray and, at first, Charlotte didn't even recognize the body as anyone at all. It was so empty—so painfully unfamiliar.

Edgar stood beside their momma's bed, cheeks pink and mouth open a little as he dragged heavy breaths, winded. For one stupid second, she thought he'd been the one making those desperate, struggling sounds. Those *dying* sounds. A little twitch at the corner of his mouth, his dark eyes wild with emotion—and she knew. It was a cold sort of knowing, catching her before feelings could follow—before fury or grief or heartache. She *knew* that he had killed their momma, even before she looked at the pillow clutched in his hands with the round saliva patch still glistening wet.

Charlotte remembered her back hitting the wall, the air heaving from her lungs, and her gaze finally falling on the woman in the bed. Dead. Vacant. Gone from her forever. Charlotte had bent forward and thrown up on the hardwood.

Edgar had left before she could get control of herself, before she could stand and look at him. She could almost pretend he hadn't been there at all and that their momma's heart had just given up. After four strokes in two years and the last five months of her being barely conscious, it would have made sense. It was the assumption everyone else had made. And Charlotte let them make it. She never said that Edgar had been there, and he pretended to be shocked when he arrived. That had been the most terrifying part—watching him fake pain and surprise so well.

For months after, until the day Edgar disappeared, Charlotte had found herself staring at his mouth, remembering that small twist of a smile, the same one she had seen that day in the woods when they were kids and he watched the fawn die.

Looking at his corpse on that table in the morgue, Charlotte almost thought she saw it—that smile in the corner of his mouth, almost there, almost formed, almost alive again.

CHAPTER THIRTY-ONE

Charlotte stood on the sidewalk outside the doctor's office, trying to catch her breath and forget Edgar's body inside. The bullet holes were gone—the one in his chest and the one in his head. Like it had never happened.

She closed her eyes and tipped her head back, trying to push down the rise of panic even as it plowed through her veins. Her heart rattled against her ribs and her skin ached as though it had been clawed raw. A chill wracked her spine, threatening to have her spill her stomach on the sidewalk.

Charlotte forced herself to drag in deep breaths, hold, and then let them out slowly. She counted in her head, with no aim or purpose. She just counted and breathed until her stomach stopped rolling and her arms stopped shaking. When she opened her eyes, she was still standing on the sidewalk in the heart of her little hometown. Down the street, The Evergreen Diner had gathered a crowd of onlookers. They peeked inside and exchanged stories, pointing at the piles of dead birds.

Charlotte patted the pockets of her jacket until she located a small bulge in one. Because it was Harvey's jacket, and not her own, there had been a good chance of a forgotten pack of cigarettes. This one was rumpled with only two passengers left. Her fingers shook when she pulled one out, putting it to her lips and searching herself for a lighter. She didn't find one and swore around the cigarette, starting down the street toward the bookshop. She tried not to think about Edgar's body, about how it was possible or impossible, and what would happen if Alice found out. Would she drag Charlotte back there again? Would she have to look at him again?

She slowed when she spotted Greenleigh and four other Wicker aldermen cutting a path for the same destination. The day was surely filling up with unnatural events. None of the city officials ever went into Harvey Darling's shop—or anywhere near him if they could help it.

Charlotte converged with the gathering, startling them when she came from the side.

Parker Whitley held the door and Deborah Rogers, Kenny Feldman, Wyatt Caro Philips Jr., and Rebecca Greenleigh filed in.

Charlotte managed a smile around her cigarette when Parker stood fast and waited for her as well, tipping his head to the side in one of those gentlemanly *"ma'am"* moments. The Whitleys and Feldmans both owned chunks of land and had been on the mountain almost as long as the Greenleighs.

Deborah Rogers owned the garbage company, now managed by her four grown children, and Wyatt Caro Philips Jr. and his family were in business with the sawmill. Of the five, Wyatt Caro Philips Jr. was the only one not actually on the city board—but likely there on behalf of his wife, Jane.

Harvey Darling perched on his usual seat behind the narrow counter, one leg crossed over the other and head cocked to the side. He blinked at the group with no signs of surprise or interest. His dark gaze considered each one, as though they were strangers to him, before turning his attention back to the book in his hand. This one had a very sexy pirate on the cover and what appeared to be a transparent ghost ship.

"Coffee cake?" he asked, monotone, not even gesturing to the plate on the counter.

"No, thank you," Deborah Rogers spoke first, voice clipped and small eyes flicking over the dessert skeptically—as though there might be razor blades beneath that crust of brown sugar and cinnamon. "We came on business."

Harvey flipped a page.

Wyatt Caro Philips Jr. seethed, fists balling against his sides as his infamous temper rose.

Greenleigh pressed past him and picked up a piece of coffee cake. "Thank you," she said, ignoring the mood of her group.

Charlotte skirted around the pack to the other side of the counter and started fishing through Harvey's desk drawers for a lighter, cigarette still between her lips.

Greenleigh shot her the *"I thought you quit that?"* eyebrow lift. Charlotte responded with a *"The world is going to shit"* shrug.

"We just wanted to get your help with something," Greenleigh said to Harvey just as Mr. Feldman inhaled to speak up.

Harvey flipped another page. "Books, pot, or cake?" he asked, sounding distracted.

"Have you not noticed what's going on?" Deborah snapped.

Harvey didn't look up. "Dead tourists. Dead kid. Dead guy. Missing guy…probably dead too." He reached into his pocket and pulled out a lighter just as Charlotte was opening a second drawer. He waggled it to the side for her, like maybe the audience wouldn't notice and she could pretend she found it all on her own.

She took it and pushed the drawers shut with a bump of her thigh.

"We need to talk to the Darlings," Greenleigh said, pulling off a corner of her coffee cake and poking it into her mouth.

Harvey stopped reading, dark eyes fixed on a point on the page before his jaw ticked and he looked up. "And you came here because…"

"You're a Darling, aren't you?" Wyatt hissed.

Harvey grinned but there was nothing happy about it. "Only when you want me to be."

Greenleigh leaned against the counter, as though she could distance herself from the rest of her pack. Charlotte stood off to the side and lit her cigarette. She didn't usually smoke indoors, but she wasn't going to miss whatever the hell was going on here. It looked like Rebecca was playing good cop to the batch of bad ones.

"We thought you could come up with us and be sort of an intermediary to help the conversation go smoothly," Greenleigh said.

Harvey's eyes watered when he held back a laugh, mouth twisting in an attempt not to grin. "What do you plan to talk about?"

"They might be able to help us find Sam and Andrew Caller," Mr. Feldman suggested.

Harvey's gaze slid over Greenleigh's shoulder to the older man. "They're dead."

"And how do you know that?" Wyatt cut in, his question loaded with accusation.

"Because you found pieces of the kid, didn't you?"

"We don't know that for certain," Parker Whitley interjected, still standing near the door.

"And Andrew doesn't get lost," Harvey continued. "If he's gone, he's dead." He thunked his paperback down on the counter and leaned forward, looking back at Greenleigh as though now she was the only one there. "If you think the Darlings did it, you shouldn't be going up there, because even if they didn't do it, they might kill you for asking."

Wyatt pushed forward, not an easy task in the small shop, but he was the sort of man used to getting his way—so he could fold space if need be. "You better tell us what you know," he growled. "What do the bone chimes mean? Why would they do that?"

"*They* wouldn't," Harvey answered easily.

Charlotte wondered if he'd been expecting this conversation. He was the wolf in a town of sheep, after all. It was only a matter of time before they turned their suspicions on him. She took a long drag off her cigarette and held it in her lungs until they burned.

"If the Darlings killed someone, you would find them dumped on your street or not at all," Harvey reminded.

It was true. It had happened before. There had been bouts of rivalries between Wicker and the Darlings long ago, the bloodiest of all being the moonshine wars in the 1920s. Four men from Wicker had been paid by a mob boss from Cyprus to go up and destroy the Darling distilleries in the woods. All four men had been drowned in whiskey, practically pickled in it, and then left propped up on posts like scarecrows along Green Street to be found in the morning—kicking off a decade of murder and vandalism between the townsfolk and the Darlings.

Charlotte had heard the stories many times from her grandfather. One of those first four to die had been a brother to her grandmother. Another had been one of Wyatt's ancestors.

Greenleigh gave Wyatt's shoulder a firm pat, a gentle signal to back the fuck up. "We just want to talk to them—maybe see if they know what's going on or if we could help one another."

Harvey barked a laugh. "Oh, *Greenleigh*, you should know better than anyone here that the Darlings don't want your help and they won't give you theirs. It's a fight to the end, isn't it? You and your town versus the Darlings? They plan to be the last ones standing. So, don't tell them you have one knee in the dirt, or they'll cut your other leg out from under you."

"This is a waste of time," Deborah Rogers declared, no great malice in her voice but a deep exhaustion.

Parker Whitley opened the door, and she walked out.

Mr. Feldman nodded to Harvey. "Thank you for your time, son," he muttered, and Harvey tipped his head in return.

Wyatt hesitated to go, grinding his teeth on his words before finally turning and leaving.

Greenleigh continued to pick at the coffee cake in hand until Parker gave up waiting for her and disappeared, the door closing with a bounce. "This is good," she admitted, poking another chunk of dense cake into her mouth.

Harvey reached out to his side blindly and Charlotte gave him what was left of her cigarette. "I mean it. You shouldn't go up there." He sounded less edgy now, but just as grim.

"There's something going on. Have you heard anything at all from them?" Greenleigh pressed instead of yielding.

"Not since the morning after the storm," Harvey admitted. "They had some damage, but the big mudslides missed their land."

"Someone blocked the road north. Does it sound like something they would do?"

Harvey shrugged. "Can't see why but I wouldn't put it past them."

"Some of the search party last night claim they saw someone out in the woods—just standing around in the dark, not responding to them but watching them."

"Anyone get a good look?" Harvey sounded reasonable now, like he might offer a name to go with the description if he had one.

Greenleigh shook her head, finishing her wedge of cake and then clapping her hands together to shake off the sugar and crumbs. She started toward the door, two steps, before stopping. "Do you think it *could* be them? Just between us. Do you think they could have killed that boy and…made the chimes?"

Harvey paused, either mulling over the idea or deciding whether or not to lie to her. "I don't know. They don't follow the same laws as you do. They don't think the way you do. There's *nothing* you should put past them. They still remember your family, Greenleigh. The grudge is real and alive, and I meant what I said about not showing your weakness to them."

Some of the color drained from her cheeks, but her shoulders pressed back and her chin high—the way Greenleigh always did when anyone spoke of her family. She nodded once and reached for the door, but it sprang open. She jumped back, barely avoiding it when Sheriff Summerfield stomped in.

His cheeks were flushed, his uniform wrinkled and smudged in dirt and dark stains. His eyes darted around the shop, bloodshot whites and blown pupils. He wasn't wearing his hat and that threw Charlotte the most. She hadn't seen Bryan Summerfield without a hat since he was deputized. When he took it off, he always held it in his hands like a shield. But now it was just gone, and he looked wrong without it.

His gaze landed on her and stopped darting, fixing like a missile ready to launch. "You need to step outside with me." He seemed to vomit up the words, like someone else had written them and his mouth was just doing the work.

All three of them blinked at the sheriff.

Greenleigh broke the heavy second-long silence. "Where have you been?" she demanded. "We've been looking for you all day!"

Charlotte might have pointed out that it wasn't even noon yet, but he was still staring at her. What did he want? Could it be something else to do with Edgar's body? Her skin washed cold and clammy. Her stomach rolled and suddenly wished Harvey hadn't taken her cigarette.

"*Now*, Charlotte," Sheriff Summerfield said, voice dipping into that authoritative bite that had her shuffling around the counter when really she just wanted to run away. He ignored Greenleigh entirely.

Harvey stood up when she moved around him, reaching for her wrist but only brushing it with his fingers. "What's this about, Bryan?" Harvey asked, using his first name like they were friends.

Sheriff Summerfield had a sheen of sweat on his brow, and when he took a step forward to grab Charlotte's upper arm, she saw he had sweat stains on his shirt collar and down his sides from his armpits to his waist. She tried to lean away from him on instinct, but he tightened his grip and hauled her forward, jerking her onto the toes of her boots. They were past Greenleigh and out the door before any of them could get out another word.

Charlotte opened her mouth, mind reeling. She could only heave out a strangled sound of confusion, little throbs of pain shooting through her arm where his fingers pushed bruises into her skin. He had never touched her before. She had never seen him lay hands on anyone unless it was to break up a fight.

Fireworks went off in her head, blurring her vision. Everything about this was wrong.

"Hey!" Greenleigh's voice boomed after them. She was a petite woman, but petite women often mustered the biggest shouts. Everyone on the street jerked to a stop, eyes turning toward the ruckus. Everyone, but Sheriff Summerfield. "What do you think you're doing?" Greenleigh demanded, close on their heels.

Charlotte tried to turn toward her, only catching glimpses as she was half-dragged toward the police car parked sloppily along the sidewalk. He gave her a hard shove, still leading with his grip on her upper arm and bent her over the hood. Her chest made a heavy thud against the metal and she winced, tears blurring her vision now. Was she being arrested? Some of the tension actually slid out of her shoulders when he pulled her hands behind her back and cuffed her wrists together, like this made sense. But it didn't.

"Are you going to read her her rights?" Greenleigh pressed, fury in her voice. She stood beside the car with her hands on her hips. "Why are you arresting her, *Bryan*?"

The bookshop door clapped again and Harvey was there in a few long strides, brow pinched under his mess of hair. "You can't just arrest her without a reason, man." He crowded in, and Charlotte could see the way his dark eyes shifted to her as he inched closer, looking for a chance to grab her and pull her away from the sheriff. Was that a good idea? Couldn't they just talk about this at the station?

And then Sheriff Summerfield turned toward the two, really looking at them for the first time. His lip curled back and, in a flash, he drew his gun from his side.

Greenleigh froze, eyes flaring and focused on the barrel, less afraid than outraged at the sight of it. Harvey raised his hands and let out a soothing *"whoa"* as he slid slowly but fluidly between Greenleigh and the barrel. He shook his head gently. "We just want to know what's going on."

Charlotte straightened up off the hood of the car, shoulders forced back by the pinching metal around her wrists. "Summerfield…" she managed to speak at last, his name small on her tongue. He didn't move, body tight and gun pointed squarely at Harvey's chest. "Summerfield, let's go. The station is right there," she said, not that she could point up the street to the brick building with flags fluttering over the entrance.

He nodded once but instead of grabbing her and marching her to the station, he took a few steps backward, past Charlotte, and opened the back door of his squad car. She blinked at it, licking her lips slowly when she found them suddenly dry. Why did she need to get into the car? The station was twenty steps away. She wanted to refuse and thought she might have if he looked anything like himself today, but with her best friend and Harvey standing in front of a gun, she didn't have a lot of choices. She bit back a rise of swear words and forced herself to walk around the open door and awkwardly duck into the backseat, arms behind her back.

He slammed the door shut and it clicked. There were no handles on the inside.

The sticky seat reeked of piss and vomit. Charlotte gagged. Summerfield opened the driver's side door and she sucked at the breath of air before he sealed them in again. Tears slid down her cheeks and she couldn't tell if it was fear, confusion, or the rancid hot air stinging her eyes. The engine started. He tossed his gun onto the empty passenger seat beside him.

She glimpsed Greenleigh's shocked face outside the window and caught the moment when her features screwed up with anger, mouth spitting swear words Charlotte couldn't hear. She twisted around in her seat to watch them through the back window as the car pulled away.

Harvey shot her a hard look, one that promised he would follow, his hand digging keys from his pocket. As soon as he tore his gaze from hers, he was running to his truck.

And then the police car drove past the station, heading toward the north end of town.

CHAPTER THIRTY-TWO

"What are we doing, boss?" Charlotte asked, forcing out the words before the silence infected her and made it impossible to ask. She leaned forward, pressing her knees against the back of the seat in front of her and almost touching her cheek to the metal partition.

The front passenger seat wasn't entirely empty. The gun lay on a bed of tangled bone chimes in a congealed puddle of vomit and blood. Her heart pounded so fast that her vision blurred when she noted the red and brown splatters on the inside of the passenger door and drying on the dash. The window to the right had been sloppily cleaned with streaks of filth left behind.

"Whose blood is that?" she asked before she could think better of it. Knowing wouldn't help her now, would it? What did he want from her?

"Not me," Bryan Summerfield said, hands flexing against the steering wheel as he drove them out of town. "It's not going to be me. Not me."

Beads of sweat joined the tears rolling down his face.

Charlotte didn't know what to say. He was obviously unhinged. What the fuck had happened to him since last night?

His bleary gaze shot to the rearview mirror and met hers by accident. He stared just long enough for her to worry they might crash, but she didn't dare look away or say anything. Sadness pooled in those tired eyes and a sob bubbled up from his chest, coming out in a strangled laugh. "Why didn't you ever tell on me?" he asked, his voice small.

He looked at the road again, shaking his head to himself once before beating his palm against the wheel three times in fast, hard succession.

Charlotte gaped. "Tell who what?" she choked out the words. *Calm down. Get your shit together and calm down.* If she riled him any worse than he was, he'd probably drive them right off the road—and depending on the turn, that could be a deadly plummet.

He let out another garbled sound between a scream and a laugh, like it got all tangled up in his chest and came ripping out past his throat in a knot. "I've thought about it every day and I still don't know why I did it. I just... I saw you and Darling, and I was so pissed."

He used the dirty cuff of his sleeve to rub sweat and tears from his eyes, one hand still on the wheel as they wound their way up the mountainside. He was driving so fast, the trees blurring and the turns making her stomach lurch up into her throat.

"I still remember the way your body fell," he said. "It was just one rock and you were on the ground, blood all down your face like *Carrie* in that movie… And you looked right at me." He laughed in a thin, high voice. "I almost thought you'd kill me with your thoughts, but you just stared. And then he picked you up and drove off… Why didn't you tell the police? Or your parents?"

Charlotte was so completely confused that for another stretch of road she couldn't think of an answer. What was he talking about?

Then she remembered prom night.

She'd never made it past the parking lot. She didn't remember seeing him or anyone else there. Had she really stared at him in those lost seconds of her life? All she remembered was the pain and the sick feeling when she couldn't tell up from down. "You threw the rock at me," she said it rather than asked it, tasting the shape of that new reality. Did it change anything? No. Bryan Summerfield had been no one to her then, just as he was no one to her now—other than the guy abducting her, of course. She guessed that would leave a memorable mark.

"What did I ever do to you?" she asked automatically, not even sure she cared. But *he* cared and right now, that mattered a lot.

He sniffled and shook his head to himself. "Nothing. The guys…" He said it like she knew who they were. *His guys.* His friends from high school. "They thought it was funny."

She nodded slowly, wondering now who thought throwing her in the back of his car was funny. Had whoever lost all that blood in the front seat been in on the joke? Or another part of it?

"I don't understand what's happening," Charlotte said as calmly as she could, staring at him through the partition.

He finally let up on the gas pedal, the car slowing to a roll and finally stopping along the shoulder of the highway. He stared at the steering wheel for a long time. Blood had dried on that soft plastic too and she saw more of it under his nails. She had mistaken all the smudges on his clothes for dirt.

"Bryan?" she said as softly as she could, fear making her voice wobble. Why was he doing this?

"I have to make the trade. I won't die on this mountain. I have to keep my side of the deal."

A lump rose in her throat, pushing fresh tears into her eyes. She shook her head when he grabbed the gun off the seat and opened his door, sliding out and not bothering to close it.

"No," Charlotte said without realizing it. He opened the backseat door, and she said it again, louder, "No!"

He reached for her, and she kicked at him, falling onto her back on the seat. When he caught her heel and then grabbed her calf, she screamed. She kicked him in the shoulder with her other boot, but he dragged her out. The back of her head thumped against the metal lip of the car and her vision instantly darkened. It was like her limbs weren't hers for a minute, all of them going limp as she slurped for air.

She wanted to call *pause*. She wanted to tell him whatever this was had gone too far, but this wasn't a game. Pain shot from the back of her head through her eye sockets.

He dragged her by one leg, Harvey's jacket taking the abuse of rocks and rough ground under her back. She spasmed when her body came back under her control, head throbbing and vision blurred at the edges. They were in the woods, farther and farther from the road. The heavy canopy of branches blotted out the day and blanketed her in shadows that cooled and soothed her rising headache.

Bending her free leg against her chest, she kicked hard at his hand, the heel of her boot digging into the fingers clamped around her and sliding off to rip her tights. He let go, dirty hand flexing at his side to shake out the pain.

Stomping the sole of her boot to the ground, she flipped over, squirming onto her knees. She was about to try to get on her feet when his hand fisted in the back of her hair, keeping her from standing. Summerfield shook her hard and her vision turned into smears of color, the back of her skull screaming.

"You just have to make a trade of your own," he panted. "You can survive if you make a trade."

"You're out of your mind!" Charlotte shrieked, anger finally bubbling up. "Let me go!"

He shook her again, ripping out clumps of her hair. "Don't be a brat! She'll give you anything you want!"

Charlotte gasped for air when he stopped shaking her. It was like she couldn't breathe when he did, the pain in her head too much for any other bodily functions to work. "Who?" she wheezed just as her vision focused on tracks in the mud. She saw the sharp hoofprints first, but over each one was a human footprint.

No.

Sheriff Summerfield threw her onto the ground and used his boot to roll her onto her back. Her arms strained behind her. She screamed when his weight came down on her, pain flaring in her shoulder until she was sure it would burst right out of the socket and maybe disconnect from her body completely. She envisioned it in a macabre moment of clarity, her severed arm dangling by the cuffs as she had to carry it around with her. Maybe she'd carry it all the way back to Wicker? Maybe she'd just keep going down the mountain to Cyprus and right to a hospital with it?

His hand wrapped around her neck but didn't squeeze. He used the grip to pin her down. She stared up at him, a virtual stranger she'd known her whole life. They had been delivered into the world by the same doctor, had gone to all the same birthday parties and schools. They had been born and raised in the same little town under Mount Bell, and she had no idea who he really was—but she was pretty sure, this wasn't it. This was not the Bryan Summerfield of Wicker. This was not even the idiot boy who had thrown a rock at her in high school. This was something else entirely.

He cried, face red and saliva dribbling from his mouth when he croaked, "Ask her to make this stop and she will." He pleaded, like *he* was the one in pain.

"What are you—" she started, but his hands grabbed at the front of her dress and pulled, ripping the buttons down the front to her waist, exposing her skin to the cold.

Distantly, she heard growling.

His hands were all over her, but her gaze skimmed the trees. What was that? The growling grew loud and deep, somewhere in the ground under her back. It vibrated under his fingers on her skin. Her breath hitched in her chest and her eyes stared up blindly at the trees. The growling rolled through her. It didn't come from the woods. It came from her chest—whispering out on every labored breath.

Sheriff Summerfield cried and panted. He sat between her legs with his hands under her skirt, groping up her hips to find the top of her tights. His dirty fingers hooked into the elastic as he sobbed, telling her to make the deal and end it.

She stared up at him, almost too confused to even be afraid or angry. Why was he doing this? Who was he talking about?

She bent one knee and planted her boot to the ground. Quickly, she brought her other leg up to her chest and snapped her leg out at him, kicking him in the face with her heel. He fell back with a surprised yelp. Her shoulder screamed when she rolled over and scrambled to her knees and then to her feet. Blood gushed from Summerfield's nose, like a ghoulish waterfall running over his mouth and chin. When she was standing, Charlotte kicked him again, this time in the stomach, and he rolled away, groping blindly at his belt for his gun.

She turned and ran, weaving through the trees.

Sheriff Summerfield let loose a guttural scream behind her, sounding more like a bear than a man.

Charlotte didn't look to see if he was chasing her. She just kept running, gaze scanning the ground ahead. Where was the road? Was this even the way they'd come?

No. It wasn't the way they'd come, but it was familiar. She thought she might be close to the Cornett Trail. If she could just find the beaten path, she could follow it out.

From the corner of her eye, she saw someone and nearly lost her footing. Her head twisted to the side, seeing the silhouette of a person leaning against a tree. The person was unnaturally tall and wore mud and shadow for clothing with wild hair and a blood red mouth.

Charlotte did not stop, not even when the monstrous creature was out of her sight, and a new wave of terror threatened to crash over her. Was it chasing her too?

A breeze pushed against her back, dragging cold tendrils along wounds adrenaline had made her forget. The back of her head throbbed, her shoulder aching, and a dozen cuts and scrapes flared to life on her legs. *"I can save you,"* a voice in the wind whispered, sounding like creaking trees and grinding stones. Charlotte let out a shaky cry. Was she going insane? Was Summerfield sick with something contagious? Or was the voice real?

"Ask me," the wind urged, and Charlotte could swear she heard a smile in those words—could almost see that blood-slick mouth grinning around each syllable.

She heard the sheriff behind her a second before his body slammed hers into a tree. Her temple thwacked against the bark, right over the scar where he had once hit her with a rock in a parking lot.

He turned her around, catching her weight before her legs could drop her to the ground. He pushed her back against the tree.

Summerfield drew in wheezing breaths and exhaled sobs, his mouth hanging open. He wrapped both hands around her neck and squeezed. She couldn't breathe. There was no chance for a big gulp of air, her mouth opening wide but getting nothing. She kicked at the ground and at his shins. Her wrists twisted against the cuffs, nails clawing at the tree behind her back. There was no more conversation. No more discussion.

"Ask me," the wind demanded and over his shoulder Charlotte saw the creature inching closer. The trees seemed to sway so that their shadows followed the monster, clinging to it like a cloak. Those bloody lips twitched, glinting white teeth. *"Just ask and I will save you."*

Charlotte couldn't think past the air she couldn't take into her lungs. Her gaze slid to Summerfield's eyes. The darkness of his pupils throbbed, and the right one grew, swallowing up the thin blue circle of his iris. It pulsed until it began to lift from his eye, bulging out of it. Something wiggled inside his pupil. She didn't want to see, but she couldn't look away.

The thin film of moisture on his eye stretched, something slender pushing against it, pressing out of that pupil like it was nothing but a void—a hole for which dark things would crawl out of his thoughts into the world. The membrane snapped and a delicate black leg poked out, twitching before bending and struggling to find leverage against the white of his eye.

Another leg and then another pushed out until eight of them writhed, pushing at his eyelid and lashes. Her vision darkened but she tried to blink it back, too horrified not to see what happened next.

She didn't even realize she'd stopped kicking and clawing. She barely twitched, her mouth open but breathless and her eyes straining to keep watch.

The gunshot clapped through the woods, louder than any thunder.

Sheriff Summerfield didn't just fall away—he was blown from her, tumbling onto his side with half his face an open wound oozing blood and brain onto packed dirt.

Charlotte dropped onto her ass. She gasped for air in ragged breaths, sagging to the side and trying to see his face again. One of his eyes was gone, lost to the gruesome hole in his head, but the other…the other had a sleek, black spider squirming out from under the lid. It was the same sort of spider she'd seen crawling all over the dead birds in the diner.

Harvey pulled Charlotte up into a sitting position, hands bracing her face to get a look at her. She stared at him blankly at first, remembering that prom night years ago. He had looked just like this—frightened and angry. She hadn't realized that her face meeting with the tree had reopened her old scar until his fingers dabbed at it, coming away bloody and sending new starbursts of pain through her face. His beautiful mouth moved fast but his words came warped to her ears. He pulled at the front of her ripped dress, mouth still moving. He zipped up the jacket she had borrowed from him. She hadn't asked if she could borrow it. She never asked and he never minded, but this time she had ruined the jacket.

He crawled away from her and toward Summerfield. Charlotte spasmed, trying to reach out and stop him before the spider could crawl its way into her Darling. But her arms didn't move. At first, she thought they were like her legs, appendages she simply couldn't remember how to use, but then she remembered the cuffs around her wrists. Harvey dug fingers into the dead man's pockets until he came back with the keys.

Cold drove down into Charlotte's bones, making her shake.

"She's not saying anything," was the first of Harvey's sentences that registered, and it wasn't even directed at her. "Her head's bleeding. We have to get her to Paulson."

Charlotte hadn't even noticed Greenleigh until then. The other woman was standing to the side of the scene with a rifle in her arms. She stared at the body on the ground. "Okay," she said. "We'll go now and send the deputies up for the sheriff…" Greenleigh managed to make it sound simple, like there wasn't a dead man in the woods. Like they weren't leaving his body behind. Like he hadn't tried to kill Charlotte.

Charlotte envied her detachment because she was drowning in the madness of it.

Harvey leaned her forward, against his chest, and unlocked the cuffs. There was another wave of pain when her arms fell forward, shoulder throbbing. He picked her up and started walking. Charlotte reached out quickly and caught Greenleigh's shoulder. Her fingers burned from the cold and her teeth chattered.

"Don't stay," she said without thinking, terrified Greenleigh would be found by whatever was in these woods— whatever had been in the wind and in Summerfield.

Greenleigh's hand pressed over Charlotte's and she nodded slowly. "Let's get you out of here."

CHAPTER THIRTY-THREE

Sheriff Bryan Summerfield inhaled. He sucked air down into his lungs, but they never quite filled, like there was a hole somewhere inside of him letting everything out. He opened his eye—the one he had left—and watched the canopy of branches glide overhead. Sunlight made the leaves glow bright yellow and orange with white light glinting between them like tiny stars.

He coughed and gurgled, spitting up blood and chunks of himself.

He couldn't move, but the ground continued to slide under him.

Craning his head back, he saw her, the god to whom he had given his body and soul. Her talon was hooked into his shoulder, fingers buried up to the knuckle in fabric and meat.

He couldn't feel it. Bryan couldn't feel anything but sadness, dread, and wonder. She looked birdlike up close, in a way that appeared fragile, despite how easily she dragged him through the woods. And those woods moved around her, changing shape and color and sound in little waves.

"What—" he croaked out in a plea for answers.

She wasn't smiling, mouth set flat across her face and gaze fixed ahead. A spider crawled up her arm and disappeared over her shoulder in the tangles of her hair. *"We had a deal,"* her ragged voice ground out, sounding like it hurt her to speak. But nothing hurt her. He was sure of it.

Bryan cried from his one eye. "I did everything you asked!" he yelled when he meant to beg for mercy. He had done so much for her. He had killed so many.

"Not for me," she corrected, lip curling with disgust as she read his thoughts. *"You did it for you. You asked not to die on my mountain."*

He heard the wolves. His gaze darted around the trees to spot them. They were giants with teeth bared in violent grins as they watched. His heart hammered against his chest and his body twitched for the first time. "Please. Please, I'll do anything," he begged. He moved one arm and reached up to clutch at her wrist. Her fingers flexed inside his shoulder, against muscles and bones. He cried harder, voice shrill with pain. "Please don't let them eat me!"

She finally smiled, and her grin shamed the wolves. *"You already made your deal. And I always keep my word."*

He shivered out relief. He wouldn't die then. He would get to leave the mountain. Bryan closed his eyes, still crying softly but losing his hold on her wrist. She dragged him for a while longer, until he heard the whisper of water grow into the churning fury of the river.

His eye flung open with terrible knowing just as she came to a stop. They were at the lookout point in the shadow of Mount Bell, where the trees gave way to a short valley and a drop off. The Aurora River snaked below, icy with the runoff from the snowy summit of Mount Grayson, joined by dozens of streams on its way past the lesser peak. Everyone had been to that spot. Every tourist came right there to take pictures with the two peaks lining up behind them. He had been there a thousand times.

The Wicker Witch drew him up to his knees in front of her, those dark eyes looking him over as though she may have missed something. He held his breath, hoping she had, hoping she would want him, and at the same time, hoping she saw nothing at all and threw him away. He couldn't meet her gaze, afraid of the madness he would find there. It was his last chance to look, his last chance to see her. Was that what she was waiting for? Was she offering him that bit of knowing?

Bryan squeezed his eye shut. He didn't want to see. He didn't want to know.

She let go of him with a shove that sent him toppling over the lip of the cliff and crashing into the dark waters of the Aurora River. It was the same river that had cut them off from escape, swollen from the mudslides and rains, washing out their only bridge.

In that split-second when the waters swallowed him whole, he blamed the river itself for everything. It had been a part of the mountain, a part of his life, and it had betrayed him completely. The icy cold stung at him like a thousand hornets, crawling into the gaping wound in his face and squirming around inside his head. The current swept him away, pushing him to the surface twice before finally dragging him down for the last time just past the ruined bridge at the base of the mountain.

His body would wash up on the banks of Cyprus and be discovered by local kids playing at fishing with marshmallows for bait. They had never caught anything before, and they would never try again after finding the body with half a face. By then, it would be too late for anyone to save Wicker.

CHAPTER THIRTY-FOUR

Fifteen generations of Greenleighs fed the Wicker Witch.

They passed down the horror of their deal, a weight that dwarfed the responsibilities of family and mountain.

They took to using the same tree in the front yard to hang themselves when the weight became too much, another legacy hidden and more secrets kept.

They saw the resentment in the eyes of their neighbors. The original families knew what they had done—the bargain they had struck for their timber throne. Lathams, Asbies, Ludds, and Crowes—they knew and they judged, but they did not leave. They had not made the deal, but they were made safe by it. They did not bring game to the mountain for the witch to hunt, but they turned a blind eye to it. They didn't prosper off the mountain as well as the Greenleighs, but what right did they have to judge?

The Greenleighs went down the mountain for church and God—to look for judgement elsewhere.

CHAPTER THIRTY-FIVE

Rebecca held on to Charlotte in the cab of the truck while Harvey drove them back to town. She passed her hands over her friend to look for wounds but the worst of it seemed to be a gash on the back of her head and her split temple.

Charlotte babbled the whole drive about a monster in the woods and a spider in *his* eye. Rebecca drank up every nonsensical word. It was hysteria, but there might be something underneath to help explain what had happened or hint at how she could help her recover. Someone had to listen, even if what she said made no sense. Did Darling feel the same? Because neither of them tried to shush Charlotte or ask for more explanations. She talked and they listened.

Rebecca tried to use her friend's mad words to block out the memory of Sheriff Summerfield's head bursting and his body going slack when the blast propelled him to the side. She and Harvey had followed the squad car up the mountain and parked behind it. The sheriff had left his vehicle running, doors open. Rebecca had popped the trunk and taken the rifle from the case in the back. The previous sheriff had used it when they had a call about a bear on the hiking trails, frightening the tourists. She'd never forgotten that it was there. She had braced it along one arm and grabbed bullets with the other, loading it as she and Harvey marched into the forest.

They hadn't known which way to go until Charlotte started screaming. Rebecca hadn't even been sure it was Charlotte at first, the sound pitching between the trees, but Harvey had set off after it and Rebecca followed. The scream choked out into silence and somehow that absence was instantly worse.

Rebecca had shouted the sheriff's name when she saw them, but he hadn't even twitched, fingers digging in around Charlotte's throat. Her face had looked purple and swollen, her head bleeding, and her clothes ripped. Rebecca hadn't even hesitated; she lifted the rifle, aimed, and fired. She had shot rabbit, dear, elk, goose, and even that bear that had terrorized the tourists years back. Not for a second had she thought she might miss, but she also hadn't been entirely ready for what she'd done. The sheriff was dead. Rebecca had killed someone, and she had done it so easily.

Why hadn't she shot him in the leg? That would have stopped him, wouldn't it?

She felt sick by the time they pulled up along Green Street in town, not because of regret but the lack of it. She had thought about that moment she pulled the trigger again and again, but she couldn't uncover a single second of doubt or horror. She had wanted to put him down, and try as she might, she couldn't find how it was any different than the bear.

Rebecca got out of the truck. Harvey gathered Charlotte and took her straight to the doctor's office.

Rebecca closed the doors and took the rifle across the street to the sheriff's station. She had to turn in the weapon and report the death. Someone had to go out and collect the body and the squad car.

"Greenleigh," Wyatt called, long legs making short work of the sidewalk between them. He had his hands stuffed into the pockets of his jacket and his cheeks were pink above his beard either from the chill in the air or some new anger.

She had known Wyatt her whole life, and he had always been angry, even as a kid. He hadn't evened out until he left home for college and started seeing a therapist. His parents had been hellbent against it when he was a teen. No Philips was going to see a shrink, because there was never anything wrong with a Philips.

"Where did you go? We're getting ready to drive up to see the Darlings," he said.

She had forgotten about the Darlings. Honestly, she had forgotten about everything. "Yeah. Give me a minute? I have to talk to the deputies."

Wyatt grabbed the door as she neared it, holding it open and eyeing the rifle in her hands. It wasn't hers and he would know since they went hunting together regularly. "Did you find that?"

She sighed. "Sort of." She stepped into the waiting room, surprised to find that it wasn't empty. Four people sat along the wall and one man, Henry Slate, beat the metal bell on the receptionist's desk as though he meant to break it.

He stopped when he noticed Rebecca, his face pinching. "Did the sheriff take the week off, Greenleigh?"

She joined him at the counter, leaning over it to look at the desk. The chair behind it had fallen over and a mug with the department logo was tipped onto its side, staining all the papers in dried coffee.

"Hello?" she called into the quiet office.

"You don't think we tried that?" Henry snapped.

"Watch it," Wyatt warned.

Rebecca tried the door between the waiting room and the office, but it was locked.

Henry grumbled, probably stifling an urge to point out that he'd tried that too.

She handed Wyatt the rifle and grabbed a chair, pulling it over. Climbing up and over the high front counter, she stepped down onto the desk. The reek hit her when she jumped to the floor, the air stale and heavy with the stink of blood and piss.

The only light came from the windows, the overhead lamps still off. She'd been in this office a handful of times in her life but never thought twice about it. There were papers on the tile floor, more dropped coffee cups in thick shards and puddles of black. Her gaze fixed on a long smear of blood on the floor, as though someone had been dragged toward the back of the office.

Rebecca held her hand out to her side and Wyatt handed her back the rifle without a word.

Henry Slate wasn't grumbling anymore, something about the situation finally pushing him into silence.

Rebecca stalked away from the desk and into the office while Wyatt climbed over the counter to follow her. She stopped when she saw another splash of red—a spray across one of the desks. As soon as she saw it, the whole room turned red. A puddle beneath an overturned chair. Splatters on the walls and an arch of fine mist on the tile ceiling.

"Holy shit," Wyatt whispered.

A large puddle behind Deputy Douglas's desk turned into a thick streak. Rebecca followed it. The streak mixed with two others, all three leading into Sheriff Summerfield's office. Wyatt signaled for her to stop, pushing his hand through the air to have her back up and take aim on the door while he sidled up beside it. He reached out, turned the knob, and pushed it open, his back to the hallway wall the whole time.

She saw inside first, and her stomach dropped. Both of the deputies, along with Mrs. Potter from reception, were in a heap beside Summerfield's desk.

Rebecca lowered the rifle and took a step back, bracing her spine against the wall and taking deep breaths.

Wyatt swung around the entrance, marching one step in before jerking back. He swore, shook his head, and then swore again. "Where—" he started and then stopped, turning a shade of green. "Where's Summerfield?"

"I think he did it," Rebecca said, voice quiet.

Wyatt nodded. "We have to find him before he—"

"He's dead. I shot him up by the Cornett Trail."

Wyatt stared at her. "You shot him?"

Rebecca nodded. "We need to get a call out to the police in Cyprus. They need to send someone up here."

Wyatt gaped at her for a long time before nodding.

"Close that door," she said roughly. "We don't need anyone seeing this. We'll tell Doctor Paulson, and he can get them to the morgue."

Wyatt continued to nod, shuffling out of the sheriff's station and pulling the door closed behind him. They both sighed, like something terrible had been locked away.

"We'll send a couple people down to the river to get cell service and make the call," Rebecca said. "And we need a few to go get the sheriff's body and the squad car."

"I can do that."

"No." Rebecca shook her head and met his gaze. "You and I are going up to talk to the Darlings."

Nothing happened on the Gray Mountain without the Darlings knowing about it, and something was definitely happening. People were going missing, bones were being found in trees, and their sheriff had gone on a killing spree.

They climbed back over the counter, opting to leave the door locked for now. Something about their expressions made it easy to clear the waiting room. Rebecca advised everyone to go home and stay there.

Rebecca dragged a deep breath when they were outside, closing the door and wishing she had the keys to lock it.

Jane Philips crossed the street toward them with a few of the aldermen on her tail, a question in her eyes. Deborah

Rogers and several others were loading up into trucks, waiting to head up to confront the Darlings.

Whatever Jane's thoughts on that plan might have been were forgotten when she saw the look on her husband's face. They told her quickly about the bodies inside the office and the incident with the sheriff.

Jane handed over her emergency keys to the building so that Rebecca could lock it up.

Someone needed to tell the families of the dead before they heard it as gossip—before they came to the station and saw their loved ones in a heap like that.

Jane offered to do the job, back straight with duty but eyes wet with empathy.

Rebecca thought it was good she took on that job, because her empathy would have no place up on the Darling property.

CHAPTER THIRTY-SIX

Charlotte drummed her fingertips against the edge of the exam table, beside her thigh. She wanted to leave, her gaze darting between Doctor Paulson and the door behind Harvey. The fluorescents were making her head buzz despite the painkillers the doctor had given her. Her shoulder had been tender but not dislocated and now she couldn't feel it at all if she stayed still. Doctor Paulson put staples in the back of her head to close-up a wound near the base of her skull and used glue on the opened scar on her temple. She shed her tights. There were more holes than fabric, anyway. Her legs were scratched and welted, red where bruises would form in the next few hours. And her knees looked almost as bad as they had when she was twelve and tried to learn to skateboard.

The doctor repeated his suggestion that she stay the night for observations, already sounding resigned to her refusal and going on about the possibility of a concussion. He said if she started seeing anything abnormal that she needed to contact him immediately.

Good thing she hadn't told him about the spider she saw climbing out of Summerfield's eye.

She glanced at Harvey. He had been standing like a statue for the last twenty-minutes; his arms crossed and his gaze fixed on her. For the first time in a long time, she had no idea what was going on behind those dark eyes.

"Okay. Okay. If I see a teddy bear riding a unicycle, I'll come back," Charlotte said, flashing a grin that sent a dull pain up the side of her face. Right. She was a mess. Attacked by a cop in the woods. That was a new one.

Doctor Paulson leveled her with a stern stare. To her surprise, it was full of concern. "I'm serious, Charlotte."

She sighed but relented. "Yeah. Okay."

He tapped her good shoulder gently. "I'll have some more painkillers ready for you to pick up on your way out." He tossed Harvey a thin smile before ducking out of the room, closing the door behind him.

Charlotte slid off the table slowly, testing her legs before standing on them fully and letting out a deep breath. What had happened? What had *really* happened?

She walked to the wall with her jacket on a hook and shoved her bare feet into her boots.

"Lotte?" Harvey asked, his voice hushed and gravelly. He sounded hurt, like maybe he had been the one dragged through the woods.

She stepped to the side, staring into the rectangular mirror mounted on the wall. Harvey had used his fingers to comb her hair before tying it up for the doctor. Red welts puffed her cheekbone, her temple, and wrapped around her neck. Blood and dirt caked her skin. She looked wild and couldn't help but think about that creature in the woods—the one offering to save her. Why?

"What?" Charlotte asked absently, brushing her fingertips over those hand-shaped splotches around her throat. The front of her dress hung open, flashing her bra as well as the dirt and sweat coated skin down to her navel. "Fuck..." she swore, trying to button it with her scraped up fingers only to realize most of the buttons were gone—ripped off—somewhere out in the woods still. The thought chilled her for some reason. Her buttons were out there, forever, sinking into the soil.

Harvey touched her elbow gently, alerting her to his nearness and turning her toward him. He buttoned the ones that were left, straightening the ruined dress on her shoulders before taking his jacket off the peg on the wall and helping her into it. "What happened?" he whispered.

Charlotte looked up at him. She tried to smile but it brought tears to her eyes. Why? Why was she crying? She was fine now. "Maybe he was crazy," she said thinly. Wasn't that what she was supposed to believe? Everything Summerfield had said and done was insane. But then *she* had seen the woman in the woods too. *She* had heard growling in her own chest. *She* had seen the spider… Didn't that make her crazy too?

Harvey's hand brushed her cheek, ghosting over skin to rub away a tear. "What happened?" he asked again.

Charlotte shuddered out a breath and, with it, abandoned all logic. "I think there's something out there. I saw it… I mean, I think I saw it. It was like he was trying to scare me into—" She squinted, and it made her head hurt even more. "I don't know. He kept talking about making a deal to survive the mountain. He said I had to make a deal. And then I thought I heard this voice… I thought I saw her." Her voice tapered off, so quiet it just vanished in her throat. It couldn't have been real. But she had seen it. What choice did she have now? She had to believe.

"Who?" Harvey asked, and she was surprised by the lack of skepticism in his voice.

She knew who she had seen but how could anyone believe her? She stared at the front of his shirt because she didn't want to look him in the eye when she said it. "The Wicker Witch."

For long seconds she waited for a laugh or maybe some joke about her head injury.

His hands were warm against hers, his thumbs running gentle tracks over her knuckles. "Start from the beginning," he said.

Charlotte looked up at him, but there was no joke playing at his features. In fact, he looked more worried than she had ever seen him before.

"Tell me exactly what happened," he said.

She nodded slowly, surprised by the wave of relief that washed through her—not because he believed her but because he wanted to hear it and she desperately needed to tell someone.

They left the exam room, picked up her prescription at the front counter, and then walked down the street to Harvey's bookstore. He locked the door behind them, and Charlotte sat in the plush chair between stacks of books. She began with the car ride and the conversation with Bryan Summerfield—his confession about having thrown that stupid rock at her years ago and all the crazy things he said about making a deal.

The hardest part had been trying to explain the sound of the witch's voice, because she couldn't remember any voice at all—just a storm in her ear and a knowing of exactly what it was saying to her.

It all ended with the spider in Summerfield's eye and to her surprise, Harvey didn't question any of it.

CHAPTER THIRTY-SEVEN

The drive up to the Darling land was quiet. Rebecca sat shotgun beside Wyatt.

They passed the sheriff's car on the way and Jordan Sutton pulled over. He and Mike Brandon had offered to collect the body of Sheriff Summerfield and bring it and the squad car back to town. The rest of the caravan continued up the winding road. Just when it began to dip down, making ready for a descent around the side of Mount Grayson, they turned off onto a barely visible dirt road that cut through the thick forest.

The branches above blocked out the sky, shadowing the narrow lane and dropping the temperature even more. The tires bounced along the uneven path, barely trampled down by use, making the rest of the drive bumpy and slow.

Along the way, Wyatt asked her how things had gone down with the sheriff.

Rebecca told him the truth—all the parts that mattered anyway. She gave a sterile, factual account and left out her own chilling lack of remorse. Not that she thought he'd judge her for it.

Almost without warning, the road ended, and the woods opened into a clearing with a large barn to one side and a scattering of cars, trucks, four-wheelers, motorbikes, and tractors in between. They drove past the abandoned vehicles and up toward the barn. Rebecca scanned each one but didn't spot anyone lurking in or around the metal heaps.

The Darlings had houses, cabins, and other barns hidden in the woods, but this was the only one that could be reached by car. They had cleared the land, like this field, with dynamite long ago.

Wyatt pulled up in front of the barn, turning his truck around before killing the engine—just in case they had to make a quick exit, she imagined.

Deborah Rogers and her two grown sons had driven up after them, with Kenny Feldman on their heels.

They all filed out of their vehicles and waited, expecting to be seen and approached. But after long minutes, still no one came out of the barn or the surrounding woods. No one popped up from the grass or slipped out of the abandoned trucks like vampires rising from shadows.

"There's no one here," one of Deborah's sons said.

Wyatt walked up to the barn. A chain as thick as Rebecca's arm looped through the iron handles on the doors but no one had bothered to close the heavy lock. He pulled the chain out, the rattle echoing off the vehicles in the junkyard. Deborah's boys came over and helped him slide the old doors open. All three men disappeared inside.

Mr. Feldman let out a huff. "Well, this is anticlimactic," he almost laughed.

Rebecca walked around, still expecting someone to come take notice of them. All her life she'd been warned not to tread on Darling territory. Now, here she was, standing right in the middle of it, and no one cared? They were definitely trespassing, and not just in the easily offended way of Darlings, but actually poking around inside their barn.

She stopped near a patch of mud where tires had destroyed the grass time and again. She crouched low to look at the tracks—not those of tires, but paws. She touched one, dipping her gloved finger into it.

"Dogs," Deborah speculated over her shoulder, the edge of her voice asking if they should be worried.

"Big dogs," Rebecca said, even though she didn't believe it. It wasn't a far stretch to believe the Darlings had watchdogs— but they had never heard any before. And these tracks were made by wolves, not dogs.

Had wolves taken the Darlings?

"There's no one here," Wyatt called, coming back out of the barn. "But they have an arsenal inside." He sounded both impressed and disturbed. "Guns, rifles, a few grenades, and a whole lot of dynamite."

"Not to mention the drugs," one of Deborah's boys said while practically giggling, leaning out of the barn.

His ma scolded him on the spot. He might be twenty-four, but he was still her boy, and they were conducting official town business.

"Why would they leave it unlocked and unguarded?" Wyatt asked the group.

"Maybe they left?" Mr. Feldman said. "Maybe they were having the same troubles as we were and took off?"

Rebecca shook her head. "They wouldn't leave. They only ever leave the mountain on errands—never longer than a day at a time and never all of them."

She was certain they hadn't just walked away. Where would they go? They barely existed. The Darlings didn't have social security numbers, driver's licenses, or bank accounts. They were born high in the mountain and somewhere out there was probably a graveyard of their dead. No, they had not left. The Darlings were a part of the Gray Mountain, just like the Greenleighs. They would die there before ever thinking to flee.

"What do we do?" Wyatt asked seriously. "We can't just leave all this. What if they are the ones kidnapping people and…making the chimes," he said, coughing out the last words instead of saying, *'killing and dismembering people.'*

"Pack it all up into the trucks," Rebecca decided.

The group stared at her, but she didn't shy away from their collective scrutiny. "Everything but the drugs. We'll lock it all up in the sheriff's station." She pointed to Wyatt before he could turn and start loading up the weapons. "Take pictures first—for the Cyprus police when they get here."

His head bobbed in a nod.

They filled the beds of both trucks.

Mr. Feldman was first to head back, Deborah and her boys following. Wyatt closed-up the barn and this time snapped the lock shut. Rebecca shut the back of his truck and was rounding it to the door when she spotted a single figure standing in the tall grass between dead cars. Her breath caught in her throat. Was she about to get caught stealing from the Darlings? Would they believe her explanation? Would they wait long enough to hear it?

But there was no *"they."* There was just one man. He looked a lot like Harvey, lean and tall with black hair and the same red slash of a mouth. He shifted, hip out and head cocked to the side, and the resemblance became undeniable. She'd always known Harvey was a Darling, of course, but hadn't quite realized why the older residents of Wicker seemed so haunted by his presence. He must have reminded them of other Darlings, ones that had warred with the town in the past.

She took a step toward him, the truck behind her and Wyatt frozen on the other side. He started to say her name like a question, but she gestured for him to wait.

"I can explain," Rebecca called.

The man grinned and she almost lost her step. His mouth was too wide with too many teeth—too many points—glinting out at her. "You're making things harder for yourself, Greenleigh," he said.

She stared hard at him. She'd never met him, but he spoke her name like they were old friends. Did the Darlings keep track of the people in Wicker? Did they know who was who? "Do you know what's been going on in the woods?"

His eyes shone yellow. She told herself it was a trick of the light winking from behind clouds. "*She* would have given you anything," he said and then laughed darkly. "Anything but what your greedy heart wants most, I guess."

"What are you talking about?" Rebecca demanded, taking another step toward him. "Who?"

"The witch," he practically purred, and she stopped walking.

"We took your weapons," she said flatly, looking for even a flicker of the anger she'd expected.

He shrugged. "They won't help you."

"We took your drugs too," she lied.

The wind moved, whipping long grass around their thighs. He didn't care that they had raided the Darling barn. He didn't care that they had trespassed on Darling land. She had never been more worried in her life than she was in that moment. What had changed so much in the game they had been playing out for generations? It was like the Darlings had called *checkmate* and she just couldn't see it yet.

"What did *you* ask for?" Part of her mind screamed at the absurdity of it. There was no witch. There were no wishes or deals to be struck.

But the Darling grinned wide and she saw all those sharp teeth again. Had he filed them to points? No. They were too long for that. And his eyes really were yellow, with black where the white should have been.

"To be wild," he said, and it came out with the pleasant rumble of a growl deep in his chest. "*She* told me to wait for you here. *She* knew you would come."

Rebecca wanted to step back, to get away from him, but she didn't dare move while he still stared at her. "Why?"

"It's *her* mountain, Greenleigh. Not ours or yours. The sooner you realize it, the sooner you can make a deal." His smile split his cheeks open in sticky red seams with more teeth peeking out. "Make a deal or die."

Her breath came out in heaves. His face opened up, cheeks gaping. How could any animal have so many teeth? His eyes grew larger and his face changed shape even as she stared at it.

She dragged herself backward in big, trembling steps, unable to look away until her back hit the side of the truck, the door still open. Wyatt practically pulled her in, the engine rumbling and wheels turning before she managed to jerk the door shut.

Twisting in her seat, Rebecca looked back, searching for the stranger in the long grass.

The man had vanished.

A wolf trotted past the rough road and darted off into the woods.

CHAPTER THIRTY-EIGHT

Charlotte went back to the trailer with Harvey to clean up.

She couldn't wash her hair because of the staples in the back of her head and she used a rag to clean her face around the gash sealed in glue. Harvey stayed in the narrow doorway of his little bathroom, talking to her and pretending he wasn't there just to make sure she didn't faint and knock her head again.

He helped her dry off and suggested she lay down for a while, but Charlotte couldn't do that, instead asking if he could find her some clothes. She always had some at his place.

If she laid down now, she wouldn't be getting back up any time soon. She could feel it, like a threat in her bones. The adrenaline was gone, and she hurt all over. Her skin sang a song of abuse, but she wasn't ready to lay herself down.

She pulled on a pair of jeans and a large knit sweater—one of his, oversized for the Darling man but just right on her. She had trouble lacing up the pair of sneakers with her torn and bruised fingertips, so Harvey did it for her.

He was frowning the whole time, trying to figure out how to stop her from going anywhere, probably. When he stood up and faced her again, he ghosted fingertips across her bruised temple before stroking some of her hair back from her face and toward the high knot on her head. "Do you want me to brush it out?"

Charlotte smiled. He was stalling. If she let him brush her hair, she would be out in seconds and she would probably just stay in his trailer until their whole town slid off the mountain and into hell. Would that be so bad? Was there anywhere she'd rather be? No. But there were still places to go and people to see.

She caught his hand, leeching the warmth from his skin and wondering if he felt the loss of it. "You really believe me?" she said, finally asking what she'd been avoiding since telling him her whole story about the sheriff and the witch in the woods.

He didn't hesitate. "Yes."

"Have you seen her?" Charlotte asked, whispering.

He shook his head once, but it didn't change his certainty that *Charlotte* had seen the monster. And knowing that he believed her was a greater relief than she could have imagined. Madness didn't feel quite as mad when she wasn't alone in it.

Somehow, she convinced him to stop by Sheriff Summerfield's home on the way back to her house.

They pulled up the long driveway between trees, parking in front of the little gray ranch house. There were dozens like it on properties snaking through the woods on that side of Wicker.

For one bizarre second, she expected the man himself to come out and ask what they were doing on his land. A jolt of panic shot through her, chased by the echo of the gunshot in her head, blowing his face apart in her memory again and again. Charlotte took the two steps up to the short porch and paused. Only then did she remember Summerfield's mom. Her hand trembled when she knocked. Was she really going to tell Janet Summerfield that her boy was dead? That he'd lost his mind and attacked her?

Harvey must have thought the same because he touched her elbow. "Lotte…" That gentle voice, calling for her to back away from this path, tapered off when they both noticed the door was open. Her knock had nudged it a few inches in, giving them a glimpse of the front hall.

"I guess that means we're not *breaking and entering*," Charlotte thought aloud.

"Just *entering*," Harvey confirmed grimly, pushing the door into a full swing. "Mrs. Summerfield?" he called, somehow sounding casual and friendly—like Harvey Darling visited often.

There was no answer.

Charlotte stepped inside. It was just as chilly indoors as it had been outside. "Janet?" she called. She had met the woman plenty of times at the sewing circles her momma used to go to.

"What do you expect to find?" Harvey whispered.

Charlotte didn't answer because she didn't know what she was looking for. She took two steps into the house before stopping and gaping at the front room.

Bone chimes hung from the ceiling and littered the floor, coffee table, and couch cushions. Bird skulls twirled on lines of thread, bumping against other small bones. They were just like the ones found dangling in the trees the other morning. Had he been putting them up? Or collecting the ones taken down?

Each room offered more of the same. Some bones were larger than birds or squirrels, some still coated in decaying flesh. The whole house stank of rot.

"Look at this," Harvey said from the kitchen. He crouched to one side of muddy prints leading to the back door—human prints with a hoof mark in the center going in opposite directions. "This is like what you described…"

"Yes," she said, taking his phone from his pocket to snap pictures of everything. The crazier this got, the more they would need proof if they were going to convince anyone else.

"Mrs. Summerfield?" Harvey called again, moving around Charlotte and back toward the living room. He paused there at the mouth of the long, dark hallway and she could see the uncertainty on him. He was compelled to check on the silent woman but hesitated to invade her home any more than he already had.

Harvey was many things, but a home intruder was not usually one of them.

Charlotte walked by him and down the hall. Her steps sounded heavy on the hardwood, echoing like they might in her own home only without the squeaky floorboard she was used to. She'd never been inside the Summerfield home before and didn't know which room belonged to Mrs. Summerfield, but she didn't bother calling out again. It felt eerily similar to hiking through the woods shouting out Sam Caller's name. Something told her no one was going to answer.

She quietly opened one door after another. An office space full of hunting gear. A bathroom with more towels on the floor than on the rack. A bedroom with a broken mirror and an open window but the bed still perfectly made. She closed each door after her, until finally opening the one at the far end of the hall. She didn't go in. She didn't need to.

Charlotte held her breath when she leaned in and saw the body of a woman on the floor. She wished instantly that she hadn't gone looking—hadn't needed to check—because she would never get that image of Janet Summerfield out of her head. The woman's eyes were gauged out, her fingers bloody to the knuckle from doing the job.

Charlotte closed the door and backed up, exhaling hard. Harvey was at her side. He reached for the door to see for himself, but she grabbed his arm and shook her head. There was nothing they could do there.

CHAPTER THIRTY-NINE

Henrietta Crowe did not love the mountain.

She had been born on it and, for a time, she had left it. She'd found a whole world beyond the foot of Gray Mountain, and it was breathtakingly large. She had seen oceans, cities, endless stretches of farmlands, and woods that were nothing like the ones she grew up in. The longer she stayed away, the more she realized how strange a place Wicker was.

The people there did not worry themselves with the business of other places. They had no religion or patriotism, aside from the Greenleighs, but that had always seemed like a suit tailored for someone else.

She couldn't remember anyone in Wicker voting on anything but Wicker matters. They ignored all other elections and calls to arms. They had even ignored the calls to war.

Revolutionary, Civil, and both World Wars had passed without much attention from Wicker. When pressed for their young men, Wicker officials had declared the boys dead. Which wasn't to say that no one ever left the mountain and enlisted, but no one had ever come from outside and successfully fetched their children from them. There was something about going up to Wicker that made other people uneasy. Tourists only stayed for short trips and spouses who moved to the mountain either made peace with the feeling or eventually left, but they never looked as comfortable there the way the Wicker born did.

Henrietta had never suggested her husband move to Wicker. She'd barely even told him where she was from. She didn't want him to have to try to fit into that little place hidden in the trees. They had lived in a small house, only a ten-minute walk from the beach. She'd had twelve years with him. Twelve years until the only man she ever loved was beaten to death for being in the wrong place at the wrong time. Bad luck, the police had told her.

There was something wrong with Wicker, but there was something worse about the rest of the world. Too much bad luck.

Henrietta went home after that. She wasn't the same person when she returned, but Wicker was the same place, and it welcomed her like a mother who had known to set her place at the table.

Wicker had its share of sadness, of lives cut short by recklessness and disease, but there had never been much room for outside wickedness. Henrietta thought often about the stories her grandma used to tell her, about the Wicker Witch. She hadn't believed in the witch before she left the mountain, but a lifetime later, when she saw the creature for herself prowling the woods and eyeing the big house, she wasn't surprised.

Bad luck had finally returned to Wicker.

She stood up from her bench on the porch of her little house and the tall, dark figure of the witch paused. It turned, eyes like shards of a broken moon glinted at her from a mess of dark hair. Fear coiled in Henrietta's gut like a living thing. It had been so long since she felt anything but the gaping wound of her loss. Her legs shook when she ambled steps closer, off her porch and to the top of the stone path leading down from her house.

In the blink of an eye, the witch moved, crossing the ground. It stopped a few steps below her but still stood a head taller. She realized then that the witch was no woman or man. It was shaped something like a human, but it had no breasts or genitals, just smooth skin and sharp bones beneath. The woods creaked and groaned in agony. Rushing water filled her ears, pressing in against her skull.

Crowes make no deals with devils, but damn her if she wouldn't have made a deal to bring back her heart.

The witch tipped its head to the side, regarding Henrietta. Red crusted lips twitched back from sharp teeth in an angry twist of a smile. *"That I cannot trade,"* the rustling of leaves and churning water in her ears confessed. *"Your heart is not on my mountain and so I cannot bring it back to you."*

Henrietta hated the tears she shed. She thought she had cried them all before she came back to Wicker, but now they streamed down her face and off her chin. Her jaw trembled and her fingers curled into fists. She had to push her head back to glare up at the monster made of shadow and hunger. Her stomach knotted and her guts clenched. Instinct wanted to run and hide. Sanity wanted to look away and pretend it had never seen this. Henrietta ignored both. She was too old to run and too tired to pretend.

Her words came out trembling, but she pushed them out all the same. "Is it true then? You can't hurt us?"

Those lips twitched and this time the teeth clicked hard, like beams of woods snapping together. One hand lifted, spreading long fingers and flashing the blades of talons in moonlight. *"Neither tooth nor claw, rabbit."*

Henrietta wanted to laugh but it caught in her chest, shaking her where she stood. She pissed a little but didn't move. Maybe she couldn't move? She was rooted under that gaze. "Then get off my land," she bit out the words, even as she continued to tremble.

The witch growled low and for a second Henrietta thought she heard the mountain shudder and crack in that sound. *"You could have made a good wolf, if you still had your heart,"* the witch said in that low rumble. *"But you will die here, rabbit, and I will own you forever as rot in my dirt."*

Henrietta's mouth went suddenly dry. She couldn't swallow. What did that even mean? "You can't hurt me," she reminded, but it might as well have been a paper sword wielded by a child.

The witch took a step back, and then another. Shadows gathered and reached with arms and fingers Henrietta could see just as clearly as the creature. Darkness coiled around the witch, and in that darkness, the witch faded away. Almost gone, it smiled, and out of the dark where the witch had been, emerged a wolf with hackles raised and teeth bared, saliva dripping off its maw.

Henrietta jerked back, almost tripping before she'd even turned. She scrambled those few steps she'd taken from her porch, her legs stiff and uncooperative. Her breath came in thin puffs, barely able to get enough for a proper scream. Her shotgun was just inside. Her hand hit the handle, slapping it down and pushing her shoulder into the door. Her body vibrated with pain, cascading from her shoulder into her chest and from her hand through her wrist. She had broken fragile bones, but she would never have the time to realize it.

She reached for her gun, falling to her knees and jarring her hip. The wolf hit her from the side, teeth clamping over her neck and the force of its weight dragging her inside.

She died fast but the wolf stayed long.

When it was full, it even slept in her bed.

CHAPTER FORTY

When Rebecca got back into town, there were small crowds in the street waiting for answers.

Deborah Rogers and her boys were parked in front of the sheriff's station with their truck bed full of confiscated weapons. The squad car was parked beside them with Jordan Sutton, Mike Brandon, and Doctor Paulson waiting just outside the building. The doctor had a duffle bag with him and a grim set to his lips.

"Should we just keep driving?" Wyatt half-joked beside her, voice stiff. It was the first time they'd spoken since the man turned into a wolf at the Darling farm.

Rebecca glanced at him. She didn't understand at first. It had never occurred to her to run from her responsibilities. This wouldn't be an easy day, or week for that matter, but she would get them through it, just as Greenleighs had always carried Wicker through bad times.

Or at least, that was what she'd been told.

Better not to think about the coffins again, empty of bodies but full of doubt.

She was out of the truck before Wyatt had pulled to a complete stop. Everyone had questions, shouting over one another and moving toward her. She pulled Jane's spare keys from her pocket and marched toward the door.

"Stay put until we get the office cleared out," she shouted to Deborah and her sons. They couldn't bring the stash of weapons they'd collected from the Darlings inside until the doctor had been in to see the bodies. They'd have to document them as best they could and then help him get them to the morgue first.

Deborah nodded and got her boys to back up and return to their post on the tailgate.

Before unlocking the door, Rebecca turned to face the little crowd. Lotte and Harvey were across the street, waiting.

Jane stood on the sidewalk with Gary Freeman, both looking solemn and puffy-eyed from crying. Jane gave her a stiff nod, signaling that the families had been told.

"What's going on?" a woman demanded, voice shuddering with the strain of fear.

"Is the sheriff dead?" Frank Wilde shouted from behind her.

Voices rolled together, crashing over one another.

Rebecca raised one arm and they quieted. "I need everyone that doesn't have business on Green Street to go home for the night." Before they could argue or demand the truth, she continued. "Bryan Summerfield, Deputy Scott Douglas, Deputy Andrea Holland, and Sarah Potter were killed today. It looks like Summerfield did it, but we can't know for certain right now. There will be a town meeting tomorrow morning and I urge all of you to come to it. We are sending people down to the river to call over to Cyprus and let the authorities there know what's happened. I need everyone to stay calm and look after your own just like you always have. Give us the space to take care of this tonight and tomorrow morning we will talk about what to do next as a town."

There was some grumbling and muttering in the crowd, but they shuffled back, nodding slowly and looking around between themselves.

"Please," Rebecca said again, not so much a request as a reminder. "Go home."

She waited for them to back up to their cars or the other side of the street and let the doctor through. He took a breath before nodding for her to unlock the door.

Rebecca flicked through the keys. "Did they bring you Summerfield?" she asked, voice hushed but steady. Jordan Sutton and Mike Brandon were waiting even as the group dissipated, no doubt expecting another grim chore. Good. They had plenty of those to go around today.

"No," the doctor answered, attention still on the door.

Rebecca paused to look at him. "What?"

He noticed her surprise and finally met her gaze. "They didn't find him."

"He was right by the trail."

The doctor shook his head. "They said it looked like something dragged him off..."

Rebecca absorbed that, fingers numb when she finally turned the knob to swing the office door open. Doctor Paulson entered, followed by Wyatt and herself. She locked it after them. They took photos and did whatever Paulson told them to. Eventually, they enlisted Jordan and Mike to fetch the gurney from the doctor's office and help wheel the bagged bodies from one building to the other.

They barely spoke during the whole process and by the time they were done with their part, it was dark out. Rebecca was exhausted, but she helped carry in the weapons they'd confiscated and made sure everything was locked up tight before finally closing the station down.

She was surprised to find Charlotte and her Darling still waiting.

They didn't suggest going anywhere to sit and talk and Rebecca was grateful. She wanted to go home. She needed to see her wife, shower, and then think about everything that had happened. She would sit down in her family office, write down every detail, and try to make sense of it.

Charlotte spoke fast but quietly enough that hopefully her words wouldn't carry beyond them. Janet Summerfield was dead, and the house had been full of bone chimes. She showed her photos on her phone. Lotte and Harvey had come back into town just before her, expecting to file a report with someone in the sheriff's station. Only there was no one left.

"Okay. I'll talk to the doctor about sending someone to collect her body." The words sounded cold but Rebecca trusted them to understand. The whole day had been a lot. She was still trying not to think about the Darling, the wolf. It wasn't possible. At least, she hadn't thought it was possible before today. But she had seen it—had seen him change—and Rebecca trusted herself.

"Greenleigh." Her friend caught her wrist before she could walk away. Lotte looked bad, the side of her face red and puffy, and her neck collared in more dark red splotches. Her eyes were bloodshot, and she shivered a little with every breath she dragged. "I know it sounds insane, but I saw the witch. We took pictures of the footprints in the house, and I've seen them before too—" She fumbled to shift through photos on the screen and turn it toward Rebecca again.

Rebecca caught it and her hand, steadying her. "You saw the witch? The…" No. *The* witch? Just like the Darling in the field had said.

Lotte bit her lip, looking away and down. Her jaw flexed from the clench of her teeth, but she nodded hard.

"Did it say anything to you?"

Her friend looked up at her, clearly surprised by the question and maybe even Rebecca's willingness to take her seriously. "She wanted to make a deal. She… *It.* I think it was baiting me. Like it needed a deal. I don't know. But I know it was real. It's here, in our woods, on our mountain."

Witch.

A witch.

The witch.

Rebecca wanted to shake her head and say it wasn't true, but that was because she didn't *want* it to be true. She didn't like the idea of anything prowling her forest and hurting her neighbours, but certainly not some monster of town legend.

She nodded, squeezing Charlotte's hand gently. "Okay. Go home and get some rest. We'll figure this out tomorrow." She needed time to think. She needed to figure out what was going on, how it was going on, and what to do to stop it.

She saw Lotte and Harvey get into their own vehicles and watched them pull down the road one after the other, splitting into different directions when they headed home.

After another moment, alone in the heart of her little town, Rebecca headed over to the doctor's office to report another body.

CHAPTER FORTY-ONE

Charlotte knew Greenleigh would never leave the mountain—wouldn't even consider running—but she suspected many others would after the meeting tomorrow.

Their mountain had changed. They had never exactly been safe, but this was different than the vague threat of the wilderness. This was more than weather and a dangerous distance from hospitals and supplies. None of those things had ever frightened the Wicker born. They had scoffed at storms and laughed at thinning food stocks—gathering at the bar because as long as they had shots and shotguns, they would make it to the next day. But nothing about this felt like those old challenges. Their mountain wasn't bucking against them to make them prove their worth; it was hunting them.

Charlotte wondered if her friend would try to keep the people in Wicker or if she would let them go without a word.

Would she let her go without a word?

There was no pride tangled up in the decision for Charlotte. As soon as they got the road north cleared, she was going to leave.

She went to her family home to gather a few things and see if she could convince them to leave with her. She planned to retreat to Harvey's trailer after thoroughly rattling the family cage.

She was pretty sure Alice would jump at the chance to leave Wicker behind, which meant she could get Miles out of there. Aunt Henri could go either way but would be unmovable once decided. Vic and his family would be a hard sell, and her dad impossible, but she had to try.

It was dark when Charlotte pulled up to the big house, lights glowing from the windows and shadows moving inside. Did they know what had been going on in town today? Or were they still cut off from the chaos and death in Wicker?

She climbed out of the truck. She'd taken the meds Paulson gave her, dialing the pain down to a constant ache. Her scalp throbbed like she had a hair tie in too snug, only it wasn't a hair tie—it was the staples holding her skin together. A gust of wind rolled through the trees, shaking branches and churning up leaves.

She was so tired that she felt sick, but sleeping was the last thing on her mind. She went over the whole day in her head again, scanning the trees in their yard and the quiet road cutting through the woods. She should start by talking to Alice.

Not just because she wanted to avoid going into the big house, but because she might actually be on her side for once.

Sam Caller was dead. His uncle Andrew was probably dead too.

Sheriff Summerfield had lost his mind and his life in the woods, but not before killing both the deputies and Mrs. Potter. Not to mention whatever had happened with his mom.

The fear in Wicker was rising.

There was a witch in the woods.

What could they even say at the meeting tomorrow? There were only a few options left and Charlotte raked over each one carefully. They could look for a killer among them. Maybe they would blame Sheriff Summerfield for all of it? Could he have killed Sam and Andrew? Why not? But from what she'd heard on the street, waiting for Greenleigh and the aldermen to return, it was clear that some of her neighbors were keen on pointing the finger at the Darlings for the bone chimes, the dead boy, and the blocked road out north.

It had only been a few days since Sam went missing, but already the town had given up on finding him or any need for evidence. He was dead and so was Andrew, but the Darlings were not presenting themselves for the blame. They had disappeared—a strange thought since it changed nothing in the relationship between them and Wicker as far as Charlotte understood things. The Darlings had always been illusive and far away, even on the mountain. The two peoples had barely interacted in her lifetime.

A quiet, melodious *clank* sent chills down Charlotte's spine.

Clank.

Clank.

There had been nothing outside when she stepped out of her truck and started toward Alice's house. The wind had blown but there had been no sounds. Nothing in the trees.

Clank.

Clank.

Clank.

The sound rattled in her ears and pushed the air from her lungs in faster and faster breaths. She looked up and around, squinting until she spotted it, right there, dangling in the nearest tree. Another chime twirled in a low branch to the right. No, not just one—a dozen.

The breeze came again and a hundred chimes rattled across the stretch of land between the big house and Alice's.

Charlotte jumped at the nearest chime, snatching it down from the tree. The jagged, broken bones rolled against her palm, cold and still wet, leaving smears of red against her skin. Were they animal bones or more pieces of Sam Caller? Or maybe these belonged to Andrew Caller?

She dropped the chime on the ground and froze, pulse suddenly racing and spine straight. She had been seen. She knew it with horrible certainty. *Something* was looking at her. Her mind raced, imagining a bear or the wolf Rebecca had told her about. Her gaze skimmed the night, turning slowly, considering every shadow until she finally swung around and found him standing right there behind her.

Charlotte jerked back, sucking a breath so hard and fast that it made her chest ache and her eyes water.

Edgar stood on the beaten driveway, staring back at her. His cheeks were flushed from the night air and his breath formed thin clouds just like hers.

It was a hallucination. It had to be. She'd hit her head in that struggle with the sheriff. The doctor had warned her about seeing things. That was it. It had to be.

He wore hospital scrubs and no shoes. The cuffs of his pants had soaked up mud and rainwater. Why would her imagination put him in hospital scrubs? She'd never seen him in any before. Why not his hunting jacket? Why not the last outfit she'd ever seen him in?

His mouth twitched and he gave a half-cocked grin. "She's considering you," he said.

Tears pricked her eyes at his voice. He was real. His voice wasn't exactly how she might have remembered it, but exactly how it was. "What? For what?" she asked, pulse pounding under her skin. It had to be a dream. She'd fallen asleep in the truck and was dreaming.

The chimes in the trees rattled all around them.

"Make a wish, baby sister," Edgar said.

The gash in the back of her head throbbed, as though to scream at her that this wasn't a dream at all. It was painfully real. She shook her head slowly. "It isn't possible."

"It's a second chance," he said. "A last chance."

She wanted to wake up now.

He took a step back and then another, closer to his house. She followed him slowly, keeping him always in her line of sight. Would he vanish if she looked away? Or would he get even closer?

A door clapped shut and a woman let out a hoarse scream of delight. Alice raced on bare feet toward them, tears streaming down her face and bloodshot eyes fixed solely on Edgar.

"It's not possible," Charlotte said again, but no one was listening to her anymore.

Alice threw herself into Edgar's arms, clutching at his shoulders and his head, smothering him in tear-wet kisses before burying her face in his neck. It was just enough commotion to draw the attention of someone in the big house, voices calling and more lights flicking on.

Charlotte wanted all of this to stop. She needed a minute to think. This didn't make sense.

Edgar held Alice, turning with her in his arms to look up at Charlotte. He flashed a grin—*his grin*—the one he'd had when he watched that fawn die and when he'd smothered their momma. The one he used to hide so carefully against his teeth.

The door of the big house flew open behind her and Victor boomed Edgar's name. Her father was soon there too and Edgar was ushered inside with a thousand questions and endless hugs.

It was a miracle, they said.

Charlotte couldn't breathe.

Alice sent Victor to wake up the Greenleighs and bring Miles home.

The news of the miracle was going to spread.

Edgar was alive.

Charlotte got into her truck, started the engine, and pulled down the long drive to the road. She thought she was running to Harvey. She could go to the trailer park and this time tell him everything. He would understand and together they could try every path off the mountain. At this point, Charlotte was ready to try swimming across the Aurora River to get out.

But when she scrubbed the tears from her eyes, she was on a different road. She hit the brakes hard. She was suddenly north of Wicker and driving upward. It wasn't possible. She'd been south of it just a moment ago.

She turned around, heading toward the town again.

This time she barely blinked, eyes fixed on the road ahead and thoughts pushing aside everything else.

There was no clear moment when it happened, no sense of being jostled or turned around, but just when she caught a glimpse of the brick buildings ahead, they vanished. She was facing north again—driving north, with her back to the town.

Charlotte pulled off to the shoulder again, almost in the exact same spot, and stumbled out of her truck. She was losing her mind. That was the only explanation now.

Her knees shook and she fell forward, landing in the dirt and vomiting up the contents of her stomach. It wasn't much. It had been a long and terrible day. She heaved again, even when there was nothing left to give.

She had to grab at a tree to get back on her feet, blinking against tears up at the moon.

It was so bright tonight.

That was when she realized there were no car lights on her anymore. She turned, looking for the truck only to realize she wasn't near any road. She was deep in the woods now, surrounded by trees and moon shadow.

Her breath came in jagged puffs. She looked for signs of a trail or landmark, refusing to search for human shapes in the night. She wasn't going to play whatever horrible game this was. She—

Charlotte swayed on her feet. The world shifted around her, unsteady underfoot, and suddenly she was on a trail turned up the mountain.

No.

She caught her breath, staring at the trees ahead. She knew the path, deep in the woods beyond the walking trails north of Wicker.

She hadn't been in that part of the forest in almost a decade.

"No," she said out loud and took a step back, shaking her head. Tears overflowed her eyes and burned down her cold cheeks.

Charlotte pressed her hands to the sides of her head and curled in on herself, squeezing her eyes shut. "No. This isn't real. This isn't real." She had been heading down the mountain not up. She would not have gone to this place—not again—not after everything.

But when she opened her eyes, she was still there, still in that place under the stars.

She had left Wicker for a couple years after her momma died. She'd had a bus ticket and a job lined-up in Cyprus. She'd just needed to get away for a while. Everyone had understood—the way they usually did in Wicker because they all knew their youths would come home eventually.

Charlotte had been sitting at the bus stop when she saw Edgar drive by in his truck early that morning wearing his favorite hunting jacket. The only thing odd about it had been little Miles sitting beside him. He'd never taken Miles with him before.

Charlotte didn't know why, but she'd followed on foot that day, jogging up the road and into the trees. She'd left her backpack near the first trail and taken care to keep her steps quiet. The whole time, she'd told herself she was being stupid. There was no reason to follow them. She would miss her bus.

But the farther she walked, the more she knew where she was going. It was his favorite hunting spot. It was the place where he'd killed the fawn to show her a part of who he really was.

CHAPTER FORTY-TWO

At five years old, Miles was smaller than most kids his age and painfully shy. But his little voice carried through the trees. It was cold. It was early. He wanted to go home. Where was his mom?

Edgar didn't shush him.

Charlotte spotted Miles first, his orange jacket a blaring star in the dim of early morning. He pouted and tapped the toe of his shoe against the base of a tree.

She only saw Edgar when he lifted his rifle. He stood just a few feet ahead and to her right. He trained the gun on Miles, that little twist of a smile pulling at his mouth.

Charlotte burst forward and shoved the weapon high just as it went off. The shot cracked thunder and birds burst from the trees. Miles wailed and huddled down on the ground with his mittens over his ears. Charlotte never stopped moving, everything happening in a matter of seconds. She pushed all her momentum and weight into him, grabbing at his weapon with both hands and tripping him with her leg around his. He fell back and she hugged the stolen rifle to her chest, her heart a drum solo high in her chest. Edgar landed on his ass and Charlotte staggered back from him, almost tripping herself.

He panted, fury washing across his features. She had never seen him look angry before. She had known when he was, but he never showed it.

"You shouldn't be here." Edgar pushed himself to his feet.

She moved the rifle in her arms, aiming it at him.

He froze.

Charlotte hadn't been hunting since she was a kid—not since he killed that fawn just to watch it die. "I can't believe I *was going to leave you with them..." she said to herself.*

What did she think would happen? Did she think what she saw, the way he'd killed their momma, had been a one time thing? An act of mercy? A desperate move to escape a terrible situation? No. That twitch in the corner of his mouth. That *twitch. He had smiled and she had known. That was why she was leaving—because she had really seen him and it haunted her.*

"We're family, Lotte. Put it down." His voice was so steady, so sure, that she almost did what he said. He had pushed all that anger and surprise away, looking like his endlessly calm self again. Edgar had always been reliable. He had been the uncontested favorite child and Charlotte hadn't even minded because how could he not be? He never fought with their

parents. He never got into trouble or did anything without a reason.

A laugh choked her, forcing tears over her lashes. "Family? What about Momma and Miles? That's your son!"

Edgar shook his head, one arm slowly stretching forward. His fingers fanned in a gesture of pleading, but those were the fingers that had killed—the ones that would kill again. "They aren't you. You're my girl. I would never hurt you or Victor. You know that."

But she didn't.

"Momma was in pain," he explained. "And Miles…the kid is weak."

He said it so casually, like shooting him would be an obvious and understandable choice. He wasn't even denying it.

"Put it down, Charlotte," he ordered, voice going hard. She took a step back but kept the rifle aimed at his chest. "I'm your brother," he reminded, that anger he'd only just suppressed coming back up like a bad meal.

She pulled the trigger and the weight of it would never be forgotten. The sound of that shot echoed through her, printed against the inside of her skull to be heard again and again.

He was her brother. He was hers. They were family. She was responsible for him. She would have gone to bat for him, would have taken care of him if he were sick, would have died for him if it came to it. So, she would do the only responsible thing, and save his son. She put him down because he was a monster and because he was hers. She had known that she could do it because he was her brother and that meant there was monster in her veins, too.

One shot to the chest to bring him down, because she was just enough like him to be able to do it, and then a second to the head to put him out of his misery—because she wasn't exactly like him.

She put the gun on the ground beside his body and went to Miles. He hadn't moved from where he crouched against the tree, little mittens pressed over his ears and tears clinging to his lashes. His eyes were screwed shut and he wouldn't open them even when she picked him up. So Charlotte just walked, not saying anything, silently praying he hadn't seen any of it. Every step, every minute, she expected him to say something or start screaming, but he just stayed pressed against her, his face in her neck and his arms curling around her neck.

The idea of getting away with what she'd done had developed in that silence between them. She had been ready to carry her screaming nephew to the sheriff's and confess to everything that had happened, but Miles wasn't screaming. He still hadn't opened his eyes. When she was close to Wicker, she pulled her hood up over her head. The streets were still empty, hours before any of the shops would open. The only windows lit up were the bakery, but the doors were still locked and the front room empty.

She sat him on the bench and hesitated. She couldn't stay with him if she was going to make this go away. She couldn't even say anything. He had his hands over his ears again and his eyes closed.

She backed into the mouth of an alley and called Rebecca. Then she waited until she saw her friend's car coming up the road before leaving. This time when Charlotte started up the trails, she grabbed the backpack she'd left by the first entrance. She hiked to the parking area where she knew Edgar would have left his truck. She took his shovel from the bed and trudged back into the woods.

How could he do this to her? He had taken so much and left her holding everything. She stopped at his body to pull the gloves from his hands, cursing him and putting them on before marching out into the forest—even farther away from the road, and the trails, and the river to the east.

When she found a clearing where the tree roots didn't lay claim to the soil, she started digging. The whole time, she thought about how at any moment someone could come along and find his truck or his body and it would be all over. The deeper she dug, the more she wished it would happen. Despite the chill in the air, she was sweating, dragging deep breaths and pushing on. The shovel scraped against stones, but she kept going, racing against her own sanity and the rumble of rain in the heavy clouds overhead. Digging in mud would be a whole new madness.

It took almost two hours, but she carved out a sloppy hole in the earth for him. When she went back to his body, the clouds finally opened up. The heavy autumn drops soaked her to the bone and made his body even heavier. She'd had the sense to pull his wallet and keys from his pockets, laying them on the grass beside his rifle before dragging him away. She had to stop twice to catch her breath, blinking back rain and tears, but eventually she got him to the clearing. And when she rolled him into his grave, it was deeper than she'd thought. He almost disappeared, curled up in that dark cavity. She carried rocks to *drop over him, weighing him down and haphazardly covering him.*

She tried to shovel the ground back in, but the downpour was filling the hole and turning the dirt to mud, so she got down on her hands and knees and used her arms to rake heaps of it in over him.

Charlotte walked through the woods almost a decade later, retracing her steps and trying to prove to herself that it had happened—that she *had* killed her brother and buried him. He couldn't possibly be in her kitchen drinking coffee with the family.

She stopped at the edge of the clearing. It had been reshaped by the storm, the ground swept away and turned from a gently rising hill into a sunken valley of rocks and the remains of felled trees.

She skirted the edge of it and kept walking, deeper into the woods.

The trees creaked and groaned and far away, and she heard chimes. *"Where are you?"* a voice called, breaking the quiet nightlife of the forest. Charlotte had officially lost her mind; there was nothing left to do but lean into it.

A silhouette moved in the corner of her vision but melted back into the shadows every time she tried to look directly at it. Was it the witch? She laughed madly through her tears. The witch had been the most terrifying thing she could think of only hours ago, but now Edgar was back, dead one day and alive the next.

A shadow moved again, there and then gone when Charlotte turned. "What do you want?" she yelled.

The forest creaked in answer.

She forced herself to stop walking and stood still, keeping her gaze fixed on a tree ahead so the shape in the corner of her vision could take form. The witch inched closer.

"Tell me," Charlotte whispered. "Why is this happening?"

"Why is this happening," the creature hummed, the words coming out strange, like they were being parroted by someone who didn't understand them as anything more than lovely sounds.

The humming grew louder as the shadow came closer. Her heartbeat quickened, the sound of the witch's voice like a wind over the ocean, harsh and booming against her eardrums, bringing fresh tears to her eyes and almost making her forget why she was out there.

"Why are you here?" Charlotte forced out the words despite her mounting nerves. "What do you want?"

"Nothing," the terrible voice whispered back in the violent creaking of trees and snapping of branches. *"It is all mine."*

Charlotte gasped for mouthfuls of air. "Why are you doing this to us?"

The shadow was beside her now, leaning its face close to her cheek, knife-like fingers ghosting up her back. *"The rabbit does not ask why,"* the witch explained in its benevolence, stones grinding in its throat.

Was that how the witch saw everything on the mountain— rabbit or wolf?

She swallowed hard but a lump stayed high in her throat, threatening to choke her with fear. Her jaw shook when she spoke, pushing her chin up with the words. "I am not a rabbit. I am a Crowe, and Crowes do not make deals with devils."

When the witch said nothing, Charlotte couldn't resist turning her head to look right at it. She expected the shadow shape to vanish again and leave her terrified and alone.

But it didn't vanish.

The Wicker Witch stared back at her, black eyes pulsing with the bodies of spiders—those sleek, black legs sliding over lashes. Its mouth was blood wet and wide, and its cheekbones fanned like birdwings under skin. A hiss rose from within the witch, the sound multiplying by the second. Charlotte could hear the earth moving in the creature's chest, ground breaking and reforming with every breath.

A crackle of lightning.

The groaning and splitting of trees.

Growling, cawing, buzzing swarms all gathered inside the witch's body.

Louder and louder until Charlotte thought she would scream if it didn't stop.

And then that bloody mouth opened, sticky lips grinning. White teeth snapped in Charlotte's face, jaw clapping like thunder.

It was the gun at the start of a race.

Charlotte was off, fleeing through the trees, running blind and frantic, arms up to guard against low branches in the dark.

A howl rose from the woods behind her and she ran harder.

A wolf pulled ahead of her to the left, far away but not nearly far enough.

Another howled, so close that she let out a strained scream.

Distantly, she realized the forest was getting darker, closing in around her like it would soon grab her up into the trees and gobble her whole. She couldn't see the wolves anymore, not even the glimmer of their eyes. The darkness grew so thick that she couldn't even see the trees, each step trusting the ground to still be there beneath her shoes.

Branches lashed her cheeks and arms, some trunks so close that she almost lost her balance and stumbled. The dark itself pushed against her back and shoulders, pressing like a firm hand. The darkness had fingers curling around her shoulders, clinging to her. She gulped and gasped, legs propelling her ever forward.

And then she burst from the forest into the blinding glow of the moon.

She tripped on nothing, legs finally giving out and dropping her onto the trimmed grass of someone's lawn. She rolled onto her back, kicking at the ground and scrambling away from the trees, eyes darting back and forth along the forest line for any sign of the wolves. She expected them to leap out and finish her, rip her to pieces or maybe just drag her in again. Honestly, Charlotte didn't know which would be worse.

But they didn't come. They didn't even howl.

After long minutes of staring, she collapsed onto her back and stared up at the sky. Her chest rose and fell with every greedy breath. The moon stared back at her, brutally impartial and unapologetic. Charlotte lifted her arm and flipped off the moon.

The wind picked up, swaying the tops of the pines and rustling the branches of shorter trees.

Eventually, she rolled onto her side and climbed to her feet. She heaved in breaths until they became almost even, until her vision cleared, and her heart stopped trying to beat its way out of her chest. The adrenaline wore off enough to let the cold seep in through her damp clothes, biting at her bones.

She gaped at the house she knew all too well, looming over the slope of the yard.

It, like many other things, didn't make sense. The Greenleigh house was on the east side of Wicker and she had been in the forest to the northwest of town. She couldn't have run a straight line there. She would have had to go around the town, passing through the hiking trails and climbing down the rock beds. And Charlotte would know, because she had mapped just about every route to Rebecca's house as a kid.

She looked at the woods again. Had they moved? Was that how she'd gone from walking down the mountain to standing north of Wicker in Edgar's favorite hunting spot? And then from that spot to Greenleigh's yard in a matter of minutes?

She shuddered out a breath and started up to the house. She wasn't going back into the forest if she could help it, that was for certain.

CHAPTER FORTY-THREE

Charlotte walked around the Greenleigh house and knocked on the front door. She could count on one hand the number of times she'd actually knocked on that door in her life but, considering what had been going on in Wicker, it didn't seem smart to go barging inside in the middle of the night.

The light over the front door flicked on and muffled voices gathered on the other side. The locks slid back from the latches. Charlotte would *not* have been able to barge in even if she'd tried tonight. Greenleigh opened the door and looked her over from head to toe. Charlotte hadn't seen a mirror yet, but she was pretty sure she looked almost as bad as when her friend found her in the woods earlier that day. She had set a particularly low bar for herself, thanks to the sheriff.

Hannah hovered behind her wife, hugging her satin robe tightly around herself. It matched her pajamas. Who bought robes that matched pajamas? Did she have several of the same color or did she have a different robe for each set of nightwear? Hannah looked pointedly pissed at the sight of Charlotte, already shaking her head like she might turn her away. But Greenleigh opened the door wide and waved her in.

Charlotte didn't linger on the step a second longer than she had to. Once in the foyer, she toed off her muddy sneakers and went straight down the hall to the bathroom.

"It's almost two in the morning," Hannah whisper-screamed in the foyer.

"Go back to bed," Greenleigh said, soft but not quite bothering to whisper.

Charlotte turned on the bathroom light and winced. She closed the door and helped herself to the towels under the sink—not the fancy ones they had on the rack, but the emergency ones for cleaning up messes. She washed the sweat and dirt off her face, being gentle with the wound on her temple. At least the glue had held and she wouldn't be getting bloodstains on Hannah's towels. Using her fingers, she combed out her hair as best she could, avoiding the back and the wound there at the base of her scalp. She dabbed it just once with the towel, to make sure it wasn't bleeding, and then left it alone.

Knuckles tapped at the door.

She opened it.

Hannah had her face set in a glare that softened just a little when she actually looked at Charlotte. She wasn't a coldhearted woman, but she was still annoyed. She held out a handful of clothes. Charlotte was about to decline. She had hips for days and nothing these two women wore would ever fit her.

Hannah seemed to realize and gave the pile a shake. "They're yours. You left them here when you were using our dryer."

Charlotte took the offering, a t-shirt and a hoodie. It had been a month since she replaced her dad's dryer and stopped using the Greenleighs'. Either the job of returning her forgotten items had fallen to Greenleigh, or Hannah had bitterly refused to bring it up. She hadn't exactly liked the intrusion.

"Thanks," Charlotte said.

Hannah walked away, disappearing into the master bedroom. She closed the double doors firmly.

Charlotte peeled off her sweat and rain-soaked sweater, the ghost of a laugh on her lips because this one would end up in the wash and abandoned here just like the clean clothes in front of her had been.

She dressed carefully, resisting the urge to look at herself too long in the mirror. She was a mess and the sight of her own skin patchworked in abuse made her queasy.

She heard the percolator before she caught the smell of coffee.

The kitchen glowed beyond the dark living room. Greenleigh put two coffee cups on the counter and then pulled a box of cookies from her stash in the narrow cupboards high over the sink. Hannah had banned anything processed from the family diet when William was conceived. She knew about the cookie stash, of course, but hadn't called Greenleigh on it. She was either saving it for a good fight or just choosing her battles.

"Hannah seems…on edge," Charlotte said quietly.

Greenleigh shrugged. "If things get worse, I'll send her and William down to the hunting cabin. You're welcome to do the same if you need to."

Charlotte nodded stiffly and pulled one of the stools out from under the tiled lip of the kitchen island. The weight of exhaustion bared down on her, making her a hundred times heavier where she sat. "Where are the kids?" She remembered something about a sleepover and the living room was a mess of blankets, pillows, and games.

"Everyone woke up about a couple hours ago when Vic came by to pick up Miles. We put the girls and William back to bed in his room."

Charlotte nodded. A couple of hours? It felt like so much less than that.

"Did you walk all the way here?" Greenleigh asked.

"Sort of." She leaned her arms against the counter and then told the whole story, from the wind chimes appearing, to Edgar being alive, to trying to drive to Harvey's but ending up north of Wicker with the witch in the woods.

Greenleigh didn't interrupt. She inhaled twice like she might, but she didn't. She poured the coffee when the machine gave a final wheeze of steam. She even remembered to put milk and sugar in Charlotte's cup despite the information overload.

Finally, she pushed the cup into Charlotte's hands and leaned against the counter opposite her. "Vic didn't say why he was getting Miles when he came…" She let her words run off before taking a deep breath and asking, "So, Edgar's alive?"

Charlotte almost laughed because somehow *that* was still the most astonishing part of the story. Not the witch or how the ground must have shifted under her feet and spit her out on this side of town—but the fact that Edgar had come home. "Yeah."

"Then, whose body did they find in the woods?"

"His." Charlotte wrapped her hands around her mug, soaking up the heat. It wouldn't be enough to chase the cold out of her bones.

"I don't understand," Greenleigh admitted patiently.

"They're calling it a miracle," she said, her voice small and unimpressed.

Greenleigh was quiet for a long time before finally setting her cup back down on the counter. "When you called me that morning and said to pick up Miles… You said to tell people I'd gone to see you off on the bus and noticed him on the bench after you left. You asked me to take my time before I brought him home to Alice. I sat with him on that bench for over an hour before taking him to the diner, pretending I was waiting for Edgar to show up."

They had never talked about it. Charlotte had never asked her what she'd done to buy the time she'd needed to get rid of his body. She held her cup tighter when Greenleigh continued.

"When Edgar disappeared, I thought… I mean, Edgar disappeared and then his body was found, and I thought…"

"That I killed him?" Charlotte's voice was flat. The gunshot echoed in her head again, crisp as ever. She'd seen his body.

She'd dragged the full weight of him through the woods to that clearing.

"Yeah," Greenleigh said with a guilty shrug.

Charlotte had called her best friend all those years ago, because she knew she would keep her secrets. She trusted her. But she had also waited all those years since for Greenleigh to ask why. Charlotte would have told her the truth if she had asked, but she never did. She never even gave any sign that it was still on her mind when Charlotte returned home a couple years later.

"Why didn't you tell anyone?" Charlotte asked. It seemed like it was time to get all the questions out. Tomorrow looked bleak.

Greenleigh stared at her. "Because you told me to trust you."

"What if I *had* killed him?"

"Then I hoped you had a good reason."

Charlotte drank a big sip of her coffee.

"You did kill him, didn't you?" Her voice was so quiet, almost a whisper.

Charlotte nodded, heart hammering against her throat. She had killed Edgar. She was sure she had, and yet, he was there, in her house again.

"Has he said anything? Told anyone?"

"I don't know."

After she'd buried the body, she'd driven Edgar's truck over the mountain and down the north side so as not to be seen in town. She'd taken the long road around Grayson to get to Cyprus. On the first day—when she'd called her dad to let him know her bus had made it down the mountain just fine—he'd told her about Edgar not coming home. Charlotte had lied to her dad, telling him she saw Edgar a couple of hours earlier in Cyprus. He'd been waiting for her at the bus station, all shook up over Momma's death and things changing.

She'd lied through her teeth, but after killing her brother, lying to her dad had been easy. Charlotte had said Edgar told her he was leaving Wicker to get his head straight. She told her dad that she wasn't sure he'd go back right away, but he'd probably be home in a couple of days.

It got easier and easier to lie about Edgar after that, especially to her dad, because knowing would have been too cruel. Let him think his boy was running away from his family and his problems—better than knowing he was a dead psycho. Better than knowing he was a murderer. Better than knowing she was too.

Charlotte had continued to drive her brother's truck for weeks, leaving it unlocked with the keys in the ignition everywhere she went until one day—*finally*—someone stole it. Coming out to that empty parking lot had been such a relief that she'd cried on the spot. For the first time since the day she'd buried him, she'd cried.

She spent almost two years away from Wicker, just wandering and working and being anywhere but on the mountain.

And then one day she'd gone home, but nothing was ever the same.

CHAPTER FORTY-FOUR

He woke—not the way a person wakes from a bad dream with a jolt, or gradually after getting enough sleep. No, Harvey Darling woke the way an animal does when something dangerous has laid eyes on it—quietly, uneasily, but all at once.

The wind rattled the thin walls of his trailer, rocking it gently. That hollowed out dwelling of metal and plastic had sat in the same spot long before he moved in years ago. It rocked plenty but it never tipped over. The trailer park was quiet under the blustering night, nothing odd about that since the mudslide chased most of his neighbors away. He didn't miss them, but he did miss their dogs barking at all the creatures great and small that came from the woods into the cleared land, chasing them off into the trees.

Sitting up slowly, his eyes searched the thick shadows for the threat that had brought him out of sleep. His heart hammered against his ribs and sweat chilled his skin. He'd fallen asleep in his boxer briefs on top of the mound of quilts. Swinging his naked legs over the edge of the bed, he silently settled his feet onto the floor. The wind made it easy to be unheard—for him as well as anyone else. He rose to his full height.

It was outside his door—whatever it was. Harvey could feel it there when he looked at the little barrier between him and the world. Stepping into a pair of boots, he never took his eyes off the door. He inched closer, stretching his arm to the side and fingering the shotgun away from the corner where it rested. It had been months since he held it, not since Vic and his idiot friends came over to try to run him off—or maybe kill him. They had been glassy-eyed, beer cans still in hand, and headlights bearing down on the front of Harvey's trailer. It was hard to know how far men like that would go if no one pulled the brakes for them.

That night, it had been the engines that woke him, the lights flooded his windows and slurs screamed at his walls. He had imagined them as wolves come to blow him away like a little piggy in the fairytale. Harvey had laughed that night, walked out in a skirt with a shotgun in his arms and told those wolves to get on their knees if they wanted to blow him. They hadn't seen the humor. He wasn't even sure the words had landed. Drunks always struggled to keep up with his mouth.

They wanted him gone. Something about *his kind*. He still wasn't sure if they'd been angry about the skirts and heels or the Darling blood. It had never mattered to Harvey because it always boiled down to the same thing—he was different.

Vic had wanted him to come for a ride with them, but it hadn't sounded like an invitation. When he didn't seem to take notice of the shotgun, Harvey shot out one of the headlights on the truck. They all took notice then, sobering just enough to jump back, swearing like he'd been the one who took a joke too seriously.

They had meant to do him harm, he was sure of that, and yet his heart had not raced that night.

But tonight, in the quiet and the dark, his pulse drummed against the roots of his teeth. He unlatched his door and popped it open. The wind swept it back, slapping it to the side of the trailer and holding it there. He would have to lean out to bring it shut again.

Harvey Darling had no intention of leaning out, not with that figure standing there and staring in. He held the shotgun but didn't raise it, afraid of breaking the moment of stillness where it only looked at him, a living shadow with starlight twinkling where eyes must be.

"Darling." His name was spoken in the sound of twigs breaking and fat raindrops pelting his roof.

There was something inescapably feminine about the creature standing in front of him, but there was nothing really to confirm that gut reaction. Cosmic eyes glinting from shadows. Its hip shifted from one side to the other, dragging its body into a series of movements. Its arms were too long, hands stretched out into talons that reached past knees.

"I made your blood a deal," the Wicker Witch spoke again, not with a voice but with the sounds of the world, building an instant ache in his skull. It took a step closer, hips first and shoulders following. Another step and the moonlight pushed at shadows, unable to erase them completely. The witch seemed dipped in tar, a coat of starless sky dressing skin like cooling wax. *"Will you live wild on my mountain with your kin, Darling?"*

He put the shotgun down, letting it fall back into place against the corner just inside the door. It could not protect him from this thing. He almost knelt, his legs aching to give out— but he was too scared of the witch taking the gesture as consent. Tears slid down his cheeks unbidden when one of those arms reached toward him, palm up, talons open. It wanted his soul. It wanted him to hand it over willingly.

"No, ma'am," Harvey said, finding the words, barely whispered from his dry throat. "I think I'd rather be free than wild."

Talons twitched and dark lips parted for the first time, despite the words he'd heard so clearly before. Sharp teeth glinted in the moonlight, white and long. The wind had not stopped, picking up dead leaves from the ground to curl into the air along with the bits of plastic trash left behind by his neighbors. The night churned at the witch's back, but he could not hear it or even feel the wind. He could only feel that gaze like rough palms rubbing over his skin, searching him for entry. It wanted him to step out of his home; he was sure of that.

Was that fantasy? Was his mind inventing rules to make himself feel even just a little bit safe?

"You will die," the Wicker Witch said, teeth clicking and leaves falling in its voice.

Harvey didn't bother to rub at the tears on his face. He nodded. "Yes, that's what happens to living things."

"Not all living things," it countered, mouth quirking in something like a smirk.

He let his gaze run over the creature again, considering that almost human shape. Was it trying to look like them? Was it a disguise? Or had people formed to look like the witch? Could there be any relation between their two species?

"I'm not so sure about that," he whispered, eyes flicking up to meet that cosmic stare again, to gaze at the stars reflected in those dark eyes. The witch appeared to be made of things he knew—the shape of a human, legs like a deer, teeth like a wolf, and fingers like the talons of a bird. Frightful, yes, but all animals that eventually died.

The offered arm dropped to the witch's side and its head tipped back. For the first time those eyes left him and turned high to the sky. The stars in the witch's gaze had not been a reflection, because when it turned its face up to look at the heavens, they vanished from its sockets. Darkness stared up at the universe. Had they been a memory printed across its eyes? Or a trick of light soaked into that abyss?

"Stubborn," the Wicker Witch mused in that gravel and wood voice, not sounding wholly unamused.

"Will you kill me tonight?" Harvey asked, surprising himself with his own boldness for the first time in his life.

Lips pulled into a full grin, still turned up to the moon. *"No, last Darling. Not unless you are ready."* It moved suddenly, too fast for him to see.

The witch closed the distance between them, face snapping forward.

He jerked back and his legs finally gave out, dropping him on his ass on the hard floor of his trailer, legs sprawled. One boot squeaked across linoleum and wedged against the doorframe.

The witch didn't step up and in, didn't even lean through the gap. It just stood there in front of the door, bent to look in at him. His heart beat so fast that his vision blurred. The witch laughed and it was the worst sound Harvey had ever heard, screams and collapsing mountainsides roared under that voice.

"You will regret denying me. But your bones will be beautiful on my land."

All at once the sounds of the storm returned, the wind rocking his trailer and then turning the other way, slapping his door shut between them. He jumped where he sat, eyes still wide in the dark. The door thumped twice and then the wind jerked it open again. He tensed, breath held so tightly that it hurt, but she was gone this time—the empty trailer park stretched out before him.

CHAPTER FORTY-FIVE

Charlotte got a ride to her truck from Greenleigh and they both drove back to town together. The road didn't move this time, and she drove right through the heart of Wicker. The aldermen were gathering before the town meeting, probably to figure out what they were going to say. Their little town had gone to hell in only three days. Charlotte doubted even Jane Philips had a prewritten speech for killing sprees and forest witches.

The whole drive home, Charlotte struggled not to change her mind. She wanted to keep going on the highway down toward Cyprus even though the bridge was out. She wanted to turn around and try the northern pass even though the downed trees were still blocking the way. Any option was better than going home, so why couldn't she take them? Why did she have to go back?

It was barely six in the morning, but her family house was in full swing.

Charlotte walked into the smell of waffles and bacon. Victor was in the kitchen with Lila buzzing around him. Charlotte's dad reclined in the family room, feet up and a grin plastered on his face as he watched the kids play a racing game on the TV. Winnie snuggled up in his lap, still in her footy pajamas. It was like stepping into someone else's dream. The rest of Wicker was in a state of terror and here was her family, going about their morning like it was Christmas Day and no one could be happier.

"Where's Miles?" Charlotte asked, dread pooling in her stomach because she knew the answer.

Her dad didn't take his eyes off the TV. "He's at his house with his parents," he said, as though he had been waiting for the chance to say it for years now. She supposed he had.

Victor tossed a look back at her from the stove. "Lotte! Want some coffee? Waffles? Jesus, what happened to your face?" he asked with a laugh—like bruises and a split temple would be attached to a funny story.

Not answering, she headed straight upstairs with her muddy sneakers still on. No one said anything, not even Lila. Charlotte went to her bedroom and pulled on the first jacket she found before pulling one of her dresser drawers almost all the way out. It was packed with jeans and tops she hadn't worn since high school. She dumped most of them on the floor to drag out a locked metal box from the back and set it on top of the dresser. Thumbing through the combination, she opened it. The little revolver had been her momma's. She'd never seen her use it, or any other gun, but it had always been there—in the back of her highest drawer, just in case.

Charlotte flipped out the cylinder and loaded it with shiny bullets from the carton. She snapped it shut and then shoved the weapon into her jacket pocket. Scooping out another fistful of bullets, she fed them into the hip pocket of her jeans on her way out. She ran down the stairs and out of the house, not wanting to see the strange, brittle happiness of her family again. It wasn't real. It *couldn't* be real—because Edgar couldn't really be alive.

Instead of following the beaten road from the big house to the street, Charlotte cut a straight line between trees from one house to the other, afraid that if she slowed down, sanity might catch up to her and make her stop. Wicker was no place for sane thoughts anymore. If she tried to form them, the effort and failure would break her.

Crossing the messy yard, she went straight up to the door only to pause there when she almost knocked. This wasn't a visit and she wasn't there to ask for anything.

Charlotte gripped the gun in her pocket and tried the doorknob. It opened and she made it one step into the house before jerking to a stop so forcefully that her bones ached. Edgar sat in the living room, staring back at her like he had been waiting. Alice hummed in the bedroom at the back of the house. Miles was nowhere in sight. She wanted to look for him, thinking he was probably in his room, but that would mean moving closer to where Edgar sat.

"Miles?" she called, finger on the trigger in her pocket. She would shoot Edgar if he stood up. She just wasn't sure if a bullet would keep him down anymore.

"I'm really happy to see you," Edgar spoke but didn't stand. Did he know she had a gun? He had no reason to doubt she'd use one.

Her skin crawled.

Miles's door opened down the hall and the boy poked his head out. Before she could tell him to come to her, Alice was out of her room and nudging him back. "Go back in and play. I'll let you know when food's ready," Alice said, not moving until Miles had retreated and she could close the bedroom door.

Charlotte had allowed Alice to distract her. The realization sent a jolt of panic down her spine and her gaze snapped back to Edgar. He hadn't moved from his seat, but he was still staring at her. Still waiting for a reply, maybe? Fine. If she couldn't grab Miles and run, she would have to dive into this.

"You're dead," she informed her brother.

Alice hurried down the hall, glaring at Charlotte. "It's *a miracle.* I knew you wouldn't appreciate it, but the least you can do is be happy for the rest of us."

The front door was still open behind her, the cold from outside seeping in. Alice hugged herself against it, but Edgar didn't seem to notice. Why would he?

"We have to talk, Alice. Send Miles over to my dad's place and we can—"

"I don't need to talk to you," Alice snapped.

Charlotte almost screamed, teeth clicking when she bit it back. "You know what really happened," she said lowly. "You knew he was dead from day one, Alice. And you knew why he died."

Alice shook her head so fast and so hard that Charlotte was certain she was right, now more than ever.

"You don't need to do this, Lotte," Edgar said evenly. "I forgive you."

Charlotte ignored him, looking only at Alice now. "He was always a little dark, wasn't he? I know you were afraid to leave Miles alone with him when he was a baby. You hovered, not because you were that sort of mom but because you knew there was something wrong with Edgar and the way he looked at Miles."

Alice scrunched up her face, her scabbed fingertips breaking open against her grip on her own robe. "No."

"He killed animals for fun when we were kids."

"No."

"He killed our momma."

Alice's gaze shot up to Charlotte's at last.

"I saw him do it, Alice. I saw him."

Alice swallowed hard and Charlotte watched her press back the tidal wave of reality. She didn't want to let her miracle go.

"He took Miles out to the woods to kill him. I think you knew it when he left, you just wouldn't believe it. He was going to shoot your boy."

Tears rolled down Alice's cheeks. "Stop it!"

"I killed him," Charlotte said.

Alice's eyes grew, losing focus. She had known, Charlotte was sure of it. She had to have known. There had been an edge of anger in their friendship ever since Charlotte came home. Why else would Alice say she owed her things? Why else would Alice be so bitter with her above all others? Why else would she hound Rebecca for details about how she'd found Miles but never, not even once, asked Charlotte about her claim that she'd seen Edgar in Cyprus that day?

"It was an accident," Edgar suggested, trying to smooth over the situation.

"It wasn't. I meant to kill him. I'm not even sorry I did it. And I wish I could say *that* wasn't him…" She glanced at the man still perched on the old recliner, looking back at her with the hint of a smile in the corner of his mouth. He couldn't hide it anymore. It was always there, curving his lips. "But it is him. It's more him than ever before and—"

"Shut up!" Alice screamed, rushing forward and pushing Charlotte back.

She staggered, heel catching on the door jam and almost tripping. "You know I'm right! You know he's dangerous!" Her voice rose as she spoke. Edgar hadn't moved from his seat, watching them like the malicious ghost that he was.

Alice swung her hand at Charlotte, tears in her eyes and cheeks red with anger.

Charlotte leaned back, avoiding the slap and taking one more step back and out of the house.

Alice's cheeks flared brighter when her swing missed, body staggering forward without the contact. She huffed, bull-like, and grabbed suddenly at the door instead.

Charlotte shook her head, imploring her one last time. "Don't do this. At least send Miles over to—"

The door slammed and she cringed, standing there for another couple of seconds while the locks slid into place to bar her from entering again.

The gun was still in her pocket, the metal warm against her hand.

Turning, she marched back up to the big house but couldn't bring herself to go inside. Feeling like the only sane person in her family was driving her crazy. She climbed into the truck, the keys stashed behind the visor, and headed to the trailer park.

CHAPTER FORTY-SIX

Alice stared at the door, her hands shaking. For a moment, she thought they would betray her and throw back the locks. She imagined running for her car, jumping in, and driving away. Her gaze fixed on the deadbolt. Alice had already made her choice.

She took a step back and tried to even out her breathing.

"Why did you do that?" Edgar asked, voice like silk over her skin. Thrilling, even if it was cold. She closed her eyes. He was alive. That was all she needed. "You knew it was her, didn't you?"

Alice let out another breath before opening her eyes and forcing a smile when she turned to face him. "Knew what was her?" she asked, but didn't want him to answer. She didn't want to know that Charlotte had murdered her husband. She didn't even want to know that he had ever been gone.

There had always been things she hadn't wanted to know.

Edgar smiled, the way he had when he knew she was avoiding problems—pretending not to see them. Why had he always liked that about her?

When he stood from the couch, he was taller than she remembered. Taller than he had been on the street last night. He opened his arms to her, and she hurried to that spot against his chest where she had always felt safe. His arm closed around her, not too tight but just firm enough so she knew he was real even when she closed her eyes.

"Don't go again," she whispered. She wanted to tell him not to let Charlotte take him away again—she wanted to swear that she would stop Charlotte herself—but she couldn't bear to come that close to reality.

Her cheek pressed to his shirt, her body leaning into the strength of him.

He stroked her hair but made no promises.

With her ear to his chest, she heard his heart.

It beat in three deep knocks, like a wolf rapping at the door, followed by a long stretch of silence where all the nightmares imaginable gathered. She waited, and waited, tears collecting behind her lids, and then finally it knocked again, three more times.

Alice jerked back from his hug and scrubbed her tears away. "I should make something to eat," she burst out, hurrying away from him and that unnatural sound. She didn't look back, because she knew that smile would be there on his face, those dark eyes studying her like he, too, knew too much.

CHAPTER FORTY-SEVEN

Rebecca met with Jane and Wyatt Philips, Parker Whitley, Deborah Rogers, Kenny Feldman, and Doctor Paulson an hour before the town meeting. Hannah had volunteered to watch the kids in one of the classrooms out of earshot of the auditorium.

The Board of Aldermen went over what options they had and found them alarmingly few. Evacuation wasn't possible until they managed to clear the road north. Doctor Paulson reported having sent several people down the mountain to the river for cell service who simply never made it, always ending up back in the town. Parker Whitley confessed to having tried to go down to the river too, thinking that maybe he could just walk across one of the foot bridges and over to Cyprus. He hadn't made it. Just as he'd come into sight of the river, he was suddenly turned around and driving through Wicker again.

No one had any idea how to explain the phenomena, so they collectively moved away from it.

They would have to clear the road north and try getting out that way.

Deborah Rogers suggested setting everyone's mind at ease by saying that Sheriff Summerfield had been behind the disappearances of Sam and Andrew Caller as well as the horrible chimes. They were fairly certain he had murdered the deputies, Mrs. Potter, and his own mother, not to mention the kidnapping and assault of Charlotte Crowe. It wasn't such a far stretch to blame him for the rest, was it? And it would put an end to talk of serial killers and witches.

Rebecca still wasn't convinced Summerfield had done it all himself, but she wasn't going to argue. This wasn't the time for any *Nancy Drew* shit.

The auditorium of the school started filling with people a full forty-minutes before seven, when the meeting was meant to start.

Jane had put on one of her best smiles and tried to greet everyone, but it soon became clear that this wasn't going to be a casual *"stay calm"* sort of meeting.

Other residents had tried to leave Wicker last night, some via the roads and others on motorbikes or four-wheelers down the mountain. They all ended up back where they started. Panic mounted with every story added. When someone whispered, *"No escape,"* it sent ripples through the crowd, turning up the tension.

Some of the townsfolk had started a list of people who had gone missing since yesterday, some having vanished from their homes in the middle of the night without a word—their vehicles left behind.

Hands raised in the crowd, one after another, reporting more family members and neighbors gone and houses full of bone chimes.

The Turners were dead, Henry Slate told them. When he'd gone over to remind his old friend about the town meeting this morning, he had found the bodies. As far as he could tell, Mr. Turner had executed his whole family in the living room before turning the gun on himself.

The hum of shock and horror, of muffled cries, didn't even last long before the crowd moved on to another frightful scene or dead neighbor.

Wicker was unraveling.

Rebecca joined Jane at the podium, trying to keep the crowd as calm as they could. They would make lists of the missing and they would bring the dead to the morgue. They would enact a state of emergency and turn the auditorium into a shelter. They could board up the windows and assign residents to keep watch at all times until they figured out a way down the mountain, or until the Cyprus police realized something was wrong and came up.

"If we can't get down, who's to say they can get up to us?" someone shouted.

A drone of panicked agreement rose in the auditorium.

"We're being picked off!" Mrs. Gary shouted.

Their voices pitched in a jumbled flurry. They talked about a serial killer hiding among them, or a madness spreading, or maybe it was the Darlings.

Jane tried to bring the crowd to order, but they were slipping away from reason and deeper into fear.

Rebecca watched them seethe, ideas rippling from one end of the mass to the other, the worst of them getting the most traction and drowning out anything resembling reason. The crowd at the town meeting was turning into a mob right before her eyes.

Her focus snagged on a shadow among the people, a faceless shape between her neighbors and friends. When the crowd shifted, the shadow vanished, only to reappear elsewhere among them. It looked like it was whispering to them, leaning over shoulders to press its featureless face close to ears.

Rebecca took a step back, bumping into the wall behind her. The shadowy figure jerked its head up and she could have sworn it stared at her and into her. And then it grinned, darkness ripping open to bare teeth.

It vanished before she could convince herself she had really seen it, and she was left watching madness spread across her community.

CHAPTER FORTY-EIGHT

Alice played house in her own home. She made an early lunch, cutting the sandwiches into triangles and piling chips on the side. For the first time in almost a decade, they ate a meal at the table together. Alice drove the conversation and Edgar made it easy with casual replies and all the right questions. It was exactly like it had been before.

Miles didn't say much, picking at his food and sneaking glances at his dad.

Edgar pretended not to notice but when Miles was distracted or talking to her, Edgar would look at their son—stare at him—his smile slipping away for a second when he thought no one saw. But Alice saw. Alice had been watching Edgar since the moment he came walking down that street last night.

He wouldn't say where he had been or what had happened, and no one seemed capable of pressing for an answer because it was all too unreal. He hadn't been missing or lost. He had been dead. They had seen his body. *Alice* had seen his body, unbreathing and hollow in the morgue.

But now he was alive and home. It was everything she had wished for. This morning, after showering and putting on his own clothes, Edgar had sat on his side of the bed and finished the book he'd left on the nightstand all those years ago. Alice laid next to him, watching his gaze slide back and forth across the pages.

None of it was real. It couldn't be. But it *felt* real, and she wasn't going to let anyone ruin it.

A knock at the front door made Alice jump in her chair. Miles's eyes widened at her, but Edgar laughed. "Babe, maybe you need to get some sleep," he suggested, standing up and leaning over to kiss the top of her head.

Her heart fluttered, just like it always had when he did that. Edgar had a way of making people feel precious—the rare few he took any time to care for, anyway.

He answered the door and Victor's voice boomed in, excited as though he hadn't just seen Edgar a few hours ago. She tried not to be possessive, tried not to show how much she wanted everyone else to go away so that she could be alone with her husband.

"There's a town meeting. Do you want to ride over with us?" Vic asked.

Alice twisted around in her chair to look at the open door, the light from outside making the house seem dark. She had gathered up all the bone chimes and swept them into the basement. Edgar had seen them but not asked what they were or why they were in their home. She wouldn't have had an answer, but he should have asked, shouldn't he?

"Do we have to go?" Alice asked, raising her voice so Vic would hear from the porch.

Her brother-in-law took a step inside, leaning over to look around the door at her. He flashed a warm smile. "It's important. Shit's really bad and we need to figure out how to set things right."

She ground her teeth to keep from snapping something about how the boys wanted to play *"rescue the town."* They had no idea what they were fighting. Did Alice? No. She had seen the creature, had heard its voice on the wind ever since, but she didn't know. She didn't understand, and she didn't want to.

"People say they can't leave the mountain. Some of the guys tried and just got turned back around," Vic continued.

"That's stupid," Alice replied. "That's not even possible. They can't leave because the bridge is out." She'd said it before her gaze slipped to her husband, the other impossibility in Wicker. Edgar didn't look bothered, he just stared back at her.

"You don't have to go," Edgar said. "I'm sure it won't take long. We can take Miles with us, and you can get some rest."

Miles stiffened beside her, his hand suddenly in hers, holding tightly.

Alice glanced down at her son. He gave a shake of his head, almost imperceptible. "No. If you guys are going to look for a fight, I'd rather he just stay here."

Vic snorted and rolled his eyes.

Edgar clapped his brother's shoulder before he could say anything. "Let's go."

Her heart jumped to her throat and she almost knocked her chair over getting up, pulling her hand from her son's in a rush to stop her husband from leaving.

He paused at the door, a thin smile suggesting he knew her well enough to know her worries before she ever spoke them. His arm curled around her, pulling her close, and he stole a kiss. All her thoughts and fears pressed back like shadows at dawn. He held her and she was safe. His forehead touched hers, those dark eyes watching her and seeing everything. "We have work left to do," he whispered, crushing her moment of peace. He grinned wider, as though that too pleased him. "See you soon."

Alice stood in the open doorway. There were two trucks on the road in front of her house, engines still running. One was full of some of Vic's friends, music throbbing out the open windows, and the other truck was Vic's. Watching Edgar get into his brother's vehicle and leave was like watching a memory from long ago—just another normal day.

The Crowe family thought Edgar was a miracle given to them during dark times. Alice had been the first to say it—but she knew it wasn't true. Edgar wasn't a gift. She had paid for his life with her soul, the absence of it cold inside her chest and the weight of someone else in the back of her every thought and action since. She knew her husband, and as much as she wanted to think there was something different about him— something wrong—she knew he was one hundred percent

Edgar. The only thing that had changed was that some of his pretense had been peeled away.

"Momma?" Miles asked, voice barely above a whisper.

She didn't look back into the house at him, still staring at the empty road where the trucks had been.

"Momma… Are you sure he's—"

"Stay here, baby. I have to go to the store," Alice said, unsure where the words had even come from.

She grabbed her keys and stepped into her rain boots. Miles didn't argue. He just sat there at the table, watching her leave while she tried not to look at him. She closed the front door and walked to her car.

Alice didn't bother with her seatbelt, just started the engine and drove away. She didn't know where she was going until she turned right onto the old highway and left Wicker, driving south toward the bottom of the mountain. Tears rolled down her cheeks and she squeezed the wheel tighter, trying her best not to think at all. She didn't want to ask herself where she was going, or why she had left Miles behind, or why she had given everything for Edgar to come home only to run away.

She just wanted quiet.

She just wanted to escape.

Halfway down the mountain, she exhaled a shuddering breath of relief, sure that whatever stories Victor had been spreading about people not being able to leave had been bullshit.

And then she saw a figure standing in the road up ahead. She began to lift her foot off the gas, recognizing the shape of a person. She heard the creaking of trees inside her car—*no*, inside her own head. The figure turned toward her, head tipped back in a dare and ink black eyes gleaming in the daylight. It wasn't a person, but it was real.

Alice pressed the gas and the engine of her little car roared as it accelerated down the highway.

The monster grinned, teeth shining and sharp, but Alice didn't slow. She wouldn't. She would run the bitch down just like any other animal from the woods that might be loitering on the road. She would find a way across the bridge even if she had to leave her car behind. She would go down to Cyprus, to her mom's place, and never look back. She would—

Alice took her foot off the gas and hit the brake hard. Her eyes widened, hands clutching at the wheel and her gaze shooting down to stare at her own treacherous body. She hadn't meant to brake. She had every intention of running the witch over.

The car jerked to a stop, tires squealing, and her pulse throbbing beneath her temples.

Alice expected to see that monstrous woman standing right in front of her car, her breath catching in dreaded anticipation, but she wasn't there. The road wasn't there either. The forest had pressed back, and Alice was parked on Green Street near the center of Wicker along with dozens of other vehicles.

She stared blankly out her window with no memory of turning around, of driving into town, or of parking.

Slowly, she got out of the car and crossed the street to the school. The doors were propped open and the auditorium was already packed with rising voices. She tried to turn away, to go back to her car or just walk home, but she couldn't; she wasn't in charge of her body anymore.

She stopped just inside the room. Everyone was yelling. They were shouting at the aldermen standing on the little stage, the same one where they had all watched their kids struggle through school pageants and bad plays.

Alice knew Edgar was in the room before even looking at him. He leaned against the wall to the right, a sly grin pulling at one corner of his mouth. He watched the scene, waiting for something to happen.

Voices rose like waves, crashing against the walls and bouncing back on them with the names of the dead and demands for rescue.

Someone had kidnapped and killed that boy in the woods. Someone had murdered the deputies and the receptionist at the sheriff's station. Someone was tormenting the town with bone chimes, and *something* had trapped them all there.

The aldermen tried to blame Sheriff Summerfield, but he was gone, supposedly dead, and this mob needed someone alive to blame. They needed action. They needed the fresh blood of justice.

Alice gnashed her teeth, feeling the mob pulling at her heart like a strong current.

"The Darlings!" someone shouted.

A chorus of agreement and rage followed.

"Harvey Darling!" came another, pointing out the snake in their garden.

Dozens of others whispered the name, breathing it like a curse.

Alice found herself nodding, tears in her eyes. There was a whisper among them, urging them on and she could hear it, but she still couldn't stop herself from joining in. "Yes," she called. "Yes!" Blame Harvey. Blame someone. Make it stop.

"We have to stop them!" another shouted, a cheer of agreement rising up.

"We have to save ourselves before they kill us all!" someone else said.

The shadow of the Wicker Witch pressed in behind her, the weight of her attention like a claw dragging down her spine, opening flesh and tapping at vertebrae. Alice heard stones grinding and the earth groaning. The demand was there, in her ear. She knew what the witch wanted her to say.

Alice cried, throat raw when she shouted, "Burn the witch!"

The mob shuddered, the words igniting a terrible need, and ending all discussion.

CHAPTER FORTY-NINE

For a while, Miles stayed at the table after his parents had both gone. He didn't eat. He just stared at the three plates of barely touched food, wondering which one would come back first.

He hoped it was his momma because he didn't know that man they called his dad. There had been pictures of him, of course, and Miles had a few memories to go with them, but there was something wrong about the person who came home. Him being back wasn't making Momma better. She smiled like she was happy, but it looked more like a grimace, and it never came near her eyes. It was the same smile she wore when she had to talk to his teachers, or the other parents, or Aunt Lila.

His gaze slid to the door and he wondered, not for the first time in his life, if his momma would ever come back. She was so sad. He tried to be good, to make her happy, but she was still so sad. And a part of him had always thought that it was because his dad was gone—that if he would just come home again, she would be happy.

But she wasn't happy.

Miles got up. He stacked all three of their plates, pressing sandwiches between porcelain, and put the short tower into the fridge. He knew the chips would get weird in there but didn't want to put them back in the bag. After zipping up his hoodie, he grabbed his jacket off the hook by the door and pulled it on. Then he sat down on the floor and put on his shoes.

The grown-ups had been saying for days now that none of the kids could go out and play or ride bikes. But all his grown-ups had gone out and left him on his own. No one had said he couldn't go too.

He shoved his phone into his pocket—more habit than anything else now that it was just a few games and a camera. He patted his pockets to make sure his gloves were in there before opening the front door.

Miles made it two steps onto his porch before he stopped.

Aunt Lila was outside of Grandpa's house. Her car was running, the doors open. His cousins cried loudly as she pushed them into the backseat. She was talking to herself, mouth moving endlessly and head ticking to the left as though listening to a reply every few seconds—the whole conversation on fast-forward.

Jeremy whined at his mom, stomping his bare foot on the ground and folding his arms, hugging himself against the cold. He was still wearing his pajamas. "Momma, why?" he yelled.

She shook her head but didn't reply, grabbing his arm and pulling him toward the car, pushing him into the front seat.

Miles took a step back.

She closed the passenger doors and then froze. Miles held his breath. Her head lifted and turned straight toward him, eyes narrowed on him from across the stretch of woods. It reminded him of how the smudge creature in the kitchen had looked at him—straight *into* him. Her expression slackened, eyes going dull. One hand lifted slowly and she pressed a finger to her lips, making a long shushing sound the wind carried to his ear. And then she grinned, so wide that he was afraid her face would split.

Aunt Lila blinked back to herself, confusion wrinkling the corners of her eyes and hand dropping away from her face. She glared at him, as though he had done something to her, and then hurriedly rounded her car, jumping into the front seat.

Miles sank back until his shoulder touched the door.

There were monsters outside.

He went back in and sat down in the living room, staring at the door and trying not to wonder which one would come home first.

CHAPTER FIFTY

Charlotte drove to the trailer park, but Harvey wasn't there. The whole *"no phone service"* thing was getting old fast. She headed into town, hoping to find him in his shop. She needed to talk to him, and they needed to get off the mountain. Greenleigh would have her hands full with the meeting today, and Charlotte had planned to avoid the whole area until it was over. Now she was trying to find someplace to park among the vehicles crammed into the little parking lots behind the buildings and lining the residential streets looping off Green Street.

She spotted Harvey's truck and parked her own right behind his, blocking him in so that even if she somehow missed him, he wouldn't leave.

Only a few steps from her vehicle, hand still stuffing the keys into her pocket, a scream of breaking glass stopped her in her tracks. The cheers of a crowd drew her closer and when she rounded the post office onto Green Street, she almost collided with the backs of her neighbors. They heaved together, facing away from her and clustered around the front of a shop. They all spoke at once but instead of a unified chant, their words became a swarm of hornets furiously gathering in the air, impossible to understand.

Pressed against a wall across the street, she saw the faces of the town aldermen. They were in a shouting match with a group of residents including Victor. The group pushed whenever the aldermen tried to get around them. Greenleigh was red-faced and yelling. She wasn't the only one.

For a split- second, Greenleigh's eyes fell on Charlotte and she froze, a thousand thoughts screaming at her through that gaze. Greenleigh jutted her chin toward the mob urgently and when Victor began to turn to see who she was looking at, Rebecca lifted onto her toes and punched him in the face.

Charlotte pushed her way into the crowd. She recognized these people, but their faces were all twisted in anger, and no one seemed to see her. She shouldered her way through but the closer she got to the front, the more they pushed back. They were kicking something on the ground, all of them trying to get closer to it.

The mob gave one more shove forward and then lurched back. She saw the body on the ground. Harvey Darling rolled sluggishly onto his side, spitting up blood onto the pavement. Red oozed from a gash on his cheek down to his jaw. He kicked at the street and rolled all the way onto his back, his sweater torn and chest heaving under it as he sucked air and stared blankly at the sky.

She was almost out of the crowd, ready to throw herself down at his side, when a hand grabbed the back of her hair and pulled, ripping some of the staples from the wound in her scalp. Pain cut a flash of light across her vision. An arm hooked around her chest, under her breasts, and lifted her, holding her back.

She finally made out the words of the crowd, screamed guttural from the pits of their madness, *"Burn the witch!"* and, *"Die, Darling!"*

Billy Benson and one of the Brandons picked Harvey up off the street and dragged him the short distance through broken glass and the open doorway into the bookshop.

Charlotte screamed again but no one heard her over their call for bloodshed. She struggled, slapping at the arm that held her. Every move sent ripples of pain through her scalp and down her neck. The man holding her shushed her, his voice low and near her ear. She froze, her skin washing cold when she realized it was Edgar. He wasn't yelling like the crowd. He wasn't calling for vengeance or justice.

His cheek brushed hers. "You could ask her to make it stop," he said against Charlotte's ear.

A flash of light off to the side caught her eye. A man jogged from the bar toward the bookstore with a bottle of vodka in hand, a rag already stuffed down the neck. The crowd inhaled when he lit it on fire.

"Save the town!" someone cried out.

"Burn the Darling!" another shouted.

The mob roared, finally one unified beast with their eyes focused on the flames.

Charlotte sank her hand into her pocket, found the revolver, and pulled it out.

"Burn!" they roared together, chanting it as the fire came closer and closer.

She pointed the gun down and squeezed the trigger, shooting Edgar in the thigh once. The sound broke the chant. He let go of her hair with a yell of surprise and she elbowed him in the side to break free, stumbling away from the crowd. She lifted one arm high and fired two more shots into the air. Like one animal, the mob flinched back.

The man with the Molotov hurled it through the air, end over end, creating a spiral of flames that vanished through the broken window of the shop. For a second, they all held their breaths, hearts in their throats. The roar came from inside, light bursting to life within the shop. They had unleashed fire on a room of old paper and, God, how they cheered to see it burn.

Charlotte moved before anyone else could grab her, running straight for that narrow door. She threw it open and rushed inside. Heat lashed at the air to warn her back, but she pressed in, the flames so bright she had to squint. Her cheeks ached, and her hair lifted and writhed against the waves of heat. The chanting started up again outside, muffled by the growl and crack of the fire blossoming in the aisles of books, reaching for the ceiling.

She couldn't see him at first, some part of her mind expecting him to be there in the middle of the floor as soon as she stepped in, but he wasn't. Curling an arm over her face, she tried in vain to shield her eyes from the sweltering heat and curls of smoke as she moved deeper into the shop, looking down the aisles for him. She had never seen anything so bright as those shelves, pages curling back and thick pieces breaking away to flutter in the air, turning to crisp leaves of ember and ash.

"Harvey!" Charlotte shouted when she found him in a heap near the wall. She put her revolver back in her pocket and rolled him onto his back. She shook him when he didn't stir, fingers ripping at the front of his sweater. Smoke choked her, tears rolling off her burning eyes and down her cheeks in streams. The shelf of books to their left creaked and began to lean toward them, a wall of fire turning into a slow-motion wave.

Scrambling to her feet, Charlotte took fistfuls of his sweater and dragged him along the wall. The smoke swirled in thick, black spirals toward the front of the shop and out the open window. She couldn't see anymore, her eyes watery and stinging. A gust of heat rolled against her left, blistering the side of her face and making the air sizzle in her ear.

She pulled him behind his desk, curling over his head when the fire-wave of books came down, sending a plume of smoke and embers barreling forward through the shop. Whatever glass remained in the ragged frame of the window went flying outward, singing across the pavement.

Harvey coughed against her chest, spasming to life with tremors she imagined came from the shock of waking up in hell.

Charlotte gave him a push, shoving him to the side, and started clawing at the floor. She kept her eyes pressed shut and every thin breath she dragged down came coughing up—rejected by her lungs. His fingers joined hers, searching the seams of the floor for the loose board. They pulled it up, and then another, and then another, tossing them away until the old tunnel was exposed.

The cold air inside reached for her like icy fingers wrapping around her wrists and drawing her down. She practically fell into the hole, crawling blindly down until darkness cocooned her. The tunnel was just big enough to sit up inside, the ground flat and damp under her palms. At any other time in her life, she might have worried about a cave-in, rats, or bugs. Today, she was so grateful to be out of the fire that she almost curled up and went to sleep in that dark, peaceful grave.

Harvey followed, coughing behind her. She crawled and every time she stopped, his hand would find her thigh or her back and nudge her forward.

The fire in the building groaned overhead, little bursts of hot air chasing after them through the tunnel. But the farther they crawled, the quieter it got—the violence of Wicker becoming something far away and muffled.

Charlotte was tempted to stop crawling before they reached the end of the tunnel, not entirely sure she wanted to be in the woods again. They were underground, someplace between Wicker and the forest, and she wished grimly that they could stay. But though the grave was welcoming, she wasn't ready to settle into hers just yet.

They inched along for what felt like an hour, slowly moving through the dark and saying nothing. She stopped when she thought something moved under her palms. *There.* She held her breath, waiting to feel it again.

Harvey tapped at her thigh, urging her forward.

"Did you feel that?" she asked.

He waited in the dark with her.

The ground pulsed again. *Thump, thump.* "That," she hissed.

"No," he coughed. "I didn't feel anything, Lotte. Just keep going."

The ground heaved under her hands and knees, against her sides, and overhead. *Thump, thump.* She was sure of it. Not pulsing but beating with the slow steady rhythm of a heart. She trembled, unable to will herself to move while it continued to throb around her. How could he not feel it?

"Lotte," he pleaded, palm rubbing at the base of her spine.

She leaned forward and turned her head, placing her cheek to the cold soil. A heart beat in the ground. *Thump, thump.* Did the mountain have a heart? Was it alive? Whose side was it on?

"Lotte, please," Harvey whispered, both hands on her now.

The beat grew fainter, farther and farther away, until it was gone and the ground steadied all around her once more. She sat up slowly but nodded in the dark, realizing that this place wasn't safe either.

She crawled and Harvey followed. He didn't ask what she'd heard—not while they were still down there. He didn't say anything at all until they reached a dead end.

"Trade places with me," Harvey said, hands on her again in the dark as they shuffled around one another so that he was ahead of her.

She heard him groping around in the tunnel and then something scraping overhead. Light poured in—not the violent firelight of the shop, but a soft glow of daylight filtered through clouds and trees. He pushed the old wood planks back, some of them falling apart from years of rot, until he could stand upright. Autumn leaves, orange pine needles, and chunks of dirt fell in around him, and then he lifted himself up and vanished.

Charlotte crawled to the end, squinting against daylight, and stood up. Her head and shoulders popped out of the hole, suddenly above ground and taking big gulps of clean air. Harvey helped her out and they both collapsed on the wet ground. For a long while, they laid there, and she wondered if the world would ever stop tasting like ash.

"We'll have to move…in case someone knew about the tunnel," Charlotte thought aloud, even though moving felt like the last thing she wanted to do. Everything hurt and the cold ground was so nice against her skin.

Harvey's hand found hers, curling their fingers together. "Did you run into fire for me, Lotte?"

Charlotte rolled her head to the side to stare back at him. He was covered in swollen red splotches, smears of blood, and a thick coating of ash. Still, he smiled at her, his lip busted and his teeth glossed pink with blood.

"I ran *close* to fire for you," she corrected.

"Where are we going to go?" Harvey asked. "They thought I was responsible for everything happening since the storm… They said it would all end if I died."

"They've lost their minds," Charlotte agreed.

"I saw Edgar," Harvey noted, seeming to remember it now.

"Yeah. Maybe we'll get lucky and they'll burn him next."

He let out a rich laugh and struggled to his feet. She watched before finally getting up too. Her head throbbed and she remembered the sensation of her skin tearing at the base of her skull. She poked tenderly at her scalp, pain shooting down her neck and around the back of her head. There was fresh blood on her fingers when she took her hand back.

"I saw the witch," Harvey said.

Charlotte looked up at him and then around, afraid the creature was closing in on them.

He grabbed her arm and shook his head. "No. Last night. It came to my trailer." He huffed another laugh, but this one came out dry. "I actually went to the bookstore to sleep because I thought it would be safer…"

"What did the witch want?" Charlotte asked, wondering if his conversations with the monster had been similar to her own.

He used his sweater to rub some of the blood and ash from his face. "It said it had made a deal with the Darlings and offered it to me too."

She didn't have to ask if he took the deal. If he had, he probably wouldn't have been the target of the town this morning. "We should leave," she said, and for one blazingly fantastic moment, she meant it. They could just walk away, hike down the mountain or around it or wherever they had to go to get away from Wicker.

Harvey smiled at her patiently, knowing she couldn't go that easily even before she was ready to admit it.

"I have to get Miles…"

He nodded. "Let's go. Road's this way." He started walking, favoring his right leg but setting a good pace. They weren't exactly in a hurry to get back to town.

CHAPTER FIFTY-ONE

His dad came home first.

Edgar stood in the doorway staring at him, and Miles wished he could disappear.

"Let's go," his dad said.

Miles stood up but he didn't want to go. "Where's Momma?"

Edgar turned and disappeared outside, leaving the door open. It wasn't an invitation so much as an expectation that he would follow.

Miles crept to the door with his hands balled inside his jacket pockets. Tears blurred his vision, but he tried to will them back. He was definitely too big to cry, but every step he took toward the truck on the driveway pounded dread through his body. He didn't want to go anywhere with his dad.

As though she heard him and came running, his momma pulled up beside the truck. Her engine turned off and she jumped out, hurrying toward them. Miles rushed to meet her, throwing his arms around her. "I don't want to go."

Her arms folded around him, but it wasn't tight enough to comfort. It was automatic and distant.

"Where are you going?" she asked, voice cracking with panic.

Miles looked up to tell her he didn't know, but she wasn't looking at him; she was looking at Edgar.

"You can't leave me again!" Alice screamed, and Miles jerked back from her.

A heavy hand landed on his shoulder, turning him and pushing him toward the open door of Vic's truck. But Vic wasn't there. It would just be him and his dad. Miles tried to twist back to his momma, but his dad caught his arm hard and hoisted him up into the cab. He wanted to jump out and run for the big house and his grandpa, but his dad was standing in the way. All Miles could do was stare past him at his momma, willing her to do something.

Edgar levelled Alice with a stare. Miles had never seen anyone do that before. He just stared at her, no more smiles, and she wilted.

"Please," she said, her voice wobbling. "Don't leave me."

Edgar held the door to the truck but instead of slamming it shut, he angled his body to invite her in. "Fine," he said coldly, watching her all the while. "Get in."

Miles panted, nodding, almost reaching for her. Yes, he wanted her to come with them. Everything would be okay if his momma was with them. But her eyes widened, flicking back and forth between the truck and her husband. Her fingers clawed at the front of her dress, at the spot where Miles had been pressed against her.

"Edgar…" she tried, but her words fell away.

"Either wait here for me to come back, or get in," he said.

She took a step back, shaking her head, and Miles lost control of those tears he'd been so desperate to hold back. Why didn't she want to come with? Where were they going? "Momma—" he started but the door slammed shut between them.

Her hand flew to her mouth, clamping over it the way she did when she tried not to cry. He stared at her but she never looked back at him. She looked at the truck, at Edgar, but never met Miles's gaze.

His dad got in and they pulled away from the curb, down the street, and up through residential roads all the way past Wicker. They were heading north, toward the trails—toward the witch bridge.

CHAPTER FIFTY-TWO

Smoke curled over Wicker, bending in slow black spires up to the gray cloud cover.

Rebecca jogged from the Greenleigh house back to the car idling in the long driveway. She tossed a bag of William's clothes into the trunk, boxes of food and supplies already packed into the backseat beside her son.

"Where are we going?" Hannah asked, shoving another bag into the trunk. They'd all but fled the town when the bookshop went up in flames and a couple dozen armed residents of Wicker piled into trucks and headed up to the Darling land. Rebecca hadn't explained what happened—not then, not in front of William—but she'd told her in fast whispers when they went into the house to pack up their most important belongings.

Hannah had shaken her head like she might deny the truth—maybe argue that their friends and neighbors wouldn't turn on each other like that—but even she knew Harvey Darling wasn't quite one of them.

They pillaged their own home like hurried thieves. Hannah took her valuables—family heirlooms and jewelry. Rebecca didn't point out that it wasn't a fire coming their way, because she couldn't really be sure that it wasn't. Rebecca packed clothes, food, and jugs of water from the storage in the garage.

She leaned into the backseat to tug at William's seatbelt and took a moment to flash the worried kid a smile. "You're going to be okay, punkin," she said and meant it. William nodded and his little shoulders relaxed a fraction. Rebecca had never lied to her son, so he had no reason not to trust her.

She closed the door just as Hannah came around the car to her, keys held out in an offer to let her drive. Hannah usually drove, but she didn't know where they were going today.

Rebecca folded her wife's fingers over the keys, holding her closed fist between them and wincing at the flare of panic in the other woman's eyes. "No one's been able to drive all the way down the mountain to get cell service since yesterday. I tried this morning after I dropped Lotte off," she confessed, voice cracking on the name of her friend. She couldn't think about Lotte yet—couldn't imagine her burning in that shop while all their neighbors looked on, cheering. "But you can make it to the hunting cabin. You remember how to get there?"

Hannah started shaking her head and Rebecca smiled because she knew her wife was lying. Hannah loved directions—mostly giving them. She never forgot how to get someplace once she'd been there.

"Down the highway until the Walsh turn off. It's a dirt road so take it easy. You're not in a hurry. You keep to that road until it forks and then take a right. You can't miss the cabin." She pulled out a pair of keys and stuffed them into Hannah's jeans pocket. "The cabin has running water and electricity. I stocked the wood pile last time Wyatt and I were down there. You can do this. The Philipses might come and it's possible some of the Crowes too." Something in her heart hardened because it wasn't possible anymore. Lotte wouldn't have told either of her brothers about the invitation to the cabin and now that she was gone...

Hannah shook her head again, tears making her eyes shine brightly. "Don't make me. Becca, *please*, just get in the car."

Rebecca cringed, letting go of her hand to cup her face. "I can't leave, and we can't hide in that cabin forever. I have to figure out how to get you and William off the mountain."

Hannah's nose wrinkled when one of her tears escaped. She tried to turn her face out of her wife's touch, but Rebecca thumbed the tear away. "You would stay even if we could get down to Cyprus," she accused bitterly, voice breaking.

Rebecca wanted to argue, wanted to lie, but this wasn't the time for it. "It's our home. It's our land."

"It's just a place, Becca. It's not worth your life. We can have a home anywhere."

"It's a legacy and it's mine. No one was ever given a spot here easily, Han. *No one.* We cleared the land and we built our homes. We held onto it through storms and wolves. I won't be the one who lost it."

"That's insane," Hannah ground out, grabbing at Rebecca's arms. "Don't do this."

"You're right," Rebecca whispered, leaning in to press their foreheads together, breathing in deep the comforting scent of her. She had never been able to get enough—not of that fragrance on Hannah's skin or all the happiness her wife had given her. But knowing that it would never have been enough, not in a hundred years or a thousand, made it easier to let go. "Even if we could leave, I wouldn't. I won't give it up." She kissed her wife before she could repeat her pleas and her logic. Rebecca understood, but she also knew there was no other way. She tasted Hannah's tears in their kiss and when she pushed her back, she didn't look at her.

Rebecca shoved her hands into her pockets and took two steps back from the car. "Don't go farther than the turn off or you'll end up in Wicker again. And don't go walking in the woods. Just wait it out and I'll come for you when I can."

Hannah was quiet for so long that Rebecca finally dragged her gaze up to her wife. She was the picture of fury and heartache. She was all soft sweater and jeans, hair in a tidy ponytail and eyes pink with tears. But she radiated waves of emotion, of anger, disbelief, and strength. "I love you," she said, and the words were hard, like a curse and a promise and a hallelujah that wouldn't save anyone.

Rebecca smiled at her. "I love you too," she said.

CHAPTER FIFTY-THREE

What should have been an easy walk to the road became an endless trek.

Charlotte could swear the forest moved around them, the ground underfoot changing from one step to the next. They passed a boulder and when she looked back, it had vanished. They were lost but they kept moving, not sure what else to do. One second Harvey was by her side, and the next she was alone. Panic stole her breath, and she spun in a full circle. She spotted him, far off to her left and staring back at her, a mirror to her own shock and confusion.

They hurried back to one another, and he asked first, "Why did you run off?"

She shook her head and they both knew it had been the forest moving them in different directions.

They held hands after that, afraid of being lost and alone.

"I have no idea where we are," Harvey admitted.

She nodded because she didn't know either.

"Do we just keep walking?"

"What else can we do?" she asked. "We'll freeze if we don't get someplace eventually."

"And to think, a half-hour ago we were worried about burning to death…" he said with a smirk.

Charlotte stopped, their fingers still laced and forcing him to stop with her.

"Do you hear that?" she whispered. It was faint, but it pricked her nerves before she could even place it.

Harvey nodded and they started walking toward the sound. The closer they got, the clearer they heard it. Children crying. That pitched whine and sniffle. The small voice of a boy asking, "Momma?" again and again.

Charlotte realized where they were, and her hand tightened on Harvey's when she spotted the road through the trees with gray daylight bouncing off the eggplant purple hood of a van. Lila's van.

They hurried toward it, only breaking their handhold when they spotted Lila making her way into the woods, away from the car and the road. She had Winnie on her hip and Summer by the hand. The boys followed sullenly, both ashen with fear and bleary-eyed. "Momma," Greg kept muttering, drawn after her as though he and his brother were on an invisible thread.

What had happened to the happy family she saw that morning?

Before Charlotte could call out, her steps gave her away and Lila jerked to a stop. They all looked in her direction. Winnie sobbed and Summer sniffled.

"What are you doing?" Charlotte asked, whispering like something would hear them any second now and come running. That was exactly how she felt. There were things in the woods other than them now, things that would not be frightened off by people.

Lila looked her over, her gaze sliding off her shoulder to consider Harvey. She shifted Winnie on her hip, the little girl still in her footy pajamas with sleep tangles in her hair. "Wicker is damned. We're going into the woods where we belong."

Charlotte shivered from the cold. The kids had no shoes or jackets on. They had to be freezing. "Lila…"

"*She* won't harm us." Lila pressed her chin high. "We are sisters. We belong in the woods with mother nature and—"

"This isn't a spiritual movement," Charlotte snapped. "The Wicker Witch is real, and she is not looking for sisterhood."

"What do you know?" Lila yelled and the boys started crying.

Charlotte thought about the witch she had seen last night—her blood wet mouth and too many teeth. *"The rabbit does not ask why,"* had been her words. Charlotte took a step closer. "We're just rabbits in her woods, Lila. If she can't use you, she'll eat you."

Greg let out a thin, choking sound.

"Shut up!" Lila said. "You're lying and it's scaring them."

"*You're* scaring them," Charlotte said, taking another step closer. She softened her voice as much as she could, pleading now. "Go if you have to but let me take the kids home. They're cold, Lila. Look at them. They're cold."

Charlotte was so close now that Summer reached out and twisted her fingers in the fabric of her jacket.

A howl echoed through the trees, and the boys jumped away from the woods and closer to Charlotte and Harvey, their faces whipping from side to side, bulging eyes scanning the trees.

Lila forced a wobbling smile. "See? She's calling to us."

Harvey swore quietly behind her, and Charlotte shook her head tightly. "She's seen you and she sent the dogs, Lila. Get back in the car."

She hissed angrily. "No! She's calling us. We are welcomed here, not you!" She started to turn away and Charlotte grabbed Summer, pulling her from her mother's grip and pushing her behind herself. Harvey picked up the little girl and grabbed one of the boys, hauling them both back toward the road and the van, away from the woods.

"No!" Lila wailed.

Charlotte grappled with her for Winnie, an awkward struggle for something precious and fragile. Lila let go when Charlotte hooked an arm around the little girl's body, shouldering Lila and turning to lift the girl away. She took backward steps, arms shaking but holding Winnie to her chest. The four year old screamed out sobs, reaching for her mother.

Lila shivered, head flicking back and forth to look at the little girl and then at the dark woods. The howling got closer.

Charlotte took steps back, vision blurred with tears. "Come on, Lila. Get in the car and come home with us," she pleaded, believing that Lila had let go of Winnie because some part of her knew she was walking toward death.

Another howl broke through the trees, echoed by half a dozen others, so close now that Charlotte could feel her bones aching to run.

Jeremy stood frozen, shaking his head and gasping at swallows of air.

Charlotte fisted one hand in the back of his shirt and pulled him along with her, toward the road. "Lila!" she yelled, trying to command the woman to follow. "Get in the car!"

Lila shook her head slowly. "I am *not* prey. I am not like the rest of you. I am part of the earth. I am… I am more."

Charlotte turned away when they reached the edge of the trees. Harvey had started the van and put Summer and Greg in the backseat. She pushed Jeremy in with his siblings and closed the door, sliding into the front with Winnie still in her arms. She spared one last glance into the woods. The shadows were moving, the wolves circling Lila as she marched deeper into the forest. "Drive," Charlotte whispered, hand cupping Winnie's face to make sure she didn't look. "Now."

Harvey pulled away from the road and turned the van around. Charlotte looked back over her shoulder, over the heads of the kids, just in time to see one of the wolves dragging her sister-in-law down into the shadows.

"The rabbit does not ask why," the witch had said.

CHAPTER FIFTY-FOUR

Harvey drove them back into Wicker, bracing for danger the whole way.

But the mob on Green Street, the one that had broken his window and pulled him from his shop, was gone. Most of their cars were gone too. Broken glass and ashes glittered on the pavement and thick plumes of smoke rolled out of the charred cavity of his bookstore. Half-burned pages littered the street and skittered in the breeze with the autumn leaves. Long fingers of soot stretched up the side of the brick building next to his place.

Harvey had always thought the townsfolk might come for him one day—might beat him to death and pretend he had never been there—but he hadn't expected them to call him a witch and try to burn him.

"Where did they go?" Lotte whispered. She still had Winnie in her arms. The rest of the kids were in the back, singing a chorus of sniffles.

Harvey shook his head. Either the Wicker folk had been appeased by their deaths and gone home, or they'd left to find more victims.

He glanced at Lotte and then back to the street. He still couldn't believe she'd gone into a burning building for him, but he shouldn't be surprised. Charlotte Crowe could do anything and she had always been different from the rest of the town. He had been so hurt and angry when she took off for two years, but it had been eclipsed by the happiness when she returned. The mountain had been lonely without her, not that he'd ever said that.

Just like she'd never said she killed her brother the day she left.

She still hadn't said it, but he knew...because Charlotte Crowe could do anything.

He turned off the highway onto her street and then again onto her property.

They passed Alice's house, her car parked in the short driveway, and went on to the big house. Vic's truck was gone. Harvey wasn't sure if he should be hoping the man was gone or at home. The car was full of Vic's kids, after all, but he'd also tried to burn Harvey to death. That sort of shit would take at least a few days to get over.

As soon as Harvey put the car in park, Lotte climbed out. She still had the toddler on her hip. The kid had cried herself to sleep, chubby limbs dangling. She opened the back door and told the rest of the kids to get out and go inside with a tone Harvey had never heard from her before. Her nephews and niece didn't argue, still sniffling but climbing the steps to the house.

"Can you go up and get Aunt Henri?" Lotte asked, voice wavering now that the kids weren't in earshot.

Harvey brushed his hand against hers, nodding and turning toward the little path that cut from the side of the house up into the woods. He had been on the Crowe property enough to know it in the dark, probably because most of the times he had been there he'd been a teen sneaking around in the night to see Lotte. If he needed to, he could probably still climb the side of the house to her bedroom window.

He clawed a hand through his hair, pushing it back from his face as if there was a chance in hell he could make himself presentable before knocking on Henrietta Crowe's door. She had never liked him, but as far as he could tell, Henri didn't like anyone. And Harvey was very used to being disliked.

Stopping at the top of the steps, he stared at the little house. The door was open and the wind brought the stink of rot and piss to his nose.

The trees were sparse enough to see far and there was no one else around—no one sitting in wait. He took another step and noticed the tracks in the mud.

Wolves.

Instinct suggested he run, but the defiant nature of humanity pushed him forward. He had to be sure. What if she was hurt but alive?

He shouldered the open door into a full swing. A shotgun lay on the floor near his boot, the barrel splattered in blood. When his eyes adjusted to the deep shadows of the unlit cabin, his gaze followed the trails of blood smears on hardwood to the mangled lump on the floor. Shredded clothing, exposed bone, and a long braid—the wolves had eaten their fill.

He crouched slowly, never taking his eyes off the room, and picked up the gun. Stepping back, Harvey closed the door behind him. The wind played music in the trees, and he glanced up to see another bone chime, this one fresh and dripping.

Did all the dead become chimes on the mountain?

He pushed that thought away, checked to make sure the shotgun was loaded, and then snapped it shut. He moved fast but didn't quite run to the big house, afraid something would see it as an invitation to chase.

In the house, Lotte was arguing with her dad about getting the kids down to the Greenleigh cabin.

The old man wanted to stay in his house. "We don't need help from the Greenleighs. Edgar and Vic will—"

"Edgar is dead and Vic tried to burn Harvey alive," Lotte argued, voice hard.

Gerard looked from his daughter to Harvey in the doorway, his face rumpling in some twisted mess of sympathy and skepticism. Harvey could hear what the man was thinking, *"That's too bad, but he probably had it coming…"*

"Dad," Lotte implored, getting his attention again. "I'm going to go get Miles and then I'm taking all the kids down to the Greenleigh cabin. I want you to come with us and help me."

Gerard stared at her, visibly torn between his child asking him for help and his own will to stay right where he was.

Lotte turned away, giving him more time to come to a decision while she went to get Miles.

Harvey stepped back, out onto the porch ahead of her, and she stopped when she realized he was alone. The door clapped shut and it was just the two of them.

She looked at her aunt's shotgun in his hands and then back up at him, the question in her eyes and pain pulling at the corners of her mouth.

Harvey shook his head once.

She looked like he'd hit her. "How?"

"Wolf."

She took a step back and turned like she might throw-up. He thought she probably would if she had anything in her stomach right now. Instead, she nodded, took a deep breath, and pushed her hands against her ribs as if she could physically hold back the wave of grief.

"I-I have to get Miles. Grab whatever food is in the fridge, and blankets, and whatever else, and throw them in the van. We're going as far from Wicker as we can get." Her words came out strained and breathy, but she managed them. She didn't wait for him to agree. She just trusted that he'd do it and started across the yard in the direction of Alice's house.

Harvey went inside.

Gerard Crowe was still standing there by the door and the boys were sitting in the living room, still in their pajamas.

"Get dressed," Harvey said, and they blinked at him in surprise. "Jackets and shoes too," he added, leaving no room for discussion.

They jumped off the couch and ran upstairs.

"I…" Gerard started, looking at the front door.

Harvey hadn't put the shotgun down and wasn't quite ready to walk around Gerard Crowe to the kitchen. He didn't trust the man with his back.

Gerard swallowed and pushed his chin up like he'd come to some revelation. "I gotta go find my boys." He took a step toward the door.

Harvey stepped into his path, eyes narrowed. "There's one car and it's not for heading back into town," he warned.

Gerard looked up at him, glaring like he might have when Harvey was a teen running around with his daughter. "Get out of my way, Darling."

"Lotte asked you to help her, and you're going to steal the car and strand all these kids up here?"

"Crowes don't run from the mountain," he rasped. "They're safe right here."

"Your sister is dead," Harvey said without mercy, watching the disbelief in the old man's eyes. "A wolf ate her in her house while you sat right here." It was cruel to say, but,looking at that stubborn old man, he felt like being cruel.

Gerard's shoulders slumped and his eyes flicked to the door and then to the side, in the direction of the little cabin behind his house. He hurried past Harvey, ambling down the porch steps and then to the right, toward the path.

Harvey went out and took the keys from the van just in case Gerard came back and decided to go looking for his wayward boys.

CHAPTER FIFTY-FIVE

Charlotte had been torn between trying to talk sense into Alice and just sneaking in the back and stealing her nephew from his room. Both plans dissolved when she reached the yard and found Alice sitting on the front steps. She must have come out after they drove by.

The woman hugged herself tightly, eyes swollen from crying and tears still wet on her face. "I thought you were dead," she confessed with a funny little laugh. "I thought you'd burned…"

"Yeah. Thanks for that," Charlotte muttered, stopping far out of reach. She hadn't seen Alice in the mob, but she wasn't surprised to find out she'd been there. Stuffing her hands into her pockets, Charlotte wrapped cold fingers around the small revolver, eyeing the open front door for any sign of Edgar.

"You shot him," Alice said, staring at the ground between them. "Again."

Charlotte looked at the rough stones of the walkway where Alice had fixed her gaze. The drops of blood were so dark against the wet rock that they almost vanished. She glanced around again. "Is Edgar here?" She almost choked on the words.

Alice smiled like there was a joke there. "No."

Charlotte nodded slowly, gaze flicking past Alice again and into the dark house. "Miles!" She would take him and run, even if he didn't want to go. She'd pick him up and carry him if she had to.

Alice let out a sob. "He's not here."

Charlotte's heart sank. They had been friends once—or, at least, family. She wasn't sure what they were now. "What have you done?" It came out in a whisper, strangled by a gut-wrenching fear of the answer. "Alice… Where is he?"

"I think she heard my heart," Alice whispered, eyes swollen from crying. "I wanted Edgar back so much. She must have heard my heart. He says I made a deal with her."

"What are you talking about?"

"A deal. A *trade.* I got Edgar back." She stared at her hands, fingertips bloody stubs of rough scabs. Thick cuts crisscrossed her palms and forearms.

"What did you give her in return?"

Alice shook with another laugh, tear wet eyes turning up to Charlotte. Her pupils were blown wide, pulsing dark, and Charlotte took a step back, suddenly afraid that one would rise out of her eye with slender spider legs pressing into her face.

"I don't remember." She heaved a broken laugh around the words. "But my basement is full of dead things. I think I made the chimes… And now," she swallowed hard, "he took Miles again. It was the same as before. I let him go."

Charlotte took a step back, and then another, her heart in her throat. "Why?"

Alice stared back at her through tears, misery on her lips in the shape of a smile. She shook her head and shrugged against her life's worst choice.

Charlotte turned, staggering down the rough walkway to the road. She struggled to think straight, pulse hammering against her ears. Her vision swayed for a second, making a blur of the trees and houses. She started walking, then jogging. She stopped when she was close enough to the big house that Harvey looked up from packing plastic bags of food into the back of the van.

"I'll bring Miles to the cabin! Just go as soon as you can!" she yelled.

His frown deepened but he didn't argue or ask questions. Harvey nodded once and she turned and started running. She didn't follow the road, chancing a corner of her own property to get to the highway faster. Would Edgar take Miles to the same spot as before? Would she be too late this time? Would he be standing over his son's body with that twisted little smile, just like with the fawn?

CHAPTER FIFTY-SIX

Rebecca stood in her backyard and waited, rifle in her arms and jacket zipped up tight. "What do you want?" she yelled into the forest.

A low growl answered.

Nerves clawed up her spine, screaming for her to run, but Rebecca raised her rifle at the woods and waited.

A wolf burst from the trees, racing toward her with lips curled back from saliva-slick teeth. Heavy paws ripped up chunks of grass with every step. She aimed and fired, blowing the beast back into a tumble that landed it almost in the exact same spot where it had emerged.

A second and a third wolf jumped forward. She took three steps back as she fired, one bullet for each, breaking skulls and sending them both to the ground.

The first spasmed back to life, kicking and whining as it struggled to its feet again. It staggered, sluggish, blood dripping off the thick tongue hanging from its maw.

Rebecca thumbed more bullets into her rifle before taking aim again.

The wolf got its feet under it, no longer shaking, and stepped closer. The other two twitched back to life on the ground behind it.

"Coward!" Rebecca screamed, not at the wolves but at the witch who had sent them. She shot the first one again, blowing a bullet through an eye socket this time.

It staggered but it didn't fall, swaying as blood rolled down its face.

The woods groaned and the wolves whimpered as though hearing a whistle she could not. They dragged themselves away, disappearing back into the trees.

She never saw the witch approach. It was suddenly there, standing at the very edge of Rebecca's yard and staring back at her.

"Devil," Rebecca whispered hatefully. "You have no right to be here."

The witch grinned.

"God is with me," Rebecca insisted. She'd gone to church almost every Sunday since she was a child. She knew God. She believed. Everyone in her family had believed. And knowing that this monster existed only made her more certain she had been taught right.

The smile vanished and the witch took a step closer, daylight doing nothing to push away all the darkness it brought with it from the woods. Rebecca wanted to lift her rifle and take a shot, but her arms wouldn't move. Cosmic eyes looked her over and then glanced past her shoulder, around her, and above her. At first, she thought the monster meant to mock her, but it was worse than that. The creature was really looking, sifting through what was there—what only the witch could see. And then those dark eyes settled on Rebecca again and the corner of that wide mouth quirked piteously. *"If you say so."*

Rebecca swallowed back a miserable groan. Never had she felt more alone. "What do you want?" she asked again, heart racing and gloved fingers holding tightly to her weapon. *Shoot. Lift it and shoot,* she screamed in her mind but couldn't convince her limbs to work while that beast still stared at her. What if she took the shot and it did nothing? Her stomach twisted, feeling sick under that gaze.

"Nothing," the creature answered.

Rebecca winced, the voice like wood splitting in her ear. "Then get off my property and away from my mountain!"

"Property," the creature tasted the word and then grinned in a flash of teeth so bright that no shadow could hide them. *"The mountain is mine. Has always been mine."*

Rebecca shook her head stubbornly. "No. We—"

"I remember you," the witch interrupted, voice grinding out like there were stones and branches lodged in its throat, pressed between slick flesh. *"I remember the smell of your blood and the sound of your greed. You want the mountain, but the mountain is mine. I built it. I moved the rocks and pushed the ground into these hills. I planted the trees and the*

bushes. I invited the birds, the bugs, and the prey. There is no village on my mountain but Wicker—no village but my village."

Rebecca shuddered, body jerking a step back without thinking. She was crying despite all efforts not to. "No."

"Yes." The ground rumbled beneath the word, waves crashing behind it, the sound straining Rebecca's skull until she feared it would crack.

"Why?" she pressed, almost begging.

The creature's smile faded, not out of contempt but boredom.

Rebecca moved as fast as she could, lifting her rifle. Her vision blurred but she aimed. They were so close. It would be impossible to miss.

But darkness swept in, like a great shadow cast from above, blotting out the woods in front of her before receding just as quickly.

The witch disappeared, leaving Rebecca alone at the edge of her yard, staring into the wild—painfully aware that the forest was no longer staring back at her.

Tears ran down her cheeks because though the witch had not answered in words, she had heard the whisper in the frigid wind. No village but *the witch's* village—there because the creature had allowed it. Because it had amused the witch.

Because it had enjoyed the easy prey.

CHAPTER FIFTY-SEVEN

Charlotte didn't linger on Green Street. She found her dad's truck where she'd left it, still parked behind Harvey's, and sped off.

She drove up the curve of the mountain, for the first time in her life feeling the sinister presence of Mount Bell looming over her, watching her every move. Was the whole mountain conspiring against her? She had heard Bell called a benign tumor on the side of Mount Grayson. Maybe it wasn't so benign, after all.

Pulling off the highway and onto the rough path toward the parking area for the trails, Charlotte held her breath. What if the truck wasn't there? What if she didn't know where to find Edgar? What if she was just too late?

The truck was there but the relief was short lived because Miles wasn't anywhere in sight. She parked behind him and sat in the truck long enough to refill the bullets in her revolver. Her hands shook. Would she have to kill her brother again? Would it take this time? Charlotte got out, leaving the door open, and trudged into the woods. She followed her memory into the steps of her past, expecting to find Miles standing by the same tree and Edgar taking aim.

But they weren't there. She turned a full circle and the forest went deathly quiet. The treetops continued to sway in the wind but there was no more sound. It wasn't hushed, it was muted.

Her skin tightened and that all too familiar chill clawed its way up her back, sending sharp pain shooting through her skull to the back of her eyes.

The witch saw her.

Charlotte stood still. The witch stepped out from behind a tree too thin to have hidden it. Charlotte swallowed back a scream, her mind fighting the unreality of the creature even as she looked straight at it.

The witch's shoulders pressed back, head tipping to the side as it studied Charlotte, seeing through her and into parts of her soul she'd never even looked at herself. The witch's mouth quirked, full lips pulling into a blood-red sneer.

"Where is Miles?" Charlotte asked, swallowing hard. She had other questions too. What did it want? When would it let them leave? Was Victor out there somewhere? Was he alive? But none of it was as important as finding Miles.

"We could trade," the witch spoke, the ragged voice curling against her ear even though the creature's mouth had not moved.

"No!" Charlotte snapped, thinking of Alice and Sheriff Summerfield. Making a deal hadn't saved either of them.

The air vibrated between them. Charlotte winced back, hands flying to her ears when the cracking of trees rammed her eardrums.

"He is mine now. You can trade or you can go without."

Charlotte cried out, rocks cracking inside her head, her hands against her ears doing nothing but holding the sounds inside. Her knee hit the ground and she heaved, spitting up what little her stomach had.

"You cannot leave unless I let you. Everything on my mountain belongs to me. Make a deal or be eaten."

Charlotte shuddered, one hand pressing into the dry leaves and cold earth. It didn't make sense. If everything on the mountain belonged to the witch, then why did she need a deal? She gulped for air, trying to get enough into her lungs to make words. She couldn't. Tears slid down her cheeks. Her skull strained, the ground shifting under her, moving through her fingers.

"Tell me what you want."

She sobbed but shook her head stubbornly. Everything on the mountain did not belong to the witch. The crows driven through the diner window had not belonged to the witch and neither did the people until they made their deals. If Charlotte made a deal, she'd be as good as dead and no matter what she wished for, this monster wouldn't give her what she wanted.

She remembered the words of her family, whispered like a warning by her mother, Crowes did not make deals with devils. Did a witch count as a devil? How could it not?

Charlotte gasped when long fingers grabbed her face, tipping her head up and forcing her to stare at the witch. Those dark eyes seethed and teeth gnashing. *"Just words,"* it spoke in Charlotte's mother's voice, a fat bodied spider crawling from the witch's hair down its cheek.

Charlotte would have laughed if only she could stop crying—if only she could breathe.

"You can make up all the words for me you like, but you will never know. You will never understand."

Charlotte sucked hard, finally filling her lungs and shuddering out a question. "Like the rabbit can't understand the wolf?"

Those lips twitched and curled right in front of her face, something between a grimace and a grin. *"Like the wolf cannot understand the stars."* The witch pulled her up off her knees by the grip it held on her face, forcing her into an awkward stance, dragging her face closer and closer until she could taste the stale blood on the creature's breath. *"You would know true horror if you could only see from my eyes."*

Tears rolled down Charlotte's cheeks and around the talons that cut into her face. "Then why are you torturing us? What do you want?"

"I am a shaper of the world. I do not waste, and I do not forget a good bloodline."

Charlotte stared. "What?"

The witch leaned in and ran its tongue along Charlotte's cheek. It traced the talons piercing her skin, lapping up blood, tears, and sweat. The beast hummed and nodded, as though confirming its own thoughts. *"Do not make a waste of yourself."*

Charlotte watched the spider crawl down the witch's jaw, long black legs reaching out and catching a coil of hair, swinging free and descending, closer and closer to her face. She tried to pull back, but the talons held fast, buried in her skin, thumb scraping her jawbone. She cried harder and her tears salted the wounds.

Gunfire exploded through the woods far to the northwest.

The witch jerked back, head turning toward the sound and eyes narrowing, as though it could see through the distance. Maybe it could. Maybe it could see the whole forest.

The monstrous hand detached from Charlotte's face, dropping her to the ground. When she looked up, the witch was gone. She dry-heaved, blood oozing from the fresh wounds on her cheeks, dotting the leaves and pine needles on the ground. Using a tree, she climbed to her feet, leaning into the rough bark while she caught her breath. The weight of the witch's attention had vanished just as suddenly as the creature itself.

Momentarily free, Charlotte started moving again, first thinking to escape and then remembering why she had come out there. She had to find Miles.

The ground jerked under her, almost knocking her to her knees again. The trees pressed back, and she stood in front of the old witch bridge that should have been a twenty-minute walk northeast of where she had started.

She swallowed hard and walked across it. From the middle of the little bridge, she could see up the hillside and make out the smokestack breathing clouds through the trees.

The house. If the witch had taken Miles to bait her into a deal, would it hide him there?

Charlotte ran up the trails, making her way north and leaving the beaten footpath when it bent to the east. She caught a glimpse of a dark, gnarled forest and then, in her next step, it was gone. The trees shifted around her and suddenly she stood one step from the witch bridge again—back where she had started.

She choked back a scream, afraid of the very real possibility that the witch would hear her if she let it out. Pushing her fists against her sides, she took a long, deep breath to calm herself. She needed to think–needed to find Miles–needed to get to that house.

There were tracks in the mud leading up to the bridge—the ones with hoofprints inside footprints, each going in opposite directions. They were the witch's steps. Which one was facing forward?

Charlotte stared across the little bridge. It had been a meeting place when they were kids, and a doorway into the woods, inviting them to explore. But back then, they had always covered their eyes or gone over backward—so the witch wouldn't see them.

Backward. She turned around, a throb of panic in her chest at not being able to see where she was going. But seeing what was coming wouldn't make her any more prepared to handle it. Sometimes, the best thing to do was just not to be noticed.

Charlotte took backward steps over the bridge and then turned up the trails. She had to go slowly, but she stayed turned around the whole way, walking up the mountain paths and working her way north—always north—until she was far from any beaten trail. The tree cover grew thicker and thicker until it seemed that day had retreated into night. She almost lost her balance, her shoes sinking deeper with every step across the soggy ground.

Giant, crooked trees curled overhead, branches reaching for the earth rather than the sky, and decorated with large bone chimes. They clanked together in a melody that tried and failed to hide the humming of voices beneath.

Her gaze cut back and forth across the dark wood, but there was no one else there and she didn't dare call out.

Another step and she was out of the twisted forest, staring down the tunnel of it in her wake. Sunlight made her wince and she lifted one arm to shield her eyes. Tall grass whipped against her thighs, the ground even soggier than it had been in the forest. Mud and blood splattered her shoes, slowly soaking in to wet her socks. Her stomach twisted at the thick stink of rot rising off the soil, her steps churning up gore between knots of thin roots.

Charlotte's back hit a wall and she almost screamed, clapping a hand over her mouth to hold it back. Her chest heaved and her eyes stung, staring across that short clearing of grass into the dark tunnel of trees that had led her there. She waited for the witch to appear, to burst from a shadow or rise from the violent soil. After long seconds, she tore her hand from her own face and pressed it against the stone wall at her back—smooth and cold.

Down the hillside, between the trees, she glimpsed a road. And, when she squinted, Charlotte made out the little creek and the old witch bridge.

CHAPTER FIFTY-EIGHT

She groped at the cool wall, turning around at last. The witch's cottage was no cottage at all. It was the exposed stone face near the peak of Mount Bell, a crooked chimney sticking out and exhaling smoke in the shadow of the mountain's snowy true peak, Mount Grayson.

Charlotte kept a hand on the stone wall as she crept around it and toward the opening. A small, frightened sound lurched up in her throat when she saw it. The doorway was a mouth carved into the rock. It grinned menacingly with flat teeth, each one the size of her hand.

One step in and the reek of smoke and blood hit her hard, filling her lungs and making her gag. Charlotte pressed forward, forcing herself inside. The floor descended into steep stone steps twirling down the throat of the mountain.

She dragged one hand along the wall for balance. With her other hand, she dug the revolver out of her pocket and held it close to her chest. Her eyes adjusted to the darkness as she continued down, the daylight above vanishing and a glow below inviting her deeper still. She moved down off the last step onto soft earth. Embers gleamed inside a giant oval hearth to one side of the round room. Half-eaten remains and picked over bones littered the dirt ground. The ravaged remains of Andrew Caller lay beside the body of a large stag, both pulled into pieces with chests opened wide.

Her breath came in quick gasps, gaze darting around the shadows and shapes as she inched along the wall. The only furniture of any kind was a huge nest on one side of the room, made of branches and moss all tangled together in a heap. Edgar sat in a squat beside it, looking infinitely patient.

Charlotte stopped moving when his dark gaze landed on her. One of his pupils squirmed, bulging with little black legs pushing at his eyelid, but he didn't seem to notice.

Amusement quirked one side of his mouth. "You actually came here for him? Why?"

Before she could answer she heard Miles whine. The boy was crouched against one corner of the hearth, hands cupping his ears and eyes squeezed shut just like when she carried him back to town all those years ago. But he wasn't five anymore. His fingers curled in the yarn of his hat, head rocking back and forth as though to shake out the new reality of the mountain.

"Why?" Edgar demanded, voice echoing in the chamber.

She jumped, gaze snapping back to him.

He stood in the middle of the room, taking the last few steps to put himself between her and Miles.

"You're already dead, Edgar," she reminded them both, squaring her shoulders and gathering the nerve to lift the revolver in her hand. Would it do anything this time? How many times could she shoot him?

"Why do you keep choosing this kid over me, Lotte? I'm your brother." Before she could marvel at the hint of hurt rattling his voice, Edgar rushed her. She fired right as his hand closed around her wrist, the barrel to his chest. The bullet blew through him, and they fell together.

"I'm your brother!" he screamed, his voice wet.

She kicked at the soft ground, trying to squirm out from under him, but the soil shifted, air bubbles breaking the surface as it changed from solid ground to thick mud. His weight bore down on her, pushing her shoulder deeper until half her chest was buried. Fresh panic made her kick harder. They were sinking. He pried the gun from her fingers. She flailed, legs going under, knees nudging sticks and rocks in the mud.

"Fuck!" she managed to grind out before his shoulder pushed her head down into the muck.

Stones jabbed at her side and when they shifted, she felt the curve of a skull. Not rocks. *Bones*. She pushed at the smooth rod of what she imagined was a femur. The bones made room for her, the weight of the mud and her own brother driving her deeper. And then she heard the *thump thump* shuddering through the ground around her, louder than it had been in the tunnel. Charlotte jerked in every direction, searching blindly for a way out, drowning and terrified of the moment she would have to inhale and draw all that rot into her lungs.

Thump, thump.

It was too steady, too loud, and too strong to be her own heartbeat. Edgar's unrelenting weight on her back pushed her deeper.

Thump, thump.

She tried to scream, the mud so thick that she could barely get her breath out.

Thump, thump.

And then she inhaled, sucking blood and decay into her body.

Charlotte gasped, suddenly standing in the hallway of her home with daylight filtering in through the front windows and the world blissfully still. She inhaled clean breaths and blinked at the room. A shadow moved down the hall, in the living room, the figure just out of sight but already she knew it was nothing frightening; she knew everything about this place and this moment.

"Baby, hurry up!" her momma called with a smile in her voice.

Charlotte trembled, tears in her eyes. She took a step forward, desperate to see her momma again, and the moment broke.

Thump, thump.

She was outside, standing in the middle of Green Street, but the town was different—the buildings sparse and the road nothing but trodden dirt. The sky changed overhead, night and day, clouds rolling in, rain falling, blue skies, more clouds, snow, wind, the sun shining, the snow melting. Her head spun and for a second, she thought she was going to be sick.

The town vanished one building at a time, right before her eyes. The trees filled in all around her. She hadn't moved from the spot where Wicker would be, but the world had slid backward around her. Wolves ran by, soundless, as though she was in a bubble only watching her surroundings, unable to hear or feel them.

Thump, thump.

Another rotation of seasons rushed by and then slowed enough to let her see the large snowflakes drifting down through the evening forest.

Movement flickered across the scene, dragging her eye through the trees to lock onto the stag running through the woods—bursting from one sliver of light to the next and leaping the ground cover. It jerked to a stop right in front of her, head high and eyes wide. Large ears flicked side to side and suddenly all that muscle went still. It listened, keen mind focused on its surroundings.

She heard nothing but that steady heartbeat in the mountain. She could only see, and from her place in the nothing, she saw more than the stag. The shadows moved, slithering behind it, and the witch neared. The stag waited and Charlotte imagined it sensing the wrongness—sensing a predator in the woods. Its head turned to the right, one antler almost piercing her bubble of time and space. The points were sharp, some still red with the blood of rivals. Not all prey were soft. But not even this beast stood a chance. The witch had laid eyes on him and decided his fate.

The witch was exactly as Charlotte had seen it today, unchanged by time. Lips curled back, colorless and parched, but Charlotte imagined they would be red again soon.

The stag lifted a hoof, hesitating to take a step, unsure which way to run. Were its instincts at war? There was no right choice. There was no way it could go that would lead it to safety.

Thump, thump.

It set its hoof down, strong body turning in the first lurch of a run.

The witch was there in a flash, one hand sliding over that strong neck. Talon fingers stroked over fur and the stag jerked back, trying to swing its body away. Another hand came up, and the witch's arm disappeared from fingertips to elbow in the animal's chest. It tried to rear back, one leg kicking at nothing. The witch, so close to the shape of a woman, lifted the stag on its arm. One hand continued to stroke, reaching up its neck to slide black fingers along its jaw while the other ripped apart its insides.

Charlotte didn't blink, trying to take in the whole scene as well as that strange face. There was nothing there she could recognize—not excitement, fear, or fury. The witch looked on, considering its prey in the final moments before the stag gave one last kick. It dropped the body, pulling its arm free in the process. Blood dripped off long talons, joining the growing circle staining the snow around the dead animal. Wet fingers curled around an antler and the witch pulled the body like it weighed little more than a paper husk.

Thump, thump.

The witch paused. It tipped its head up at the sky. Charlotte stared, unable to look away. The whole world shuddered around her. For a moment, she understood. She knew the witch was not a witch, but something old and inhuman—something that would devour as it pleased and live forever wild. This creature had played games with the people who had come to the mountain and tried to settle there; it had made bargains out of amusement, to build the world just as it pleased on a foundation of bones and broken hearts. The witch had lured the deer, wolves, and bears to the woods with plants and smaller prey just as it had lured the humans with seams of gold in the rocks.

But though the witch had built the mountain, it did not control the weather. It was a beast of this world too. And just as the storm had cleared the mountain and released the witch from its home, so had it once brought the rockslide that caged it. And from the puddle deep in the cave, the witch had watched the mountain—just as Charlotte watched it now, time rolling and knotting in all directions.

The witch, standing in the place where Wicker would one day be built, in a time long before Charlotte's own, turned and looked at her. Its head tipped to the right, birdlike and predatory. Talons twitched at its side and that long body pivoted away from its meal, facing Charlotte through time.

Thump, thump.

Charlotte tried to back away, tried to run, but she was frozen in place.

The witch's mouth curled into an offended snarl, and it lurched toward her.

Shaking her head, she tried to speak, but could only spit up mud, suddenly choking on it.

The witch thrust both arms at her, talons slicing through the air, and Charlotte feared it would snatch her right out of time.

She jerked back, chest aching where she was sure she had been shoved by the witch. Everything was dark when she lifted her heavy head from the muck, coughing up gore in a desperate bid to clear her lungs and get air.

Edgar cursed and fell back, slipping off her and into the mud.

Charlotte scrubbed a hand over her face, shaving the sludge from her skin and opening her eyes. The ground was only inches of mud now, no longer a sinking pit of it. Edgar crawled to his feet, almost as drenched as her and looking frightened of the depth that had been there moments ago, driving him to the edge of the room once more. Had he seen something in it too?

Charlotte shuddered, rot staining every breath she drew. She was covered, head to toe, in the gore of the mountain. Crawling away from her brother, she made her way toward the opposite wall. In the filth underhand, she found a slender bone and kept it, hiding it clumsily against her sleeve when she struggled to her feet. Her legs shook, her breaths still so loud that they echoed in the stone chamber.

"I didn't choose Miles over you," she croaked, trying to distract Edgar while she caught her breath.

He was on his feet and stalking toward her, skirting the middle of the room. She had forgotten how tall he was—probably because she had never been afraid of him before, not like this, not for herself.

"I didn't kill you to save him." She panted, standing now, her legs still trembling but managing to hold her up.

He stopped, almost sliding in the mud.

Charlotte met his gaze, tired down to her bones and beyond the shock of having her reality turned upside down. She could do insanity. She had done it before—for him. "I killed you because I love you. Because you're my brother and my responsibility. You are mine and I was the only one who could do it—the only one I would let do it."

He stared at her, surprised and maybe a little disbelieving. She imagined the concept would be hard for him to understand. Her brother only saw the world from where he stood—from his own wants and needs. Rabbits and wolves. She slid the bone she had picked up along her thigh, lowering it until she fisted the thinnest part. She dragged deep another breath and then moved it in front of herself. Grabbing it in both hands, she snapped the bone in half. The ends splintered into jagged points, gleaming white like teeth from their coating of filth.

"And I'll do it again, Edgar. I'll kill you every damn day if I have to."

Betrayal rippled across his features and he launched himself at her, closing in fast. When he reached for her neck she let him have it. He continued to pedal the ground, driving her back until she hit the stone wall. With a roar, he lifted her off her feet and closed her airway in his grip. Large, shadowy spots stretched across her vision, her skin electric with all the bruises and cuts she'd gathered over the last two days. His fingertips dug into her neck, but she didn't struggle. She didn't reach for his wrist or kick at his legs.

She stabbed one of the bone shards into the side of his neck.

Two times.

Three times.

He screamed but he didn't let go.

Charlotte's lungs were going to burst, her face hot and her eyes blinking wildly against the loss of vision. He squeezed and she realized he meant to snap her neck like she had snapped the bone. In his right eye, the spider legs flailed, past his lashes and pushing at his lid, feeling out the shape of his socket in a frantic bid for escape.

Escape.

Charlotte suddenly hated that spider. No one was going to escape if she couldn't get Miles out of here—not even the spider.

She brought her arm up and stabbed the second bone shard into his eye, right into the spider's back, shoving it in until the legs were gone, stuffed back inside her brother's skull.

Edgar flung himself away from her, falling onto the floor with a sudden splash, the muddy center of the hut deep again and waiting to be filled.

She landed on her feet, almost falling to her knees.

Edgar began to sink.

Breath wheezing in her throat, Charlotte lunged forward, grabbing one of his legs with both hands and pulling hard. She slid and kicked at the loose ground to keep him from going under. She hugged him, grabbing at limbs and wet clothes until she pushed them both to the solid edge, away from any chance of escape. He twitched, gurgling sounds that were almost words. She rolled him onto his back near the steps and cringed, the knob at the end of the bone pressed into his socket like a bloated, sightless eye.

He stared up at her with the other, body twitching and jerking in her grip as blood gushed from the jagged tears in his throat.

Charlotte leaned over him and stared back. "I love you," she reminded him, but there was no kindness in those words. It was a threat. "Don't come back."

The light went out of his eye and a final breath rattled from his chest, quieter than the gunshot that echoed in her memory from the last time she had killed him—but loud enough to stay with her forever.

CHAPTER FIFTY-NINE

Charlotte staggered back a step and then another, leaning against the wall and taking deep breaths. For too long she stared at the puddle in the center of the room, her memories of what she had seen in there already adopting a dreamy quality—slipping away from her as though her mind simply didn't want to keep them, afraid the madness would infect the rest of her memories. When the mud pulsed in quiet, calling heartbeats, she recoiled.

Her gaze landed on Miles and, for a split-second, she was surprised to see him there. She had forgotten him. He hadn't moved from his crouch against the wall near the hearth. He screamed when she pulled him to his feet, but she didn't stop to console him. She didn't have the air for it in that pit. They needed to get out. They needed to get far before the witch came back. Charlotte dragged him along the side of the room to the stairs and started climbing, never letting go.

"Aunt Lotte?" Miles half-choked out the words, arm still jerking against her vice grip on his jacket sleeve.

She looked back at him once, mud wet hair slapping her cheek. He heaved a little sigh of relief when she met his gaze and, finally, he stopped dragging his feet. The climb up was harder than the descent, the stairs steep and her body so battered and tired that pain rippled from every limb, but she never even thought about stopping.

When they got to the top, they stumbled blindly out of the dark into the bright gray daylight. She still didn't let go of his sleeve or slow down, dragging him across the soggy field and through the dark patch of forest. She started running with Miles in tow when they reached the woods.

Gunfire came in bursts to the west—automatics and shotguns. Less than before and somewhere not far off at all, she heard a man screaming at the top of his lungs. Wolves howled in that same direction, answering one another.

She pulled Miles away from the sounds, staggering toward where the trails should be. She needed to get him to a road, find the truck, and take him down the mountain to the Greenleigh cabin—out of the way while they figured out what to do next. *Next.* That seemed like an impossibly faraway concept.

The ground changed and both she and Miles tripped, falling to their knees.

"Where are we?" he asked in a hushed voice.

Charlotte blinked, recognizing nothing until she realized they were facing north rather than south.

The sound of gunfire and wolves were to their left now, farther away. She forced herself to get up again. Every inch of her hurt, from skin down to bone, and her throat burned. She wanted to stay down and sleep. She wanted to close her eyes and give up. But instead, she grabbed Miles by the arms and hoisted him to his feet.

"That man…" he said. "I don't think he was my dad."

"He's dead," Charlotte replied, because it was the only thing she could think of. His dad was dead. That man, that monster, *his dad*, was dead. Charlotte pulled Miles into another hurried walk, away from the howling and screaming. She looked around at the trees, frantic for some sign of a road.

Miles squeezed her hand. "Can we leave?"

She laughed before she could stop herself, her voice raw when she spoke, "I'm trying, kid."

The forest changed again, and she bit back a scream, pausing to listen for the sounds of wolves or people. This time there was only the creaking of trees and whistle of birds. The ground sloped gently, so she followed it, down to where the bushes grew thick and the trees thin. It reminded her of the woods behind the Greenleigh house.

Hope had barely begun to bloom in her chest when she spotted the edge of a yard and the silhouette of the house at the end of the clearing. She mumbled a *'thank you'* to no one at all and pulled Miles into a run toward the lawn beyond the trees. Maybe Rebecca hadn't sent Hannah and William down to the cabin yet. Miles could go with them. She pushed back branches and kicked her way through the bushes. She was almost there—only two steps from breaking through the edge of the forest and landing on the imagined safety of that trimmed grass.

The gunshot clapped against her ears, leaving a ringing behind that stunned her into stillness. No. That wasn't right. The sound hadn't stopped her—the weight against her chest had. It pushed and pushed, and she landed hard on her back, arching when the weight bearing down on her turned into pain. She half-expected to sink into the ground like she had in the witch's cave.

Miles stood over her, his eyes so wide they strained his face, bulging with tears rolling right off them and down his cheeks. Charlotte tried to scream but her lungs were in a vice. She was still in the woods, staring up at the swaying tops of the trees. Finally, her breath heaved out of her, forming a cloud against the cold air, leaving in a gust like her soul itself rising from her body.

No, she thought, hands groping at the pain in her chest, as though it were something she could wrap her fingers around and toss aside. Heat gushed out of her, between her fingers, and she blinked hard to see past a rise of tears.

Greenleigh slid to her knees beside her, shaking her head. She pulled Charlotte's hands away from her chest and turned a shade of green-gray. Rebecca pushed her palms down in their place and Charlotte opened her mouth wide, wanting to scream but only getting out a breathy gurgle that sounded wet and tasted like iron.

Greenleigh's lips moved, apologizing and promising to get her to the doctor.

Charlotte knew at once what had happened and she gave all the credit for the mastery of her death to the witch in the woods. It was cruel—to see her survive Summerfield and Edgar only to be shot down by her own best friend. It was just as her family had always warned: *"That Greenleigh will be the death of you, Charlotte Crowe."*

"We have to get you up," Greenleigh said. "We have to get you to the car."

The trees swayed overhead, and this time Charlotte could see an eagerness to their movements—an excitement that made their branches quiver. She had never known before how wicked trees were.

"Can't feel my legs," Charlotte wheezed out. "Can't-Can't move them…"

A wolf howled, close by. Greenleigh's head snapped up to scan the woods and Miles pressed his hands over his ears again.

Charlotte coughed hard, trying to breathe but her lungs were wet. She was drowning again.

Greenleigh continued to hold pressure to the wound on her chest, but her expression changed, eyes narrowing. Charlotte knew that look—she was trying to think of a plan, of a way to make this work when she already knew it couldn't. Greenleigh knew there were no options left. They both did.

Charlotte heard her name on the howling of the wolves. She could hear it like a voice so clear that she didn't understand how she had ever not understood before.

She reached up and grabbed at the sleeve of Greenleigh's jacket, pulling until her friend looked down at her, eyes wild with guilt and fear. "Take him," Charlotte gargled the words, tears making her vision blurry. "And…" She convulsed, pain ripping through her chest, squeezing her lungs and drumming her heart.

One of Greenleigh's bloody hands cupped her cheek, leaning over her with tears in her eyes. "I'm so sorry."

It was a small relief, that she wouldn't argue. Charlotte knew if it had been just the two of them, Greenleigh would have stayed and tried to defend her even after she died—just to keep her from the dogs. But they weren't alone. Greenleigh would understand that there was no choice left. The wolves were coming, and Miles was still standing there.

Charlotte grabbed at the back of her friend's neck, dragging her face down close. "Go backward. Her home. Close the door again. She was trapped before," she choked out. It wasn't close to enough explanation, but she couldn't get the air for more. All she had left was a hissed, "Run."

She let go and Greenleigh nodded, her hand leaving Charlotte's chest. The wound bled freely. Greenleigh pulled Miles from Charlotte's sight, just as the howling grew deafening.

Charlotte would never make it out of the forest, let alone off the mountain.

The wolves growled, the sound low and close—so close that the heat of their breaths puffed across her icy skin.

The trees lashed at one another high above. Greedy for the best view? She had been so close to the end. So close to making it out.

Something crawled hurriedly across the ground toward her head and she winced, expecting the jaws of a wolf to clamp over her face.

But the body that scampered to her didn't strike. The witch leaned on all fours over her, its blood-smeared face appearing upside down over her own. The tangles of mud-clumped hair curtained both of them, brushing the dirt and crisp autumn leaves on either side of Charlotte's head, blocking out the woods and making those seconds together horribly private.

"I heard your plea," the witch cooed with all the gentleness of crushing rocks.

"I didn't plea," Charlotte choked out, her words wet and barely audible.

The witch grinned, black tongue rolling along Charlotte's bottom lip to gather up blood and filth. She hummed thoughtfully overhead, as though considering something in the taste. *"Yes. I accept your terms."*

Charlotte twitched, trying to swallow but there was too much blood in her throat. She coughed hard, splattering both of their faces with red rain. The witch didn't appear to mind the misting. "No. I asked for nothing," Charlotte tried, barely able to recognize her own voice, each word more mangled than the last.

"Oh, but I hear it in your blood, in your failing heart, in your dying body…"

"I'm not…" Charlotte tried but this time she couldn't get out all the words. She couldn't get air when she sucked. She clawed at her own chest, body jerking side to side on the ground. Tears rolled off her eyes as pain and panic became one in the agonizing thrash of her shoulders before her body slowly sank back, giving way.

The witch arched overhead, becoming a blur of color and then darkness. It howled in terrible triumph, and it was the last sound Charlotte Crowe heard before she died.

CHAPTER SIXTY

Rebecca sped down the dirt road, trying not to look for monsters lurking in the thick woods on either side. They were there, somewhere, and she knew that now. She had looked back in her yard to see the shadows come for Lotte. The witch had taken her, the forest shifting around them until they were out of sight.

Rebecca had left her best friend to that fate—not to die alone, but to die with that monster.

She squeezed the steering wheel, gaze darting to the rearview mirror.

Miles had curled into a ball on the backseat, his face buried against his knees.

More than once, she opened her mouth to say something, to soothe him or apologize or promise that everything would be okay, but she choked back the words every time, teeth clicking shut and teary eyes fixing on the road ahead. What could she say? She had shot his aunt and had no idea if destroying the witch's house would get them off this mountain or just prolong the inevitable. If they couldn't break her hold on them, couldn't get down to Cyprus, they would all just be waiting their turn to die.

Lotte had said to go backward. What did that mean? Literally walk backward up the mountain?

Rebecca turned off the dirt road and up a curved driveway to a house much like her own, large and picturesque among the trees. The Philips home had one of the best views on the mountain, overlooking a drop down one of the slopes from the back of the house. She parked in the middle of the path, both Jane and Wyatt's vehicles still in the driveway.

"Stay here for a second," Rebecca said, but Miles gave no sign of having heard her.

She got out.

The front door flung open, and Wyatt marched out with a gun weighing down his right hand.

She stopped beside the truck and waited. Had it been a mistake to come there? Maybe their friendship didn't extend to a small-town apocalypse?

Wyatt's gaze moved over her, fixing on her bloody gloves and the red smears on her jeans. "Are you hurt?" he asked but didn't come closer.

Rebecca looked down at herself, not having realized just how much of it there was. "No."

His frown made his beard twitch, but he didn't raise his weapon, looking past her to the truck. "Are Hannah and William okay?"

"Yeah. I sent them down to the hunting cabin. Is Jane still here?"

He nodded once, shoulders tight. "We were getting ready to go down to the cabin too." There was a question in there—an inherent uncertainty that came with reality doing a handstand.

Rebecca sighed a breath of relief. "Can she take Miles with her? He got…separated." She swallowed, the echo of that gunshot still ringing in her ear. The moment she saw Lotte fall, she knew she had made a mistake—that it hadn't been the witch come to call on her again. She could argue that her friend had looked like the monster, drenched in mud and running through those trees toward her, but what point was there in that? She had pulled the trigger and the cost had been the life of someone she loved since childhood. No excuse or explanation would change it.

Wyatt took a couple steps closer, relaxing. She had no idea what convinced him she wasn't a threat, but she was grateful. "Of course. Do you want to come inside?"

"I can't," Rebecca said before she could be tempted. She needed to keep moving. She needed to get this done before nightfall.

"Where are you going?"

"Sheriff's station," she swallowed hard. "I'm going up Mount Bell to find the house." *The witch's house*, she corrected in her thoughts but couldn't bring herself to say it out loud.

She thought Wyatt would question her sanity or try to talk her out of it, but then he nodded once and asked, "Do you want help?"

"It's not safe."

"*Greenleighs…* You may have settled the town, but my family came not long after. This is as much my home as it is yours."

It was a relief to have someone understand this place and what it meant to her, but that was even more reason he might not want to join. "I don't know what will happen to Wicker."

"Better to destroy it than let someone else have it," he muttered and turned back to the house. "I'll grab some things. Put the kid in Jane's truck and I'll be right back."

Jane came out of the garage, sensibly dressed and carrying two hiking backpacks stuffed to the brim. She gave Rebecca a nod and tossed the bags one after the other into the loaded truck. "Girls, let's go!" Jane called to the house.

Josie came jogging out, a pillowcase full of boardgames cradled in her arms and her little sister on her heels. She slowed when she saw Miles through the window. Her mom nudged her along, into the truck.

Rebecca returned to her vehicle, opened the back door, and leaned in. "Miles," she said his name and was surprised how steady her voice came out. "I'm sorry."

He sniffled, dragging in a breath. "She's still out there…" he muttered. "She's out there with the witch."

Rebecca cringed, remembering Lotte on the ground in the woods, blood bubbling from her mouth and a gaping hole in her chest. She was dead by now. "I know. You have to go with Mrs. Philips. She'll look after you."

"She's still out there," he whispered.

Rebecca stared at the boy, not sure if he meant Lotte or the witch. She peeled off her gloves and reached out, pulling his hat off his head. She brushed tangled curls back from his face. "I'm going to go find her, okay? Your aunt wanted me to get you someplace safe. So, I need you to go with Mrs. Philips, that way I can go back for her."

"For Aunt Lotte?" he looked up, his eyes wide with brittle hope.

She cradled his cheek in her palm, thumbing away tear tracks. "For the witch, Miles. I won't leave her in the woods with the witch."

Hope drained from his small face, but a grim understanding took its place and he nodded. Sometimes people just had to settle for the best they could get.

She stood and stepped back. Miles crawled out of the truck, shoulders hunched. She put his knit hat back on him and he nodded once before making his way up the driveway. Jane waited for him by the truck with a gentle smile. She helped him up into his seat beside Josie, buckled him in like she would have for a much smaller child, and then closed the door.

Wyatt came out of the house wearing his thick hunting jacket. He had his rifle bag in hand and put it in the back of Rebecca's truck before kissing his wife and daughters goodbye. Rebecca got into the driver's seat and closed the door before she would have to hear the exchange of *'I love you'* and promises to be safe.

On the drive into Wicker, Rebecca told Wyatt everything—even about how she had shot Lotte, thinking she was the witch and what Lotte had said.

"Could just be the shock talking…" he suggested quietly.

Rebecca shook her head. "She'd been there. I could see it on her." *Literally.* Lotte had been covered in blood and mud with bits of bone stuck to her clothes and tangled in her hair.

The houses along their way into town were either abandoned or boarded up. Most of the residents had planned to die on this mountain someday—a right of their birth there—but none had expected it to be like this.

Rebecca parked along the sidewalk, without a thought for the painted lines designating spots. She pulled the heavy keyring from her jacket pocket on the way to the front doors of the sheriff's station. The bookstore was still smoldering. It was hard to believe that had happened that morning. When the world as she knew it went to shit, it had gone fast. Rebecca was still fiddling with the keys when three men came around the corner and up the sidewalk in a jog. Wyatt pulled out his handgun and bellowed a warning in their direction. Rebecca focused on getting the door open.

"We saw it," Victor Crowe called, voice wobbling. "We saw the witch. She… And the wolves… Fuck, the wolves…" He was crying.

Rebecca found the right key and turned back the bolt in the door, only looking up when she was half inside.

Victor's pants were splattered in blood, but from his steady walk, it didn't look to be his own.

Henry Slate and Billy Benson were on his heels, looking scared in a way she thought suited them fine. They had formed a mob, tried to burn a man to death in his own shop, and then taken their rampage up to the Darlings. They had wanted to play with death and now they were neck deep in it.

"Did you find the Darlings?" Rebecca asked, hearing the contempt in her own voice.

Henry Slate cringed and Victor shook his heavy head. "They're gone. I think the wolves got them. They were everywhere."

"The Darlings are the wolves," Rebecca muttered.

Wyatt was still standing between her and them, gun in hand, but the three that had gone cowboy made no move to raise their own weapons against him. If they had any sense left, they'd all know better than to try.

"What are we supposed to do?" Benson asked. "I think we're the only ones left…" It came out in a small confessional whine.

She wanted to laugh at them—or spit at them. *Now* they would listen? They hadn't listened to her, Wyatt, Jane, or anyone else when they started the day. They had decided they knew what was best and that the best thing to do was kill people. She wanted to call them idiots, tell them they were damned, and turn her back on them. But she didn't have time to be their judge, not yet. She needed to blow shit up, and she needed gunfire, and if these boys had proved themselves good at anything, it was causing a scene.

"Any of you know how to use dynamite?" Rebecca asked grimly, certain that they all did.

They perked up a little and shuffled into the sheriff's station behind her, Wyatt never taking his eyes off them. It still reeked of blood and piss inside the building. They had moved the bodies yesterday, but no one had cleaned up the gore, and the windows and doors had stayed locked.

She went straight for the evidence locker where they had stashed all the weapons and explosives they seized from the Darling barn. Everything was still there, dangerous but forgotten until now.

After they divided up the jobs and loaded their vehicles with supplies, Rebecca turned on the city evacuation alarm. She had only ever heard that screeching siren on the days it was tested—twice a year, just to make sure it still worked. Wicker had never heeded an evacuation suggestion before, but today the siren didn't stop after two rounds of signals. It kept going, echoing through the city and the trees and the forest all the way down to the base of the mountain.

She wondered if the sound would escape whatever curse held the people from leaving. Would the residents at the far edges of Cyprus and the bottom of Mount Grayson hear their signal? Would any of the residents still holed up in Wicker listen to it and get as far away as they could?

Wyatt dropped Rebecca off at the old bike trails. "You're sure you want to go alone?"

She laughed dryly because she wasn't sure at all. "You have your own job," she said, pulling a backpack on and giving Wyatt one last look. She wondered if she should say something noble or maybe thank him for his friendship, but it all sounded too lacking in her head. His half-smile suggested he was thinking the same thing. Finally, she shrugged, and he laughed with a nod.

The blast of a grenade went off down the mountain, followed by gunfire.

Backing away from the car and the highway, she headed toward the bike trails. Wyatt pulled away from the shoulder and continued along the winding road north.

She hadn't been out to the old witch bridge in years. Hannah didn't like that they called it that. She had tried to bring up giving the little bridge a proper name years ago, but no one had listened. It wouldn't have mattered what they named it—it would always be the witch bridge and children would always tell the story and cover their eyes when they crossed.

Lotte had been afraid of the witch back when they were kids, but she tried to hide it. She had gone looking for the house with the rest of them, calling out to the wicked spirit in the trees. Rebecca had not believed in it. None of them had, not really, or they never would have gone looking.

Turning around, she took a deep breath and then started walking backward. If she couldn't see the witch, then maybe the witch couldn't see her. That was how it had worked in their childish games, right?

The gunfire and blasts continued to the south and if she was lucky, it would distract the witch long enough to save what was left of Wicker.

She walked backward up the slope of the mountainside as quickly as she could, but it took more time than she would have liked. All the while, she strained to hear gunfire and blasts down the mountain. How long could they keep the witch distracted? How long before she noticed Rebecca or Wyatt? The ground under her boots plateaued off and the deep shadow of a twisted grove of trees swallowed her up, the heavy chime of bones clattered overhead, and the path became soggy and red.

CHAPTER SIXTY-ONE

Charlotte should have been dead.

She knew it even when she opened her eyes, dread gathering in her chest where that bullet had run her through.

The air was cold, the sun sinking low and the sky draining of light behind the heavy clouds.

She stared at the forest, not the one she'd grown up with but the one that always had been here—that gnarled grove of crooked trees dressed in bone chimes. Her back was to the stone face of Mount Bell beside the entrance, a cluster of footprints in the mud beside her left by the witch who had dragged her up there. Why? Why keep her alive?

Charlotte coughed, lurching forward but unable to lift her hand to her mouth. Her limbs felt distant and unattached. She could see them, but she couldn't quite sense them.

Something caught in her throat when she coughed, making her eyes water and panic flare across her mind. She was choking!

Coughing turned to hacking, a spray of fine red misting her muddy shirt, until the lump finally heaved up her throat and dislodged into her mouth. It clanked against her teeth, heavy on her tongue, so she spat it out into her lap.

The bullet rolled wetly over her muddy jeans and into the grass. She tried to catch it, but her arms still weren't obeying her.

And then she saw a figure in the tunnel of shadowed trees heading toward her. Panic drove a thin sound from her, close to a scream. There was definitely something wrong with her body if she still couldn't muster the power to move now.

The figure stopped at her sound and Charlotte realized instantly that this was not the witch come home.

After a few still seconds, the shadow started walking again. It was moving backward, toward her. No, not toward *her*— toward the witch's home. Charlotte cried. Rebecca had understood her and come to finish it. She opened her mouth to call out to her but no sound came.

Rebecca reached the wall, so close she almost stumbled over her, and then finally turned her head to look at her. Charlotte had never seen so many emotions on that face before.

"Lotte?"

Charlotte blinked away tears but more came. She wanted to nod or reach for her, but all she could do was hold her gaze.

Rebecca exhaled hard and dropped to her knees beside her, running hands over her and whispering gratitude and prayer.

"How are you alive?" Greenleigh asked, taking Charlotte's face in her hands. "We have to get out of here."

"Did you bring it?" Charlotte asked, voice raw and startling herself. She hadn't meant to ask that. Bring what?

Greenleigh nodded and dragged the pack off her back. She set it in the grass between them, unzipping it to show that it was full of dynamite sticks and a couple cans of kerosine. "I wasn't sure what to expect…" she explained.

Charlotte smiled, and at least that was real. "Always prepared."

Her eye throbbed, sending a shudder through her whole body. Charlotte looked down at her hands. They weren't in her lap anymore; they were on the bag. She could see her fingers gripping the canvas but she couldn't feel the fabric against her skin. "No…" she whispered, but it was too late. She was on her feet, hugging the bag to her chest.

"Lotte?" Greenleigh barely got out her name before Charlotte shoved her back.

She tried to scream—tried to stop—but she couldn't. She ran.

A wave of motion sickness sloshed inside her. There was no connection between her movements and her muscles. She ran, panting, and unable to stop.

She tried to let go of the bag, she even tried to trip herself on the uneven ground, but it didn't work. It wasn't fair. She hadn't made a deal, not really, not intentionally. She hadn't traded her life for this, had she?

Greenleigh chased her, calling for her to stop.

Charlotte couldn't. She felt the witch smiling somewhere far away in the forest.

She ran faster when she hit the solid ground beyond the dark woods, sprinting through the trees. At first, she didn't know where she was going, but then she saw the clearing up ahead.

Greenleigh screamed for her to stop, voice pitching in panic when she too recognized the drop they were nearing. How many times had they been to this spot? How many times had they dared each other to stand at the edge and look down at the river?

Charlotte stopped suddenly, body lurching to a halt with the toe of her shoe over the broken lip of land. For a moment she thought she'd gotten control of herself again, but she hadn't. The Aurora River snaked below, the churning anger of its current pushing cold air up the cliff face.

"I'm sorry. I can't stop. I'm sorry," Charlotte cried, body leaning over the edge, feeling the witch pull at her like a puppet. She had survived just to die like this?

"It's okay," Greenleigh said, winded.

Charlotte looked back at her. Or maybe it was the witch looking through her? The other woman had stopped only a few yards away, flushed from chasing. She lifted one arm high and pressed the button on a handheld airhorn, sounding it off through the woods like an echo to the emergency siren still ringing through the trees from the town below. Greenleigh smiled at her confusion, making her words a promise when she said it again, "It's okay."

Charlotte opened her mouth to ask how this could possibly be okay, but the question was stolen from her by a huge popping sound that vibrated through the air. She turned away from the river, still hugging the backpack, and stared over the tips of the trees at the rocky peak of Mount Bell. Lights flared one after another, smoke and rubble bursting out after each one. The explosions came in a ripple, each one setting off the next, cutting a line along the top of that lesser peak. Their peak. Their mountain. A half-second of stillness followed before the whole hillside rumbled—as though the mountain itself were screaming.

Charlotte dropped the bag onto the soft ground at her feet, the witch releasing her in a fit of panic. The ground cracked and the trees lashed toward them in the deafening roar of destruction.

Greenleigh lunged those last steps to her, colliding with her and hooking an arm around her middle. She pulled her off the cliff and as they fell, Charlotte continued to stare up. The ground rushed after them, bursting straight off the ledge above and blocking out the sky just before they hit the river. They went under and the cold stung at her skin like a million tiny needles all pushing in and wiggling.

The current spun them away but Greenleigh clung to her. They both gulped blindly at air every time the river pushed them up to the surface. Charlotte wrapped her arms around the other woman when she realized she had control of them again. She strained to look back, trying to see the mountain, but all she saw was a cloud before the river dragged them under again.

CHAPTER SIXTY-TWO

They washed up on the muddy banks of the Aurora where the river widened, pooling against the edge of Cyprus. Rebecca dragged Lotte out of the water, both of them shaking hard, lips blue from the cold. The fairy lights strung along the veranda seating of a restaurant glowed brightly in the early evening, reflected on the dark waters. For long seconds, Rebecca gawked. They were off the mountain. She knew it, because she had never seen those lights before—never been to that spot or that restaurant.

Someone noticed her and she fell back onto her ass on the bank beside Lotte. Strangers shouted down to them, promising to call an ambulance and then arguing with one another about getting down the overgrown slope to the water. She stopped listening.

"Are we dead yet?" Lotte asked.

Rebecca looked down at her. The river had washed the mud and blood off her. "Not yet."

Lotte stared up the mountain—nothing but a giant shadow in the night from where they sat, thick clouds of debris rolled off it, like smoke from an all-consuming fire. "She's gone again."

"How do you know?" Rebecca asked, even though she desperately wanted to believe it.

Lotte absently touched her face, poking at one eyelid. "I just know."

Rebecca nodded slowly, accepting the vague explanation. They were off the mountain, so something had changed.

"Thanks for coming back, Greenleigh," she mumbled, sounding sleepy now.

Rebecca nodded, sirens blaring through the night, growing louder and louder on their way to them. She hadn't expected to find Lotte alive in the witch's cave. She had gone to double their chances of success. If one of them had been caught and killed, the other could still blast the witch's home or the hillside. "Thanks for not being dead."

Lotte smiled, eyes still closed and breath hitching in the cold. "Yeah. Let's not mention the part where you shot me to anyone. This is going to be hard enough to explain without that miracle."

"Agreed." How *were* they going to explain it? What stories would the other survivors of Wicker tell?

Blue and red lights spun through the night, pushing back the shadows on the riverbank. Officers and ambulance personnel called down to them, reassuring as they made their way through thick foliage.

"Everything is going to be okay," the strangers said.

Both women laughed, because they were right—but they had no idea why.

CHAPTER SIXTY-THREE

The dynamite had crumbled the peak of Mount Bell and caused a rockslide down the mountain that buried the entrance to the witch's cave, the trails they had walked as kids, the town of Wicker, and the Greenleigh estate. The blast was felt all the way down in Cyprus. When the cloud of debris finally cleared, and those below could see the mountain again, there was only one summit left—only Grayson.

The handfuls of families who had evacuated down the side of the mountain before the explosion survived. Most didn't wait for emergency personnel to set up a temporary bridge for vehicles—they took what they could carry and crossed on a footbridge before dawn, leaving their vehicles along the last stretch of road.

The mayhem in the days between the storm and the rockslide were blamed on Sheriff Summerfield and the Darlings. Even the rockslide itself had been pinned on the reclusive family high on the hill. A manhunt ensued, but no Mountain Darling was ever found—none but Harvey Darling who had been repeatedly questioned and then finally released.

Wicker was not rebuilt as it had been before. It was no longer a town, even though many of the surviving residents returned to the mountain. They built their new homes lower, closer to the mill and with a little distance from the graveyard of the old town.

Only the Greenleighs and the Crowes climbed back up to the spots where they had always been. Greenleigh rebuilt her family home, with its windows facing the woods, and Charlotte finally went home to the big house she'd been avoiding since her momma died.

Together, she and Harvey cleared it out of almost everything that had once been. She kept a few boxes of family photos, the weapons, and her momma's quilts. Everything else was either hauled down the mountain to Cyprus or burned. Her right eye never fully recovered, the pupil blown so wide that her iris was nothing but a thin ring. Doctors couldn't explain it, and in her nightmares, the spider squirmed around in there, trying to push itself free.

Alice disappeared after Mount Bell fell. Charlotte didn't know if she made it off the mountain or not. For a while Miles lived with his maternal grandmother in Cyprus, only visiting the old house for a night or two at a time. Eventually he stayed. Eventually the mountain called them all home.

Victor didn't die in that last battle to distract the witch and her wolves, though he often wished he had. He settled into a house near the mill with his kids, low on the mountain where he could tell the story however he liked. He woke often to the howling of wolves in his dreams and the memory of teeth in his skin. He never went back to the big house or spoke to his sister again.

The Darling Pack stalked the north side of the mountain and spent their winters near the old homestead. Charlotte wondered if they remembered who they used to be. Even if they did, she doubted they regretted their choices. Nothing in the relationship between Wicker and the Darlings had changed.

Every so often the wolves came down the south side to get a look at Rebecca Greenleigh.

She shot them if they came within range and, as far as Charlotte had heard, they didn't get back up anymore. Greenleigh liked to say they were reminding her that they were still there, but Charlotte suspected it was the other way around.

The Darlings still meant to be the last on the mountain and now, more than ever, Charlotte suspected they might be.

Charlotte and Harvey burned the little house where her aunt had died, and Charlotte spent two months in the woods every day looking for her dad's remains. He had refused to leave the house with Harvey and the kids—insisting on waiting for his boys. When she found him, there was little left to identify, but she gathered all of him up and took his remains to Cyprus to be cremated.

She wouldn't leave him on the mountain. She wouldn't leave any of them there.

There was a reason the people of Wicker had never buried their dead on the mountain. What slept in the ground there, under their homes, held claim to it all. And she knew now, why Crowes didn't make deals with devils.

THE END?

Not if you want to dive into more of Crystal Lake Publishing's Tales from the Darkest Depths!

Check out our amazing website and online store or download our latest catalog here: https://geni.us/CLPCatalog.

We always have great new projects and content on the website to dive into, as well as a newsletter, behind the scenes options, social media platforms, our own dark fiction shared-world series and our very own webstore. Our webstore even has categories specifically for KU books, non-fiction, anthologies, and of course more novels and novellas.

AUTHOR BIOGRAPHY

Cheryl Low might be a primordial god, building the world around her with her bare hands and making sketchy deals that only ever favor herself.

…Or she might be a human on a bus somewhere listening to a horror audiobook. The answer might surprise you! But it probably won't.

Readers…

Thank you for reading *The Wicker Witch*. We hope you enjoyed this novel. If you have a moment, please review *The Wicker Witch* at the store where you bought it.

Help other readers by telling them why you enjoyed this book. No need to write an in-depth discussion. Even a single sentence will be greatly appreciated. Reviews go a long way to helping a book sell, and is great for an author's career. It'll also help us to continue publishing quality books.

Thank you again for taking the time to journey with Crystal Lake's Torrid Waters.

You will find links to all our social media platforms on our Linktree page: https://linktr.ee/CrystalLakePublishing.

MISSION STATEMENT

Since its founding in August 2012, Crystal Lake Publishing has quickly become one of the world's leading publishers of Dark Fiction and Horror books. In 2023, Crystal Lake Publishing formed a part of Crystal Lake Entertainment, joining several other divisions, including Torrid Waters, Crystal Lake Comics, and many more.

While we strive to present only the highest quality fiction and entertainment, we also endeavour to support authors along their writing journey. We offer our time and experience in non-fiction projects, as well as author mentoring and services, at competitive prices.

With several Bram Stoker Award wins and many other wins and nominations (including the HWA's Specialty Press Award), Crystal Lake puts integrity, honor, and respect at the forefront of our publishing operations.

We strive for each book and outreach program we spearhead to not only entertain and touch or comment on issues that affect our readers, but also to strengthen and support the Dark Fiction field and its authors.

Not only do we find and publish authors we believe are destined for greatness, but we strive to work with men and women who endeavour to be decent human beings who care more for others than themselves, while still being hard-working, driven, and passionate artists and storytellers.

Crystal Lake is and will always be a beacon of what passion and dedication, combined with overwhelming teamwork and respect, can accomplish. We endeavour to know each and every one of our readers, while building personal relationships with our authors, reviewers, bloggers, podcasters, bookstores, and libraries.

This is what we believe in. What we stand for. This will be our legacy.

Welcome to Crystal Lake Entertainment.

Also from Torrid Waters...

Can the past hold sway over the present?

When artifacts connected with the violent death of the Russian sorcerer, Grigori Rasputin, come into the possession of three ordinary souls, echoes of the past become powerful voices in a deadly realm.

Tatiana is demure and ineffective as a Manhattan advertising executive, but when the unusual historical find of her dreams is procured, she puts a whole new spin on office sex and politics. Can she handle the ability to manipulate events?

Father Brett Elysian is a dynamic and popular addition to the staff at Saint Stanislaus, so why is Pastor John McCaffrey uneasy? There's the young priest's sudden transfer from a distant parish, as well as some bizarre incidents to contend with…

Newly widowed Hank Stanton writes journal entries daily to the dearly departed love of his life. He's troubled by the loss and the dreams tormenting him since he found the old Russian dagger in the attic. He has a dark appointment with destiny, one that will bring together all three tales!

Also from Torrid Waters...

Come for Thanksgiving Dinner. Stay for the Feast.

Sierra's first American Thanksgiving promises to be unforgettable when her college roommate, Zoe, invites her to the Samuels family feast. But as the ten-hour banquet unfolds, it becomes clear this is no ordinary holiday gathering.

With everyone bound by a chilling rule—eat and drink exactly as served, and enjoy it, or face dire consequences—the traditional celebration quickly takes a dark and macabre turn. Will Sierra survive the Samuels' sinister hospitality or become part of a feast far more horrifying than she could have ever imagined?

Question Not My Salt is a gripping tale blending the terror of *The Texas Chainsaw Massacre* with the culinary horror of *Hannibal* and *The Menu.*

THANK YOU FOR PURCHASING THIS BOOK

www.ingramcontent.com/pod-product-compliance
Lightning Source LLC
Chambersburg PA
CBHW070402310726
48977CB00003B/524